Jar Baby

For Adam

Jar Baby

Hayley Webster

ch
Dexter
Haven

Published in 2012 by Dexter Haven Publishing Ltd
Curtain House
134–146 Curtain Road
London
EC2A 3AR

ISBN 978-1-903660-10-2

A full CIP record for this book is available from the British Library

Typeset in Sabon by Dexter Haven Associates Ltd, London
Printed and bound by CPI Group (UK) Ltd, Croydon, CR0 4YY

Nothing makes us so lonely as our secrets.
Paul Tournier

One need not be a chamber to be haunted,
One need not be a house;
The brain has corridors surpassing
Material place.
Emily Dickinson

You must trust and believe in people or
life becomes impossible.
Anton Chekov

Prologue

Stella is in Rohan's workroom. She is being fitted for a tailored bolero jacket, trimmed with dark ostrich feathers, as she has been every Saturday afternoon for the past five weeks. She will wear it for her *Vogue* photo shoot with her husband behind the lens. It is Rohan's idea of a joke. Making his mark. Stitching out his territory in rich plumes across his married lover's shoulders.

I saw it once in an early manifestation, when it was still in two neat pieces, dismembered. I pulled away its protective cloth when Rohan was out of the house for an early swim. It grasped the shoulders of the mannequin; separate feathers reaching like fingers towards invisible collarbones. The sleeves shone under the light, glossy as Stella's hair, and I stroked its length until my palms were damp and the place where my hand had been was a slick of navy blue.

Now they are locked in there together, Stella and Rohan. They have left the window open and I try not to focus on their gulps for air and exhausted chest laughs. I am under strict instructions not to disturb them under any circumstances.

In the Mercedes on the driveway Drake, Stella's driver, sits with his feet up on the dashboard smoking a hand-rolled cigarette. We always seem to be left like this, two outsiders on the gravel. He has tuned the long-wave radio to a station from far away, to a woman singing something languid and gasping in French. I think how I would love to let him into Rohan's workroom, to see him stroke all that silk for Stella's future dresses, where his fingers could pucker those smooth lengths to shreds.

'Cherry brandy,' he says and grins. People say that Drake is very good looking. He has thick, curly dark hair, tipped at the ends with white and silver. He has the type of lined face that shows the history of his smiles. Everybody likes Drake. He is the life and soul of the party.

'Hmmgh,' I say, because the brandy is hot and makes my throat contract.

'Smoke?'

I lean against the front wheel of the Mercedes and say, in my best impression of Drake, 'Don't mind if I do.' I find it easier if I pretend to be Drake. I do not know why.

He laughs. He always laughs at me, but I do not take it personally. He knows the truth about me. He has told me often enough. He leans over to put the cigarette in my mouth and lights it for me. I am breathing his breath: tobacco, brandy and, unexpectedly, lemons. His body is wet with a faint film of sweat and I am once again aware of his own strong smell. It reminds me of the big wooden crates Rohan is sent from clients or cloth men in other countries. That trapped air from another time and place, which rises up like an out-breath when the lid is prised from its mouth with a crow bar. Finely stitched material, so many reds, exotic tealeaves – free from their caddies in soft mounds – candle wax, brown paper, dust.

I cannot explain it, this odd sensation, but as I smoke and lean against the wheel, for a moment I feel I am Drake. I part my legs, swing one arm over my left thigh with the hand dangling down, hold my cigarette between my thumb and first finger, and squint as I inhale. All of me feels like Drake, like a man whose job it is to drive a privileged woman around in a black Mercedes, who has entertaining stories about bar brawls and a different woman in every town or village, who can tell people what to do and make them do it. There is sun in my eyes, and smoke, and the sting of brandy. Maybe if I transform myself into Drake I can be free of myself, free of everything.

'Come and sit with me.' He pats the seat between his legs.

I do not know how to say no. I have known Drake nearly all my life.

On the seat next to him is a well-thumbed magazine with the familiar pictures I do not want to see.

'Why will you never look like this?' says Drake.

'I don't know,' I say. I close my eyes and try not to think of those orange-skinned women stretched out and bent over, parting slick mouths, long legs, beautiful and not like me.

'Don't tease me Diana. You know full well.'

'Because I am ugly,' I say. 'Because I am not like other girls.'

'That is right,' he smiles his wide smile. 'And that's nothing to be ashamed of. It means when people want to do these things to you they will do them because they can see past your ugliness.'

'Yes,' I say. This makes sense to me. I have heard it often enough. Everything Drake says makes sense.

'Although, remember, I will probably be the only one who can ever see past it.'

'I know,' I say.

'Which means…?'

'I am lucky to have you.'

'Yes. So…?'

'Thank you Drake.'

'You're welcome.'

He puts his hand on the zip of my jeans. 'You're welcome Diana. Anything to make you happy. I do make you happy, don't I?'

'Yes.'

He uses his driver's hat as an ashtray while he unbuttons the front of his trousers. I know what to do. I have been doing this since I can remember. Since the first time I sat on his knee. It used to make me vomit, litres of clear liquid that fell from my mouth by the toiletful, so much puke I thought I would shrink to nothing and be a pile of cloth and skin and dead hair. But that was a long time ago.

But this time is different. This time he puts it in me.

A French woman sings of unrequited love, wanting to forget through bursts of white noise. A slide show: the sound of Stella and Rohan. Drake's unpolished boots on the dashboard. My half-smoked cigarette on the gravel. Drake's sweat dripping into my face from his forehead. And the feeling: you have brought this on yourself.

'Do you want the dog?' he asks, rolling another cigarette, sprinkling Stella's husband's tobacco into the fold as he buttons himself back in. 'Or we could have another go?' He winks.

I say nothing.

With a conspiratorial smile Drake shrugs his shoulders, and at the touch of an electric button whirs down the partition between the front and back seats of the Mercedes. There, a sign of hope, is Ruskin. Stella's dog. He pants, oblivious, and jumps up to lick my face. I ruffle his hair with joy and relief.

'What do you mean?'

Drake puffs out smoke rings, 'Well, lovely Diana, I mean why don't you take the dog for a run?' His eyes are closed now. He leans back in his chair and taps out a swing beat accompaniment on his knee.

'OK,' I say. I feel now grateful, and almost say thank you, but the words stop in my head and never reach my lips. I click Ruskin onto his purple leash, turn away from the car and walk very slowly, without looking behind me, towards Hat Cove – that other part of the beach, that secret stretch, which only Rohan and I know.

The tops of my legs are sore and sting wet.

The dog looks up at me with happy eyes. The little silver bell engraved with his name that hangs from his blue collar tinkles as his head trembles.

'What do you say?' Drake is looking at the magazine again.

'Thank you Drake.'

'It's a shame you will never be like these women Diana. These are the women men really want. But ah...' He strokes his thighs with the back of his hands. 'We must do the best we can with what God gave you.'

'Thank you Drake.'

As I reach the pine trees which separate the house from the sand, Drake turns up the radio and sings along in caustic French. Above a falling clarinet solo he calls something out which I do not quite hear but sounds like, 'Ask Rohan about your real mother. Go on – I dare you!' I do not ask him to repeat himself.

An afternoon to myself, a dog of my own, hiding on the private beach, skipping and bounding between the rock pools and glutinous seaweed. We run and play and fetch sticks and shells. With each return of a piece of driftwood in Ruskin's mouth I start to imagine that he is really my dog, one I share with my real parents. It's not really a kidnapping, as such. I have been given permission.

Time escapes.

When Rohan appears just as it is getting dark, looking for me, or maybe for the dog, I panic. I have been watching tiny, near-invisible crabs skate and scrabble in a rock pool, but now I hide behind the rocks as he calls my name. With each shout the dog begins to whine, and I know I have to keep him quiet. Above all things, I do not want to be found. I am not ready to be found.

I hold my hands over his soft face and keep his body still with my own.

'Shh, Ruskin. Please be quiet.' I am nearly on top of him, slowly stroking his face at first, then wrestling with his limbs to keep him still. There is a quickening of the thud, thud of his tail which slows, then stops.

One final thud and a cloud of sand.

When it is very late, when the sea is quiet and there are no gulls, I return to the house. Remnants of an un-thrown party for three are stacked on the kitchen counter. Balloons, flat in their plastic packets, rolls of crêpe paper – tightly wound wrinkles of red, blue and green – a cake on the table, painted with food colouring to look like a face, a row of lit candles for a mouth, burning to stubs. A plate with several half-eaten sausage rolls scattered with curls of pastry, covered with taut cling film, and, beside the cake, three elasticated paper hats, pink and silver spiralled cones. I have never had a birthday party before.

Rohan sits at the table, dark in the candlelight. He looks tired. His red hair is twisted with grease and, I think, secrets, his eyes threaded through with bright veins. He wears an open-collared shirt with stains like shadows along its front: coffee, butter, lipstick. He has bare feet and his trousers are rolled up to his calves. The copper hair on his legs is thick, and I know if I touched it it would spring back in my fingers like moss.

'I was worried about you,' he says.

'Sorry.' I do not sit down.

'Have you seen Stella's dog?' He pushes the cake slowly across the tablecloth.

'Ruskin?'

'Ruskin. It's just Drake said Ruskin ran off. I wondered if you'd seen him.'

'No,' I say. 'I didn't.'

'You're sure?'

'Yes. I think I'll have a bath.'

Rohan sighs and stands up. 'Blow these out first, will you? It's bad luck to leave your birthday candles burning.'

Half-heartedly I lean towards the cake and breathe onto the candles. I forget to make a wish.

'Let's go swimming.'

'What?'

'Let's go sea swimming. Night swimming.'

I nearly say no. I think I have had enough of the beach, but the thought of the sea in the dark – the cold water and salt of the sea – makes me change my mind. I nod.

'Come on then,' he says. We are both suddenly very cheerful.

We run to the beach and the sand is cold. I kick off my sandals as we run, fully clothed, towards the water, all the time saying nothing, just running, running, then swimming. The cold water is everywhere and I swim hard, as hard as I ever have done. My head thumps with the rush of blood and me holding my breath under the water for too long. Everything is black, but I know the landmarks by heart, I do not need to see. My lungs ache. There is smoke on the horizon, and bubbles, and enough thick green and grey to push my eyes closed forever. I do not even flinch at the stroke of seaweed in the murk. There is just cold and dark and water and the sound of my breath held tight in my chest. Everything feels clear and bright and wonderful.

When I eventually stop I am a good way out. My eyes have adjusted to the moonlight, I can see the orange lights from windows in houses along the shoreline. The sand is a flick of brown on a black wash landscape. The current is strong. I look about for Rohan but he isn't there, so I panic slightly but only for a moment because soon his head is above the surface and he treads water beside me. He looks happy, although his mouth is submerged in the water. His eyes are bright, no more bloodshot. We stare at each other through the night.

'Rohan,' I begin. Maybe it is time to tell him about Drake. Maybe he can make it stop. Maybe Drake is wrong and I won't be sent away and locked up or worse. But nothing comes. I cannot risk it. I do not want to be sent away. And Rohan is not strong enough to hear it. I know he is full of his own sadness.

It is a long time since we have swum like this.

Gold moon and sand like glitter between my toes and in my eyes. Salt water in my mouth. Our legs kicking furiously to stay above water.

Rohan closes his eyes and pushes his head backwards into the sea. His red hair spreads outwards in the water like sun-dried seaweed, like tarnished foil, a Sun King let out at night. He smiles and opens his mouth as though to speak, but instead, for just a moment, puts one hand at the roots of my hair. I feel the scuff of his fingers against my ear, grooved and dry like driftwood. I wish I knew what it was like to have parents.

'Happy thirteenth birthday Diana,' he says eventually, as I scull the dark like water. 'It will be a better year this year.'

1

On the evening of 14 March 2012, in the skies over the South Downs, a chartered helicopter travelling from London to the coastal town of Cowling suffered engine failure. Within a matter of seconds, thin strands of spring fog, flames and burning aluminium fell from the sky onto the footpath below. Among the debris was newly knighted fashion designer Sir Rohan Rickwood. A day that began with champagne, recognition and validation ended with broken glass, rubble and molten metal. Two occupants of the craft, Rickwood and the pilot, were found dead at the scene. Stella Avery, Rickwood's wife, the model and seventies style icon, avoided the disaster, having changed her mind at the last minute and stayed in London.

Rohan Rickwood: tailor, man of silk. Uncle Rohan was dead.

I used to think my mother was a mermaid with a slick tail. It is strange to think she ever lived, breathing air and not sea water. Secrets are more dangerous than truths. Truths are tangible and you can hold them in your hands until they make sense. Secrets leave room for reconstructions and interpretations. My entire life was made up of the interpretations of a lonely girl looking for meaning.

I never knew my real parents.

I still have the photograph Rohan gave me when I was a child. It is creased now, multi-folded through time: a faded black-and-white couple in Arran jumpers walking along the beach, a milk-furred golden retriever at their heels. Rohan said he took it himself when they visited him one autumn at Cowling. Before I was born.

He rarely talked about his sister and even less about her husband, but when he did – when his unpredictable temperament allowed – Uncle Rohan would regale me with elaborate retellings of my parents' accomplishments, their discoveries, their adventures across continents in the name of marine science. Dog whelks and sea slugs were their shared speciality. Also ragworm and dune beetles and parched fronds of sea-holly. My mother – Dr Alice Everett – loved, and made her life's work, coastal flowers: charted the life cycles of Stork's bill, Scurvy grass and Lesser sea-spurrey. My father – Dr Will Everett – was England's foremost expert on Guillemots. Apparently he could do the most uncanny impression of their distinctive call. A favourite party trick.

Will and Alice Everett died not long after I was born. A boating trip while on a scientific research trip. The bits of them I knew, snippets, anecdotes, flashes of their brilliance, were Rohan's memories, passed to me across the kitchen table over soups and stews, over ginger biscuits and dark coffee, over the tailor's dummy, pins at our feet. It was clear to me that Rohan's feelings towards my dead father were of ambivalence, if not disdain. When he talked about my mother he would ring his hands in tight loops, or squint his eyes into tight creases. 'She was beautiful, your mother,' he would say. 'It was taken from her. She couldn't live the life she was destined to live.'

'Do you miss her?' I did not feel I had the right to miss what I had never known.

'I miss what she was, what she could have been,' he would say. 'Before …' A fist on the table and more whisky.

Once I asked if her hair was really that long – it is way past her hips in the photograph – and he said yes.

'What colour was it, her hair?'

'Reddish brown,' he said. 'Just like yours. Your mother was beautiful and funny and intelligent and kind. I could not have wanted a better sister. Life can be cruel Diana. It can take things from you before you are ready. It can leave you with dust.'

I liked to hear about her hair. It made her seem more real. More like me. When I brushed my own, I imagined hers threaded tight amongst the bristles. When I felt the sun on each strand, hot like polished coins, or when I tied mine up with a shoelace to take the damp thickness away from my neck on a sunny day, I wondered if her hair felt the same. I imagined she washed out the curls in her hair with soapy water that final morning. One last time. Fingers with suds at the roots.

Will and Alice Everett were scattered at sea, so I never visited a grave. I suppose I always thought they were out there somewhere. Especially my mother, her hair curling around her like pond weed, a cocoon for a new birth. On her way back home from cold Canadian waters. A tide mother. I never knew how long it would take, but have always known the sea works this way. It brings things back to you. In time.

Where was I when I heard the news? I do not remember exactly. There were newspaper sandwich boards propped out in the street: 'Designer killed in chopper inferno', 'Just knighted: design world mourns tragic Rohan'. There was rolling news on the radio, the TV, but it didn't really sink in. Not at first. Over the years, I had become skilled at evading most mentions of either Rohan or Stella, like those adults you see who still, without realising, effortlessly miss the cracks in pavements in case some long-forgotten, imagined childhood terror should catch up with them. Interviews, showcases, TV documentaries all passed me by, myself safe in the knowledge that things were better now, that I need not cling to the past or their way of living. That I had recovered. But this time it was impossible to avoid. One phrase was repeated over and over, a dated expression that drew me in, 'no suspicious circumstances'.

Rohan's funeral was held, just over a week after his death, at St Joseph's church in Rain, a small village between Cowling and Brighton. I only heard about it from a Radio 4 arts programme I'd seen mentioned in the newspaper. It had been put into the schedule before his death, and kept in as a sort of tribute. His name, stamped out in black and white under 'Pick of the day' made me feel something, a stirring, a curiosity, combined with an unexpected, unwanted, need. I think I just wanted to feel a connection. I had seen neither Rohan nor Stella for ten years.

Ronnie and I had listened while doing the washing up. It had, for once, been mostly about Stella, how she had contributed considerable cash to restore some especially rare organ pipes at that church: ornate, blue, Rococo cylinders which rose high up into the rafters and were carefully embossed with leaf-gold birds of paradise. Apparently, said the narrator, the restoration was part of a bigger project across the South East to relaunch monumental, ecclesiastical buildings as tourist attractions rather than places of worship.

'So God is truly dead,' laughed Ronnie. 'Coincidence about the name. *Rickwood*. You're not related, are you? You've always had such *style*.'

I shook my head but didn't say anything. A movement of the head is not the same as a lie.

The church's squat round tower, of tightly packed grey and brown stones, was certainly picturesque. I approached the graveyard from the nearby train station, stopping to read a poster stuck to the gate which proudly informed passers-by that St Joseph's was to be one of several Sussex locations used in a new BBC adaptation of *Middlemarch*. I wondered if Stella had parted with all that cash because she had imagined, in some far-off future, the look of their coffins as they swung dramatically through those substantial wooden doors. Never too late to make a grand entrance.

It seemed good form not to wear black to a tailor's funeral. I dressed in purple, bright like they use in church during Advent, with a low-fitting, wide-brimmed hat that hid my eyebrows but not my eyes. I painted my lips scarlet in honour of Stella, a sort of joke that didn't even make me laugh. I considered wearing dark glasses for disguise, but I soon realised I need not have worried. On the shingle outside St Joseph's nobody knew me.

In clusters around the church stood mourners in elaborate, or self-consciously understated, apparel gathered in mini communion, rearranging stoles, asymmetric hats, sweeping haircuts coloured in neat lines away from tight skin. There were people I recognised immediately, television personalities, singers, actors, models with silk handkerchiefs at their eyes, arms draped around older, over-groomed men. People who had, as Ronnie and I would have giggled together had she been there, *had work done*. 'Freshened up' is what magazines call it, although in real life there didn't seem anything fresh about it. There was something rather sorry about it, about trying to hold time still in a stitched skin bag, something that made me feel I'd forgotten something important.

Although they showed no sign of recognising me, I immediately knew several faces of guests at Rohan's many soirees. I remembered them, women clinging to his words with the wine and the smoke, and laughter, always laughter and shut doors, beds unmade, eyes at keyholes, ears at walls. I tried to remember names, but I didn't really know them, these women. They were similar now to what they were then, but their hair was slightly higher, their make-up slightly thicker. I could not help but admire the coiled green felt-and-wire hat on the head of a woman in a white flared trouser suit. It crept up from the top of her ears, round and round, until it reached a summit about a hand's length above her head. It came to an exacting point, and was capped with a green PVC ball that made me think of olives in Martinis.

These women reminded me of the rows of females in Rohan's fitting room. I caught glimpses of them through the keyhole. There were always women in Rohan's fitting room: ladies in fine dress, girls, wives of rich men from our village, from faraway towns and cities. They were indistinguishable from the mannequins. Women came from miles around to be pinched in at the waist by him, to be cut off at the knees. They paid good money. But behind their backs he raised his eyebrows. Silly women. Always caring about their figures, trying to tempt a man, to entice him, with their narrowness, their controlled curves. 'You are better than that, Diana,' he said to me. 'You are not like them. Your mother was not like them, and neither are you. She wore clothes because she loved them or because they amused her or because she liked the colour of the lining. The first ever dress I made was for her, and she wore it to weed the garden.' He sighed. 'I have never been more pleased with any other piece I've made. Never. No. She was not like these women. And you are not like them.' I was never quite sure how this made me feel. It was like Drake said. I was different.

'Pardon?' A man in a wonderful deep blue suit cut slim at the waist turned towards me. I was startled. Nobody knew me.

'Sorry. Nothing,' I said. 'Talking to myself.'

The man in the magnificent suit stared at me, a flicker of recognition on his pink face. We knew each other.

Sir Jimmy Trowse. Stella's first husband. Rohan's best friend.

'Diana!'

'Sir Jimmy.'

He looked me up and down. I remembered a time when he didn't see me. When he flung words out of his mouth, above my head, to the loveliest of Rohan's rejects in the smokiest corners of the most lavishly decorated rooms. I was invisible then, a clump of child who could watch, could wait, could see. Suddenly I was one of those grown-up women, stitched into fine cloth, stroked in silk, sucked in at the waist in stiff darts.

'You have some...' he reached out to take a piece of invisible fluff from the collar of my dress. His fingers stayed there, resolute, on the purple downturned flap.

'Thank you,' I said. New Diana – Dee – the Diana I had become since leaving Cowling, would not stand for this uninvited contact. I would have laughed at him. Told him off for being an old letch, fake-shuddered and made a joke. Together Ronnie and I would have rolled our eyes and slipped our arms around each other's shoulders. Instead I stood before him with his fingers on me, blushing, quite red. There was a unexpected thrill in it. In being chosen.

'Have you seen my darling ex-ex-wife? She hoped you would be here.' Sir Jimmy let his hand fall from my dress, speed-reading pearl buttons with the backs of his fingers.

'No,' I said. I looked around sharply with an impulsive fear that the woman who had stolen my home would be there, over my shoulder, catching me with her once husband's hands upon me. But there was no one.

'She's about here somewhere. She'll be delighted to see you. You've been quite invisible, haven't you, these past years, despite her best efforts?'

I did not want to engage Jimmy Trowse in any conversation about my new life. I did not want the words 'despite her best efforts' to raise fury in me. Efforts? I pulled my hat further down my forehead and began to step away.

'A little, I suppose,' I said. 'I'm going to look at the church. Gather my thoughts.'

'Of course. Of course.' He didn't mention Rohan or offer condolences. He shrugged and twinkled.

Before I had a chance to say anything more a woman stepped onto the gravel who took all of my attention. A vision! Like the ascension of the Virgin in the illustrated Bible. This woman: mid-fifties with an intense mouth, fairly wide hips and turquoise glasses on a red string around her neck.

'Who's that?' I said. 'That woman?'

'Who?' Sir Jimmy looked about him and didn't seem to see her. How could he not?

I nodded in her direction. 'The one by the steps with the big specs.'

Sir Jimmy frowned slightly and gave a little shrug. 'Oh her. She's nobody. Nobody of any interest anyway. That's Glenys Pimm. The academic. Married to Victor Eve.' He turned and looked towards a tall, young brunette in four-inch heels and a grey fur coat. 'Jodie!' He bellowed and started towards her. 'OK Diana. Looking forward to seeing you at the wake. Nothing like a bit of dinner and dancing, eh?'

I laughed a small laugh. A polite, disinterested laugh. 'No, nothing like.' But he was already gone.

Glenys Pimm, I thought. What a wonderful name. Pimm. You couldn't say it without parting then pressing your lips together. Pi-mmm. Glenys Pimm had shoulder-length chestnut hair that she'd segmented off and pinned up into neat whorls with – I imagined – old-fashioned bobby pins. She wore scarlet lipstick – like Stella's – and did not lift her glasses onto her face. They sat, askew, the metal rim of the arm, surely, against her left nipple. I tried, through the people gathered about her in their power groupings, to see what kind of shoes she was wearing. I imagined them to be high-heeled, crossbar leather, perhaps brown, or unexpectedly, playfully, Robin Hood green, but before I could really see she had disappeared with the rest of the crowd into the arched doorway.

Inside the church the stained-glass windows refracted coloured light onto the thick white walls. The high-arched roof, made with fat beams linked at their tips, seemed to hold something cold and quiet, a different kind of atmosphere. As I sat, in one of the pews towards the back, I looked upwards and imagined surveying the whole thing from on high. I had an unchecked thought that maybe Rohan, the ghost of Rohan, was up there in the thin air, transparent, watching us make a show of grief below. I tried to meet his gaze but immediately looked away, my eyes drawn swiftly to the patent of my shoes.

What would I say if he really were there? I had believed, hoped, when I first moved to the city, that he was sorry I had gone away, that he often thought of me, that his life was not complete without me in it. I saw it as a sort of punishment for him. I imagined him coming to find me, rescue me, beg me back. Maybe that belief had sustained me all this time. When I heard the funeral announcement on the radio, when there had been no phone call, no one asking me to be there, no apparent desire for the long-lost niece to return home for the burial, I wondered if he had actually *forgotten* me. Or worse, that he didn't care. This thought had filled me with terror. That I could disappear completely, that he could live without me just as I'd learned to live without him. It was unthinkable.

A string quartet, seated near the carved wooden font, played something beautiful yet overtly grand, Beethoven I think. If only Ronnie were there, to tell me. The church was full now. Packed tight. So many people had arrived for the ceremony that some stood at the back and along the sides of the church, against the walls. Fashion-packed.

And in came the coffin.

The lid appeared to me a trap door just waiting to spring open, to send pieces of him tumbling out along the aisle like contents of a dropped suitcase. I remembered his shoulders, round rocks for swimming, and could only think that this heavy box, carried by unknown dark-suited men with bowed heads, held pieces of him, legs, arms, shoulders, hair, all blood and mangle from the accident. For the first time since I'd heard of his death I allowed myself to imagine those last moments, his body, ripped, burnt – what? Orange and pink pieces of him falling from the sky like body-part confetti, his final thoughts. Of what? Of whom?

How could I live now I knew I would never see him again? I had thought, believed, I never wanted to see him again. This was easy when I knew where to find him, when I could imagine him in his house, in his workroom, standing out by the sea. As his coffin passed me, silver handles waiting to be rapped like doorknockers, I wished I was somebody who cried, like the women in bright hats in the rows in front of me, but there was nothing apart from a dull ache in my legs and hands. A scraped-out stomach and mouth. Tired and dry. I had lost Rohan a long time ago.

And then, when I thought I might get up and leave, when I knew this was nothing like an easy goodbye, that there was no place for me at a funeral where I was anonymous, unwanted, I saw, amongst the mourners who walked with the coffin, side by side, Stella and Toby.

That face.

He looked just the same as he did when we were teenagers: the same black hair, now shorn to his scalp. That body, dressed in what Rohan would have undoubtedly labelled 'a cretin's idea of a fine suit of clothes'. I could tell he'd gone to the trouble of having it made especially for him, that he couldn't, after all these years, bring himself to buy something off-the-peg. I imagined his lovely-limbed body being fitted at a gentlemen's tailor, probably on Jermyn Street or Saville Row, one with a good reputation but not one with flair. Rohan always said Toby had the potential to look truly exquisite in clothes, if only he had the imagination and inclination. He obviously still had neither, but he did look appealing. Stella would think he *cut a dash*. And his eyes – oh those eyes! – as blue as block colour in a fresco painting; a perfect slot of time cut out from the past and patched neatly into the present. You could hardly see the joins.

And Stella. Stella was dressed mostly in black: a silk shirt-dress over wide-legged trousers, pointed green leather boots with brass buckles, leather bangles up her left forearm. She had a long, olive-green silk scarf wrapped around her head, a turban with only a pale slice of hair hanging out behind one ear. Still the same Stella. Bleak and breathtaking. My whole body shook with rage and resentment. I was shocked to feel how much I hated her.

Pinned to Toby's left lapel was a crimson tulip, wilting: his own tribute to Stella. When she first moved in she had insisted on fresh tulips every day of the year, no matter the season. Rohan used to send me to the florist to pick them up and I used to spit onto the stamens. As a child, and then a teenager, I called her the Human Broom. In public she always wore her hair in a huge, fat chignon, with extra hairpieces pinned on top for good measure, on some days even sporting ridiculous hats for extra effect. Her locks resembled a carefully constructed celebration cake, her body was as narrow as a pole.

When the vicar began to speak, I couldn't stop staring at Toby and the Human Broom.

How could they?

The day I saw them together was as vivid in my memory as if I'd caught them, then, embracing in the aisle of St Joseph's. The two of them stood, by Needle Rock, far out on Cowling beach, bound together, like a couple in a sepia photograph. Despite the heat there was a vicious wind from the sea. Stella's white-blonde hair whipped around her, slapped against her cheeks like seaweed against rocks in a gale. Toby's hands were on the back of her neck, a thumb on her chin; so much worse than if his palms had been pushed into the trifle frills of her skirt – a sign of tenderness as well as lust. I had replayed this image in my head many times. Sometimes I would vary what they were wearing, or the length of Stella's hair. Sometimes I would make her fat, or old, but nothing could take away its potency. It was always the same kiss. Their hands and lips. Connected.

I knew then it had been a mistake not to bring Ronnie.

People I had never met, or seen before, stood up at the lectern to tell unknown anecdotes about the man who had taught me to tie my shoelaces, to eat with a knife and fork, to thread a needle and make a hem. A woman in her fifties in a grey ball dress and bare feet. A young man with blue twists of long hair. A teenage girl in a pair of long cotton shorts and a ruffled lemon blouse. An old man with black-and-white striped trousers and an intricately decorated walking cane. Each began with, 'The thing about Rohan Rickwood was...' as though each of them held the secret to his soul in one easily digested turn of phrase. I couldn't make out how any of them were related to Rohan or Stella. None of them introduced themselves, as though it went without saying who they were, how important their link to the coffin on the stand before us.

Jimmy Trowse, when it was his turn, got a happy cheer as he stepped up in his special blue suit.

'Well here lies as spectacular a champagne socialist as there ever has been.' Pause. 'And I should know. I taught him all I knew.'

Nervous laughter. A few loud voices from the back.

'I know it is not long since he died. I know the temptation is to weep and wail and quiver with a rush of grief. But I know he would not have wanted it. Not Rohan. Not Stella – I'm sorry my darling to speak for you but do forgive me. You were both far too stylish for any of that.' He held up his hands and she nodded. She looked neither happy nor sad. Her face was still, and expression seemed to have been washed from it. Botox, I mouthed, then held back an inappropriate giggle. 'Try and imagine them, as they were that night, before it all happened. Smug, happy, pissed.'

Stronger laughs.

'I would not be surprised if many of you are thinking that if this accident had happened twenty years ago, the police would have been rummaging in my briefcase for wire cutters by now…' More laughter. 'But that was the great thing about Rohan Rickwood. He could make you forgive him anything. Make you laugh with some unexpected turn of phrase, or just seduce you with a mere swish of his crimping shears.' He ran his hands through his thick hair. 'He had that universal quality, that earthy charisma, a desire for self-improvement that cut through any challenge. And, of course, if that failed he'd just ply you with enough good booze so you'd forget why you were angry with him in the first place.'

There were loud laughs and nodding heads all around me. Jimmy Trowse showing off at Rohan's funeral, and me, hidden at the back, extraneous.

'Oh,' and he pointed at the congregation, 'and don't forget, the main reason we all loved him: he sure as hell knew how to make the fairer sex look like she needed a good *fuck*…' He slapped his hand over his mouth, feigned shock. 'Oh, sorry Vicar, sorry *God*, for my *naughty words*, but being *men* I'm sure you are both well aware of what I'm talking about…'

A lot of laughter then. Jimmy Trowse pulled a hipflask out of his jacket pocket, raised it, then took a good swig. 'I'll miss the bastard. And as for Stella, I'm sure I speak for everybody when I say that you are not alone. And nobody wears a Rickwood dress quite like you do.'

And then, this man who had behaved, in front of the altar, in front of God, in a way that would have been unacceptable at any normal human being's funeral, aimed a round of applause at the coffin of my dead uncle. After a few solitary claps he was joined by others, then others, until soon it seemed to me from my seat at the back that the entire body of the church was full of the sound of hands coming together, loud, enthusiastic, full of something I could not be part of, full of joy for what they believed, what they thought they knew, to be a life well lived, cut short, but worth something.

I sat completely still. I do not remember if I clapped. I had thought I wanted to say goodbye, to let go once and for all, but now I had so many unanswered questions. It did not help that my name – and those of my parents – were not mentioned once in the whole sycophantic, revisionist retelling of a life. Just one nod towards me, just one simple mention of the old life, would have pacified me, would have stopped the sear of fury in my chest, the scorch of injustice in my lungs. I had always believed I had rejected the old life. Sitting in a wooden pew at St Joseph's, I realised that the old life might have rejected me, and that was different.

'As you all know, Stella has decided not to speak at the funeral,' said Jimmy as the applause subsided. 'She has said that there are not enough words, that they would be wasted.' Stella was looking down at her hands. I thought it odd that she wore no hat. She was always such a one for etiquette. I could not see the whole of her face, just shots of her like she was appearing through one of those old-fashioned slide projectors. 'She is happy to speak to anyone at the wake. Bring her a glass of champagne and give her your favourite Rohan memory. That's all she wants.'

In my head the words: what about *me*?

I had intended leaving after the funeral, but Jimmy Trowse cornered me in the doorway on my way out.

'Crematorium, then wake,' he said. 'Come in my car with me Diana.'

'No. No thank you. I need to get back to town.'

'Nonsense. You're coming with me.' He held on to my cuff.

'No, really. I'm not going to the crematorium.'

He shrugged. 'The wake then. We're having it at the Metropole.'

I looked blankly.

'Let my driver take you. To Brighton. He knows where it is. He's got keys to my room. Have a shower, a couple of gin and tonics. Freshen up.'

I found it unbelievable that I had been 'chosen' by Sir Jimmy. I knew the routine. Rohan had told me about it in the pre-Stella days, drunk, boasting. He and Jimmy would survey any public gathering and choose a list of three women each. First choice and two reserves. In the unlikely event that none of the three women were interested, Rohan and Jimmy would swap lists and give the other's choices a go, by this time too bored or too drunk to care. There were variants of the game, like the time fifteen models of similar age, frame and features came to the house for a week to be fitted for Rohan's spring collection, and to be photographed on Cowling beach. Jimmy challenged Rohan to start at one end of the line-up, he at the other, and see who got to the centre model first.

'OK,' I said. 'Thanks.' I wasn't going to *do* anything. I wasn't even going to go. It is just easier, with someone like Jimmy, to consent and then make a deft escape.

'Great!' He raised his eyebrows. 'Wonderful.'

To the sound of strings and a trumpet the mourners at Uncle Rohan's funeral stepped out onto the shingle. There were photographers weaving in and out of the various groups, as though it were a wedding. At least the coffin was not being buried. Rohan was afraid of being buried alive. Not much chance of making that mistake here.

It was time to go home. To make my escape. I took one last look for the mysterious Glenys Pimm, but she was nowhere to be seen. I felt disappointed. I would have liked to have seen her shoes.

'Diana!'

I turned to see Toby Farrow striding towards me, his too-short trousers pressed against his body in the wind, the outline of his legs drawing my eye.

'Toby.' He swung towards me, tried to embrace me. I think he would have tried to lift me and swing me about if it wasn't for my crossed legs and hastily folded arms. 'I'm so glad you're here. I didn't know how to get hold of you. We didn't…Look! It's you!' He held his arms wide and shook his head. 'Diana!'

The trousers of Toby's suit skimmed the top parts of his ankles, and the creases in the sleeves were not quite close enough to the seams. The jacket's lapels were sixties-style, thin and insubstantial, unsuited to his now clean-shaven head. Despite this, despite the bad choice and bad fit,

I liked the material of his suit: some kind of cheviot, textured and a very dark green, the colour of moss on a tree.

'Yes, it's me,' I said. 'I wasn't going to come. It was a last-minute decision.' This much was true. 'I thought it was the least I could do, to come.'

'And you're coming to the crematorium?' He looked over his shoulder and threw his head about as though looking for something, or someone. 'It may not be too late for you to do a reading...or say something...'

All eyes upon me.

'I'm not coming.'

'What?! You've *got* to. You can't just turn up and disappear like Cinderella.'

I laughed, but my voice came out horizontal, monotone. 'I can't come. I have to get back.' All these dull, flat phrases. The opposite of sparkling conversation.

'Oh. Oh. Yes. Of course.'

It's Toby! Toby Farrow! Say something clever. Anything.

'But can we stay in touch?' He pulled an empty chewing-gum wrapper from one of the pockets in his trousers and a short pencil from his jacket. 'I've been trying to get in touch with you for *years*. I've been working on something. I didn't know how much you knew. I don't want you to get the shock of your life. Today is not the time for it. I haven't been able to talk about it...Oh, I'm rambling like an old woman...Just tell me we can stay in touch.'

Say no, that's all you have to do. Go home to Ronnie. Be happy.

'OK.'

'I want to talk to you about this film I'm making.'

'OK.'

He handed me the pencil and wrapper. 'Give me your number. I know I can't trust you to call me.'

I wrote down our actual phone number on the blue paper. It would have been so easy to slip in a wrong digit, to make up an entire row of numbers.

'I'm off,' I said.

'Yes. Right. Well. Good to see you. You sure you don't want to hang around and say hello to Stella?'

Good God no. 'Not this time. I'll miss my connection.' This was a lie. My ticket allowed me to catch any train I liked. An afterthought: 'Oh, is your mum here?' I looked about for Trudy. Plump, honest, reliable Trudy. She had lived in the house opposite ours through much of my childhood and had never failed to provide me with cakes, tea and the teenage magazines that Rohan had so forcefully forbidden me from buying.

'No,' he said. 'She's back in Cowling.' He looked about him for a moment. 'This isn't really her scene.' His face darkened and then he nodded. 'Well you take care.' Then two neat kisses on either side of my mouth. Hands on my shoulders.

'Bye Toby.'

'Bye Diana. I will call you.'

I ran along the church path, away from the flash of blonde hair I caught in the corner of my eye.

On the train I thought of Toby's legs, of that curve of skin behind his ear between his hairline, his hands on my shoulders, searing holes like cigarette burns through my dress. I thought of Stella's thin face, her fine bones and expressive fingers. Rohan in pieces, thrust into a hot furnace, no longer real, or even *there*.

At Victoria I changed into jeans and white shirt and wiped off my make-up, stuffed my dress and hat into my backpack. No need to provoke questions when I got home. Ronnie thought I had been at work. I walked home through Holborn, just as it was getting dark. There were rubbish collectors on every corner with sacks and big gloves and stubble. Central London is the only place I have ever lived that the binmen don't whistle at girls, although there was one man, one man in a small white electric sweeper who drove very slowly around the streets where we lived, collecting glass. He followed me sometimes, on my way back from the tube, drove alongside me. He seemed harmless, would ask me, endlessly, on dates, where I worked, what I did, who I was seeing. His name was Carson and he was from Nigeria. He was there this evening. The usual questions. This time I told him I was a journalist for the *Times*, that I wrote pieces on theatre and high fashion, that I really could not stop because I was on my way to interview a famous playwright over dinner.

2

Rohan Rickwood: tailor, man of silk. Uncle Rohan was dead.

The morning after the funeral, Saturday, Ronnie woke me up with breakfast on a tray. She'd cooked smoked kippers and poached eggs and opened a jar of her mother's homemade jam to spread on wholemeal toast. She'd put a copy of the *Guardian* on the tray and left it open on a piece in the 'Review'. A piece about Rohan that gleamed with black-and-white photography, a history in well-staged montage.

'You sure you're not related?' she said, putting the knife and fork in my hand. 'You look a bit like him. If I screw my eyes up and lean backwards.'

She laughed. I had not even grown up as Rickwood. I had been Diana Everett like my parents. Rickwood was the one bit of Rohan I had taken for myself once I left Cowling.

'Sort of,' I said. I felt uneasy about my previous lie. Maybe I could ease her in gently. I had got away without telling her about any of it, had recreated myself from remnants, anecdotes, TV soaps and bad radio plays. I had made myself all the things I had wished I was, and she'd believed me. I wanted everything to be separate. To keep things separate. I wanted to be a perfect me. Nothing like the real me.

I scanned the double-page spread, topping up yesterday's fury at the discovery that I was, once again, unmentioned. *Rickwood's muse, Stella Avery, is head curator at the Museum of Twentieth Century Fashion in West London. She is currently working on a retrospective of Rickwood's designs.* I did not know what I wanted. An acknowledgement would have been a start. Something. *Rickwood famously wooed Avery with a dress a week for an entire year, while she was still married to photographer Sir Jimmy Trowse.*

I saw Rohan's face scowling out at me: him and Stella, him and Jimmy, him and various *celebrities* at various *functions*, and I knew I'd left it too long. If I didn't make myself known soon I would be less than an ink-stain on the rewrite of the story of his life. Why did this matter?

'Sort of?' She bit a piece of toast, half a triangle in one mouthful. 'I was *joking*!'

'He was my uncle, Ronnie. My mother's brother.' I turned the paper over so I couldn't see his pixelated face, a picture taken after I'd left, staring at me, making me lose my appetite.

'Your *uncle*!' She bounced on the bed beside me. 'Rohan Rickwood! How come you never said! I know we don't *do* the past but – your *uncle*! How well did you know him?'

'Not that well,' I said. 'Not really.' It came out before I'd had a chance to think.

'Oh.' She seemed to accept this, and leant back into the headboard. 'So you're OK that he's dead then? You weren't close?'

'Not really,' I said. 'I hadn't seen him for ten years.' A truth.

'Your *uncle*!' She shook her head. 'You are a constant source of surprise, Dee Rickwood.'

Something I must explain about Ronnie is that she is a very beautiful thing – not beautiful like Stella, pale and unobtainable, but beautiful like fruit, like a slab of plum cake, like cream. I have never grown out of wanting to be surrounded by beautiful things. Sometimes, when we were at the supermarket dropping potatoes or carrots into plastic bags, or picking out shades of paint in DIY shops – terracotta, olive, sundrop yellow – I looked at her short nutmeg hair and the girth of her wholesome hips and thought, 'Mine. She's mine.' Not the healthiest, most loving of thoughts, I know. I could pretend it was something else I felt, something more salubrious – I'm sure many people do pretend to themselves about their own relationships – but I do not need to pretend about Ronnie.

'I've got a week off,' I said quickly, trying to slip this in behind the Rickwood revelation. 'Last minute. I had some holiday left over and Sylvie told me to just take it. You know Sylvie. Spontaneity personified.'

'That's unusual for her,' she kissed my forearm. 'But great. We can do lots of things!'

'Yes we can.'

Smoked kipper is a very specific taste – you have to be in the right mood, and I wasn't. It was a garish yellow, fluorescent, with the feathery, stained bones along its centre curling up in a puddle of tainted butter. It brought out the worst in the yellow of the walls, the worst in our carefully applied burnt-orange skirting boards.

'You should go to the National,' said Ronnie, clearing away trays. 'See some proper paintings.'

'Yes,' I said. 'Yes I should.'

I immediately crossed off the idea of going to the National Gallery. Last time I went at her suggestion I spent the entire day between the gift shop and the café. I didn't have the heart to traipse around neatly labelled sections or to pretend the art had any effect on me without her, other than to make me inexplicably want to creep around carefully wielding a scalpel. Shhhhhvit, shhhhhvit, shhhhhvit: neat tears in canvas.

Instead I pictured myself secretly spending my day looking through second-hand shops for interesting patterned material, making myself a new skirt, or blouse in mint green or sky blue. Maybe it was time to bring out the sewing machine, now Ronnie knew Rohan and I were related.

Sylvie Aldiss had not given me a week off. I had called her the day before the funeral and told her I had broken my leg. It was the first thing that came to mind, the most failsafe reason to be off work and completely unarguable. To make sure there would be no working from home I said I also had concussion, that I had fallen down the stairs and was covered in splits and bruises. She had said she was very sorry, that she hoped I was better soon, and could I keep her up to date on my progress. I didn't feel bad. If I *had* broken my leg then I would have been *entitled* to those days off. And it would be a treat not to stare at the computer and that endless roll-call of food words.

Succulent.

Juicy.

Drizzled.

Plump.

Slathered.

Moist.

Dark.

Smoked

Frothy.

Hot.

Ronnie cleared up and took the trays downstairs, rattling about with dishes, hot water and bubbles in the sink. I would have the day to myself. She would be off to the university to see Bob Routledge with more work on her PhD. 'Sex in the Garden of Eden: Milton on beauty', or something like that. It was hard not to get carried away by Ronnie's enthusiasm. She lived and breathed *ideas*.

Ronnie was actually my first girlfriend. I'd had flings, obviously. Especially when I first came to London and leapt from one bed to another, hating every moment but unable to say no. But with Ronnie it was different. It was not about the sex, which I could just about do if I focused on making her feel good. If I switched off. But when we were not in bed she made me feel like the world was full of wholesome, hopeful things. She made it possible for me to enjoy cooking, reading quietly by the window, chatting about the news. The sort of things other people – people not like me – did. Too good to be true, but it was true. It was how she lived. A proper grown-up. And now we shared a home, that was the most important thing, our small and perfect flat in the middle of the city; rented, old workers' quarters that had been taken on by the council and later sold on to property developers, mass landlords. We made up the interior – accidentally at first – to look like the gingerbread house, the woodcutter's cottage, bonding over our shared love of mismatched ephemera. We held small dinner parties for her friends, sausage and mash and Scrabble. We often had our breakfast at cafés on Russell Street, slipping out – less than five minutes from our flat – on free mornings and spending leisurely, precious minutes eating creamy puff pastries and strawberry-topped sponges, drinking spiced coffees and iced lemon tea.

Before she went she came up to give me a kiss. 'I've put some coffee on. When you want it. I'll see you later.'

'Love you Ron.'

'Love you too,' she blew an open-mouthed kiss from the doorway. 'Oh, a parcel came when I was washing up. I've left it on the windowsill.'

After I heard the front door swing shut behind her, I felt a rush of elation. Time stolen feels so much more full of possibility than time given. The thought of Sylvie Aldiss keying my number again and again was unexpectedly pleasing. Let someone else find new ways to make food look more like food. I went downstairs in my pyjamas.

As I poured coffee from the cafetière I glanced towards the sill. There, next to the unopened packets of herb teas and mixed nuts, was the parcel. I had to check three times to make sure I was not imagining it. Why was the past creeping in everywhere now he was dead? Please no, I thought. It's the jar baby.

When I was at home – I still think of Cowling as home – for as long as I could remember Uncle Rohan kept a dead baby in a jar on the shelf above his desk in the study. Part of his collection. I cannot remember what I thought the first time I saw it. I cannot remember ever first seeing it. It was always just there, this thing in a jar. I had always been fascinated with its lucent skin, with the thick furrows where the bloodlines had begun to form, with its droopy sack-body, veined like blue cheese. I remember likening it, at various stages of my youth, to wrung-out tea-towels, to AA road maps, to sponge cake soaked in sherry: the beginnings of a trifle.

When I was very young and yet to realise that human babies could be kept in jars, half-ready, forever awaiting birth, I thought it was some kind of mad scientist's experiment, some kind of rodent crossbreed, like in a cartoon. It was too big to be a normal mouse so it seemed logical that Uncle Rohan had somehow managed to get hold of the offspring of a mouse mating with a cat, or a badger, or, more appealing at the time, a golden retriever. Stella's golden retriever, Ruskin – named after her soon-to-be-ex-husband's hero – with whom

I would run on the beach and feed special treats from the sweet shop while Stella was being fitted for new clothes. I was forever pestering – for ten years or more – Rohan to get me one of my own. I would have called it Sable, like fur, or Rever, like lapels. But Rohan was very allergic to dogs. They made his eyes bleed pink, watery blood and his skin smell like creosote. They brought his fingers out in blisters.

The jar baby gleamed under Rohan's desk lamp like something warm and precious, like Ruskin's coat, and I imagined the relationship between rodent mother and her canine lover as being something of a grand romance. I pictured them kissing over spaghetti and their little baby appearing – rabbit-from-a-hat-like – the next morning. I was too young to consider the monstrous, bloody notion of a mouse giving birth to a swollen puppy, too young to associate myself with flesh, or even with having a flesh-and-blood mother – mine was a regenerating mermaid floating off the coast of Canada. I had dreams of Uncle Rohan lifting the mouse-baby from its mother's belly and placing it into the jar when its parents – caught up in the joys of mutual adoration – were not looking. For seven days, until he won me over in that way of his – that soft, coiled-up way – I considered Rohan nothing less than a murderer.

'Don't look at it Diana. Don't be morbid. I have enough morbidity for the both of us.' He tried to make a joke of it, but did not hide it away.

But the parcel was too small to be the jar baby. What a relief! What a silly thought! I didn't pick it up, couldn't touch it. I just bent over the counter, pushed my face right up close, examined it without actually having to become part of it. I knew it was from Rohan – the front was etched in the familiar brown ink, his thorned italic script spelling out my name, where I lived and a capitalised command: 'NOT FIRST CLASS'. I stared at the parcel for so long, for hours maybe, assessing it with my eyes. The subtle grain of the paper grew tighter, swelled with movement. I knew each little tear and scrape from its travels through the postal system. I knew every crease and bump and sticky-taped fold. I could almost see the place where his tailor's fingers had sealed the edges, where he had neatly tucked in the ends. He had always drawn lines on plain paper to keep his writing straight, and I could see the faint pencil outlines under his wording of my name, how he had tried, and failed, to scratch them away with the insubstantial rubber on the end of one of his yellow 2H pencils.

I could not guess what was inside. While it remained unopened I had the strange feeling that it was *him*, that somehow *he* had been wrapped inside the brown paper, tied up with string and postmarked Brighton with no return address. I owned him at last, but could not face him. I knew it wasn't *literally* him, I wasn't deluded. But I did think it might be some essence of him, some vapour that, if let out, would seep into all things and never leave me in peace. A packet full of magic dust.

He had not forgotten me.

For the rest of the day I didn't move from the kitchen. I made myself coffee. I watched the parcel. I could not escape the memory of the jar baby.

This went on for hours.

When Ronnie got home I was relieved. I swivelled round and hugged her tight, kissed all those silly little curls around her hairline (the rest of her hair was glass flat, apart from those never-growing whirls).

'Let's go out for dinner,' I said. Kiss, kiss, kissing.

'Not tonight,' said Ronnie, her hands around my waist. 'I've got too much to do here. What was in the parcel? Did you go to the National? What did you look at?'

'No I didn't. Not today,' I said. 'And there was nothing in the parcel. I mean I didn't open it.'

'Whyever not? On both counts.' She was undoing the buttons of my jeans.

'Because it's probably a load of old junk. It's from my Uncle Rohan.'

She stopped with my buttons and creased her nose.

'Oh, is it from his solicitor? Do you think you've *inherited* something?'

I looked at her, was no longer in the mood. I could see my face reflected in her spectacles. It was distorted, forehead-heavy, like a deflating balloon. My eyes were flicked ink.

Eventually I said, 'No.'

'That's odd,' she said. 'Funny he should send you something so close to when he died...'

'I suppose,' I said. Ronnie had just put into words what I'd been thinking. It didn't make sense. What was he trying to tell me?

'You suppose? You *suppose*?' Ronnie started towards the sill. 'You haven't rattled it or anything?' She reached out her hands, to touch it.

'No!'

We both jumped at the sound of my voice. It was like a conjuror's projection. It seemed to come from somewhere else. I pulled her towards me, coo-ed. 'It might be fragile. I'm sure it's nothing.' I kissed her ear. 'Tell me what you talked to Professor Routledge about today. I want to hear all about it. And show me what you've been painting.'

Ronnie sat down at her easel and pointed out a new wedge of green oils that she must have applied that morning. She kept her head tilted to one side, put her long squirrel brush in her mouth between her teeth and her lids screwed up tight under her brow. Her eyes were like slots or, I thought, surgeon's incisions. She looked happy though, paused as a statue. Like one of those silver-sprayed street mimes who stand about the Plaza on upturned crates, strapped to delicate wire wings. Ronnie needed little encouragement to talk about her ideas.

'We talked about the eighteenth century,' she said. 'About how the twenty-first century could be its mirror.'

I nodded. Why would Rohan send me something in the post after all this time? How did he find out where I lived? Why had he died so soon, so near to getting in touch? The parcel on the sill let out its own low frequency. A hum. It was louder than Ronnie.

'Do you remember when Elton John got all dressed up like one of those men at the Sun King's court, with a huge wig full of silly boats and sails? It was so heavy he had to have it held up with special pulleys! And nobody said a thing! How Marie Antoinette is that?'

He had touched that parcel. With his hands.

'Bravo Elton! Bravo! The Emperor's new clothes! Even now some people aren't afraid to spend their money, like a new kind of aristocrat. You look at all those Boucher paintings, that frothy Greuze. You look Dee…'

It is a message. A message from beyond the grave. I shook with that thought.

'…You look and you'll see it's true. Successful women were expected to have fat thighs then – to show their wealth. Successful women are supposed to have thin thighs now, to show their restraint. It's the same, but different. It's the same, but worse, because people think we are better now. They just stick the word "irony" on the end like it's a heal-all.'

It watched me from the windowsill, and I, in return, watched it.

'So you agree then?'

'What?' I blinked. 'Oh. Yes. Definitely.'

'I knew you would. I told Bob that even though you don't know much about the exacting details, you are philosophically tuned in to this stuff.'

'You did?'

'Yes. Yes. Of course. You're always giving me new ideas.' She kissed my neck. Three wet circles. 'He said I was lucky. His partners aren't interested at all. That's what happens when you become a sugar daddy. I've tried to tell him.'

'I like to think I'm of use.' This was a funny thing about Ronnie. I knew next to nothing about her favourite subjects, but, by nodding, saying 'Yes', or 'Really?' I had somehow given her the impression that I was thinking deeply about her intellectual questions. Her talking gave me time to think. I loved the sound of her voice when she thought she was coming up with new ideas, as if her rush of adrenaline was contagious, a shot to my system.

'You're being kind to call them "partners",' I said. 'Conquests would be more apt.'

'Ah Dee. The cynic between two thorns.' More kisses. 'Oh. Did I tell you the new thing about the serpent?'

'No.' There were only two words in my head. Suspicious circumstances. 'Tell me the new thing about the serpent.'

She patted her knee and I slid onto it. 'Well... The serpent in the garden wasn't unappealing like everyone thinks. What would be the point of that?'

I nodded.

'It has to be something more than that, right?'

'Yes.' Rohan in pieces. Flames between his fingers.

'Well I've got this Milton reference...'

'Really?'

'Yes... "So varied he of his tortuous train Curl'd many a wanton wreath, in sight of Eve, To lure her eye..."'

Maybe there were answers inside the parcel. Why did Stella change her mind about the helicopter? As Ronnie talked and I pretended to listen, I promised myself that I would open it tomorrow. If Rohan wanted me to know something, it was my duty to find out what.

3

The next morning Ronnie got up before I did, went off to university and left some cold boiled bacon out on a tray for my breakfast. She wrote a little note:

Off now. Sleep tight Sweet Prince. Love you.
Enjoy the National.
Stella Avery (!) called for you, early. I didn't want to wake you. Told her you'd ring today and I put her number on the pad by the phone.
Mwahhh.

Rx

Stella? Great. Thanks Toby. Don't ring yourself. Get Stella to do it. And why was she ringing now? There were times during the last ten years when I would have begged, indeed did beg, to hear from her.

I considered opening the parcel. The time wasn't quite right. I knew I had to leave the house so I wouldn't have to share any of my space with it. It was too loud, there on the sill. It filled the flat with a low murmur. I couldn't hear my own thoughts.

I tapped in the number Ronnie had left for me. A switchboard operator answered.

'Good morning. Museum of Twentieth Century Fashion. How may I direct your call?'

When had Stella started organising the Rickwood retrospective? Before the accident?

'Hello? Is anybody there?'

'Oh. Yes. Sorry. Can I speak to Stella Avery please?'

'Can I ask who's calling?'

'Dee. Dee Rick...Everett. Diana Everett.'

There was a click and then a Strauss waltz. I imagined myself dancing to it. Satin slippers. A proper picture-book heroine.

'Diana?' Nobody actually called me Diana any more.

'Stella.'

'Diana. Yes. It's me. Toby gave me your number. How are you bearing up?'

So intimate, as though we were still close. Just like Toby. He could never leave Stella out of it. 'I'm fine. Things are good.'

'Right.' She paused.

'I'm OK. Work is getting me through.' She sounded weaker than I remembered. In my mind, those past years, Stella was like a cage. Bars to keep everyone on the outside.

'You want to get some coffee?' It was me. I suggested it.

'Oh, yes. I could get you lunch. You could come here.'

'Where's here?' I tried to find amusement in her assumption that she would have to get me lunch, as though it was obvious that I would never match her fiduciary success, the career and 'lifestyle'. Rohan hated the word 'lifestyle'. He said it made a mockery of the true value of existence.

'The museum,' she said. 'Near Holland Park.'

'Right. What time?'

'Come at midday. I can take a couple of hours.'

We both hung up. I thought, oh good, Holland Park, I can go and watch the squirrels. That was what Ronnie and I used to do. In the beginning.

The Museum of Twentieth Century Fashion was new, with lots of honeycombed glass and clean sheets of steel. It looked like Stella, immaculate and moneyed. There were clusters of people – from all walks of life, multi-nationed – in little groups around the entrance. Some children on a school trip, dressed in purple blazers with a yellow cord trim, took it in turns to walk in front of the sliding doors: open, closed, open, closed, open.

'Just stop it!' said a man in a navy polo-neck jumper. He was trying to shout but not draw attention to himself at the same time.

'Just stop it!' said one of the boys in a rather impressive imitation of his teacher, then pushed past me, smelling of too much after-shave, sweat, hair-gel and swagger. The whole group, about ten in all, boys, got into a line beside Jumper Man. He looked relieved and scribbled at his clipboard of notes.

In the foyer of the museum there was a tall bronze statue of an excessively thin woman. She was faceless, had delicate elbows, knees, long tapered limbs. She was draped in a piece of blue-and-vermilion shot silk. I thought, that's Stella. The statue was labelled *Offsprung*, and was by a sculptor named Victor Eve, a name that seemed faintly familiar although I could not remember from where. I felt sure it was of the woman I used to know. It was typically Stella to put something so centred on herself in prime position. I looked at the silk, it was perfectly cut, hung straight and neat, like it could have been made of something hard, something solid. I reached out to touch it, wanted to let my rough fingers catch on the smooth material, to make a run.

'Don't touch! Please!' It was Stella. She appeared from nowhere, was next to me without making a sound. That's what it is to float on air.

'Sorry,' I said. 'It's beautiful.' Fool.

'Thank you,' she smiled, blushed even. 'Victor made it especially. He's doing a whole series of the things.'

We hadn't agreed where to meet. I had imagined approaching the reception desk, sounding important: 'Could you tell Ms Avery that Ms Everett is here to see her?' I don't know what got into me. I think it must have been all that glass and steel, the fountains and flower garden that grew in a semi-circle, welcoming visitors with a lilac-bloomed smile.

Stella was now a more severe version of the immaculate woman I used to know. She now had the drawn face that is the curse of the very thin after their mid-forties, although it was obvious that lotions and bronzers and powders gave her a look of health and kept her photogenic. She wore a tight black suit with sailor's trousers and a white shirt with oversized lapels. She had a series of antique brooches – a peacock, a daffodil, a snake, several unidentifiable, jagged silhouettes – pinned to a bright green sash tied around her waist. Her long hair was ironed straight, pinned back in loops behind her ears with onyx hair slides, and she wore long, gold-hoop earrings that hung past her chin. I shrank at the thought of my own work wardrobe. V-neck jumpers and black boot-cut trousers. Cakes at the desk. My job to get the copy done, invisibly, on time. To source photographers who could make an egg custard look like pure joy. It was Stella's job to be the shiniest button in the sewing basket, to flash and glitter and shine.

'Shall we go somewhere else?'

'OK,' I said. I wanted to look around the museum, to see her office, the people she worked with, but I didn't want to see any of Rohan's clothes. Not yet.

At the main desk an attractive girl, about twenty-four, was showing a leaflet to a group of French exchange students. She wore a black-and-white striped sweater, off her lovely freckled shoulders. I made a point of catching her eye on the way out. She smiled. A blush?

Usually, I am a very monogamous person.

Stella and I walked along Abbotsbury Road and past Ilchester Place.

'Can we say a quick hello to the squirrels in the park?' I said.

Stella nodded, but seemed rather preoccupied. I thought of the opera Ronnie and I had seen at the park theatre last summer. They'd produced it in a fifties style, although it was still as lavish and bright as the music, and we watched it greedily, lapping up the flaming voices and hurtling orchestra. I'd never been to an opera before Ronnie was educating me.

'I saw *The Marriage of Figaro* here last summer,' I said.

'Ah *Le Nozze di Figaro*,' said Stella in a slow, correct voice. 'Wasn't it *wonderful*? I saw it with Rohan.' She sighed.

The houses stood back from the pavements, with large, slabbed steps leading up to the doors: white, cream, and long deep-set windows that reminded me of wedding cake. The houses were tall, were probably flats now. I wondered how high the ceilings were compared to those in our flat.

In the park Stella and I stood on soft grass and watched a child feed a squirrel dry bread.

'Have you seen Daniel Young recently?' said Stella.

'No,' I said. 'Have you?' Daniel Young was the son of a friend of Stella's I once went out on a few dates with when I was sixteen.

'Yes. Yes I did. He came out. Living with his boyfriend in Muswell Hill.' She gave me a sidelong glance.

'Really? Good old Richard. Good for him.' Was she trying to imply that I'd turned him gay? Or that she knew he was gay when she set us up? That would be just like Stella. I remembered my dates with Daniel. Pizza Express, dough balls, chatter about his work as a sports correspondent. One time in his car he tried to rip me out of my dress and called me a delicious tease. Luckily it had too many buttons and he'd had one vodka tonic too many and he gave up before he got past my midriff.

'What about Lucy Bowers? And Joey Rendell?' She tapped each name out on a different finger. 'Or Peter Woodward? Or Jamie Ulrich? Do you ever wonder whatever happened to him?'

Names I hadn't heard or thought of for years. This is what people do when they have so much to say they do not know where to begin. They talk about everyone else.

'Peter's in the army,' I remembered. 'I heard he plays clarinet in the marching band. Three children, all with names beginning with A. Archie. Alfred. Annabel. Can you believe that?'

'What's his wife's name?'

'Alice?'

We laughed a little.

'Jared Robinson said he saw you a few years back.'

'Did he?' Nonchalant.

'Yes. He said you were at a hotel in Warwick. Away for a murder mystery weekend. You were the murderer.'

I thought about this. 'No I wasn't. I was the murderer's scapegoat.'

She raised an eyebrow. 'He was adamant you were the glamorous murderess. He said he marked you off on his card from the moment you walked in.'

'Nice. But he was wrong. I was the murderer's lover, if I remember rightly.'

'He said you didn't remember him.'

'I was in character. He probably got confused.'

'Maybe.' I had been there with Ronnie. It was an anniversary present. She had been the murderer and I'd been her lesbian lover for whom she'd killed her rich, stupid husband. I had been annoyed we had been cast to type. Ronnie had laughed and said it was because we both looked so damned straight. Jared Robinson had been cast as Ronnie's husband and had remembered me in the bar. He'd bought Ronnie and me a drink – without asking – and laughed that maybe we could act out our roles in the privacy of his room. I had sat, startled, and said nothing. Ronnie, clever Ronnie, had said, 'What, we quietly kill you and have lots of sex in the shadow of your dead body?' If only I could say things like that. I just froze. I had the horrible feeling that without her I would have ended up in his room for lack of something to say in retort.

'I never liked him much you know.'

'What, Jared?'

'Yes. He was a nobody who thought himself important.'

'Yes I suppose he was. A lot of that crowd were a bit… You know, I wish you'd stayed in touch,' she said. 'I wanted to talk to you.' I'd always thought our first meeting after all this time would be melodramatic, exciting, fireworks in dark skies. Instead it was calm acceptance; another piece of the past patched neatly into the present. You still couldn't see the joins.

'Talk away,' I said. I was determined to let her do the work. If she thought I had forgotten those times I tried to get in touch, those desperate phone calls asking for help, then she was wrong. And as for Toby. That was unforgivable.

'You have to learn to look after yourself Diana,' she'd said the last time. 'You can't keep calling here every time you break a fingernail.'

The cuts on my arms and legs were serrated like the edge of the bread knife.

'I was ringing to say hello,' I said. 'To see how you both are.'

'We are fine. We are good. Very busy. It's nice having all this time to ourselves. What are you doing?'

I nearly said, 'I am sitting on the floor having cut my arms and legs to pieces. I cannot look after myself. I can barely get out of bed. I want to come home. I want you and Rohan to come in the car and pick me up and let me sleep to the sound of seagulls for a hundred years.'

I actually said, 'Working, sleeping, working. You know.'

'Well, keep at it. You can make a good life for yourself.'

'Yes Stella.'

'Well take care.'

'You too.'

'Love you.'

'Love you too. Tell Rohan I...'

She had already hung up.

Now she was breathing slowly, picking at the skin around her fingers, almost destroying a perfect manicure. Almost.

'You make it difficult...' she said. 'I thought you'd get in touch about the funeral. That maybe you'd do a reading. Anything. But you didn't. You didn't do anything.'

'Me?'

'Yes. You've got all this...*face*,' she said.

'*Face*?'

'Yes...I want to talk to you about...things...we need to work out what to do with the house. If we can make a claim. It's going to be given to...What is it?'

I had stopped walking. '*Face*?!'

She turned, her red coat a bright swirl of woven wool. 'You left without a word,' she said. 'How could you do that? Without saying anything. Rohan was a nightmare when you left. You made what should have been the best time of my life utterly horrendous.'

'*I* just left *you* there?' Rohan was a nightmare when I left? Something about that pleased me. I had thought they had enjoyed their alone time.

'Yes.'

'Stella...It was a long time ago. Things are different now. I'm different now. I barely remember anything about it. It seems like another time completely.'

She shrugged. 'Rohan was not everything you thought he was. There is a lot about him you don't know, and it is not necessarily my place to tell you. *I* didn't know most of it, in the beginning.' I stared at her. I could feel my eyes burn.

'Let's eat,' she said. 'It doesn't matter. You're here now. I know where you are now. You're not going anywhere yet.'

We stepped away from the squirrels and back onto the pavement and walked.

'Here?' Stella stopped in front of a small Italian restaurant called Tentare. I thought I knew what the name meant, but could not remember. The windows were deep-set, the frames painted dark to look like antique wood. The glass panels were splashed sporadically with round swirls, making the lit candles from the inside gleam out, from various angles, either warm and twinkling or distorted and sad. There was creeping ivy around the door, with big plastic cream blooms stapled to the vine, and baskets of artificial (or very stale and plasticated) bread at the entrance, accompanied by onions, tomatoes, leaves of basil – all fake, glistening with gloss varnish. I make it sound dreadful, but it wasn't. It had the illusion of being somewhere very fine indeed.

As soon as we were inside I felt better. It was easier to be in her company with a silent audience.

I ordered miniature pancakes with smoked haddock to start, Stella ordered sweet and sour baby onions. I was teetotal then. I had given up drinking for around eight years, since I had first got together with Ronnie, so was surprised when Stella ordered a bottle of red and I allowed the waiter to fill my glass. Just the one. Make this whole meeting a little less starched. I'd not had a drink for so long, I was bound to know when to stop now. That was the problem before...not the drink itself, no, drink is just drink...but knowing when to stop. The promise I'd made Ronnie, well, it probably didn't count any more. I'd made that promise when I was a different Diana. When I needed her help. When I needed to prove that I was worthy.

'Sassicaia 1999,' said Stella. 'Cabernet and Sangiovese. Delicious.' There were tiny wrinkles around her lips, and the skin on her neck was thin and like used cling film.

'Lovely,' I said. I had absolutely no idea what she was talking about and, considering my job, felt a fraud. I usually recommended wines from suppliers who'd done nice deals with the buyers. That is the way these things work.

I watched her pick at her food like I had seen her do so many times in the past. There was no Rohan there, and I felt exposed. There was nobody to filter our actions and reactions through. We both drank steadily. I helped myself to more bread.

'You not hungry?'

'I don't have a big appetite. You know that.'

I thought of the slender statue. Who was Victor Eve?

There were many reasons I left the beach house at Cowling. Many of which I had purposely avoided since I moved to London aged nineteen. It was the passivity I'd hated. My passivity. I wanted to be somebody who made things happen. Not somebody who let things happen around her.

Stella visited Rohan every week for several years before they married: a glamorous, red-lipsticked model, married to Jimmy Trowse, who spent most of his time in other countries or in other women. After a while, behind her back, Uncle Rohan always said what terrible taste Stella had in clothes, that she had no ideas of her own. She wanted, like many of his clients, to look 'like she had stepped from the pages of a magazine'. This, I came to realise, was one of Rohan's worst insults. It was really his way of saying women were like static puppets, waiting for someone to bring them to life.

I wasn't supposed to go into the fitting room when clients were there, unless specifically called for by the jangle of Rohan's servant bell. I used to bring tea and a china plate of Lincoln biscuits – which were usually only eaten by him – long before they arrived. I would slip in, stealthy, practical in my shirt and jeans, and set out the tea things. Sometimes they would request black coffee, peppermint and camomile infusions, or hot water with sliced lemon and shavings of ginger at the bottom of the cup. He made out orders for me on tickets of pink paper like I was a waitress. It was always important to Rohan that I stayed out of the way. *They must not see you Diana. Keep out of sight.* When I was very young I wondered if they had something wrong with their eyes, until I worked out it was because of something wrong with *me*.

When it was just Rohan I would take a pot of black tea and a jug of goat's milk as he sat there with his dressmaker's dummies, mannequins draped in cloth, in taffeta or cotton, most often silk. He would have pins hanging out of his mouth and his work glasses pressed precisely onto the end of his nose. It was only after they'd gone that I was allowed in for any significant amount of time, ushered in. While Rohan entertained Stella in the finer rooms of the house it was my job to trawl the carpet of the workroom for errant pins. With my fingers adorned with thimbles, coloured like gems, I would tug at the flat-weave floor and pull out the hidden silver spikes. They were packed into the carpet like mesh armour, hundreds buried tight into the grain.

'So, what have you been doing?' Stella dabbed the corner of her mouth with a napkin. There was a faint ring of lipstick on her glass.

'Oh, you know. This and that,' I said. 'I'm a food writer now. For Fair's Fare, you know, the fair-trade-y supermarket for people with too much money and too much guilt.'

'Really? Sounds interesting. What do you do?'

'Oh you know. Source recipes, collect photography...choose ingredient of the month, that kind of thing.'

'Sounds fun.'

'It is.' Was she being sarcastic? I knew Fair's Fare was hardly glamorous. But glamour wasn't part of mine and Ronnie's life. Glamour was irrelevant. This reminded me of something Toby once said to me. 'Do you hate glamour because you think it is a waste of time and resources, or because you wish you were a part of it, but feel you can't be?' I had had trouble answering him. If I had answered him I would have had to tell him about Drake.

I wasn't supposed to end up in food pornography to part shoppers from their hard-earned cash. I think Rohan had always thought he would train me up, get me nifty with patterns, and pins and fine lines. For a while I even – and I bet that shiny curator Stella didn't know this – did some finishing: I sewed the button holes, felled the lining and stitched the edges. I started off on men's and was about to start on women's when I ran away. As well as the infamous women's workroom, Uncle Rohan had another room entirely separate for men's tailoring, where I was allowed to come and go as I pleased. I had more responsibility in there, and liked it because it was plain, with clear wooden floors and shelves stacked with books as high as the ceiling. There were big, thick books, full of places, dates, addresses and names, although Rohan never let me see them. There was one old-style tailor's mannequin. It had a bald, faceless head and it always wore a slanted Humphrey Bogart hat. Sometimes I would pretend it was my husband. He was a kind husband who didn't expect me to do anything I didn't want to do. And he made me laugh, belly laughs that shook me till I had tears in my eyes.

My mobile began to buzz in my jacket pocket.

'Oops. Sorry,' I said and pulled it out to switch it off. 'SYLVIE' was flashing on the screen. 'Actually, I'd better take this,' I said. 'Give me a second.'

Outside by the plastic food I accepted Sylvie's call.

'Dee. How are you?'

'I'm OK thanks. Bearing up.'

'Poor thing. Everyone sends their regards. Unlucky you.'

'I'm feeling a bit better today. The bruises are going down, at least that's something.' I scratched at my knee. 'But it itches like hell, Sylvie. This damn plastercast. I look like something out of *Star Trek* with an elephantine leg.'

She laughed. 'At least you've not lost your sense of humour. What about your head? Do you feel up to doing some work at home?' I touched my forehead, feeling for impossible bumps. 'I know you'll be missing us…I could get some stuff sent over if you feel up to it. I wouldn't want you to get bored.'

'OK,' I said. 'But my head is in a pretty bad way. I find I can't remember where things are in the kitchen. Coffee in the tea jar. Biscuits in the fridge.'

'Poor thing…Lucy, poor Dee is going senile…No, seriously. I hope you get better. And if you need anything, just shout.'

A voice called something out in the background. 'Lucy says to tell you it's not the same without you.'

'Tell her it's not the same without her either.'

'It's not the same without you either.' She laughed. 'Ahh. She blew you a kiss. How sweet. Well, if you get any thoughts about this new Food for all Seasons campaign let me know. Any good puns for slogans will be much appreciated.'

'Will do, Sylvie. Thanks for calling.'

'No probs. You rest up Dee. Make sure that Ronnie takes good care of you. Byeee.' Several voices shouted Goodbye behind her.

'Bye. Send my love to everyone. Ooh. Wait. Sylvie, are you still there?'

'Yes.'

How about *Season's Eatings*?'

'Dee. You are a genius. Season's Eatings. Great. Now, rest up.'

Back at the table Stella had poured the last of the wine.

'Sorry,' I said. 'That was work. They want me to go on this thing to France. To source recipes for a new farmhouse cookery leaflet.'

'Very nice,' said Stella. There were so many familiar things about her. How could she have changed so little? I felt I was completely different, but she, she was the same, with skin like antique manuscript.

'What about you?' I said. 'This exhibition about Rohan? How long has that taken to set up?'

'Oh, you know.' She looked out of the window. 'I've been working on it for about a year. Rohan gave me lots of things for it. You must remember what a hoarder he was. And I've got nearly all of my dresses from the year of dresses.'

'Wow,' I said. 'A lot of work.'

'Yes. I've got some things to sort out, mostly because he's dead. It makes it different.'

'I bet.' The interest in the exhibition was bound to have significantly increased since Rohan's death. As far as I'd heard he had hardly been setting the catwalk alight the past few years.

'Look,' she paused. I wondered if she had been about to make a confession. Or an apology. Or anything. Instead she said, 'I'm having a party tonight at Toby's flat.'

The waiter took our starter plates, and as Stella ordered coffee I realised she had considered them our mains.

'Right.' I thought she was explaining why she was eating such a meagre lunch, but she was inviting me.

'I'd like you to come.' She picked at the threads on the tablecloth, destroyed some hand-embroidered lilies.

'Right.' I wasn't prepared to say yes or no. I thought of Ronnie.

'There will be loads of people who are interested in Rohan's work, who have helped me, the *museum*, pay for rare items.'

'Right.' Had she told her friends about me? Not so invisible after all.

'So you'll come?'

'OK.'

'Would you like to bring a guest?'

Quickly, 'No.'

'Diana…' Stella put her hands over mine across the table. 'What happened? Are you ever going to tell me what happened? Everything would have been so much easier if you had left nicely at the time we discussed. Disappearing – that was selfish. You didn't think of what you left behind you.'

How could she twist everything? 'Stella, you must know. I don't need to tell you.'

'Indulge me.'

I didn't know what to say.

I stared at her and wondered if she remembered that last night as vividly as I did. She looked slightly different now, but I could still see her as she was then, on that night the entire house was decorated with rolls of velvet and fake diamonds. They would have used real stones if they had not been afraid of people stealing them. 'It would be nice if we *did* have diamonds to give away,' Stella had said. 'The ultimate gesture. But we do not.' Instead I had sewn sequins on the curtains and glued them onto the wine glasses set out in the kitchen. Silver streamers were hung from ornamental chandeliers as I took small pastries from the oven and dusted them with icing sugar.

Rohan and Stella's engagement was announced in *The Times*. It made the BBC evening news, but as I did not have regular access to a television I never found out what tone they took. I imagined that people thought it a Good Thing. Lovers entwined together after all those years of faux-secrecy. And they'd had Sir Jimmy's blessing.

Stella had even brought me a suitable dress for the occasion. She stood in the doorway of the kitchen with a purple, leather vanity case and two suit bags curled over her forearm.

'I'm here to get us dressed,' she said, smiling. 'I've found some perfect shoes for you.' I wanted to enjoy the moment but I was suspicious. Was she doing this to make herself look good? The perfect guardian in the eyes of the world. Nothing to do with how she felt about me.

In my bedroom Stella stripped me to my underwear. She shook her head at my grey bra – 'The wrong size my darling! How have I let this pass so long?' – and loose-elastic knickers. She had brought me everything, right down to the insoles to go in the spike heels she let me borrow. Stella's feet were a whole size larger than mine, a fact that at that time brought me great comfort.

We stood before each other in our underwear. Stella nearly naked was not beautiful; her body was strange and sunken, small breasts and sharp collarbones. I thought how much more beautiful she looked in clothes. Her hair hung over her shoulders like cut, pressed silk. I wanted to stroke it. I remember that urge, now, the urge to put my hands on it. To swap bodies and to know what it would be like to be her.

She had stood ready before me like a trophy. She looked younger than her forty-two years in a peppermint, backless dress with gold heels and matching earrings. She had a Chanel clutch bag, grey leather with a big golden buckle. A Tiffany hairpin fixed a side parting and her make-up finished her. Her eyes were vivid and wet. She had a strange look. 'This will show *her*!' she said triumphantly.

She had been speaking more and more nonsense in the weeks before the party. Nonsense about imaginary women and imaginary laws. I had wondered if she had been taking drugs.

'Do you remember the party?' I said.

'What, our engagement? Are you *joking*?'

'Yes. You were wearing the peppermint dress. You leant me your shoes.'

'You posted them back without a note. That's how I knew you were in London.'

'I couldn't keep them. I've never been a silver stiletto kind of girl.'

'But you *wanted* to be. I knew you wanted to be, but you never *stood up* to him. But it made no sense. For you to run like that.'

'I hardly *ran*, in *those* shoes. I want to know what you thought you were doing,' I said. 'Why you felt the need to mock me?'

'When did I ever mock you? All I ever did was *help* you.'

'Dressing me up like a ...' I drank more wine. 'What is the point of going over this? We both know what happened. I don't want to think about it.'

Stella sat up straight in her chair and slid a pale slice of hair behind her ear. 'I want to know what you were doing with Jimmy.'

'What?' Had she seen us at the funeral? Had she heard me say I'd go back to his hotel?

'That's what's bothering me,' she said quietly. 'I want to know what you were doing with my ex-husband.'

'One thing I can assure you, Stella,' I said, 'is that nothing has ever happened between myself and Sir Jimmy.'

'It was like you wanted to upstage me,' she said. 'The two of you. I don't know why you would do that after all I did for you.' I had absolutely no idea what she was talking about. This was about her betrayals, and if she was not going to acknowledge what had happened the night I ran away, I certainly wasn't.

'What time?'

'What?'

'What time tonight?'

'Oh. Well. Seven thirty. Bring a bottle. Or two.'

'OK,' I said.

'I want to give you this.' She pulled a brightly coloured gloss catalogue from her bag. 'We can talk about all this properly another time. Not in such a public place.'

It was a brochure about her Rohan exhibition. A photo of him on the front, arm around her in a scarlet fishtail ball gown. They were laughing. Rohan's shirt matched Stella's gloves.

Stella was already at the door, taking her dark-red coat from the stand and air-kissing the waiter, a man she knew. As the shape of her, the slender shape of her, disappeared into her green city, I thought just how much the statue looked like her.

I had been left with the bill. And less than a glassful of wine.

'I'd like to order a main course,' I said to the waiter, finishing what was left of the bottle. 'And another bottle of your...' I looked at the label. 'Sassicaia 1999.'

4

The man sitting opposite was called Benjamin Burne, but he went by the name of Benjy. Benjy Burne worked in fashion journalism. All Stella's friends gathered around the table worked, it seemed, in what she called *the style industry*. Most of them were younger than her. She dragged me through the door as a special guest because I was, she said, not only her sort-of stepdaughter – what?! – but an honorary member of the *fashionocracy*. Her word.

I realised straight away that, as though all those funeral wishes had been granted, I was no longer Dee Rickwood, Food Editor for Fair's Fare supermarkets, but Diana Rickwood, niece of the glamorously dead and fêted designer Rohan Rickwood. Nothing excites the masses more than tragedy and glamour, and the story of Rohan and Stella was that incarnate.

All I needed to know about Benjy Burne was in his dandelion-print tie and olive Bengaline suit. Jaunty. Very Stella. I didn't listen to him. He flicked his fingers as he talked, gesticulating not unlike Stella herself. It went without saying that his hands were elegantly long. Stella always had a thing for artistic hands. She would coo over Rohan's hands like a wood pigeon.

I noticed, pretty speedily, and perhaps drunkenly, that Stella's dinner party was all about acting and expressing wonder. *Darling, how wonderful. Have you met Ivan? Here, Izzy, isn't Jane's clutch bag completely wonderful. Go on Diana, tell them about Rohan's workroom. Wasn't it just wonderful?*

That was another realisation. Stella was staying with Toby in his flat in South Kensington. I could not believe they were being so blatant. Could nobody else see what was going on?

I poured myself some Rioja. It didn't feel like a bad idea. I had been self-controlled for so long, tried so hard to make myself a better person, surely I needed a day off. I had missed the drink. Benjy, who popped out smoke rings that rose up towards the wrought-iron lampshade, was talking about a Lelong-style dress Rohan had made for Stella in the year of fifty-two dresses.

'It's amazing he managed to make so many in such a short time,' said Benjy. 'How the devil did he do it?'

I remembered the dress he was talking about: its indigo, pointed sleeves, its thin hem and sweeping neckline. I wondered what he had been buried in. Was it something I'd helped finish in the other workroom?

'Determination,' I said. 'Bloody-mindedness.'

Toby appeared from the kitchen, carrying champagne. He looked old in the newness of his flat. It was very Stella. He must have been programmed into it, just *must* have been. Whatever happened to *his* taste? My old feelings about her stirred with the wine. This house had polished wooden floors; blonde, Scandinavian? I had no idea. There were lots of chrome shelves, made up of tubes, lots of beige – and its daring variants, mushroom, taupe and fawn – sofas and cushions and even a chaise longue. There was no clutter anywhere. I knew this must be a fashionable look, and I knew that Ronnie would hate it. Neither she nor Toby would ever look right there.

Stella was dressed in dark silk – it was one of Rohan's. The fit told me he'd made it especially for her. All of Rohan's clients wanted to be dressed in silk. His workroom was full of dummies and thread and yards and yards of silk. Brocade, cire, crêpe, faille, foulard, gauze, grosgrain, peau de cygne, peau de soie: a litany of silk. But that – and this is what none of them realised – was *just one room*. There was more to Rohan than clothes. Anybody who had ever bothered to get to know him knew that. Rohan was a talented painter, for one thing, although he always seemed to destroy his paintings when they were done.

And Rohan had his secrets, hidden, locked away in cabinets and drawers, a whole other life nobody, not even I, knew about. Sometimes I would imagine I was a spy and it was my job to work out just what he was hiding. I would hunt and sneak and forage, but I never found anything that made any sense. And I could never be sure. I was certain, as the jar baby sat on his shelf, that it must have had something to do with it. I caught him, on more than one occasion, singing lullabies to it, soft words and melodies that he murmured barely moving his lips. 'I am living the wrong life,' he would say. 'And you are not even living yours.' But my investigations brought no answers. The jar baby was a riddle. And now Rohan was dead the whole thing was unsolvable.

Benjy Burne was talking a lot about a book he was writing on Rohan. He said there was a market for it now, since the death. He said unashamedly that the story had everything: glamour, aristocracy, fashion and death. He had a tape recorder on constant whirr. Every time he asked me something I knocked back more wine and fed him false information.

'How many hours a day did Rickwood spend working?'

It depended – sometimes one, sometimes fifteen. 'Ten.'

'Who was his favourite designer?'

He didn't have any, but he was a big fan of the Romans. 'Jean Paul Gaultier.'

'Who was his inspiration?'

Jane Russell. 'Bette Davis.'

'Did you ever have any reason to suspect he was having affairs with anyone other than Stella?'

Well, only if the many other women counted. 'No. Not at all. He adored her.'

'Was it always his aim to get a knighthood?'

No, he was a socialist. 'Yes. He talked about it all the time.'

'How did he maintain his friendship with Jonathan Trowse?'

They pulled women together. 'Good-heartedness.'

Little things, exaggerations, outright lies, all sucked up into his cassette recorder for later use.

Stella came and sat between us and touched both our arms. I knew instantly that she and Benjy were having an affair. Of course they were. Toby would never be enough for her. It was all about the chase, about the getting, for Stella. I was about to challenge him on it. Ask questions in his own style.

'So how long have you been fucking Stella Avery?'

'How often do you do it? Do you think she fakes it?'

'How do you maintain your hypocritical friendship with Toby Farrow?'

And then, through the door walked the woman Sir Jimmy had named as Glenys Pimm.

'Sheriff of Nottingham,' I said. 'She looks…lipstick.' I could not put my words together in any kind of intelligible order.

'Pardon?' Benjy was gesturing to Toby, who was passing us with a bottle of champagne.

'Nothing,' I said. 'I'm just going to the toilet.'

By the time I got to where Glenys Pimm had been she had gone, and I wondered if I had imagined her. Instead I stood in the queue outside the bathroom as Toby came past, with his bottle.

'Diana?' He waggled the green bottle in front of me.

'I've left my glass. Other room.'

'Have mine.' A woman in a blue pleated pinafore handed me her glass, a splash of red wine in the bottom. 'I'm moving onto the *hard* stuff.'

'Don't tell me,' said Toby. 'If you don't tell me, I won't be able to judge you. Or stop you.'

'Malk. You're so tightly sprung.' The pinafore woman put her arm around Toby's shoulders. Malk?

'Nahh,' said Toby. 'Just careful…' He slipped out of her grasp. 'Diana…' He poured the drink into my soiled glass. The red rose up in a twist and turned the bubbles pink.

'Toby. Toby!' I pulled his ear towards my mouth. 'I know about Stella.'

He put his mouth right by my ear, his lips almost upon my earlobe. 'You do?'

'Yes. I'm so sorry.' I wanted him to know that Stella was cheating on him. To tell him before they made a fool of him. I wanted to ask the question that begged to be asked. Did Stella kill Rohan? And the one that begged not to be: did you have anything to do with it?

'I can't believe you ever thought otherwise,' he said. This made no sense, so I thought I heard him wrong.

'Someone once told me that I'm the type of woman one expects to make the first move…'

'Pardon?'

Music came from the front room. A guitar solo, a Moog, Mancunian vocals.

'First move…I'm not…it's pride…move.'

'It's good to see you having a good time. A lovely drunkard.' He ruffled my hair. Why was he ignoring me? I was trying to tell him something important.

'I have to be a good host,' he said. 'Speak later?' He kissed me then, on top of my hair, light. His lips didn't press hard enough to meet the skin.

I drank my champagne in one swallow just as the woman in the pinafore leant out of the toilet door, voice dropped low. She hissed, and grabbed the strap of my top.

'Come and join me,' she said. 'I hate doing it alone.'

Laid out on the toilet were two neat lines of cocaine. I stared at them for only a second before watching her fling her head down, her hair around the bowl. One long sniff and then a laugh. One high-pitched laugh.

'Why does that always feel so *good?*' She laughed. Her blonde hair fell back over her shoulders and she reapplied her mascara in the mirror. I thought she looked familiar, that I'd seen her on an advert for some accident-pay-out law firm. She passed me the rolled-up twenty-pound note and smiled. 'This one's on me.'

One sniff couldn't hurt. After all, this was *fun*, and it was so long since I'd had any *fun*. I let her hold my hair away from my face, her thumb at the nape of my neck. Self-belief in one snort.

'Doesn't it always make you feel like your knickers are on fire?' She laughed again and we stroked away the last remnants from the lid. Before we opened the door we kissed a little. Open mouths. Teeth.

As we closed the door behind us she put out her hand. 'It was nice to meet you.'

'Nice. You too,' I said. I put my fingers up the inside of her top, under her bra. Just for a moment. Neither of us said our names.

The party unfolded in a series of foggy pictures, single frames through my unclear eyes. Bright colours. Laughter. Loud music. Toby and Stella dancing to somebody playing folk guitar. Benjy Burne with his notebook and his ears up, like a dog.

It all seemed so familiar. But this time I was inside it. I remember thinking one word. Victory! And then another. Love!

Benjy was in the corner drinking clear liquid from a tall glass.

'What's your tipple?' I said. 'Can I have some.'

'Tap water,' said Benjy, and passed it to me. I pretended to take a sip and nodded thanks.

'You can ask me some more questions if you like,' I said.

'Pardon?' He took his pencil from behind his ear.

'I'm ready to answer some more questions.'

Benjy put one hand on my shoulder. 'If you want to, just talk, and I'll write down anything that might be useful.'

'He didn't love Stella,' I said. 'At least not exclusively. If you know what I mean.'

Benjy said nothing. He held his Dictaphone curled up in his palm.

'He was at it with practically *everybody*...' The model from the toilets wandered past. She had a glass of champagne in one hand and the hand of a thin man in pinstripes in the other. I tugged the hem of her pinafore dress and smiled up at her.

She looked down at me. 'Hey sweetie! I could really do with another trip to the ladies'.' She winked.

I giggled. 'You couldn't get me one of those could you?' I gestured to her champagne.

'Have this.' She passed me hers. The pinstripe man held tightly to her other hand and pulled her in the direction of the toilets. 'My turn,' he said angrily, and she looked back at me, rolled her eyes, and gestured with the little finger of her right hand.

'Catch you later?'

'Too right,' I said. I downed my champagne as quickly as possible. My head rolled around in small loops. It felt like I had all the answers to all the questions in the universe.

'I am back with my people,' I said to Benjy. 'These are my people.'

'Pardon?' Benjy put his pencil back behind his ear. 'Look, Diana, are you OK?'

'Yes. Yes. I'm great. Ronnie is too boring. She won't let me have any fun. If she were here she wouldn't let me...'

'Is there anything else you want to say now? We could arrange a meet for another day?'

'No! No! Wait!' I grabbed his wrist. 'It's about Stella,' I said. 'You should really know, if you're going to be spending as much time with her as you seem to be, that she cannot be trusted.'

'What are you talking about?'

'I caught her, you see,' I said. I was laughing loudly.

'Caught her doing what?'

I looked up to see her talking to Toby. They leant towards each other, were flicking through a pile of vinyl records, holding up shared favourites, laughing. Shameless. Brazen.

'I caught her on the dragon-footed piano,' I said. 'I thought someone was playing Stravinsky. There were all these chords, you see. I could hear them from the corridor.'

I was still staring at her. She looked so blameless. If only she had said sorry at lunch. If she'd admitted she had been in the wrong, that she had betrayed me, I wouldn't be swaying here next to the ridiculous Benjy Burne.

'It wasn't Stravinsky. I had convinced myself them on the beach was my imagination. That I'd twisted it. Misconstrued. But that night it was her arse on the keys. She was there, on the baby grand...her peppermint dress bunched up around her legs, like a, like a, I don't know. Like a prostitute in a painting, like a flower with its petals being pulled off. He had his hands around her waist...his face at her neck.'

'Diana, I can't hear what you're saying. Shit! My tape's run out…
Diana?'

'She was crying. She started crying. It must have been the guilt,
see?'

My head swung back into a magazine rack. 'She was fucking *Toby*
in *our* music room. At her own *engagement* party.' I wanted to jump
up and point at her, call her out for a duel, but I couldn't feel my
legs.

'And that's the truth about the lovely Stella. She fucked my best
friend Toby. In our house. With her future husband in the other room.
And she didn't say sorry.'

I remembered something, slight, significant. 'She gave me
something… When I caught her … she gave me something that couldn't
be true because …'

'Look, Diana, my tape has run out … I'm sorry. I … look, I couldn't
make out what you were saying. Can you meet me later in the
week?'

I jolted, the memory gone. I was furious. 'If you can't be fucking
bothered to listen …'

'No, seriously, Diana. It's loud in here. The environment's not
right. But I would really like to speak to you.'

'You missed your chance, tie-boy,' I said and laughed.

'What?'

'Sure,' I said and stood up. 'I'll talk to you some other time.'

I reached out and we shook hands. 'And one more thing,' I said
mysteriously. 'Don't you think it *strange* Stella changed her mind
about the helicopter on the day of the accident? Don't you think it
strange she is playing happy dancers with a man half Rohan's age?
Don't you think she seems a little too *happy?*'

Mournfully, as I staggered away and saw couples kissing and
stroking and laughing, I remembered my only real attempt at a
relationship before Ronnie. His name was Liam Roundhouse. He was
lovely. I met him in a pub in my early days in London. He smiled at
me while I was picking up spilt tobacco from the wooden bar.

'Are you always this messy?'

'I could lie and say no – but yes. I can't help it.'

'There's worse in life than a messy woman.' He paused. 'A really tidy, house-proud woman. Now that is worse.'

'You sound like you know what you're talking about.'

'Not really,' he says. 'But I can imagine.'

Liam Roundhouse was twenty-one years old and he worked on a market stall. He supported West Ham. His favourite food was his mum's spaghetti bolognaise. He liked Kronenbourg, bar snacks, films with big explosions and doing the *Sun* crossword. He made me laugh all evening and I agreed to a date. Then another. We kissed by the River Thames on the Embankment. Proper kissing like the girls at school used to do. Lips and tongues and hand holding.

'I love your body,' he said. 'It's so…' And he brought his fingers to his lips and did an extravagant Italian-style air kiss.

'You don't think I…?' I wasn't sure how to finish the sentence.

'You smell so…' he said with the same kissing gesture.

'You don't think I smell…?' What? Warped, polluted, unclean?

But then we went to bed.

In the kitchen I drank a glass of orange juice that had been left on the counter. Maybe I needed to sober up. Just as I thought this, a thick arm reached past me and opened the cream Smeg, pulling out a bottle of continental beer. Whoever it was smelt of rolling tobacco, lemon soap and gin.

'Want one?' said the man, passing me a beer. I was going to say no, as strictly speaking I was, even by my own standards, past my limit, but he passed it in such a way that I thought I would only seem impolite and not-his-sort-of-woman if I didn't.

'Oh yes,' I said, and waited for him to pop off the top with the wall-mounted bottle opener.

'Smoke?' he said, pulling a scarlet pouch of foreign tobacco out of his back pocket and rolling a cigarette in liquorice paper with just one hand.

'Oh yes,' I said. 'Neat trick.'

He passed me mine and lit it with a cooking match from the box Toby kept beside the stove and said, 'Always beware of men who can do neat tricks. They are bound to be self-obsessed with too much time on their hands.' Then I realised the man in the kitchen was Jimmy Trowse.

'Do you have too much time on your hands?'

'Absolutely,' he said. 'I do absolutely nothing every single day unless I believe it will improve the already near-perfect canvas of myself.'

'Oh,' I said.

'Don't worry,' he said. 'I'm sure you know by now that I am completely and utterly insincere. We never got to follow up our date, did we?'

'No, we didn't.' The beer and the cigarette tasted sour. I had to lean against the kitchen sink to stop myself from sliding backwards. 'Maybe now's our chance.' I tried to pull what I thought was a suggestive face, but blew smoke in my own eye and had to squeeze it shut to stop the acrid pain.

I felt the sudden urge to wet myself. A very clear thought: if you piss yourself now, well, it will dry over the rest of the evening, and it won't really matter anyway. Nobody would believe you'd done it. Social etiquette and disbelief will save you. As wet heat spread around my lower body and trickled from the hems of my dark jeans, I whistled the opening strains of *The Rite of Spring*.

'Should you really be doing that?' said someone – I thought it was Sir Jimmy – and I said, 'I don't see why not. I've always had perfect pitch.'

'Drinking beer?' It was somebody else. Benjy Burne. 'Wouldn't you say you fancy a coffee?'

I looked up. There was no sign of Sir Jimmy, and I tried to stand in front of the piss puddle I'd created. I wondered if Benjy, offering me coffee, could hear the quiet trickle of liquid as it dripped between the floorboards.

'You're right,' I said. 'Silly me.'

'Talking to yourself?' he laughed. 'It sounded like you were chatting yourself up.'

'Yeah. Well. I thought myself the most attractive prospect here… Didn't want to waste any time before someone else stepped in. You know how it is.'

He laughed.

'I want to show you a picture of my real mum and dad,' I said, reaching and scraping in my pockets but unable to find it.

Then for what seemed hours I leant over the sink with my eyes closed.

I think I left without saying goodbye. The last thing I was sure I saw as I reeled into the street was the glorious Glenys Pimm being nuzzled in the neck by a short, black-haired man with a beard. I meant to shout out, 'Not good enough for you!' but instead I swaggered along the street, squinting for an orange light, which thankfully soon came.

I staggered from the taxi to home.

When I got back to the flat Ronnie was already asleep.

In the kitchen she had left me a glass of milk and a cascade of kisses on a post-it note. I felt guilty.

While I slept I dreamt I had opened Uncle Rohan's parcel. It was a glass box full of his odd objects, random things I'd forgotten he'd owned: a coral whistle he'd picked up on a visit to New Zealand, a thimble made of fish scales that he liked to say was a gift from Neptune himself, a pile of ageing coins – he never carried English pounds and pennies, just seemed to swap Things for Things – and scraps of leather cut into careful circles that he used to save for patching holes in his clothes when they wore through. Bits of Rohan, things I'd seen every day for nineteen years of my life, all squashed into the package in my dream and all – and this was what struck me most – padded out with curl after curl of glossy red hair: beautiful, vibrant, lustrous, more vivid than anything I'd ever seen in real life. It didn't seem to end, his hair. It just kept spiralling out of the paper, glistening between my fingers. It curled tightly behind the glass and I pressed my fingers into it, cold tips on smooth strands. I woke with a start, longing to touch it, just one last time.

On waking I was entangled in the covers, sloppy and agitated and hot. Ronnie was shaking me lightly, 'Dee, Dee, Dee-eee,' and my first thought was, Fuck, I've pissed myself, and I flicked my legs open and shut like scissor-blades, somehow thinking – in my blurred, just-woken state – that I could push the wetness down into the mattress.

'I'm all right,' I said.

'No you're not,' said Ronnie. 'You were screaming.' She showed me a rising welt on her shoulder, juicy with blood, 'And you bit me.'

5

You can recreate your past in words, but you can't recreate it in your memory. It just follows you around, like a ball of wool, slowly unravelling or being wound up, getting bigger and bigger, then smaller, distorted, distended, but still, always, no matter what you do to it, the same yarn.

I grew up in a beach house full of old things, with a duvet stuffed with peacock feathers and the taste of sea salt on my lips. I grew up sharing a king-sized bed with a red-haired man because we were both afraid of the dark, in a house full of candles and open fires because he didn't believe in excess electricity. A house where if something useful broke, you could turn it into something beautiful – unusable, but beautiful. A house where there were floorboards that creaked in the night, boxes of buttons and trails of thread between the cracks in the plaster. *The Cowling Place*.

Ronnie was watching me. Waiting for something. I meant to say sorry, but I laughed. I found the bite hilarious for some reason. Hysterical. My dream was confused, people kept turning into other people and faces shifted. One thing that stayed the same, one thing that felt safe, was Rohan's hair. It was soft and warm and I had been relieved to see it. It had made wonderful sense. But to wake and see the perfect pattern of my well-kept incisors and molars set deep into the pale skin on Ronnie's dependable shoulder seemed, inexplicably, funny. Her bright eyes in the dark seemed funny.

'It's not funny,' said Ronnie, getting out of bed to make us early coffee.

'Yes it is,' I said, but could not tell her why.

And then it hit me, what I'd done, and I panicked. I wanted to take it all back. I may have lied to Ronnie before, I may have lied to Ronnie constantly, but it had always been to make us better, to stop me messing things up. Because I wasn't good enough. This was different. If she knew what I had done at Stella's party it would hurt her.

Rohan's house was full of things, of seemingly random old possessions, which were all, every last one of them, part of his collection. *He* was part of his collection. *I* was part of his collection.

When I was twelve I asked him how much it was all worth.

'Nothing to most,' he said. 'Priceless to me.'

He winked and turned back to his work, his wide shoulders bunched up like drawn curtains, his tufts of red hair like broom bristles, like dried fox fur. Rohan was neat and taut and precisely built, athletic with muscle upon muscle, lean like a runner from his daily swims in the sea before I'd even got out of bed. His eyes were the colour of beach pebbles, and he wore his hair long over his shoulders, like a pelt. I watched as he labelled a packet of sunflower seeds with the familiar brown ink from his fountain pen made of rhinoceros horn. It was carved to look like a snake, and if you pressed the tip of the tail, a bright scarlet ribbon, threaded through with wire, would coil out of its mouth like a forked tongue. On the seed packet Rohan wrote '*MAGIC BEANS*', and then looked up at me, the scar above his top lip a sliver in the light. I raised an eyebrow like I'd seen him do at the women when they were not looking. I thought I was beyond his jokes and tall tales then, thought I didn't believe a word he said. I tutted and flounced away. Magic beans indeed. Who did he think I was?

'Here.' Ronnie was back in the room, handing over coffee. 'I know it's none of my business – and don't, whatever you do, take this as an accusation or a criticism – but when did you take up drinking again?'

I went quiet. I had been intending to deny it but the piss-coastline on the undersheet betrayed any of the false nonchalance I'd had in mind.

'I didn't mean to. It was a one off.' I thought about this. 'And I'm so much better now.' I remembered the taste of the no-win-no-fee model in the blue dress. I wished I could wipe her from me. That I had three faces: one for Ronnie, one for everyone else and one just for me.

She'd brought the coffee in those green and maroon mugs I'd bought from the French market that summer. It's only now, now I remember the tray in her hands, her green eyes pale and concerned, that I realise they wanted to be that Rothko painting: that the wedges of colour reflected on her face like shame.

'I love you,' she said, and settled back on the bed. 'Budge up this way and we can clear that side up later. Have a hot drink first.'

Toby had been in my dream too. Vivid colours and sensations down my legs and round my ankles. Sweat and goosebumps. Toby had been trying to kiss me, but my mouth was full of cotton wool. I thought, 'This is supposed to be the most romantic moment of my life and I can't even get it right.' Then I castigated myself for being so naive. Every time I tried to spit out the cotton wool my mouth would just fill itself up again, dry fluff soaking up all the wetness of my tongue. I could barely reach his lips.

'You were shouting "Mine!" in your sleep.'

'"Mine"?' I said.

'Yes. You were sucking the pillow and shouting "Mine!"'

'I was dreaming about you,' I said quickly. 'I dreamt that you wouldn't let me kiss you, and your lovely lips were only an inch from mine. I just wanted to kiss you.'

'Come off it,' said Ronnie.

'Seriously,' I said.

She sat up and leant against the headboard. 'Look. Why don't you open it?' Ronnie reached under the bed and pulled Rohan's parcel on top of the duvet. 'I know you said you didn't want to, but look. It's here now. It will be fine.'

'I don't want to.' Better not to know.

'I'm here for you. It'll be OK. You can trust me.'

Another opportunity, a chance to make a good decision, to get out of the harmful spiral, to rid myself of the Rickwood coil. But I didn't want to disappear, to let things go. I didn't want Stella to take everything once again. I couldn't let her get away with *murder*.

'Maybe…' I said and put my hands on the brown paper. I felt nothing. There was no microscopic vibration, no jolt through my fingers.

Ronnie sighed. She was wearing her purple striped pyjama bottoms and a thin-strapped grey vest that was a size too small.

It made her breasts look like jellies pushed against glass. Her nose was red.

'Have you ever heard of the Death Instinct?'

She chose the wrong time to bring out her Let's Teach Dee hat.

'No,' I said, pulling the parcel onto my own lap. I considered what would happen if I never opened it, if I left it wrapped like that at the back of one of my drawers in the chest for years and years and years. Then my children could open it when I was dead and discover what it was their famous great-uncle had wanted their mother to see. They, with distance and clear heads, could set about unravelling the mystery. If the police said there was no foul play, and seeing as Stella herself hadn't been in the helicopter when it crashed and had no connection to any of what happened, well, it was an open and closed case and nothing I thought of – despite what I knew in my guts – would change that. Then I remembered that I would never have children and that my womb was probably barren and that it had probably given up, spluttered into nothing, like the wombs of all women who dare defy the rules of nature. 'Imagine you as a *mother*,' laughed Drake in my head. 'Who'd want to waste good seed in *there*.'

'It's Freud.'

I exaggerated a yawn.

'Thanatos,' she said.

'Gesundheit,' I said, an easy joke.

'It's the self-destruct button, it's...' She trailed off. 'You don't have to press it, no matter how much you want to. Not if you identify it.' She smiled at me. A big over-bright smile. 'You can trust me.'

'I know.' I touched her knee.

With one tear, one slide of my thumbnail, the paper packaging fell open.

'Oh!' said Ronnie. 'It's beautiful.' She reached out to touch, but I pulled it away. Inside the parcel was a blue cape made of lovely soft fur.

Rohan, despite being a man of cloth and stitches, had never made me anything to wear. Not until now. Or at least I hadn't known it until now. It wasn't that I had never wanted him to – sometimes I would pray, hands folded neatly on my bedcovers, that he would – and it wasn't that he didn't want to either. It was just the *wearing* of clothes was not what we were about. It would have seemed out of place. And as he said to me once when I dared to ask him if I could have perfume for Christmas, 'I liked it when you asked for stationery. I liked it when you asked for Lego. Don't spoil what makes you *you*.' I felt he was trying to keep me a child, or maybe he was confirming what Drake knew to be true, but I shoplifted cheap perfume from the shelf at the local chemist. I never dared use it in case he smelt it, but would open the lid and breathe deep in secret. The smell of the imaginary woman I could never become in my nostrils.

Ronnie was right. The cape was beautiful. It was distinctive, not quite like anything I had ever seen before. It was, oddly, very 'me', whatever that means, inasmuch as I couldn't imagine, say, Stella wearing it. It would swamp her, not just because she was thin. It would flap about her, leaving her squeaking like a wet reed.

The cape had a detachable, felt, funnel neck and seams across the collarbone which gave it the look of a half-sized coat. Its diagonal row of big, round, cobalt buttons on the right side of its front stamped a path between my chin and my shoulder. It wasn't so much a cape, nor one of those shrug shoulder coverings, but a sort of mantle, a nearly-wrap. The detachable neck, when in place, changed the feel of it, made it more like a bridle, a fabric prison. It would make me austere. Without it, the cape was something to keep my shoulders warm, to make me look pretty. With it, the cape was something to keep my neck straight.

'Wow,' said Ronnie. 'A genuine one-off piece of Rohan Rickwood.' For a moment I thought she was talking about me. 'Aren't you going to try it on?'

I undid the buttons and spread it out in front of me. 'I don't think so,' I said. 'I'm not ready.'

'It's a lovely gesture, don't you think?'

I nodded.

'Why do you think he would have sent you that?'

I shrugged my shoulders.

'Hmm. Do you think it's a message?'

On my first night in the city I slept on a bench outside Victoria coach station, still in my party dress and Stella's heels. I spent hours watching people's emotional goodbyes and hellos. I saw one man weep heavy tears as his wife and child disappeared on a bus labelled Newcastle, only to see him cheer delightedly ten minutes later at the arrival of another woman and child on a bus from Poole. The child – a boy with thick freckles that seemed like an extra layer of skin – called him 'Daddy'. I saw a young woman, a teenager probably about the same age as I was, sink to her knees as her tall boyfriend with burgundy-dyed hair and a guitar over his shoulder went off to Glasgow. I remember she wore a long green scarf and had her hair tied into a ponytail with a pink elastic. She didn't move for twenty-three minutes.

I timed her.

'Are you going to tell anyone about this cape?' Ronnie was clearing away the mugs, had given up trying to touch Rohan's present.

'Like who?'

'I don't know... Some journalist or something? It's a rare Rickwood. It might be worth something.'

I glared at her. 'Are you saying I should sell it?'

'No! Of course not. No!' She stepped towards the door and looked back at me. 'I was just thinking that maybe you would want to find out more about it, where it fits in with the rest of his work. It could be a chance for you to forge some kind of ancestral link. That was all.'

I shook my head and held the cape to my chest. 'I don't want to tell anyone about it,' I said. 'I want to keep it for myself. I don't want anyone to know about it. It's our secret. Promise?'

'Promise,' said Ronnie. 'Of course.'

My body was sore, scooped out. My limbs one minute heavy, the next tingling as though light, airy. So I slept. I must have slept all day, because when I woke again the light outside the window was shadowy and grey and the streetlights sent orange throughout the bedroom.

Ronnie had made a grand supper with a salmon starter, chicken risotto, chocolate pudding and a platter of cheese. She had set candles up on the table, snug in new holders, had tied the cutlery together with coarse strands of green gardening string. She had laid a tablecloth and put cushions, in new red covers, on the dining chairs. There were two yellow-and-red tulips in a cleaned-out mustard jar in the centre of the table. Coincidence. Rohan always said he didn't believe in coincidences.

'Ta da!' she said, and dipped a curtsy. There were pans fizzing on the stove. The kitchen smelt of leeks and melted cheese.

'Ooh,' I said, dazzled by the display.

'I thought you could do with a night of "us" stuff,' she said. She came over and took my hand. 'Come and look at my painting.'

I moved to the other side of the kitchen. Our flat was all corners, fair-sized rooms with all sorts of knobbled edges and places to bang errant elbows or knees. Ronnie's canvas stood on its easel, casual, at first glimpse, and I wasn't equipped for what she had created.

The entire painting had changed from a careful consideration of what it was to be beautiful – her original self-imposed brief – to a wild, excessive, pulsating chaos. There were figures, stretched, contorted, depicted in various states of undress, their limbs at angles and attached to the wrong sockets, some fat, some thin, some variants of the two. There was a long clothes line – Ronnie had painted the cord in intricate detail so that you could almost imagine the whoosh of your hand as you ran it along its length – running between the top two corners. Along it were little coloured pegs holding socks, boxer shorts, frilly knickers, tights, vests, all knotted, straight from the laundry to the line with no care taken over their placing. Their owners had other things on their minds. The figures were submerged in orange and red water, which at first I mistook for fire, but was definitely water: Ronnie had rippled the oils, made the colours move, made you want to dive in. That was what the people in the painting had done. They'd been lured into the water, were trying to swim, their underwear swinging in the breeze, torn limb from limb.

'Oh,' I said. I didn't know what she wanted me to say. I realised that I hadn't actually looked at Ronnie's painting for the last week. All this time she'd been adding to it, changing it entirely, and I hadn't noticed a thing.

'It's beautiful,' I said finally.

'Thanks,' said Ronnie. I was being pulled into the painting. I thought of Rohan's dummies, of unfinished patterns pinned to cloth, of my endless search for lost pins. I thought of the lullabies he sang to the jar baby and never to me. I thought of peeling off my skin, then my flesh and then grinding my bones. I thought what it would be to disappear entirely.

'I had this idea – I suppose it came from that story about your uncle in the news – about clothes and what they do. They lure the eye, Dee. Very Milton. But without them, the naked body lures the eye. But we're so used to seeing people naked that we're becoming immune. I had to make them disfigured to do it, to make it not look like one of those paintings you buy in a gift shop to go over the sofa. I had to put their limbs in the wrong sockets, their eyeballs between their collarbones. I had to fuck them up, basically.'

I continued to stare at the painting. It seemed to spin on the canvas. I wasn't sure how Ronnie did it. She was walking, talking, brilliance. She shone bright, brighter than her painting, and I knew then that if I had wanted to experience safety and kindness for the rest of my life I should never have given Toby our phone number. If I had truly intended to extricate myself from the old life, I should have stayed out of it. Going back made a mockery of everything I'd made since. But, seeing her painting, thinking of Stella's pale hair and Toby's blue eyes, Rohan's body in fiery pieces, I knew it was impossible. I wanted everything to be separate. To keep things separate.

Whatever was in the pans let out thick steam: tarragon, coriander, garlic. I put my hand onto the table, the cotton cloth, to steady myself. The fabric was rough, puckered, seemed to lock my fingers to it with tiny thread fastenings. Everything was too much. I had to get out. Anything to be away from the painting, which heaved in my stomach like rising dough, a bucket of maggots, too much brandy.

'It's a shame you have to go back to work,' she said, and I knew then that I couldn't. My days of deliciously yet accurately describing easy-cook dishes for the twenty-eight to fifty-five demograpic were, for the time being, over. I also knew, with the swell of the fire waves on the canvas, that Ronnie had been trawling my dreams for inspiration.

In the window above the stove, I saw the reflection of the jar baby. I remembered the way it changed colour depending on the weather. On sunny days, flecks of yellow and orange would shift inside the glass like liquid amber, like homemade marmalade. When it rained, the baby's juice would sit milk-still, and I would watch the small fingers press into the glass. I could see little fingerprints; tiny dots and swirls and half-formed grains. When there was frost, strands of grey smoke and slits of violet would settle on the toes and fingers, along the scoop of the ear. And always, never changing, always open, was the jar baby's big, bloated eye: black, fish-like, a polished pebble, molten tar. Depending on his mood, Rohan would give the baby different names. Sometimes it would be Horatio, sometimes Jemima. At other times it would be Philip, Little Pip, or Squeak. Occasionally he called it 'our bundle', although this would make him frown and pull me to him, his chin in my hair. 'It's not right,' he would say. 'It's not right at all. What some people go through. The stupid laws that govern us all. We think we are free, but we're not.' It was sexless, the jar baby. It could be whatever you wanted it to be. It was a boy-girl. A birl. A goy.

Eventually I said, 'Shall we have a glass of brandy?'

Ronnie didn't say or do anything to show she disapproved. I was a drinker again. I'd remembered the brandy I'd bought the previous week, before I'd been to the funeral. I had bought it to flavour a cake, a cake I was going to make for Ronnie. It still sat, unassembled, unbaked; dry ingredients in the various cupboards of our kitchen. We drank, in silence, listening to Classic FM on the wind-up radio. Ronnie preferred Radio 3, but it was my turn to pick, which was lucky, because they were playing my favourite bit from *The Marriage of Figaro*. I don't know what it's called. Every fifteen minutes or so one of us would stop to wind the handle on thirty times.

I try and remember that now, our Last Supper, with the food turning to pulp on the stove, the smell of cooked vegetables, the smart at the back of my throat from the brandy, all performed before Ronnie's troubled canvas. She was squinting in the light and got up to rotate the blind so the slats pushed the beams upwards instead of into our faces. She wore a pair of navy cords, a polka-dotted yellow and green shirt, and had a purple cotton hairband pushing her short hair from her face. It stuck up, behind the material, like foliage on the horizon, the remnants of crop burning. What else? She had no make-up on, had put on a bit of weight. I watched the little ridge of her belly pucker and settle above the button on her trousers. She had a warm middle, no sit-ups for Ronnie. She was wholesome, pretty, fresh-faced. What else? She dipped the tip of her index finger into the hot pools of melted wax around the candle wicks. She let the mixture cool and form a new fingerprint, then held it close to the flame, letting it melt from her finger and back into the pool. What else? She wound the radio on and hummed to Mozart, crumpled lips, raised jaw, a little clod of excess flesh hanging under her chin, joining her neck without definition. Freckles on her cheeks, her brow, her ear lobes.

'Ronnie,' I said, putting Stella's MTCF catalogue onto the table. 'There's something I have to tell you.'

6

I tried to think of when it all changed. When I had a glimpse of freedom. I wanted to remember what it was like when it was just Rohan and me. How it had been before Stella had moved in properly. Our home, *the Cowling Place*.

Rohan said he'd chosen our house over others because of three things: the distance from the main village, the sound of the wind, and the proximity of the abattoir. I once asked him if he thought it strange to have a slaughterhouse so close to a public beach. I wasn't squeamish about the blood and the noise – it had always been there and, after all, I had known nothing else. It was no wonder there were few visitors.

'It needs to be somewhere,' Rohan had said, nodding in the direction of the abattoir as he made a chopping motion with his hands, laughing like Vincent Price, a comedy ghoul miming a kill. 'And it made this lovely house cheap. A bargain for a skinflint like me.'

Things changed when I moved schools. Big school, with its extracurricular activities, its many-peopled corridors, its vastness that bred easy lies.

Rohan picked out a school for me in Evenham, a town to the east of Portsmouth and on a direct rail route from Brighton through Cowling. The night before my first day, we sat at the kitchen table drinking cocoa and eating chocolate digestives. Rohan was agitated, rolling cigarette after cigarette, tapping ash into an upturned gravy boat, and lolling his head back to push smoke out towards the ceiling.

'There are over a thousand people at your new school,' he said.

'Oh,' I said. I could not imagine what a thousand people might look like, let alone how they would all fit inside a school. My only concept of a school was the one-roomed Cowling village school where I had cooked cheese straws on greaseproof sheets with Mrs Mundy, who also taught arts and crafts and homemaking, or grew vegetables and picked weeds in the school allotment with her husband, who also taught woodwork and how to look after our bicycles with grease and an adjustable spanner.

'Lots of them will have had a very different upbringing from you.'

When I was eleven, despite seeing all the people who came through the doors of our house, I did not really believe anyone had a different upbringing to me. My life was everyone's life, and everyone in the world lived by the sea with their uncle and helped him with pins; could chant the names of seaweeds, fish and crustaceans, knew how many pieces of material it took to make a flattering, well-structured waistcoat. And nobody had a mother.

'You might be a figure of fun,' he said. 'You might stand out because you are so...' He shot smoke out of his nostrils and did not finish his sentence. Even now I would have loved for him to finish that sentence. What was it he thought I was? Why did he think that would make people make fun of me?

One afternoon Drake had said, 'Just remember, if you see anyone laughing they are probably laughing at you.' Rohan had now confirmed it.

'Just tell me if anybody so much as puts a finger on you,' said Rohan. 'I will be able to tell if they do. You won't be able to hide a thing from me. Don't let anyone corrupt you. Don't let them manipulate you. And you tell me. Tell. Me. Everything.'

He picked up his deck of cards and began to shuffle. I presumed he was about to suggest a game of whist, or piquet, but he just continued shuffling and never dealt, constantly slotting the cards in and out of the neat stack. The back of each card was decorated with a picture of a cotton reel and read, 'SEW WHAT for all your tailoring needs', with a central London telephone number underneath it.

'I'll be fine,' I said. It felt familiar to reassure Uncle Rohan.

'Oh, I know you'll be fine,' he laughed. 'It's about time you went to a school that could actually teach you something. It's the others I'm worried about. People can be so...'

He tailed off and pulled a face that looked like he might cry.

I felt calm about my new school, having spent days of so-called 'school' on the beach, categorising scurrying creatures, gathering the remnants of cuttlefish to use in collages, or having skimming contests with Jeremy Willis or Tom Root. No matter what Rohan said, I thought I had nothing to worry about. How different could it be?

Abruptly, from nowhere, Rohan said what was really on his mind. 'If you are ever going to have sex with a boy, could you please tell me about it, and I will get you the pill.'

He was very serious. He looked at me with his big, pop-up-book eyes and tried to smile, but could not quite manage it. 'I'd rather you did not have sex with a boy at all, but you don't want to be pregnant. You never want to be pregnant.' He stood up then, and turned his back. 'I know how they think. I know what they want. Remember that.' He left the room.

I really had no idea what the pill was, but knew it had to do with sex. Rohan and I had never talked about sex in relation to me, despite his many late-night descriptions of his indiscretions, or confessions and accusations when he was drunk. Despite my years of fumbles and fondles and mouthfuls with Drake.

I had never kissed a boy. I knew I was behind on this because despite the backwater nature of my school the girls did talk about it. Part of me knew I was not that interested in kissing a boy because I did not know how to do it, and because I thought they would see through me. I wanted to be around them, play on the beach with them, laugh with them. I wanted to talk to them like I talked to Rohan, at the table with cards and coffee and cigarettes. When I was alone I was more likely to imagine boys I liked kissing a girl who wasn't me. A headless girl with a soft, clean body. A body like Stella's.

Men do not fall in love with women who do not look very nice. Aged eleven I was certain this was a fact. I also knew I did not look very nice. There was no comparison between me and those women in Drake's magazines. I thought, 'I never want to have to talk to Rohan about sex again, ever, ever,' and vowed that I would not, unless under pain of torture or death, and even then only if I did not have to look him in the eyes as I said anything incriminating.

I have often wondered why I connect so much with my eleven-year-old self. My first day of school is so clear to me, not just things I saw or smelt or heard, but how I *felt*. How things seemed to me. How things *were*. I remember I tried to avoid the kicked-out legs of older children and the laughing of two girls in my form class about my lack of bra. 'I can see your nipples. Bullets. Bullets.' Rohan was right. I should have listened. Or, I felt angrily, he should have prepared me.

After lunch – which I ate in the canteen alongside a girl called Tammy with a pinched-up face, a blunt fringe and who told me I had to be her best friend – I met Toby.

The magnificent Toby Farrow!

I was late for my first ever Chemistry class. I had been cornered in the girls' toilets by Marie Powers, one of the girls in my form who had mocked me for not wearing a bra. She tried to unbutton my shirt, but I squirmed from her grasp and ran off. She ripped a hole in the sleeve of my bottle-green jumper. The school badge I'd sewn into the chest the night before hung from its corners like a mouth.

'Nice to have you along,' joked the teacher, Mr Dance. He was amiable and I was relieved. Any grown-up men in school were greeted by me with a sense of relief. They were familiar. I thought myself safe with them. Tears from the toilets faded.

'Sorry Sir.'

'No matter,' said Mr Dance. 'It's your first day after all. Find a seat and sit down.'

I chose a stool near the back of the room at a long wooden bench with gas taps and pulleys and neatly wound reels of ticker tape on it. I unpacked my pencil case and a notebook. When I eventually looked up, not really listening to what Mr Dance was saying about Chemistry being concerned with the make-up of the material world all around us, I saw Toby Farrow.

He was grinning at me from the other side of the bench, the first person to smile genuinely at me all day. He had lovely, thick, black hair. He had huge blue eyes, bigger than Rohan's, and lovely soft, big, lips. He had a sort of wonky nose. I stared at him and wondered what this meant: he was obviously perfect, because I went so red that even my fingernails changed colour. I smiled back, and he smiled even wider. I said nothing. I didn't want to break it.

'I'm Toby Farrow,' he said. 'But you can call me Mr Farrow.'

This made me laugh. 'I'm Diana,' I said. 'Diana Everett.'

'I'm delighted to make your acquaintance, Ms Everett,' he said, and made a big show of kissing the back of my hand. 'Now, do keep our relationship to yourself, as I don't know what I'd do if my wife were to find out about you.'

'Your wife?'

'Yes. Luckily she lives on the planet Ugg and I commute here each day to go to school. It's a long story. You age backwards on Ugg. I am actually fifty-three.'

I laughed. 'What is your wife's name?'

'Zog,' said Toby. 'Don't worry. She's not a patch on you. She has three heads and her eyes are on her ribcage.' He let out an over-acted shudder. 'She's a good cook though. I'll give her that. I've got grilled Martian in a red berry gravy for dinner.'

Toby Farrow made a quiet, high-pitched noise and answered an invisible telephone from beside a gas tap.

'Yes. Yes. Hello darling. Yes, I'm fine. I'm learning about the material world all around us. No. No. I'm alone.' He held up a finger to his lips to request my silence. 'Of course I'll walk Rex later. Yes. Yes. Love you.' He crossed his fingers and rolled his eyes. 'See you later.' Toby hung up.

'She wants me to walk my androig,' he said. 'He's taken to biting her tentacles.'

I laughed again. 'Don't you like her?'

'Of course not,' he says. 'Nobody likes their wife. They prefer their *mistress*.'

He said the word mistress like a promise.

I thought about Rohan, and swiftly covered the name tag attached to my pencil case with my address on it. I could not bear the thought of Toby turning up unannounced at the Cowling Place only for Rohan to see him off with a knitting needle or crimping shears, blabbering on about the pill. Why did he have to think the worst of everybody? And what would Drake say if I brought home a boy. He might tell him our secret, and then everybody would know.

For the rest of the lesson I imagined what it would be like to kiss Toby Farrow. It was not an unappealing thought. I picturing him holding his mouth against mine for a long time, the tips of our tongues touching slightly, his fingertips marking a pattern along my neck. I stared at him, secretly, and hoped he would not notice.

At the end of the lesson we packed away our things.

'See ya,' said Toby, swinging his sports bag over his shoulder. 'See you tomorrow.'

'OK,' I said, and watched him leave.

I thought about Toby all the way home. It was a new feeling, this feeling that my life might not just be Rohan and Stella and Drake and the Cowling Place forever and ever. That things might happen to me. That I might, one day, have a life of my own. Separate. Even good.

That evening when Rohan and I sat at the table to discuss my day, I intended to tell him everything. I had never, consciously, lied to Rohan in my life. Drake was my only secret, and if I had thought he would understand I would even have told him about that. But I knew if I did the sky would cave in.

'Some girls say I need a bra,' I said quietly, ashamed.

'OK,' said Rohan. 'We'll sort that out. Silly of me not to notice.'

I folded my arms across my chest and then I told my first ever lie to him. It was not so much a lie, as such, more a retention of detail.

'Met anyone interesting?' He looked at me over the rim of his glasses.

'I have a new friend called Tammy,' I said. 'She seems nice.'

I told him nothing whatsoever about the existence of Toby Farrow.

I didn't know why, but this seemed important. And I can now see that this moment was when everything changed. When my head split in two.

7

I chickened out a little. All I did was open the catalogue and say, 'The woman running this is Stella Avery.'

'The model? Rohan Rickwood's wife?'

'The very same.'

'She called the other day.'

'Yes.' I said. 'I've been seeing a bit of her recently.'

Ronnie looked at me over her glasses. '*Seeing* her seeing her, or just meeting up with her?'

'Oh, meeting up with her. Ronnie! Don't be *silly*.' Other, more relevant confessions took a back seat.

'So...'

'Well, I thought maybe you should meet her.' I was surprised by this. 'And Toby. He was one of my best friends growing up.'

She stared at me.

'I know you're always wanting to find out more about my past. I thought it was time.' This wasn't strictly true either. I didn't want Ronnie to be part of any of it, but it was becoming impossible to keep her separate. If I wanted to hold onto what we had – and I did, didn't I? – then I would somehow have to play it out with her feeling, at least, like she knew where I'd come from.

She hugged me. 'I would love to meet them,' she said. 'Anyone who's been important to my Dee is important to me.'

We kissed.

'You could wear your cape.'

'No.'

She recoiled at my raised voice and pulled back. 'It was just an idea.'

Stella and Toby were waiting outside the restaurant.

We sat together. I was really quite calm about everything, all things considered.

'Mussels in garlic,' I said to the waiter, who was dressed all in red, with a diamond-pierced ear and long, brown hair tied into a ponytail. 'And a white beer please.'

'Moules Espagnol,' said Stella, correctly. 'And a bière blonde.'

Everyone giggled, high spirits. I started eating rye bread with mayonnaise. The mayonnaise was warm.

'You OK?' Ronnie nudged her knee against mine under the table.

'Yeah,' I said. 'Fine…Great.'

'Cheer up!' Stella said. She was resplendent in an indigo wrap dress and chandelier earrings, her normal get-up for a Friday afternoon. Around us several people muttered and pointed. Stella acted oblivious, even if she was not. She must have been used to it. Revelled in it, no doubt.

Jealousy overwhelmed me. A physical sensation like needing to vomit, like a snort of cocaine, like all of my nerve endings fighting their way through my skin.

'God, Diana has always been so highly strung,' she laughed. Ronnie nodded in friendly agreement.

'Did you ever notice how she always has to do the exact opposite of someone else, just to prove she's an independent thinker?'

'Yes!' said Ronnie.

'And the way she sticks her fabulously pretty bottom lip out and pouts whenever someone says something she doesn't like?'

'Yes! Yes!' Ronnie agreed.

I was, for the first time in my life, in the situation of having people who knew me from different times comparing notes.

There were too many pockets of time to keep apart.

'I'm going to the toilet,' I said and got up. The music – seemingly one man and his Casio playing hits of the eighties – plodded out familiar riffs in homogenised rhythms, extending the fashion for irony, surely, one step too far. As I walked I lamented the birds. In the house by the sea I had risen at 6.30 every morning to the sound of birdsong, a contrapuntal chorus with the sea on percussion.

I had always been an outsider.

I stood in front of the mirror and looked at my face. Had I changed much in the last ten years? There were a few lines around the corners of my eyes. I seemed to get more spots on my chin and around my nose now I was older. My hair, short in my youth, was long, reddish brown, though more red under the bathroom's spotlights.

Sometimes things happen so fast you don't get a chance to consider how you would like to act. You just act. I have always had an ideal me. A calm, unthreatened, kind and empathetic me. It's just it has always taken a back seat to the knee-jerks of anger, envy and fear.

'Adapt,' I told the face in the mirror. 'Just adapt. You've done it before.'

I spent the next five minutes washing my hands. I took a squirt of perfume from one of the pink bottles on the edge of the sink, and a foil-wrapped chocolate Brazil from a big bowl by the door on the way out.

At the table everyone was laughing.

Ronnie was touching Stella's earrings.

'Do you think I should get mine pierced?' she said as I sat down.

'If you like,' I said. Pierced ears and Ronnie didn't seem right to me.

There was beer and smoking outside. Ronnie had brought her pipe and was puffing away at it like the intellectual lesbian she was. I had always thought she looked good with it, thought she carried it off, but next to Stella she looked like a staged sidekick. Stella smoked menthol cigarettes from a red coral cigarette holder. If only she looked like the wannabe she was, that the effort she obviously put into her appearance made her look like a fool, but it didn't. She looked in control, elegant, like the first woman ever to have made herself look good with the use of clothes, make-up and carefully chosen props. In fact, she didn't look like she had carefully chosen props. She looked like she was born into the world with these glamorous things around her. That they were as much a part of her as marrow, tissue, bone.

'And then...' Ronnie's voice was breathy, she was laughing. 'And then I looked up at the screen only to find that the university computers' spellcheck wanted to change *Trompe l'oiel* to *Trompe L'Oreal*. As if a brand is more of a word than an artistic concept!'

Ronnie laughed, Stella laughed. Oh how we all laughed. Back at the table the waiter brought my mussels, *moules*, followed by a bottle of champagne in an ice bucket. 'Lady Rickwood,' he said quietly. 'This is from our manager Karl Timmins. He is very sorry for your loss.' He coughed and glanced sideways. 'As are we all. Um, yes.' He began to step backwards. Embarrassment and awe.

Stella nodded and smiled slightly. 'Thank you,' she said. 'Your concern is appreciated.'

The waiter looked relieved and made his way back to the metal hatch.

'Well that was nice,' she said, pouring champagne into each of our glasses. 'People are being so nice. I feel, slightly, that I am supposed to be on show. That people want me to look constantly pained. But Rohan would not have wanted that, would he? He would want me to get on. But I hate to think I'm seen as insensitive.' She sipped her champagne through tightened lips. 'Because it does hurt. For various reasons. I dedicated my life to that man.'

Toby and I were silent and I sat on my hands. It was Ronnie who knew what to say. 'Who cares what people think?' she said. 'You know how you feel. You have to deal with it your way. Christ. We are not put on this planet to make people feel comfortable.'

Stella smiled. 'Ronnie you are a tonic.' She finished her champagne and poured another. 'Rohan used to give these fabulous parties, didn't he Diana?'

I nodded slowly.

'They were something else. Themed. Glorious. Resplendent. A house full of fine wine and beautiful people.' She paused and looked down at her plate.

I continued to nod. I hated his parties. Hated that I had to stay out of the way. Hated that they always ended up with his cat cries into the night, and a cautious female bumping into me on the landing first thing in the morning. Hated that, without fail, they ended with washing up for me to do in the light of day. Began with music, laughter and my head pushed firmly under my pillow to block out thuds and echoes. The worst evening of all, the engagement party, with myself invited for the first time, saw Stella slipping between the laps of every man there assembled, easy, flirtatious, laughing. Me, solid, lumpen, cold.

'You never said you'd grown up with all these illustrious individuals,' said Ronnie, who then whispered, '*You said you barely knew him.*'

'Ah well,' I said. 'None of it seemed that illustrious at the time.' I mouthed, '*I'm sorry,*' and she shrugged a little.

The restaurant was set out in the basement, like a wine cellar mixed with a canteen, long tables and benches, which meant you could end up sitting elbow-to-elbow with someone on the next section you had never met, would never properly meet, yet had shared intimate contact, body, breath, air.

'Don't you think, Diana?'

'What?' I hadn't heard what they were talking about.

'That we should all go to the National to look at the Titian?'

Titian now was it? I couldn't keep up with all the intellectual namedropping that seemed to have invaded the conversation.

'We can look at Actaeon,' said Ronnie. 'You can see what Titian thought of your namesake's finest hour.'

'All right,' I said. It wasn't as though the afternoon could get any worse.

They walked, warm from beer and food and chat, through Covent Garden, towards Trafalgar Square. I was with them but I was cold right down to my toes. I felt a wrench at the sight of the buskers and street mimes, the musicians and magicians juggling with fire. They were different now. It seemed not long ago that I had innocently swung my shopping bags through strands of spring sun that fell through patchy clouds onto my shoulders, glimpses of brightness between all those old buildings and the new, striking my eyes, making me blink with brilliant optimism.

Not this day. On this day the crowds bothered me, swarmed, clattered like dried peas poured into an empty pan. Falling out between the gaps and cracks of the shops and other people, spilling out from doorways. Everybody's heads seemed too large, lolling on their shoulders like over-sized bowling balls. I longed for a time that had gone and would never come back.

'Ice cream in Trafalgar Square?' Stella was smoking and walking, getting admiring glances with every footstep. Her colourless hair, pale and fair, was down over her shoulders, the layers a serpentine line dissecting her back. Her eyes should, considering the colour of her hair and her skin, have been pale and watery, or ice blue. Instead they were brown, dark brown, with glints of gold and green around the pupil. Magic-potion eyes, as Toby had sickeningly described them the first time I let them meet, when we were twelve. I had wanted to keep them separate too, had thought, despite my hatred of her, that Stella was *my* grown-up sophisticated friend from the city who had stories about politicians and artists and movie stars and who once gave me a string of unwanted beads – they were last season and too chunky – which I never dared to wear anywhere but inside my bedroom. I was thirteen and spinning, naked, plump, in front of my mirror, coloured plastic beads marking bright patches along my naked torso. Was Drake right about me? For a moment, with the beads cold against my body, I let myself imagine he was not. Of course, I had always been afraid that Stella would make Toby fall in love with her like she did Rohan. It had never crossed my mind that it would actually happen.

We walked, they talked like old friends. Ronnie and Stella. Stella and Ronnie.

Toby walked in step with me. 'You're quiet,' he said. 'Not like you.'

'A lot can change in ten years,' I said.

'I wish you'd stayed in touch,' he said. 'I missed you. You were my right-hand man. My best pal.'

Even then, when it no longer mattered – when it was over ten years since I'd stared out of my window to watch the sea curl towards the shore under moonlight thinking of his face, his voice, his hands – it still mattered.

'Well, I had to get away,' I said and looked up at him, our feet stepping out over cracks. 'I was never going to live in the same house as the Human Broom, was I?'

He laughed. None of it mattered any more because I had Ronnie, and we loved each other, and she could paint pictures of swirling bodies in an orange sea, and she loved me.

Ronnie's face was bright; she was aerated with the joy of joining my past, excited at new company, new potential links, interactions. It was always Ronnie who invited people round for dinner, who arranged group trips to the theatre, or to see some new arty French film. It was always Ronnie who thought that life involved groups, clusters of people circling the core, the nucleus, us, and that without others we would shrink, diminish, and lose our selves in sheltered misery. I always thought it would work best of all to be just two – no temptations, no head-turning – but I let her make us friends. It seemed to make her happy.

'You *grew up* with Rohan Rickwood?' she whispered, trying to link her arm through mine.

'I suppose so,' I said, blocking the gap in my arm, making her pull away.

'Why didn't you say?'

'I suppose I was still in shock from his accident,' I said. It sounded plausible.

'Poor thing,' said Ronnie, and stepped backwards, in sync with Stella.

We didn't eat any ice cream in Trafalgar Square. We agreed to go to the gallery's café after we'd looked at the paintings. I was already used to being around people who knew so much more about everything than I did, it hardly registered that Ronnie and Toby had started to talk about Shakespeare, that they were rattling words and names off that meant as much to me as a vocalised line of binary code. I suppose I could have asked, could have learned. I never thought it was possible to admit that I didn't know something. If you show your weakness, your enemy knows where to strike first and hardest, but I was happy we'd agreed to go to the café, the café being the one part of the National Gallery I really knew well.

They took me straight to the Titian. At the time I presumed the three of them were inhabiting a happy little bubble that really didn't need Dee, me, Diana, as part of it. I wanted to be sea-swimming, to be in the water and feel my body float and hang, unsinking, weightless; to glide through the water, lovely with grace.

'*The Death of Actaeon*,' somebody said, and then, with a brilliance I couldn't have expected, it appeared, larger than I would have imagined, as big as me.

The first thing I saw was the prominence of Diana. She stood at the left of the painting, mighty, the foreground; a bold, luminous figure, draped in a loose-fitting, rather flimsy and romantic pink dress. She was strong and graceful, the perfect woman, with broad arms and legs, but an unflinching female shape, with pleasing dips and swells. Not fragile she. The rest of the painting was dark, a mass of bark and leaves, and the Huntress dominated the canvas, took it in her stride. She was aiming her bow.

I moved further back, I was too near to see clearly, and from my new spot I could make out more. The trees and leaves unfurled, as though I had stepped into the forest with them, and I followed the sight of her bow. There was Actaeon, head already stag-like; his legs half-turned, his glistening torso still that of a man. His face was gone, his body staggered, useless. There was no chance for him. The hounds were long and sleek. I thought they could almost have been jumping up at him with love, as though he had just come home and they were happy to see him, like regular domesticated dogs. But there was desperation to it. He is desperate for them to see it's him, and they do, they see it's him as a *stag*. Actaeon trained them to hunt the stag, to hunt himself. Diana was smart.

It was impossible, I discovered, not to keep coming back to her one naked breast. It sat, round with its fantastically small and perfect nipple, on the top of the neckline of her dress. I tried to see if it had slipped out, if Titian had it happen by mistake, a titillation for the viewer, but the gown seemed to be tailored that way, seemed to be designed for the display of this one faultless breast. I marvelled at this, got caught up in the consideration of Diana's flesh on display. I remembered Ronnie saying something about the Amazons cutting off one breast so they could carry their bows. Was she teasing Actaeon? Was she showing him, one last time, the very thing he died for? That didn't seem enough somehow; although I was convinced Diana had a sense of humour, that this was the kind of thing she might do.

I stepped backwards again, and truly I felt that I had stepped into Diana's forest myself, that I was observing Actaeon's death from *within*. If this was the case, I had seen Diana's breast, not just from outside the painting – where I was safe, where I could shudder at the horror of her cruel handling of the accidental Peeping Tom – but from inside it, where Diana herself resided; where she knew I was watching, waiting, where she wanted me to know that it would soon be *my* turn.

I jumped, spun around. Ronnie had put a hand on my shoulder.

'Well we've done all the paintings we wanted to do,' she said. I noticed the word 'we'.

'How?'

'Well you've been staring at poor old Actaeon here for at least forty-five minutes.' She laughed. The other two popped their heads up behind each of her shoulders, an angel and the devil.

'I have not.' There was no way I had been standing in front of the canvas for more than ten minutes. The time had flashed by; I had been inside the painting.

'You have too,' said Ronnie. She showed me the pink Flower Fairy watch I'd put in her stocking the previous Christmas. It was a quarter to four. This is my first memory of time changing speed, of me losing time, in adulthood. It happened often as a child but I thought I had grown out of it. I tried to make a joke.

'It was Diana's tit,' I said. 'I was getting a good look.'

We ventured down to the café, past the visitors, standing, on chairs, in front of canvas, staring at guides, hooked up to headphones. I felt different about the gallery. I wanted to stop and stare at more of the paintings. I wanted to see more Titian.

At the table I ordered a slice of chocolate cake and a double espresso. I wondered if I was drinking too much coffee, if that could explain my lost minutes. Stella came up beside me, and asked for a sparkling mineral water and a banana.

'I never guessed you were gay. Why didn't you tell me?' she whispered, setting down her beaded clutch bag under her chair and giving me a quick touch on my shoulder. 'Is that why you left? Because I was trying to set you up with Toby?'

'What?'

'After everything, I should have seen you were never interested in boys,' she said.

Bluffing, I thought. She is trying to find out, in that egotistical self-deluded way of hers, if I ever fancied *her*. I turned, saw the tidy curve of the tip of her nose in profile, her long, mascara-extended lashes, a strand of pale hair across her cheek.

'I'm not gay,' I said. 'I'm indiscriminate.'

I turned to Ronnie as quickly as I could. She was beaming because she was talking to Toby about Shakespeare's fixation with Time. They were bonding over the sonnets.

'Shakespeare was obsessive about the passage of time,' she said.

'I know!' It was Toby's time to get excited, each of them with their little theories on how the world is and what it is to be human. 'It's a recurring theme. I love it, all that "I have wasteth time and now time wastes me" stuff. I like to think all art is about mortality, mostly, and that there is nothing we can do about the fact we are hurtling towards obscurity and death.'

'Except,' said Ronnie, getting quicker, her cheeks flushed, 'if you're an artist!'

'And yet to times in hope my verse shall stand, Praising thy worth, despite his cruel hand.' They said it unison.

'Beautiful,' I said, sarcastically. 'Whose cruel hand?'

'Time's,' said Ronnie. 'Sonnet 60.'

'Basically Shakespeare wanted to catch out Time. He wanted to be immortal,' said Toby. 'To make beauty immortal.'

'It worked too. In a way of sorts.' Ronnie smiled.

The waitress brought our orders on a grey tray.

Stella's chandelier earrings caught the light and made me, momentarily, blind. I tried not to catch her eye. I felt she was watching me.

8

Whenever I am sure I have found equilibrium – a perfect balance of the way things should be, to the horizon a clean sweep of calm blue – something inevitably comes along to unbalance it, to overload the tentative harmony, creating something lopsided and new.

I have wondered whether you can only recognise that perfect time of balance, that moment when everything is just right, after the scales have been tipped. Some call it hindsight, the point when you know you had it, could have had it, but have let it go forever.

For the next two days Ronnie worked on her thesis. She sat at the kitchen table into the early hours, scraping away at her notebook with blue biro, with pencil and washes of blue and pink highlighter pen. She said something about changing the thrust of her argument, that she was going to introduce Shakespeare in with Milton.

'There's something in it,' she said, not looking up from the page, not even when I touched her knee. 'There's something about being lured and not wanting, but wanting, to die.'

I wondered if Rohan wanted to die, when the flames came. I saw Stella with a fire extinguisher, blasting the burning helicopter with bursts of thick foam. After the smoke got thicker the foam turned to fire, and she smothered the wreckage with thick orange. I pleaded, silently, with Ronnie to pass the test. To say one thing, anything, that showed her disdain for Stella. That showed she understood. That it was her and I against the world. But she didn't. She just wrote notes about things I didn't care about, not once flirting with me for ideas.

'There's something about the knowledge of death making everything more vivid, more alive. Alive doesn't count if you don't have death.'

'Thanks for that Ronnie Truism Peterson.'

'Pardon?'

'I said you seem to be getting somewhere at last.'

She looked at me. 'Do you realise how many times Shakespeare mentions the word "Time" – be it capitalised or no – in the Sonnets?'

'No,' I said. Of course I didn't.

'Fifty-seven,' she said triumphantly. 'I counted them myself.'

'Well done you,' I said.

She didn't look up. 'I don't mean to be a pain, but could you leave me for a bit. I think I'm onto something.'

I wandered off to make a cup of tea. Ronnie's painting was under a red cloth on her easel. I thought perhaps she had covered those bodies so they didn't jump or slide into our kitchen, tiny legs and arms and lips twirling and dancing on the Formica.

I wanted to ask her if she thought Stella looked like a murderer. Did she have that distorted cranium, those head bumps that gave it, so neatly, away? Did she move across the room in slow motion, in black and white, like all those villains they show on the TV news? If only perpetrators moved so distinctively in real life. I could imagine Stella turning her head in gravel-grey light, looking at her exhibition with narrowed eyes, suspicious slits that told the truth of her intent.

Instead I forgot Ronnie had asked me to leave her alone and said, 'Do you have a theory on who Shakespeare was writing the Sonnets to?'

Ronnie sucked in saliva through her teeth, put down her pen and turned to me.

'It doesn't matter,' she said. 'I'm interested in the words on the page, not revelations worthy of an Elizabethan *OK!* magazine.'

'Gossip is the glue of society,' I said.

'No,' said Ronnie. 'Not for me.'

'Sorr-eee,' I said, a teenager.

'I'm just telling you what is important to me,' she said, and put her arms around my neck. I felt her fingers trace indifference and apathy along the top of my spine.

'I thought *I* was important to you.'

'Oh, for the moon's sake Dee, you are. You are the *most* important thing.' She kissed the freckles on my earlobe.

Ronnie is the only person I've ever known to say 'for the moon's sake'. She is the only person I ever knew who will only drink hot drinks if they are served in cups or mugs with white interiors. She is the only person I ever knew who squeezed spots that didn't exist and wondered why her skin would pucker with misdirected blood vessels.

'Sorry,' I said. 'What did you think of Stella? You didn't say.'

'She seems nice. I liked her.'

'Yeah,' I said. 'That's right.'

Rohan once, drunk and back from a late-night swim, said of Stella, 'She is not the love of my life, Diana. You have no idea Diana – no idea! – what some people do in the privacy of their homes and for what reasons. What stupid, shallow, fucking *cruel* or cowardly reasons. I'm a coward. A proper snivelling coward. You should know that about me.'

'You are not a coward,' I said. 'You are the best person I know.' I patted him sympathetically even though, as usual when he was in this kind of mood, I had no idea what he was talking about and he slightly scared me.

'But *I* know Diana. I have seen it all. The things people can't even speak about, let alone do. I could have had the life I dreamt of, dreamt of since I was a little boy, but I didn't. And do you know why? Because I am a coward.' Then he stared at the jar baby on the shelf and sang a soft tune, incoherent and full of sorrow.

I kissed Ronnie's hand and went into the living room, where I sat on the sofa sipping gin with Rohan's blue cape spread across my lap like a cat. I stroked it and stared at the ceiling. I watched the cracks and flaked paintwork long enough for them to take on strange yet familiar forms. Humphrey Bogart wore a fedora low over his eyes and chewed on an ear of corn. Marilyn Monroe sucked a bendy straw attached to the tail of a tiny Tyrannosaurus Rex. A woman with long hair hid baby Jesus in her relaxed perm and a headless mannequin with an extremely long neck smoked a fine Cuban cigar. All of these shapes were the pattern on the back of a long coat. The picture rail was a structured collar. The skirtingboard an upturned hem. The coat was on the back of a Titan who stepped over puddles, and people, in Covent Garden, its shadows the size of rain clouds. The hem swept along the street picking up litter bins, cigarette butts and people in its wake.

'De-eee!' Ronnie called from the kitchen. The cape jumped from my lap and I blinked. 'The phone!'

I put the cape and bottle under a cushion and hoped it was not Sylvie with more requests for work I had no intention of ever completing.

'Thanks for the space,' said Ronnie. She squeezed my arm as though she meant it as she passed me the receiver.

'Are you doing anything this afternoon?' said Toby. 'I want your help.' He gave me an address in W11. 'Do you have a good camera?'

'Of course I do,' I said. 'You want me take some pictures of jellies, breads and soufflés?'

'Not quite,' he said. 'Be there at one. The best thing for you to do is see.'

The security guard in the green hat typed in a six-digit code. He looked at me longer than felt comfortable.

'What?'

'Nothing,' he said as he pushed open the door. 'It's just odd to see so many girls who look so …' I cut him off with a slam. I knew what people saw when they looked at me.

But there in the springboarded studio were couples waltzing. The mirrors around the walls reproduced them over and over. Pairs and pairs of lean men with shoulder-length orange hair and their arms around tall, dark-haired girls. Young women. One, two, three. One, two three. A Strauss waltz came from speakers in the corners, hung up on chains from the ceiling.

One, two, three. One, two, three.

I stood with my hands in my pockets. The couples were wearing stripes, like deckchairs. The women in short skirts with bustles at the back and green corsets. The men in Victorian swimming costumes, blue and white, with their uniform hair at their collarbones.

One, two, three. One, two, three.

I, of course, presumed I had fallen asleep on the tube and this was a product of my imagination. I had been losing so much time recently that I thought perhaps this was reverie, some kind of hallucination brought on by lack of sleep, too much coffee, too much booze. It wasn't until Toby, shirt-sleeves rolled around his elbows, jeans and brown sandals, clapped his hands together and each couple froze where they stood, arms outstretched, hands on shoulders and waists, that I realised the scene was real.

'Diana!' He came to hug me and as always I stopped him with folded arms. He hovered in front of me, nearly fell as I refused touch.

'Toby...' I held my camera at my chest, fiddling with the lens cap. 'What are you doing?'

The girls all looked just like Stella. Her pale skin. Expressionless faces attached with greasepaint. Except they all had dark hair. They all had eyebrows painted high on their foreheads. They all seemed surprised, horrified and strangely attractive.

'I want you to help me choose my Rohan and talk about Stella.'

'Um...' I lifted my camera and began taking snaps of each couple's feet. The music continued in the background, swooping strings, and Toby clapped the dancers into life. The girls' skirts frothed at the thighs like beer foam, the men swung their hair about their necks like the fringing on stage curtains. 'Why talk about Stella?'

'Don't you remember?'

I shook my head.

'Don't you remember your caricatures of her? Your one-liners about what she was wearing as we sat and wrote out recipes in home economics?'

'Ah,' I said. Memories of the stories I told of them at night, how I couldn't sleep for the noise, how she dressed up for him like brightly foiled Quality Streets or cling-filmed chicken pieces. Her damp skin as she poured coffee in the morning and the holes in her thin stockings. 'Of course. OK.'

'I think he made you see her like that. I don't think you ever saw Stella through your own eyes.'

Toby would say that. He had been corrupted by her. I was affronted, but could not think of anything to say in retort. We sat on one of the cushioned windowsills. He poured us tea from a thermos. 'What do you think?'

'Well…'

One, two, three.

They dipped and rose, up, down, around and around the studio. All the faces looked the same, all the wigged Rohans had been given the same face. I closed my eyes quickly and tried to remember his real features. I saw nothing but a blank expression with a mass of hair. Reassembling him from disembodied parts was impossible. All I could see was the gaudy make-up on the dancing men in the studio.

'I'm making a film,' he said. 'About Rohan. Well, about Cowling and…I've received funding already. I've shot a lot. I would love it if you would help.'

I stared at him. I felt slightly ashamed that I had not asked him what it was he actually *did*. I had presumed that he was living off the spoils of the ever-moneyed Stella.

'Um…'

'There are going to be all these musical set-pieces. Like this.'

I said nothing.

Toby nodded. 'I wanted to show you. Have you see what I was thinking.'

'I can see,' I said. 'Something…'

'I was worried that if I told you about it you would just say no.'

I continued taking pictures of the dancers. None of them were body shots, instead I lined up frames of their backs in the mirrors, their knees, their tidy ankles.

'It looks…startling,' I said.

'Yes.'

'What is supposed to be happening here?'

'It's a fantasy scene,' said Toby. 'They are building a sandcastle on the beach.'

Whose fantasy?

'I wanted to say that even though you appear in the story, it's not about you.'

It was hard to believe this when two of the main characters of my childhood were there stepping about the floor, the mirrors adorned with Cowling beach props.

'It's about how Rohan went about making clothes. How he looked at the world. It's a fantasy...Lots of dance and music.'

'OK,' I said. What did Toby know about how Rohan went about making clothes?

'It's not actually Rohan's story though. It's the story of someone close to him, someone he didn't want close to him. What do you think?'

'It looks impressive.' Whose story? I was too afraid to ask.

'Do you mind if you're in it? I want you to be in it.'

I had always wanted to touch Toby's leg, his neck, the top of his head. I lifted my hand as though I might, but could not. I had thought of this before, how it was better to imagine than know the truth. The thought of rejection, of not living up to his standards, of him putting his hands on me and seeing I was broken. That thought was enough for me to leave him to Stella forever. He would have had to fight to have me. He would have had to pass a hundred unpassable tests.

One, two, three. One, two, three.

The faces on the dancers appalled me. They were stale and fixed on. Their eyes were opened wide, big and blue, with more eyes painted on their eyelids for when they blinked. They were like the masks at an eighteenth-century ball, exaggerated and cold like terror. What was the dance saying? After every twelve steps the wigged men would nod at the Victorian women. After another twelve steps she would shake her head coyly, avert her gaze. Throughout it all they grinned like Harlequins, their bodies moving in loops and their clothes pinned tight to them, like wrapping paper at Christmas.

'I will let you put me in it,' I said. 'But only because it's you.'

'I won't make you look anything but wonderful,' said Toby.

I wanted to say that I was anything but wonderful but instead said, 'I should think so too.'

'Does this mean you'll be there for the real Rohan audition?'

'This isn't the real Rohan audition?'

'Nope. This is just dancing Rohans. I've got different Rohans for different bits.'

'I'll be there if you think I'll help.'

'You always help.'

'I need to go,' I said. The air was fat with dance sweat. 'I've got to be somewhere.'

'Call me later?'

'OK.'

Toby kissed the air goodbye.

On the way home I found myself entering the wooden doors of the National Gallery. I went straight to the leather bench in front of Actaeon. There were six other paintings in that room, all hung on long chains and symbolically, yet not practically, protected by a green rope attached to dark-stained wooden posts. I thought it horrifying that somebody might walk through this part of the gallery and not notice Titian's Diana. To this day I could not say what other paintings are in that room, and I'm glad.

I sat still and stared. It didn't matter how long I spent in front of the painting. The afternoon was mine. I could sit there until the museum closed if I liked. Something about that was reassuring.

On this viewing I was particularly taken by a figure on a horse in the distance among the trees. I hadn't seen him on first viewing, but now he seemed significant. I had the feeling that whoever this was had answers. Could tell me things. Why was he so far away? Why didn't he gallop in to save the man being attacked by his own hounds?

The longer I looked the more the trees made me unsteady. My head was full of Strauss and brightly painted faces.

I was about to try and stand up when I felt certain that someone was shooting tiny arrows into my shoulders. I didn't want to look around, for fear that I would see Diana with her bow. So instead I sat motionless, staring at her authoritative pose; making sure her sights were still set on the stag-man.

'Die! Die! Die!'

A man was shouting. I knew at me. And he wasn't in the painting, he was in the real world of the gallery. He was commanding me to drop down dead. I whirled around, terrified, and was ready to protect my body to the last blow, expecting an arrow through my middle, through one of my eyes, through my heart. Instead there was a short man with black, gleaming hair, a carefully groomed beard and moustache, dressed in a navy-and-white pin-striped suit – bespoke I could tell – waving at me from beside a security guard. For a horrible moment I thought, I've damaged it, I've torn Diana, and had visions of myself hacking at the canvas, around the radiant silhouette of her body, and felt in my shoulder bag to make sure I hadn't done anything quite so extreme.

'Die! Wait there!'

Perhaps it was Death himself, catching me out in an art gallery, sweeping through to get me, to finish me off, once and for all. I looked about me. I had no choice. There was nowhere to go.

Death puffed towards where I stood and stopped next to me, the top of his head the same level as my chin. I remembered him then: the man with the beard kissing Glenys Pimm at Stella's dinner party. I *had* seen them, they were not another figment, which meant the shouting man knew me. He wasn't coming to sweep me away to the underworld. Unless Death was a familiar guest at Stella's dinner parties. I shuddered.

'Di! Good to see you!' He said. Immediately it all made sense. Di. Not Die.

'God,' I said. 'Nobody's ever called me Di.' The surface of the man's hair was darker than it should be. It made me think of those terrible adverts for men's hair colouring, where the businessman is suddenly top-notch, making buckets of money and picking up hot women at award ceremonies, just because he'd made his head resemble an upturned river otter. I considered telling him that hair always looks better if it remains white once nature has turned it that way. White stands for remembrance.

'I thought Stella called you Di,' he said by way of explanation. I wondered how old he was. He could have been anything between forty and seventy.

'Not that I've heard. Call me Diana,' I said, changing myself, without consideration, back to what I was: casting off Dee.

'Diana,' he said, placating me, taking my hands in his. 'Would you do me the honour of accompanying me to the canteen?'

I slipped my arm through the handle he had made with his.

The man did most of the talking. We ordered coffee and walnut cake and a pot of tea. He asked for a side-serving of whipped cream to go with the cake, but not to bother if it was from a squirty canister.

'I liked what you were saying about the link between what we view in a painting and the concept of us ourselves being viewed *by* the painting,' he said, stirring a second sugar into his tea.

'What?' I had no memory of a conversation with this small, bearded man, let alone some kind of philosophical debate about art.

'You know. At Stella's dinner. You said that the best works of art make you feel like you are not just looking at them, but that you are part of them, inside them. At best you, the viewer, is the object of study and the work of art is more real than you are.'

It didn't sound like something I would say. 'I said *that*?'

'Yes. You were eating the salmon at the time.' He leant forward and whispered, the brown icing on his cake luminous, a solid wedge of butter and sugar. 'You took a line of cocaine from the back of Glenys's pocket mirror.'

I took more cocaine? Not just with the model in the toilet? And I didn't remember that either. That was the night I awoke in a pool of my own piss with teeth marks in Ronnie's shoulder after a dream of curl after curl of glistening red hair. Ah, Ronnie, I am sorry. I can't go back. I wish I could go back. I have ruined us forever. Tears and guilt hung from my lashes. I stared at the man and he winked. He took a bite from his cake and I pushed a fork into mine. I have never liked eating sponge cake with a fork. It seems to take the fun out of it.

'Oh yes,' I said. He had a sense of focus that intrigued me. I didn't want to admit that our apparently wonderful evening had had no effect on me whatsoever, so I asked him a question. 'What's your name again?'

'Victor!' he laughed. 'Victor Eve of course.'

The name rang a bell. 'Did you do the *Offsprung* statue at the MTCF?'

'Ah yes. You like the silk on bronze, you said.'

We'd already talked about that too? I remembered why I'd chosen sobriety all those years.

'Who was the model?' I imagined his strange eyes on a naked Stella.

'Surely you know?' He raised his eyebrows high, like two French accents. I could see he plucked them that way.

'Stella?' I said.

'No,' he said. 'If you don't know already I don't think it is my place to tell you. Not until we know each other a little better. I will tell you some other time.'

The statue must be Stella. It looked just like her. He was probably playing with me. Worse, maybe he was in on the whole plot to kill Rohan and appropriate his reputation. Maybe Stella had sent him to see how much I knew. Maybe she had been having an affair with *him* for years too. I could imagine her pointed fingernails in the roots of that too-dark hair.

It seemed to me that other visitors to the gallery moved around us in a variety of overdeveloped poses. The green glass tables and walls, and the smoky stone-tiled floor accompanied by the half-ellipse lighting suspended from the ceiling made me think of hospitals, of supermarket packaging, of a movie-man's idea of our world in the future. My seat faced the entrance and the wall, which was decorated with a blown-up black X-ray of Seurat's *Bathers at Asnières*. I didn't know what it was called then, but I looked it up in the catalogue afterwards. Later, when I had grown accustomed to which paintings drew the biggest crowds, I knew why I recognised it. It was a *famous painting*.

The painting had never done anything for me, but it is hard to take in a painting without knowing its history. I got that from Ronnie. If you know something about it, about the artist, about the thinking on art at the time, you see all sorts of things you would not otherwise see. (But there is someone – a woman? – to the centre-right of the painting, half-in, half-out of the water. She is showing me her back. Diana?)

Ronnie said something about taking the high arts and subverting them for the lower orders. She said that the Salon snubbed it, afraid Seurat would start a revolution. High art and the masses were supposed to be separate. Us and the gods were apart. We were not to look for messages for ourselves upon the canvas. At least, I think that's what she said, although she didn't like *Bathers at Asnières* either.

'I need to be going,' said Victor Eve. He was refolding a purple satin handkerchief, which he arranged deftly in his pinstriped suit-jacket pocket. I wondered if he had said anything important and whether I had missed it.

'OK,' I said.

'You will come and see me soon?' he said. 'Glenys and I? There is so much we want to say to you. It has never been the right time but now…Well, things are different. We are all older and wiser than we once were. We have been carrying this thing around with us for far too long…You have borne the brunt and it's not even your fault.'

He stood up and I could see he really was only the height of my shoulder. He carried himself with a confidence that made him seem more attractive than he was. He was very well groomed, although there was something about his gleaming hair I could not stand. I wondered how the shimmering Miss Pimm had such a partner, tried to imagine them in each other's arms, his substantial fingers pressing into her flour-and-sugar skin.

'Yes.'

He pushed a green business card into my hand and left me with half a pot of tea remaining. 'It was so good to see you,' he said. 'You have turned out to be a very likeable, attractive young woman.'

'Yes,' I said, although it didn't sound much like me.

Victor Eve left in his fine suit swinging a National Gallery carrier bag. You could see his scalp between the Brylcremed strands of hair, brushed slick in furrows.

When he was gone I was alone and confused. I longed to touch Ronnie, to pull her body towards me, to press my fingers into the lovely fat at the tops of her thighs, to stroke her great white back. To make amends. I knew I loved her. How could anyone not love Ronnie, but the sex... had I ever really, truthfully enjoyed sex with Ronnie? It wasn't something I wanted to think about – in any case Ronnie was at home writing about death and Milton, thinking admiring thoughts about Stella Avery. New best friends.

In front of me somebody's phone rang. It was Beethoven's Fifth. It played for the two opening Dah dah dah dahhh, Dah dah dah dahhhs and then began again, destined never to get past the first four bars; trapped forever in its opening bravado.

Behind me, a women, unexpectedly, shouted out, 'Answer the bloody phone!'

She was scribbling at a pile of notes, working on a God-knows-what of great importance. The man in front, who wore fashionable narrow glasses and a wholemeal sweater, was sharing afternoon tea and scones – with his mother? – and reached in his bag, retrieved his phone and turned it off. He curled around to see his attacker.

'Get a life,' he said firmly, shocked.

'Get a new phone,' said the woman, which didn't really make any sense.

'Get a life,' said the man again, but quietly this time. He turned around and poured tea into the cup of his female companion. Two pretty girls giggled at the table behind. From silence came the clank of cutlery and ceramic and the faint rumble of art tourists.

I finished my tea slowly. When the waiter – young, attractive, with his long hair held back in a black fabric Alice band – took away Victor's cup and saucer and his plate scattered with walnut remnants, I had no tangible evidence that he had ever been there. The longer I stared at the empty seat, the more I was sure I had imagined the whole meeting, along with the waltzing Rohan's from Toby's studio.

To my left, the top of Nelson's column appeared in a corner of the window. I could see the great man himself, his back to me, addressing an imaginary air-bound audience. The sky was white and full of cloud. I thought how marvellous it would be if Nelson shimmied down his column and started hacking away at pigeons with his sword.

I sat there until the café, and the museum, closed. On my walk home, reluctant to see Ronnie or think, I stopped in a dark bar to drink.

9

I slipped out of bed before Ronnie was awake. She was snoring and had one arm behind her back with a pillow over her head. A text message on my mobile, timed at 4 a.m. said, 'Thanks 4 the memories!! x' It was from somebody saved in my phone as Pub. I deleted it and had a strip wash in the bathroom basin. I ran the blue bar of soap over my belly, my legs, under my arms, through matted pubic hair. I sprayed myself all over with cheap body spray and stared at the grey folds of tired skin under my eyes and a red-wine and tobacco-yellow tongue. I could not remember his face although I knew he had sandy-coloured hair and a short nose. All else was gone. I knew he had winked at me as he sang *Eye of the Tiger* at the Karaoke machine and swung the microphone during the instrumental like a fat tail; then an alley, split bin bags and my knees on concrete.

Once, before Ronnie, after Liam Roundhouse, I was dragged from a club to an alley by my feet. A tall man in a blue shirt and gelled hair stood over me with his trousers around his ankles. He burned holes in my breasts with his cigarette and kicked me in my ribs. The next morning I tried calling Rohan and Stella from a payphone.

'Hello it's Diana,' I said.

'Ah, hello Diana,' said Stella. 'How are you?'

'I'm OK thanks. Yes. Fine. How are you?'

'Good. Busy.'

'How is Rohan?'

'He's in Venice.'

'Oh.' I paused. 'I had a hard night last night,' I said.

'Best you give up the booze Diana. It has never brought out the best in you.'

'No.'

'You need to sort out where your life is going. Did you ever look at what I gave you? Before you ran away?'

'You're right. I need to sort my life out.'

'Fine. I need to go. I have a photographer here. You need professional help. Don't just call when something is wrong.'

'OK.'

'Bye Diana.'

'Bye Stella. Tell Rohan I…' She had already hung up.

The three of us met in a café on Old Compton Street. Toby, myself and that irritating wannabe Benjy Burne who had so rudely missed his chance to probe my memories at Stella's party. We were to discuss a) Stella's impending exhibition; b) Benjy's book about Rohan; and c) Toby's mysterious film.

'Look,' said Benjy, dishing out liquorice cigarettes from a silver holder. 'We put Rohan in our Barometer on Sunday.'

In front of him, splayed out over discarded sugar granules and wet coffee rings, was the *Sunday Times* magazine. There, on the style page, at number 2 of the 'going up' section, were the words 'Rickwoodian glamour'. The accompanying text read, 'His nipped, tailored, chic style is back firmly on the agenda for this summer. Impractical as it may be, think heels and waists and red lipstick. Think *Dallas* if it had been made in the 1930s – sans shoulder pads. Think Baby Jane before whatever happened to her.'

There was a square black-and-white picture of Benjy in the corner of the page. He had his fashion-specs on: thick, perspex, clear-glass and his hair gelled into a sort-of quiff. Today his hair was messy and limp over his face and he wore no glasses.

'Everyone is buzzing about Stella's exhibition,' he said. It was utterly apparent to me that Benjy Burn and Stella were clambering all over each other in the dark. How could she have an affair? How could it ever occur to her to even begin to cheat on *Toby*? But then how could it ever occur to her to even begin to cheat on *Rohan*?

'Well that is good news,' said Toby. 'The whole thing is practically ready. All the hard work has paid off.'

'I was hoping to corner some people at the shindig. I've been gathering information,' said Benjy. 'And I'd like to talk to a few people – Glenys Pimm, Victor Eve, Eddie Drake…Does anyone know what happened to him?'

Drake's name, unexpected, uninvited, brought me out in a red rash across my chest. Shame on my collarbone. Whatever had happened to him? I tried not to think of it. He had still been there, Stella's lackey waiting in the wings.

And there were Glenys and Victor's names again, this unknown couple who suddenly seemed to be in the background of all my current interactions. Toby spoke brightly.

'Oh, no. He moved to Australia and never stayed in touch. No luck there Benjy.' Toby's eyes glanced left, at me. *He knows,* I thought, and shook with shame.

'Well, the others at least. And your mum, Toby. Will she be there? Is she up for contributing to my grand tome?'

'Um…I suppose,' said Toby. 'I mean, maybe. I don't know.' He was doodling on the cover of a thick exercise book. Trudy. How reassuring to hear her name. The only sensible woman I'd ever known. Reassuring in her corporeal normality.

'How is your mum?' I said.

'She's good.'

'Where does she live now?'

'Still in Cowling.' He looked up at me. 'But she's moving house soon.'

I nodded.

'We need to organise a trip to Cowling,' said Toby carefully. 'I've been meaning to mention it anyway. Stella wants help organising everything. Boxing it. Getting rid.'

He must have seen the look on my face. 'But she is not going to get rid of anything without consulting you first, Diana. That's why I want you to come with us. You can help. And maybe we'll find some interesting things for my film.'

'And my book,' added Benjy.

'Yes. And your book.'

'Maybe,' I said. Outside I thought I saw Ronnie wave at me through glass, but it was just someone who looked a lot like her, adjusting her hair at her reflection in the window. It couldn't be Ronnie. Ronnie would never adjust her hair in a shop window.

'Tell me a bit about your childhood,' said Benjy, leaning forward and tapping his cigarette. 'Imagine I'm your shrink.'

I couldn't think of anything worse, at that moment, than Benjy Burne being my shrink. I wondered if he remembered my drunken ramblings. If any of it had stuck.

The shells on Cowling beach are the colour of toenails. They lie in clusters, scooped out, open, cracked at their rims. Sometimes a mollusc clings to their centres. An orange-brown curve that falls out then in, like a lung. There are baby crabs, tiny, white, pink at the knees. They flicker across rock pools like plastic toys on strings, playthings for passing toddlers. Sometimes they reach adulthood, but sometimes not. They die and shrink into little balls the colour of worn ashtrays in car dashboards.

In summer ice creams gleam white from the shacks on the seafront. The wind blows out skirts and wrappers and helium balloons shaped like monsters. A dragon with a golden tail rises above a li-lo child. 'Look!' he says as he toes the water like the bath at his grandmother's house. The blue string is just out of reach, like a lost memory. In winter the joggers wear sunglasses. Their Lycra shines back from the pathway like camera flashes at a football match. The dog-walkers bend and show off their puppies' coats like mothers at school gates.

The whitewashed houses crack and leak because of the sea. Everything – lips, hands, air, thoughts – tastes of salt and Queen Victoria.

But Benjy wouldn't want to know that.

'No,' I said, finally.

He shrugged and lit a cigarette.

'The Rohan of the first wave of Stella's exhibition is very much a *bon viveur*,' said Benjy. 'Colourful, passionate … poor boy done good.

She would love you to be available in the gallery to talk to visitors. She would pay you…It's just a living relative would make it so much more *credible.*'

I was reminded of a conversation I once had with Ronnie. 'As an artist you can take something that matters very much to you,' she said to me one morning before we'd even got out of bed, 'and make it turn out exactly the way you'd like.' She stroked the top of my hair in little taps and sweeps of her thumb. 'Or the opposite. You can make yourself suffer again and again by having your characters play out your mistakes forever in vivid Technicolour.'

We were both naked, gripping each other.

'That's art,' she said. 'The process of art at any rate: grasping at your uncontrollable world until you make it unchangeable. What is actually true about a story, told from a certain point of view, that ends before death? That is not true, Dee. Life doesn't end before death.' She shook her head. 'Who in their right mind would think they could describe the world *as it is*? They only know how it is *for them.*'

'I have no idea,' I said. I was uneasy, was pestering her for sex with the back of my hand. I just wanted her to stop talking.

'Each and every one of us is the same. But our own hurts and fears don't let us see it. We all think we are the heroes of our stories and that there are villains, comrades or the prince on the shining horse.'

'Hmmm?' My fingers free-styled the slope of her hip bone.

'Do you think the Ugly Sisters of your story see themselves as the Ugly Sisters? Not fucking likely.' She sighed melodramatically. 'Everyone is Cinderella Dee. That is the secret.'

'Do you mind if I lick your belly button?'

'Oh Dee.'

There were many stories I could whisper to Benjy Burne across the glass table of that fashionable café. The glitter of Rohan's life was full of endless revelations. The women, for one – some of them very well known and married to people more powerful than a photographer. There were truths that would change everything anybody had ever written, discussed or printed about Rohan Rickwood. But, for the time being, my lips were sealed. Stitched with white cotton. Pins between my fingers. Secrets between my palms.

But Benjy had asked me about my childhood. It was impossible to think of me then without Rohan. Rohan, waiting for Rohan, watching Rohan, was my childhood. And the endless shadow of Drake reminding me I was different, reminding me I was a parentless child, that I was born to be forgotten.

I had always been certain that there was more to my uncle's relationships with the women in the workroom than he ever told me. Why would ladies need fittings in the middle of the night? In the early hours? Why was I never allowed to meet them? Why was I unseen? I remembered one in particular. Fiona was the name I was given. She wore a silver charm bracelet with ballet shoes and leaves and half-hearts hanging from the emerald chain links and had her face covered with a thick, black lace veil. Rohan had ordered peppermint tea and insisted I took it in to them in my nightdress and dog-face slippers. She had been sitting in the corner, next to an open ledger book, with just her hands and her ankles on show. I did my best not to look – as were my instructions – but I caught the bouncing of her knee in my peripheral vision, her hands wringing the purple velvet of her skirt, the catch of the charm bracelet in the light.

Afterwards, when I asked him why she was crying, he said, 'Wedding gown. Ruined with spilled oil. I have to make one from scratch.' But I didn't believe him then, and I didn't believe him now.

'After opening night we should go on the trip. Back to Cowling,' said Toby. 'You could bring Ronnie.'

'Ronnie?'

'Yes. The four of us. And Stella.'

'Maybe we should,' I said. I thought if Rohan was trying to send me a message then maybe there would be clues left in his house. If Stella hadn't rifled through them already. Wiped them clean. But if the cape was the first in a chain, if his death really wasn't an accident, maybe it would be there for me. Maybe he'd suspected something, maybe he'd been afraid. The thought of Rohan afraid made me tremble. I had seen Rohan afraid in the past, curled up on the kitchen floor and howling. I couldn't leave him like that now he was dead.

'And we have Tobe's film,' said Benjy. 'The next big Brit-flick, with rolling scenery and wit and vibrant colour and musical numbers and intricately reproduced period detail.

'Now now,' said Toby, smiling.

'He's ever so humble, our Mr Farrow,' said Benjy, patting Toby on the sleeve. 'Won't even accept praise now he's an award-winning filmmaker.'

'Award-winning?'

'You must have heard of Malk Blancossier,' said Toby. 'BAFTAs galore. An Oscar two years ago for Best Adapted Screenplay.'

'Malk Blancossier?' I said. Of course I had heard of him. The darling of the British film industry. 'That's *you*?'

'I suppose it is,' said Toby. 'I sort of think of him as someone separate from myself, an aspect of me, but yes. Malk Blancossier is me.'

'You directed *Mariage à la Mode*?'

'I did. You going to get involved with this film then? Now you know I have acceptable credentials?'

'I said I would.'

'Good. Perfect.' He put his hand in the air to attract a passing waitress. 'The bill please,' he said to her, then to me, 'Now enough of this self-aggrandisement…I just want everyone to be aware I'm working on this film and to keep their eyes open.'

'Aye aye Captain,' said Benjy.

'Sure thing,' I said.

'*You're* Malk Blancossier?' I said.

'Yes, yes. I'm Malk Blancossier. Now forget about it. I'm exactly the same Toby Farrow you knew at school.'

With the bill paid we all agreed, some more reluctantly than others, to a trip to Cowling. We would go the day after the exhibition launch when it was still fresh in our minds. With handshakes and cheek kisses everyone went their separate ways. I said I had to be somewhere, and watched Benjy stride off into Soho with clasped hands. Toby came up behind me and touched my arm. I stood in the doorway of the café, unable to move.

'Seeing as we're both here,' said Toby, 'do you fancy getting some chips? For old time's sake.'

I nodded my head.

'And then you can come and help me audition Rohans.'

I nodded again.

We bought polystyrene cups of fried potatoes from a kiosk on the edge of Soho. For the first few moments I swelled with the ease of eating chips in the rain with Toby Farrow. Everything was vivid and right: the crunch of the salt and the sting of the vinegar, the wet hems of my flared jeans against my ankles, the colour of the dark regrowth across his scalp. Our legs in sync. I wished, rather pointlessly, that this was the beginning. That we'd met the day before and this was our first date. I thought how good things can be at the beginning when you haven't given much and you can walk and eat chips in the rain without history on your fingers. Anything might happen. You might just walk like that forever, with rain on your lashes and the smell of fried food in your nostrils. He might smile at you and kiss your neck, a trail of hope from lobe to throat.

'Salt,' he said. I had a crystal of salt on the end of my nose, and he reached to push it away.

'Thank you,' I said.

'You know what we should do?' he said, licking the tips of his fingers.

Myriad much-yearned-for options flitted through my mind. 'Eat more chips?'

'No,' he laughed. 'No. What we should do is set ourselves the challenge of finding the worst second-hand ornament on those charity stalls down there.' He gestured to a row of temporary tables emblazoned with charity banners set out at the mouth of the road. He cracked his polystyrene cone into pieces and dropped them into a public bin.

'What?'

'I'll show you,' he said and led me to them. Twenty steps forward: a time machine to how it might have been between us in a world without Rohan. Or Stella. Or Drake.

Toby Farrow and I stood in front of a fold-out table and together contemplated a row of ceramic figurines. Toby elbowed me in the ribs and pointed at the ramshackle selection of ornaments that were set out in no particular order on the smoothed-out plastic and labelled with yellow price stickers. A ceramic man and woman garbed in eighteenth-century aristo-wear sat next to each other on an ornate bench. The man pushed a rose into the woman's hand as her face turned coyly away. Or, at least that's what would have happened if the colour transfer applied to the molding hadn't been so out of sequence: the couple's eyes were on their cheeks, leaving white orbs in their sockets where the pupils should be, the red of the lips was on their chins, like they'd been kissed by a glamorous and demonstrative aunt. The detail on the dress was supposed, perhaps, to look like ochre taffeta and skirts and petticoats. The effect was one of mould on a bathroom wall.

'*Par exemple*,' said Toby in mock French pointing at the offending item. 'Could you please, Miss Everett, tell me what this is supposed to be?'

I looked at it carefully. 'Two accident victims strapped to a marshmallow?'

He laughed. 'Quite right, well done.' He put his face close against the table. 'Do you know why somebody would want this on their mantlepiece?' His eyes were bright and his gaze drifted upwards. He tapped at his chin with bitten fingernails.

'They wouldn't, would they,' I said. '*I* wouldn't.'

I put my hand in my back pocket and pulled out some change. I paid £1.20.

'Here,' I said. 'A present.'

Toby took the gift and smiled at me. 'I did miss you, you know,' he said.

'I know.'

'Did you miss me?'

'What do you think?' I shrugged. I was about to say something, anything that could move us forward when I saw the familiar flash of a lemon-yellow raincoat. Sylvie Aldiss. The boss I had been avoiding for near on a week. She stood on the pavement opposite and stared. I smiled at her and she frowned, began to stride towards me in lace-up Edwardiana.

'Dee?'

Toby turned towards her.

'I need to get going,' I said. 'Thanks for the chips.'

'Diana, I want you to come to the audition.'

I did a strange thing then. I reached out and shook Toby's hand. 'Back at the café in five mins.'

As I began to jog along the pavement, half affecting a limp, I could hear Sylvie's footsteps quicken, but I didn't stop. I knew she wasn't the sort to chase for more than a couple of minutes. I would have to hand in my notice properly. I wasn't even sure if they could sue you for breach of contract. I thought of Lucy and the morning cakes. I thought of my telephone with the cut-out picture of Sean Bean stuck to the headset. I thought of the broken wheel on my swivel chair. I missed the office then, because I knew I could never go there again. It would be someone else's job to drizzle and slice and sauté. Another unhappy ending.

'What was that about?' Toby leant against the window smoking a cigarette.

'Not much,' I said. 'You remember the excuses I used to make up at school?'

'Like the one where you found a dead person in your duck pond which meant you had forgotten your ingredients for HE?'

'Yes.'

'You haven't changed that much.'

'No. Are you going to show me those Rohans?'

'Yep.'

10

There was one time, a time near the beginning, when something, a mere flicker but still something, happened with Toby and me. I have held onto it like an old receipt at the bottom of a handbag, or a fallen button put in a drawer to be sewn on.

'Nice pants,' said Toby. I looked down at myself in my green bikini. I tried to imagine what the exposed blocks of skin – belly, thighs, breasts – looked like from his perspective. Naked. Flesh. And there stood Toby from school, my secret friend, the one bit of life that was mine, just mine, fully clothed, grinning and smoking a cigarette. On Cowling beach. He was out of place, not in school uniform. A rabbit out of a hat.

'Thanks,' I said slowly. It was a hot day. I did not have a towel with me. I usually ran from the sea to the house in my swimsuit and let the sun dry me off, or wriggled, hidden from view, on my front in the sand, crunching myself into the grains. I quickly wrapped my arms around my belly and hunched my arms forward to make my breasts retreat against my torso. The images of the women in Drake's magazines writhed in my head and mocked me. What had I been thinking wearing a bikini? There would never be a day I could be free. There would never be a day I could be unwatched. 'What are you doing here?'

'Here's where I live,' he said, stretching out his arms to suggest the whole beach. I almost believed that he did live on the sand, that he rose up from a dune in a cloud of dust each morning and magic-carpeted his way to our big concrete school in Evenham. He flicked the top of a silver Zippo lighter up and down with the back of his thumb. The breeze did not allow a flame.

'*Here* here, on the beach?'

'Yeah. I'm Mr Sandman,' he said and blew smoke towards me. I breathed in a little through my nostrils. That smoke had been inside Toby Farrow's *lungs*, right down inside him where his breathing began. I shivered.

'Oh,' I said. Was he making fun of me?

'We've just moved into the White House on the hill.' He pointed to the building on the small mound opposite ours, the one with the Grecian columns either side of the door and the flat, white roof.

'Old Mr Lewin has moved?' This seemed highly unlikely. Albert Lewin had lived in the old white house since before the war. He was born there. As was his father. And his father's father.

'Must've done,' said Toby, stamping out his cigarette with his bare foot. 'Unless my mum has moved out here to the middle of nowhere to be with the man of her dreams and hasn't told me.'

'Mr Lewin was about a hundred and eight years old,' I said.

'That's never stopped her before,' he said and laughed. 'That was a sort of joke.'

Everything I knew I could be fizzed with hope and possibility and utter joy at the thought that Toby would now be my next-door neighbour and that maybe this was all *meant to be*. The very fact that he was standing just across from me, beautiful and unkempt, and I was barely inches away from him, practically naked, nearer than I'd ever thought I could be. I willed him to reach out and stroke my belly with the tips of his tobacco-stained fingers.

For some time we just stood there in silence. I could feel him watching me, scanning my body for signs of…what? I tried to place myself in a way that was appealing but gave up because I knew I had nothing that was appealing to any boy, let alone Toby. I was used goods, I was nothing, I was a body that should never have been born, caught up in a jar for eternity never breathing one breath. Stella had said that I should not presume a boy won't like me, but it was different for her. She looked the way she did and I looked like this. The girls Toby liked were always of the permed, eye-linered, lipstick type. Pretty. Girly. Girls like Drake had shown me in the magazines. He was turning into quite the ladies' man. The sight of me in a bikini was not going to change his mind and make him see me any differently than he ever had done since I'd known him. Best. Pal.

But he *was* watching me.

I had always thought of the beach as mine. Mine and Rohan's. Drake never troubled me on the beach – he was always expected to be in his car, his own private prison that was the one thing that protected me. And nothing had been seen of him in the two months since that last time when I took Ruskin. Now there was this boy standing there in long grey shorts and blue shirt, no shoes, with his uncut black hair swept up into an involuntary peak, as though he had always been there. Comfortable. Too comfortable maybe.

I had a horrible thought that I would, from that moment, be less free. I would have to worry about what I did at the beach, how I looked, what I said, because the boy I would one day marry would be able to observe me at all times and I did not want to fail any secret tests. I wanted to pass with flying colours: red, gold, green.

'Do you like ginger cake?' he said eventually. He looked up at his house.

'Yes.'

'Do you want some?'

'OK…' I looked up at Rohan's house, which glared at us from above the growing pine trees. Put some clothes on. You are not for public consumption.

I was about to suggest a need to go home to get dressed when Toby said, 'Wear this,' and produced an oversized man's shirt from his back pocket, which he helped onto my shoulders.

It was coarse cloth, the shirt, blue with thin white stripes. The sleeves hung way past my hands and I stuck my thumbs through the hole above the buttons to wear the cuffs like fingerless mittens. The smell of it made me gag. I threw it off me onto the sand and had to do everything I could to stop myself from being sick. I could not explain my extreme reaction, but the shirt, the feel, the touch, the smell, sickened every molecule in me.

Toby didn't say anything about this strange display. Instead he took off his own shirt and put that on me. His shirt smelt lovely, like rainwater, cracked pepper and cheap soap. I wanted to wrap myself in it over and over like a shroud.

'Well, come on then,' said Toby, leaving the other shirt. 'Trudy's got the kettle on.'

Trudy.

Everything in her kitchen was homemade: cups, plates, tablecloths, cakes, bread, plaster.

Everything about her said, to my mind, mother. She was what I imagined when I dared to imagine my own. Capable. Strong. Kind. A story-book mother. A mythical being (although my fish-fin mother was beautiful and Trudy was not). It was all I could do to stop myself from falling at her feet, curling around her ankles and begging her to adopt me. Imagine: homemade gingerbread, kind words, laundry that was warm from the airing cupboard.

'I'm plastering this buggering wall,' she said. 'Nearly done.' She covered the clawed-out hole with four quick slathers and wiped plaster from her chin with the back of her forearm as though it were icing. 'You must be Diana,' she said, and held out a hand.

'Yes,' I said, shaking it firmly. 'Pleased to meet you.' I was excited that she knew my name, because this meant that Toby must have spoken about me at home, to his *mum*, which meant he must have thought about me when we were not at school, which meant I was not invisible, and that I was, maybe, even a little *important*.

'I've made cake and tea,' she said.

'That's how I lured her here,' said Toby, pulling out a chair for me at the kitchen table.

I liked Trudy immediately because: a) she said nothing about the fact I was standing in her kitchen with her son in practically just my underwear; b) she wore ripped jeans, a black T-shirt, a paint-stained shirt and had long, very black, unruly hair tied back into a pony tail. She also wore flip-flops with not a frill, tuck or bustle in sight; c) she was overweight and did not seem bothered about it; d) she was Toby's mum, which meant that without her Toby Farrow would never have existed.

'Your Uncle Rohan,' said Trudy over her shoulder. 'What's he like?'

I didn't think twice about answering her. Usually I was tightlipped about Rohan. I didn't want people befriending me in order to get close to his needle basket. Or worse.

'Well, he's clever, and good with colours,' I said. 'He collects things. He makes clothes – you may have heard of him – for all sorts of people and he swims a lot. He likes the sea. He has red hair, hair the colour of the wrappers on chocolate coins at Christmas. He never cuts it. He sometimes ties it up with a velvet ribbon, like Dick Turpin, like a highwayman. He's good at making up stories. He wrote a book for me once, when I was small, about a rich man who ended up with nothing because he kept throwing his money into puddles for fun. He drew pictures to go with it, but wouldn't send it to any publishers. I think he could have had it published. He's like that. He can do *anything*. He can make a drawing look exactly like something with only a few strokes of a pen. He has the nicest handwriting you will ever see. He only writes with italic pens and brown ink and he has these big books in which he writes and writes and writes. And he doesn't believe in money. He likes to barter, which means he has to carry stuff around with him all the time that might be worth something. He says that the trick is to find the things that are financially worthless in general, but priceless to people he needs things from.' I stopped for a breath, jubilant. 'I have lived with him my whole life, ever since my parents died at sea.'

I stopped. I leant on the table for balance.

'He sounds like quite a character,' says Trudy. 'Doesn't he Tobe?'

'Yeah,' said Toby, who flicked at his bare toenails with his fingers.

'He is,' I said, embarrassed.

'I'm sorry to hear your parents died at sea. It's the sort of thing that happens in movies.'

'Mum,' said Toby with what I thought was a warning tone.

I shrugged. 'I never knew them so I can't miss them.' It was a phrase I had repeated many times in my life, so often that I nearly believed it.

Toby leant back in his chair and smoked another cigarette. Trudy did not reprimand him for either of these activities.

'Do you want a beer?' he said. 'I'm done with tea.'

'Why not?' said Trudy. 'Diana?'

'Um…' Rohan did not allow me to drink alcohol with anyone but him. And Drake's brandy was our secret. 'OK.'

In Toby's room we listened to music by bands I had never heard of. At home we did not even have a TV, and I spent most of my time listening to radio on long wave. Tchaikovsky, Borodin or the one, two, threes of a Strauss waltz. Most of Toby's music had guitars and electric organs and men singing in out-of-focus echoed voices. I liked it. In part because it was like nothing I'd really heard before, and in part because Toby liked it, because this was what was inside his head when someone said the word *music*.

We drank more beer. I was still in my bikini and Toby's shirt.

'That other was my dad's shirt,' he said.

'Where is your dad?'

'I don't know,' he said. 'He's, well, he's not around any more. But he's never been around much. He's always worked away. I don't think I'm the son he asked for at the baby bank.'

'Do you mind that?' My head was swirling with my fourth beer. Toby's walls with posters of pretty models in pastel-coloured lingerie that I could never live up to rose up and up and the floor slowly disappeared, down, down. I felt the heat and adrenaline of jealousy. I had thought better of Toby, but those women were like Drake's. Unlike me.

'Thank you Drake.'

I have him to thank for my impeccable manners.

'Not really,' Toby shrugged. 'You don't miss what you've never had, do you?'

'I suppose not,' I say. I missed all sorts of things then. The folded-up photo of my mother and father and their dog was the only tangible evidence of their existence. Trudy with her ginger cake, her jeans, her wide belly. I wanted to say Toby was wrong. That you can miss something you have never had more than something you've lost. I wanted to ask, 'What is it like to be held by your mother?' but I simply could not.

Toby moved nearer to me on the bed. I wished I had only been drinking tea and that my mind was clear enough to know how to behave. My body was pricked all over with pin-points of heat and Toby's shirt was stuck to me with sweat while a kaleidoscope of pretty girls with tanned skin clicked in and out of shape on wallpaper the colour of sand and sky, ceiling with flaked paintwork, light fittings shaped into rose petals, items of Toby's clothes slumped in a pile on a chair, my own bare legs, white goose-bumped.

Toby's hair, dark as oil, shiny as polished shoes, both dry and greasy from the sea air; the smell of beer, salt, white spirit.

'I didn't know, you know,' Toby said quietly. 'I really didn't know any of it when I first met you. I want you to know that. I really want you to know that. It has changed everything. Knowing. And be careful of Trudy. She is not like...' He trailed off.

A riddle. I had no idea what he was talking about. My mind was slumped with bubbles and beer. I felt his fingers on my knee and the length of my body went cold, then hot, and I thought perhaps he had set light to me with the end of his cigarette. I patted my legs for flames but he traced a pattern with his thumbnail on my thigh. My heart was so loud, so fast, that I expected the walls to shake and crumble, for the White House and my body to split in two.

And then I passed out. Or fell asleep. Or whatever you call it when you get properly drunk for the first time and lose track of time, place and all sense of reality. I woke up at 2 a.m. to find the bed empty and me still in my bikini and the shirt. I snuck out and ran home, shivering and repulsive. We never spoke of it again.

This incident, for reasons that are unclear to me, is intrinsically linked in my memory with an entirely separate incident with Stella's engagement dress.

Rohan was making a fitted bodice dress from emerald silk. It was for Stella to wear to their engagement party. A week before the night itself I had an idea.

The dressmaker's dummies in the women's workroom were all of the same sort: limbless torsos with a huge split down the centre. A hollow carcass with only dials to change the dress size. Turn the dial left to make the dummy body bigger, turn right to reduce.

I decided, quite suddenly, to reduce.

The dummy was set to Stella, mini-woman, compressed style. Rohan was yet to make his final measurements. He always finished the final bits of pattern-cutting using the dummy. I was not sure why. Maybe he just could not get enough work done when measuring up Stella in person. Couldn't keep his hands off her. I did not need to do anything drastic, just tighten the seams a little, an ever-so-slight twist of the dial.

Stella put so much effort into staying that narrow. I wanted to see her reaction to the thought she was losing control. It was not as though she could eat any less.

I did it in the morning, when Rohan and Stella ate breakfast in the front kitchen. Rohan's bread and jam, Stella's coffee and cigarettes. Rohan had promised a morning swim. I stood, at the kitchen door with my towel and my shirt dress over my swimsuit. Grapefruit and egg whites and rejection on ceramic.

I turned and left them to it.

The dummy was always set to Stella. It was a guaranteed revenge.

Just under a week later, the day before the party and Stella dressing me up, I saw the results of my handiwork.

Stella, lipstick smeared around her face, mascara wet and sooty, in a beautiful green silk dress with a split seam.

She sat on the back step drinking a glass of champagne, smoking a cigarette without a holder – always a sign of distress. I sat down next to her and put my hand on her shoulder.

'I've put on weight,' she said. 'Look at me! I'm hideous! I'm vile. I'm *gargantuan!*'

She looked exactly the same as she always did: refined, polished, very thin.

'You look lovely,' I said.

'I don't fit into this dress. I'm a mess. Rohan will notice. He will say something.'

'He will?'

'Oh yes. He'll see. He always sees.' She looked down at her hands. 'You can't be a designer's Muse and put on weight. You see? His clothes are for me as I was. Not like *this*.'

'I'm sure he can fix it,' I said.

'So am I, but then he'll *know*. He knows so much already. He sees everything. I don't want him to see *this*.'

'Have you got something else to wear?'

'Nothing special enough. And I am supposed to wear this. It makes a statement. And Jimmy is wearing a matching tie...A sort of joke on their part...to show Rohan won fair and square. I have to get it right. Do you see?'

I did see, although I did not want to, as it sounded terrible from Stella's mouth. Like Rohan was a villain in a cartoon.

'I could sew it up for you,' I said. 'I'm sure I can adjust the seam a little. Make it more comfortable.'

She looked up. Powerless. 'You could?'

'Yes.'

So I let Stella hold onto my arm as I took her, and the dress, into Rohan's workroom without permission. The lights were out, the mannequins were lined up, limbless with their scraps of silver and thread, nipple-less breasts peeping through ragged cut-outs shaped like leaves.

'Autumn, literally,' she said. 'He is taking a risk with this one.'

I wanted to say that I thought he never took risks, not with his clothes. He knew precisely what he was doing and why, but I didn't. I took her towards the footstool and stood her on it. I made her put her hands in the air, long white tubes with no shape and fragile ends. I didn't pull back the curtains. I lit the oil lamp on the wooden desk and jumped at the shadow of the jar baby. Why was it here in the workroom? It didn't belong here.

It held one, gentle finger up to its blue lips. Shhhhhh, it said. Shhhhhhhhh Diana. I turned, quickly, and told it, in my head, to be quiet. This was none of its business. It had held its silence for this long, now was not the time to interfere.

There really is nothing to it. The seam split because I had turned the dial. The difference was negligible, but Rohan's dresses for Stella were always such a perfect, tight fit. He would often stitch her into them and undo the seam when she returned. In this instance there was enough material left behind the stitching to let it out. As Stella stood there with her arms in the air, her stomach pulled tight, her small knees apart, it took me all of four minutes.

When I was done, as she still stood in her strange, rigid pose I said, 'That should do it.'

She looked at me before dropping her arms. Her eyebrows fell low, and with a look which said, 'Are you sure? Are you really sure? Could it really be that easy?'

'That's done it,' I said again. 'You will be fine now Stella.'

Her arms dropped back to her side and she put her hand on my shoulder to help herself from the stool. She stood, green as a wreath, in the yellow light of the oil lamp. 'Thank you,' she said quietly with a smile. 'Really, really thank you.'

I was about to tell her that it was no problem, that it was nothing, that I was glad to have been of help – which strangely I was – when she said something odd, something I did not understand.

'This will show that woman,' she said. Then, 'This will show both of them. How long does one person have to suffer? When will I ever be enough? Each time he raises the bar. It's a limitless bar. I will never, ever…' She crumpled, the whole of her shaking, 'ever jump high enough. He's twisted Diana. He is obsessed with an old life, a warped life.' She shook so vehemently that I thought she might break in thousands of pieces. 'And she doesn't have to try. She isn't even *here*. But she's everywhere. Do you see?'

She was angry then, some power returning to her voice. 'I wish we could spend more time together like this Diana. But he would never allow it. And I can't. It's too painful. I know it's not your fault. And as for that *retard* next door…'

She jumped up then, animated like an intricate marionette. 'Ah ha!' she said. 'I have something for you that will change your life. You can't be held a prisoner forever.'

Then, before I could say anything, before I had time to feel bad about tricking her, or think about those long white arms, or concepts of a mystery 'She', she was across the workroom, rummaging in a drawer full of scrap paper.

'I know it's here somewhere… It's the catalyst, my darling. It's all you need to work it out… You could have come across it yourself. You *might*. I can't get in trouble for that.'

With that she thrust into my hand, triumphant yet trembling, a piece of thin paper with the same photograph repeated on it five times. There was hole in it, where a sixth copy had clearly been. I looked at it, held it there, flipping it over and back like a strip of redundant fish skin.

And then she was at the door and gone, a thread of her perfume left in the space where her body had been. She was laughing, a strange, hollow laugh. I wished I had dared to ask what woman. Dared to ask what she meant by being with me was too painful. I wished I had opened my mouth and asked her if it was really true that she and Rohan had asked Drake to show me the ways of the world like he said. But I did not dare. I never dared.

The piece of paper in my hand was too much, too heavy.

'No,' I said firmly, running to the jar baby and staring it straight in its big black eye. 'This is not for me.' I folded it small, into a neat square parcel. I folded it tight. Then I lifted the jar with the baby inside and I put the paper underneath it. It would be safe there. It would never need to be seen again.

'You look after it,' I said. 'It's not for me.'

Out of the workroom, preparing the Cowling Place for the elaborate party, I tried to write the incident off as the ramblings of a paranoid anorexic. A manipulative, shallow has-been desperate to please her man. I pushed my doubts, my questions as deep as they could go. I knew Rohan better than her. Oh yes I did. She was upset because she thought she'd put on weight. A few days on menthol cigarettes and coffee and she would be back to her controlling, inexhaustible self. And that piece of paper was a lie. A mirage. A phantom that could never return.

11

Toby opened the door to his office and scooped up a pile of papers from a swivel chair.

'Sit here Diana,' he said. 'Sit here, and when they come in, watch them and wait.'

The small room overflowed with papers, folders, plastic sleeves and photographic transparencies. A lightbox in the corner, switched on and glowing white, was spread with small, bright squares; flashes of red, gold and green, too far away for me to see any detail. The walls were crammed with row upon row of books and the odd poster and postcard of Malk Blancossier's work. The award-winning actor, Daniel Dervish, in tight curled wig, green stockings and rouged cheeks winked at me, large and looming, from the promotional shot for *The Rake's Progress*. The tag line, in looped eighteenth-century script read, 'For some too much is still not enough.'

'Do you want me to take notes?' I said.

'No,' said Toby, lifting a thick script from a shelf and setting it on the desk. 'I just want you to go by gut reaction.'

'OK,' I said.

'And by the way, Rohan's called Stephen Provost in the film. It's not a direct bio-pic. It's a proper story.'

The first actor was called Thomas Reed and he was dressed in a white shirt and a pair of dark jeans. He had his sleeves rolled to his elbows and shoulder-length, dyed, auburn hair which he had tied back with a ribbon. A try-hard touch, I thought. Very specific if not a little pretentious. He had obviously done his homework.

'Hi Tom,' said Toby.

'Hi Malk. Good to see you again,' said Thomas Reed. 'I've worked on the speech till my eyes bled. I dream about needles and pins. Last night I thought I was flying on the back of a seagull.' He laughed. He had a large, swollen voice and a thick-set chin. He was a broad man, not wiry like Rohan, and his hands were short with fingers that made me think of broken clothes pegs. I took an instant dislike to his hands. Someone with hands like that could never play Rohan. Hands like that could never run through cloth like water.

'I don't want you to do the speech today,' said Toby. 'Just a chat really.'

'Ah, yes. Of course,' said Thomas Reed. 'The infamous Blancossier chat technique.'

'Ha,' laughed Toby. 'Barely a technique. Just a chat.' He did not look at me or introduce me. Thomas Reed did not look at me either. Perhaps he thought I was a secretary. Perhaps he thought I should be offering cappuccinos. Perhaps he didn't even see me at all.

'So,' boomed Thomas Reed. 'What would you like to chat about?'

'Stephen Provost,' said Toby. 'I want you to describe your Stephen, how you see him, in ten words.'

Thomas Reed leant back in his chair and put his hands behind his head. The gesture reminded me of someone but I could not think who. The stretch of his arms and the tension in his shirt around the armpits gave me a jolt of repulsion. No, no, no. Thomas Reed would never do.

'Well, off the cuff that's quite difficult,' he said. 'If you'll excuse the pun.' I swallowed a cough and sat on my hands. 'How about, and this is just off the top of my head so it would probably change if I got the part, and probably change from scene to scene because, as we all know, no character could ever really be described in ten words.'

He had a strange smell, Thomas Reed, like a summer evening on the underground, that clasp of heat that grabs you halfway down the escalator and doesn't let go until you are out of the turnstile on the concrete of your destination. The longer he chose to ignore me the more I disliked him. I imagined pulling out his stubby wooden fingers one by one, shaving them down in an electric pencil sharpener.

'Brilliant, genius, chutzpah, focused, ambitious, obsessive, sexy, enigmatic, brazen.' He paused to place his ugly hands on his knees. 'And, I shall link these two words together with a hyphen: in-love.'

He nodded to himself and to Toby. 'Yes, I would say, at this point, that's how I see him. At least they are words that I think relate to him at various points in his story. For me it is a love story, this script, although having only read the first half it could turn out very differently. But no, I'll show my hand and say I see it as a love story.'

Toby nodded. 'OK. Just for argument's sake Tom, could you tell me why?'

'Why?'

'Why you see it as a love story.'

Because that's what he's read in magazines and seen on the news, unimaginative, fat-handed ape.

'Because he loved her no matter what. It shaped his life. But it's not just his love story. It's Julie's too. Because she dedicated her life to them,' said Thomas Reed. 'That woman dedicated her life to someone else's love story. She knew no different. From a child. It's dark, that's for certain.' He leant back in his chair again. Small circles of sweat had appeared in the seams of his armpits. His voice was still loud, actor-bombastic, but his body language had changed. I thought he could see he had failed. Knew that he had messed up his chance by going with cliché and not using his imagination, or the words on the page. I automatically presumed Julie was the name Toby had given to Stella.

'That's why I said obsessive too,' he said quickly. 'Because it's not right, really, is it? To do all that. It doesn't feel like sanity.'

Toby smiled then and gave Thomas Reed the wedge of script he had in front of him. 'Thanks Tom. I want you to read the rest of the script and I will see you again. When you read the rest of it you will know why I asked you, at this point, how you saw Rohan.'

'OK,' said Thomas Reed. 'Great. Looking forward to it. I just think this part is unique, you know? A part like this for an actor of my age...it's a gift.'

'Yes,' said Toby. 'That's why I want an unknown. And don't forget the exhibition launch. I think it would make sense for you to be there.'

'Of course.' Thomas Reed stood up and went to the door without once looking at me. It made me furious to be ignored like that.

Toby did not say anything, but instead pulled another script from a shelf. I opened my mouth to say – what? – I did not know. Before anything had escaped, in came the next Rohan. With him came the smell of mint and biscuits.

'Hi,' said the big man with scruffy dark hair, long at the fringe and at the ears, wearing knee-length shorts, trainers and a blue T-shirt. T-shirt! Rohan never wore a T-shirt. Not once. Not once in the whole time I ever knew him. It was always shirts for Rohan. Or a bare chest, thick with orange wool. But I liked the shape of this man. He was tall, broad, with strong arms. He stood with and without purpose.

'Hi Richard,' said Toby. They shook hands.

'Hi, I'm Richard Milk,' said T-shirt, putting out his hand to me.

'I'm Diana,' I said, glancing cautiously at Toby to see what I was allowed to say. He was looking at the script, so I added, 'Diana Rickwood.'

'Ah, yes,' said Richard Milk. 'The niece, right?'

'Right.'

'Some people call me Rich Milk. Like a delicacy.'

He smiled at me, an open-mouthed, white-toothed smile.

'Gosh you have amazing teeth,' I said, then blushed.

'They don't come cheap,' he said. 'And I had to give up coffee and red wine for these beauties.' He stuck his bottom lip out in a pout. 'Don't get me onto the topic of fags though. Giving them up is another matter entirely.'

I nearly said that giving up anything was impossible for me. I thought of drink, the amount of times I was sure I would never have another, then my elbows on a smooth bar and the thought, 'Just one.' Would it ever be just one? Could it ever be?

'Tell me about it,' I said and grinned back, direct, touching my hair.

'So Richard is my assistant,' said Toby. 'He's in the process of sorting out some issues with the script. Libel issues you might call them. How would you describe Stephen Provost in ten words?'

Richard Milk had an easy energy about him. He sat with his wide hands on the armrests of the chair. He was so big, everything about him was big – his eyes, his arms, his thighs, his back. I found myself staring at his upper arms, imagining him lifting things, heavy things, with one easy movement.

'OK,' he said. 'How about: creative, witty, affected, jealous, illegal, dark, heavy drinker, obsessive and,' he paused and took a side glance at me, a flash of mischief, 'ginger.' He laughed. 'There's no denying he was ginger.'

I laughed and blushed again. Witty. Was Rohan witty? I tried to think of one time we ever laughed together, he and I, but could not. He was funny in a room of people. He was entertaining in interviews, at parties, on TV. In the Cowling Place he could go for many days without ever saying anything. Sometimes it would be weeks without a smile.

'Thank you Richard. I presume you have got everything done that you need to for the exhibition launch?'

'Yes,' said Richard. His hands were large and his fingers had rough knuckles. His nails were bitten down. The skin on his lower arms and hands was very white, and the veins in each hand stood out, thick like medicinal tubing. I thought I could see his heart beating.

'I'm having problems finding out whatever happened to Eddie Drake. He sort of vanished.'

Drake. His name. His face. Was he part of the story? I had never told one person about the Drake years, the times in his car and his ever-present words. I felt ashamed. I felt like a child about to be embarrassed in front of the class by an unprofessional teacher. I felt like I was about to be revealed as the villain not the protagonist. No, Diana. Nobody knows. He will just be a passing character. A chauffeur who disappeared into the night with a dead dog.

'Hmm,' said Toby. 'He's a slippery bastard. I don't care. He's not likely to come forward and complain now is he?'

'No.' Richard looked at me kindly. He looked, to me, like somebody who could lift up the whole world in his hands and still be able to roll a cigarette. 'What about Julie?'

Stella's code name.

'Ah, she goes on about the law and documents and wills but...' Toby looked at his hands. 'She must know what she's done is illegal.'

Was Toby saying Stella killed Rohan? Was he saying that? Right then?

Toby didn't say anything but reached out his hand and put it around Richard Milk's competent fingers. Richard Milk's hands were the loveliest hands I had ever seen.

'Till the launch,' said Richard. 'And you, Diana,' he said, turning to me and reaching out his hand. 'It was lovely to meet you. You are exactly as I imagined.'

I shook his hand and felt his thumbnail stroke my knuckles. I smiled at him and he smiled back. 'Yes, good to meet you,' I said, and I meant it.

'I'm sure we'll meet again,' he said and turned to leave. I missed him immediately.

I wanted to ask Toby about 'Julie' and the word 'illegal', but then in came a second Rohan.

'Peter!' Toby leapt out of his chair and came to the other side of his desk. He and this older man, a man whose age inexplicably revolted me with his first step onto the green carpet, embraced in front of me. Arms tight. Eyes closed.

'Ah Toby, Toby,' said this Peter, addressing him as his real self and not as director. 'So you think you have a part for me at last?'

'Maybe. Maybe. Hopefully!' said Toby. He turned towards me. 'This is Diana! Diana this is Peter Wallace. Actor extraordinaire, all-round good man and long-term confidante to this once wannabe director.'

'*The* Diana,' said Peter Wallace, shaking my hand and clasping me at the elbow. 'Well I never.' When he said *the* Diana I thought of the Titian. I thought of her skin, of her one breast, of her hair in tight curls around her forehead. I thought of the hounds, and her arrow. I thought, as I shook Peter Wallace's warm hand, that I would like her to set hounds on him. I did not like the ease with which he spoke to Toby. I did not like the ease with which he spoke to me.

'Pleased to meet you Diana. Toby and I go way back. I've heard all about you.'

Despite my revulsion I had a flush of pride, brief yet potent, at the fact Toby talked about me to people who had never met me. 'All bad I hope,' I said, then regretted it.

'Oh yes. All terrible. I know all about how you…'

'Peter was my landlord. I slept in his attic,' said Toby quickly.

'Those were the days,' said Peter.

'They certainly were.'

Boring small talk, and Peter Wallace could never play Rohan because he was too fat, and too old, and he smelt like eco-detergent and patchouli oil. Although as he took off his coat I realised that he was not fat. He was tall, with wide hands and wide feet. He was slim at the hips and had a flat stomach.

'Stephen Provost, in ten words,' said Toby. 'Go!'

'Intelligent, scheming, user, dangerous, duplicitous, articulate, talented, sexually potent, handsome.'

I watched him with anger. Where had he picked those ill-suited Rohan words from? I thought perhaps he was trying a different approach to get the part. Trying not to fawn, or fuss, or go on about love stories and creativity. Surely this would not work for Toby, friend or no friend. It was obvious to me, and I should know, that neither of these actors could play Rohan.

'You know I appreciate you giving me this chance Toby,' said Peter Wallace. 'I know I'm not quite…'

'Don't mention it again,' said Toby. 'I've had you in mind for this role for years. It's not in the bag, obviously. You know that. But you are in the final two for these particular scenes, and I know you know the role of Rohan better than anyone else there is.'

Oh no! No! Let this man play Jonathan Trowse. Yes. Peter Wallace would be a perfect Jimmy. Tell him that, give him that. I understand you like him, but no, not Rohan. Not Peter Wallace for Rohan.

'You've already got the whole script, and I'm guessing you've read it.'

'Twenty times at least.'

'Great,' Toby smiled. 'Shall the three of us go for drinks?'

In the bag. I hated Toby then. Hated him for nepotism and despotism and directorial rights and privileges and blindness as to what made Rohan *Rohan*.

'Let's,' said Peter. 'Diana?'

'Let's,' I said. Just one.

'Great,' said Toby. 'I just need to talk to Peter about a few things, and we'll be right out. Take a look along the corridor. All sorts of nonsense along there.'

I nodded. Secret-talking without me. So there was Rohan Rickwood for the silver screen right there, looking, sounding and talking nothing like Rohan at all. Even peg-handed Thomas Reed had bothered with hair dye and a ribbon.

I had barely taken five steps along the corridor when I spotted Richard Milk coming out of a toilet. I stopped to watch, thinking he was about to walk away, but he turned, smiled and came straight towards me. He walked with long strides, his broad arms still at his sides, his fingers clenching and unclenching.

'Hi,' he said.

'Hi,' I said. I felt shy and could not think of anything to say.

'Can I have your number?' he said.

'Pardon?'

'I think it's best to just come out with these things. So can I have your number, then?'

'Um, I don't know if that's a good idea,' I said. If only I knew how these things were done.

'Of course it's a good idea.' He put his hand in his pocket and produced a shopping receipt and a pen.

'I won't give you my number,' I said. 'Not now.'

I loved the smell of him. Could imagine my mouth at his neck, his arm around me, the dents in the mattress after a night's sleep curled up at his hip.

'Ah ha!' he said. 'That was not a definite no.'

'I meant it to be definite.'

'But it wasn't,' he said. 'Which leaves me with one option.' He knelt down on the carpet and ripped the receipt into four. He wrote the same number on each piece.

'You can call me when the definite becomes a maybe.'

'It won't.'

'But it might.' He grabbed my handbag and began undoing pockets and zips.

'Excuse me!' I said, tugging it back towards me as the strap strained at my shoulder.

'Nearly done,' he said, slotting the last piece deep into my bag with a long-armed flourish. 'There,' he said. 'Now you can call me.'

'Not that I will.'

'But you might,' he said and winked. 'I think you like me.'

'I won't call you,' I said.

'You might,' he laughed and turned his back to walk away.

'I won't though,' I said.

'Methinks the lady doth protest too much,' he said without looking back. I said nothing, just watched his blue T-shirt disappear through the door at the end of the corridor.

I was still standing, watching the space in which Richard Milk had asked me out, thinking of mint and biscuits and a blue T-shirt on the floor next to a crumpled bed when Toby and Peter Wallace came out of the office.

'See anything interesting?' said Toby.

'Maybe,' I said. 'I don't think I will go for that drink. I think I'll go home to Ronnie.'

'You sure?'

'Yes. Another time.'

'You will be at the launch tomorrow?'

'Yes.' I did not really want to go, but I wanted to see if Stella would show her true colours, if I could discover some evidence that would shed light on the strange situation that surrounded Rohan's death and the parcel and the fact that everybody thought they knew the real Rohan Rickwood when really none of them did.

12

It seemed implausible that I might live another fifty years and never see Rohan again.

I don't believe in life after death. It is a strange thought, a thought that made me consider what Ronnie and Toby had said in the National Gallery café about death and Shakespeare and a war against Time. Rohan looked set to last forever with his clothes and through his relationship with a famous woman. But it wasn't *my* Rohan that was lasting. It was a horrible creation that people fawned over, told clever jokes about. It was Rohan as icon, as drama, as glamour, as sex. It was a Rohan that could be played by Peter Wallace or Thomas Reed and be believable. I didn't want Ronnie to get caught up in it. It is hard not to get caught up in that stuff. It seeps in. It starts off as a friendly coffee and cigarette. It ends up with entire bottles of gin and snorting cocaine off a glass table through £50 notes. Ronnie was supposed to be the calm, wholesome escape. She was supposed to have saved me. Now what had I got her into?

If Rohan barely spoke about my parents he spoke even less about his own. He told me early on, as soon as I could talk or comprehend, that the subject of his parents was out of bounds. 'As far as I am concerned I never had parents,' he said. 'They are dead now and that is all there is to it.'

In time I knew better than to push him. I certainly did not dare ask about my grandparents on my father's side. For all I knew they were out there somewhere knitting Mr Man jumpers and watering snapdragons in some Wimpey home back garden. I waited hopefully for drunken revelations but he only spoke in riddles.

'When somebody you trust lets you down you never recover,' he said. 'You carry it with you forever. It cuts you down. It changes the way you think. I've seen it destroy people. My sister, she...' He made his hand into a fist. 'I promised myself I would never let anyone I care about down again. I would not be a coward. Being a coward is the worst thing any human being can be – I assure you that. More damage is done by one coward than a thousand Hitlers.'

Cowards were one of Rohan's favourite drunken topics of conversation. I looked at him expectantly at the mention of my mother but he said nothing more about her. I was always hoping for scraps about her. Those scraps, other than the photograph, were all I had.

'Well I sorted them. They are so ashamed of me they'll never show their face in polite society again,' he said, about whom I did not know. 'And I will sort out anyone else who cowers behind the façade of being a pillar of the community. Rock the boat Diana. Rock the boat as much as you can.'

I patted his arm and nodded. I knew that his wish for me to rock the boat did not include me rocking any boat he had carefully constructed for me. I wanted to say, what *about* your parents? What does this have to do with them? And what does it have to do with my mother? But I asked none of these things.

'Tell me about your new collection,' I said calmly. 'I saw all the blue wool O'Connell delivered. What's the theme?'

He perked up, sat up straight, rolled his sleeves up. I hoped he would make himself a coffee – whenever I went for the pot in these situations he would turn on me, a frenzied look in his eye. 'I am not a drunk. Do not ever imply I am a drunk. I can handle my drink. Do not *fuss*.' Then he would apologise like he always did. 'I'm sorry. I'm sorry. I'm sorry for everything. I've failed you. I've failed everyone. We shouldn't be living like this. This half life. If I could change this…' On this occasion, however, he said, 'I'm thinking of something aquatic. Not the sea but freshwater. How much do you know about carp?'

I ignored Ronnie while she dressed to get ready. I didn't mean to but I was finding it more difficult even to look at her, let alone talk. She gave me so much space, but with every bit of space she gave me I slipped further away. Part of me – a part that wanted to cling to her feet with numb fingers – wanted her to sweep me up and lock me away where

I would be safe. That same part of me wanted her to fight for me, to keep me by her side, not to let the past pull me away from her.

She wore a blue polka-dot dress with a belt around her middle and stood before me in all her glory. I said nothing. I sulked, and pretended to read her book of Shakespeare sonnets.

'I'll meet you there,' she said. 'I understand you would want to go alone. This must be so very difficult for you.' She was not angry. I ignored her and she was not angry. So fucking understanding. Why, when I was in this sort of mood, did that bother me so much? As she shut the door to leave I still said nothing. Unnecessarily petulant. A compliment would not have hurt and yet nothing could have made me come up with one.

As soon as she was gone I fell back on the bed and stared at the ceiling for what could have been hours or minutes or neither. I imagined what it would be like to float in nothing, falling, with no material substance around me to gauge my own size. Falling like that I could be as big as the universe or smaller than sand. Without anything to compare myself to I could easily be nothing, non-existent, air. This thought terrified me, and I pushed my fingers into the duvet just to prove it really did exist.

At some point the telephone rang.

'Hello?'

'Hello Diana.'

It was Stella. I was late.

I leant back on the bed and pulled a pillow over my belly.

'Are you coming to the gallery?' Stella talked fast and I could hear clinking glasses in the background. I remember once, in an interview she gave about modelling for some photographer or other, the journalist wrote, 'If Stella Avery were a word that word would be *vital*.'

'No,' I said.

'Why on earth not?' said Stella, raising her voice.

'I've got a hot date with *The Archers*.' I kept my voice straight.

'Hmmm,' said Stella. '*The Archers*?' I heard her tap at the mouthpiece with something hard. 'Are these Archers world-famous, of-the-moment and sexy-as-hell?' I found her self-consciously young language faintly embarrassing. You are old, I wanted to say. You are creased and puckered and old.

'Sort of,' I said. I'd never really been particularly interested in *The Archers*. They were another bi-product of Ronnie's upbringing.

'Have these Archers shown interest in getting your face out there on TV?'

'No,' I said.

'Do these Archers have all kinds of fabulous connections and want to make you the toast of the town?'

I shook my head and said nothing.

Stella tutted loudly. 'You are so *stupid* Diana! For God's sake – you're always cutting off your nose to spite your face.' She became more excited. '*Rohan Rickwood* was a famous fashion designer. *Rohan Rickwood* is the subject of this exciting exhibition that everyone is just dying to see! *Rohan Rickwood* was your…uncle! *You* are the only one still around who lived with him when everyone had forgotten who he was. *You* Diana. You are Diana *Rickwood* and there are people here who would roll over and *die* to hear stories about the old days. And this is your chance. Your chance to discover truths about your past, about your *life*, things you have never even bothered to ask yourself about. Things you *should* ask yourself about Diana. Before it's too late for you.'

'There's a scandal about home-brewing in Ambridge, and I can't let myself risk missing it.' I said. What on earth was she talking about? I was well aware of Rohan's faults. I had lived with them, manoeuvred around them, made myself slip in between and outside them. But I loved him. And would have done anything for him before Stella stole him from me and built our life around her lies and deceit, bringing her driver and his opinions on the truths of men and women with him. She was trying to trick me. She was trying to direct my attention from her involvement in his death.

'Acchh,' said Stella, and I could hear her scowl. There was something inexplicably gratifying about teasing her. There have not been many times during our acquaintance when I've had something she's wanted. Not to her knowledge.

'That's all very well, but if you keep going like this you're never going to get anywhere with anything. You're going to be one of those people who wears a pinny and cleans out your oven with marigold gloves on a Tuesday afternoon.' She paused. 'Or worse, you're going to be homeless and jobless living off the remnants of your own bitterness. I truly thought, when I gave you those photos, that you'd do something with them. I thought you *had*, right up until we met again…I thought you disappeared because you'd gone in search of the truth, but you did the exact opposite. You're in a cocoon, Diana. It may have worked when you were a child, but you are a woman now. And Rohan is gone.'

'I happen to be a fan of pinnies and marigolds.' I wanted to rewind time, back, back, back to the sea. Back to the beginning. *I do not want you to be friends with Toby Farrow. I do not want you to be alone with him. I forbid you from being alone with him*, as Rohan patrolled my bedroom, in the cupboard, under the desk, under the bed, looking, looking, for signs of debauchery, of sex. And yet he never suspected Drake. He looked for villains in the wrong place. And I was too good at covering my tracks.

'Uggh,' said Stella. 'You just don't know your own power, that's your problem.'

Power. Yes, that was more like the real Stella. I twisted the fringe on the orange cushion and saw myself at my bedroom window in Cowling, staring out, wishing something would happen, cursing the crashed boat in Canada, cursing my mother for dying without me.

'You could have people eating out of your hand Diana. Your hand!'

'I don't want people eating out of my hand,' I said, wiping my palms on my jeans. 'What are you talking about?' I wanted to get off the phone and have a cup of tea and Marmite soldiers. To hold onto something tangible and good. Ronnie and I didn't even have a television, and I never bought magazines so I could avoid this kind of thing. And because the women in them still filled me with rage and shame and inadequacy. I know what I am like. I am easily led. If I went to that party I knew that would be it. If you cannot trust yourself you have to avoid situations that will make you act on your untrustworthiness. Diana's first rule of trying to be good.

'Look, it will be fun. It *will*. I know that for a fact. And *Toby's* here with his endless wit and sarcasm. And your Ronnie – the belle of the ball. You'll have someone to mock everything with if that's what you want to do. I'm not asking you to take it at all seriously.'

I didn't like the way she said Toby. Like she was rubbing it in. 'I'm not going.'

'Diana,' Stella said sadly. 'It's such a great opportunity.'

'Why don't you just enjoy it without me?' I already knew I would go, but there was no need to tell her at that moment.

Stella paused. 'Oh hell, I'm not proud: people are asking specifically for you.'

'Nobody knows me,' I said. 'I could lie and say I'll go to get you off my back and then not turn up anyway if you like.'

'Don't be stupid.'

'Well then, I'll say I won't go and won't go. Simple. So I'll see you tomorrow. Maybe you'll let me drive your BMW.'

'You'll regret it.'

'I doubt it.'

'Diana!'

'Bye.'

I hung up and went upstairs to put together an outfit that was specifically 'Dead-designer-with-a-compelling-sex-life's-niece'. I thought it was about time I unveiled my new cape. I wanted to test all those Rohan Rickwood experts to see if they really did know his work as well as I did, and laugh at them when they proved they didn't.

I decided to wear the violet Miss Jean Brodie dress. It was still in the green cardboard bag with rope handles, wrapped up in pink tissue sprayed with vanilla perfume. I'd bought it in a boutique in Covent Garden when I decided to go to Rohan's funeral but felt it was too much and had never worn it. At these sorts of things – and I must admit that even though I hated them I have spent long years observing the etiquette – it's a question of looking effortlessly 'together'. It's something I've never mastered. Why would I want to humiliate myself? But this dress showed off my shoulders. Ronnie was always telling me I had great shoulders. Swimmer's shoulders. So, I slid on the dress, flattened out the wrinkles, and put on a green pendant, bangles and a few silver rings. I dried my hair straight and spritzed it with this shine spray we'd somehow ended up with in our bathroom.

I completed the finishing touches, painted my face; smoky eyes, thick black lashes and a smear of lip-gloss. I put on some heels and looked myself up and down. For a moment I almost believed I could pass as someone attractive, at least I could if you didn't look too hard: I matched, accessorised and glimmered. I felt wonderful and terrible at the same time. I thought of Rohan. *You're not like them Diana.* Drake would have laughed to see me like this. I had learned not to trust mirrors. Whenever my reflection told me I looked good I knew it was my mind playing tricks on me.

I remember dressing up for a school disco. It was compulsory, something to do with some 11-plus exams and a presentation. I remember Drake offering to drive me. I remember Stella saying, 'How kind.' I remember Rohan saying, 'Just this one time. This one time. But I want you back early and Drake will keep an eye on you.' I remember climbing into the car, nervous, nearly hopeful, and Drake's eyes on me in the rear-view mirror.

'Jesus Diana you scrub up well,' he said smiling.

I looked at him shyly, folding my hands in my lap.

'Really?'

'God yeah. You look like a beautiful young woman. You're really blossoming. All the boys at your school are going to be gawping at you.'

I flushed, red-cheeked, wide-eyed.

'Really?'

He caught my eye in the mirror, looked at me long and hard and licked his lips. 'Of course not.' He laughed that loose, easy laugh. 'You look your usual self with a bit of window dressing. But you know that's never mattered to me. I've always fancied you despite your shortfalls.'

'Oh.' I shook, embarrassed to have dared think boys might gawp at me.

'What do you say?'

'Thank you Drake.'

Before I left I took my cape out of my sock drawer and smoothed it out on the duvet. I wrapped it around myself and did up the big buttons. The material was warm and strokeable. I left the funnel neck behind. It would have been too much too soon. The blue and the lilac reminded me of the reflection of sky on car windows. What was it made of? I'd never seen Rohan work with fur because of his allergy. I hoped it was replica, and believed it must be.

I walked up the cobbled street to the gallery and saw the temporary fake flames in makeshift torches on the pavement, and nearly turned around and went back home. Perhaps I should leave it be. Remember the sober Dee: girlfriend of a brainbox, in a flat of Mediterranean colours and soft textured upholstery. What happened to her? I thought of the without-me, post-funeral article in the *Guardian* and stepped forward.

'Isn't this exciting?' somebody in a very tight green, seamless mini-dress said in front of me to her friend, who had exactly the same straightened, honey-highlighted hair extensions.

'Not really,' I said under my breath.

'Do you think we'll see Robbie?' said Nubile #2, pulling down the sky-blue velvet of her dress and tucking a strand of dark hair behind her ear.

'Maybe,' said Nubile #1. 'I mean, I hope so.' She paused and fiddled with her invite, her mobile phone and her pearl-beaded clutch bag. I'm thinking of starting the rumour that you were one of Rickwood's Muses.' She laughed.

'Wouldn't that have been brilliant?' said Nubile #2. 'Everyone knows he used to have sex about seven times a day.'

I shuddered. Could I do this? What had Stella created?

I imagined being a Muse and thought of Ronnie, that if I had any scrap of artistic talent I would capture her on canvas. I thought of a static woman suspended in air, carved from white soap, mute, with foam at her bare feet. As I tried to picture her face, all I could see was the blended features of an amalgam of Stella throughout various stages of her life, young as she was when Rohan first met her and holding back time in thin skin as she was now. I remembered the sculpture in the doorway and had a horrendous thought that I had to disregard before I'd even thought it. The day I had seen Toby and Stella on the beach was the day before the engagement party, but maybe these were not the first times these two had been together. Maybe it started earlier. Maybe it had carried on for years. Maybe, the day Rohan's helicopter fell out of the sky, the two of them had laughed between the same sheets before she tinkered with the engine.

I could hear the yap of her laugh. I considered making a sculpture of her to go in the entrance of the Museum of Twentieth Century Fashion as I saw her: defiant, pieced together with broken bits of blue and pink and pearl, her limbs in all the wrong sockets. A traitor's smile.

'Promise me you won't snog Harry, OK?'

Nubile #1 giggled and smacked her lips together to even out her gloss. 'There's no point me making a promise I can't keep. The press will say I did anyway.'

I was glad to give my invite – a round, bright-yellow affair made from a plastic pouch filled with glitter gel – to the attendants on the door and leave the groomed girls behind.

As soon as I was in I was overwhelmed by a) the number of people crowded around the entrance, drinking champagne; and b) the blown-up photographs of Rohan and Stella set around the walls, or hanging from the ceiling on invisible wires. I thought I might be sick, and would have been if I hadn't heard the 'Diana!' come gliding over well-coiffed heads. It was Stella. She was, as ever, immaculate, long, languid, pale. She wore a simple white shift dress over a pair of green, mid-calf-length culottes, a severe pair of ruby leather boots, and had a Pucci silk scarf around her neck. She had piled her long, pallid hair into a big ball of loose strands on top of her head and had painted her lips the colour of blackberries.

'I knew you'd come!' she exclaimed joyously. 'I told them to look out for you on the door.' She seemed to be hooked up to some tiny earpiece that meant she could talk to any of the staff in the gallery at any time. She stared at me. 'You look utterly, utterly, *wonderful*.' She touched my arm. 'No really. You've scrubbed up beautifully.' That degrading phrase. Scrubbed up.

'Now you convinced me to frou myself, I deserve a cocktail,' I said.

Someone Stella didn't see, someone obviously so efficient as to be invisible, tried to take my cape, but I shook my head; someone else pushed a champagne flute into my hands, and a silver tray of miniature Yorkshire puddings filled with tiny sausages appeared before me as though hovering on air.

'Yes please,' I said to the waitress as Stella shook her head dismissively and pushed her head high, presumably periscoping the room for networking opportunities. Waitresses and waiters hurried past with trays of elaborate, delicate food: baby portions of sushi piled up in pyramids, pork or apple pies the size of marbles, fingertip-sized loaves of bread, silver bowls of pistachio nuts and mixed berries. A waitress, dressed like a fetishised coastguard in a red-sequined bikini and a doll-sized plastic lifering in her hair, fixed me with a look that said, I thought, *get me out of here*. Stella was talking to a man in a well-tailored suit, laughing at things he said that couldn't possibly be that funny.

'Are you happy?' I whispered into one of her ears laced with real diamonds.

'Of course I am darling. The whole thing's a *hit*! And you will never talk to me about anything real in any case, will you?' She smiled brightly and I wondered if maybe, just maybe, she actually wasn't happy at all? Maybe even Stella could experience guilt. But as soon as I thought it, she was gone, with the words 'I'll be back in a min.'

As far as I could see there was nothing there about me at all, and I was standing by myself in a room full of people wearing a one-off, very special, piece of clothing made by the person they were all there to celebrate. Yet I was invisible. Stella had been happy to drop me at the first opportunity. I looked about for Ronnie, who would, at least in this, understand. But she was nowhere to be seen. I regretted my sullen reaction to her earlier dress-up.

With more champagne and a Surf Boy cocktail on its way I wandered over to take a look at some of the exhibits. The gallery was dedicating the whole of its downstairs space to Rohan Rickwood: man of silk, and the temporary walls had been pushed to the side to make way for the guests. The main exhibition was through in the side gallery, under lock and key and still closed to the swelling throng, but there was one big frame in the centre of the bubbled-glass floor. It sat, I guessed, about six-foot high and six-foot wide, hidden beneath a huge hessian curtain. Something amazing in there, I thought. Maybe it's his body, pressed flat and laid out between glass or pieced back together in mock-Picasso. I ambled towards it, grabbing a yellow drink from a tray, and thought I'd take a sneaky glance. But as soon as I got nearer I realised that the frame had its own bodyguards, and they had begun to wheel it towards the main exhibition.

So this is what happens when you join the big league, I thought, and pictured that famous Rohan photo in *Vanity Fair*, standing in his workshop, his hair done differently, sort of swept upwards and backwards, his body faux-relaxed, his eyes made wide with mascara. That was five years after I moved to London. I had to not leave the house for a month, until all the covers stopped staring out at me from shop windows, from display racks at the tube, from the arms of glamorous women and gay men.

'He was remarkable really,' a woman with a glass of whisky filled with ice-cubes shaped like dolphins said to my left. 'A real talent. And he didn't give a flying fuck what people thought of him!' The woman laughed, loud, unapologetic. 'I mean, I heard he shat on a plate and gave it to the Prime Minister at that South Bank bash.' The people around her screeched. 'I mean, you have to be a certain type of person to defecate in front of the PM...' She took a sip of her whisky and threw her head back.

'You mean he shat on a plate *in front* of him?' A man next to her said loudly.

'That's what I heard,' said the woman touching the man on the shoulder. 'I heard he stuck the sheet of toilet roll he wiped his arse with afterwards on the wall at Number 10 and labelled it *Stand and Deliver* in red biro.'

They all laughed and leant in towards each other. Who was this man, *this* Rohan? I stopped a passing waitress, who had a decorative starfish woven through her hair, and requested another Surf Boy.

The people in the gallery mingled and swarmed, and I started my next cocktail. I was getting drunk fast, which felt like all I could do. I turned to one of the glass tables covered in brochures and picked up a neatly typed piece of green-ink, seaweed-decorated paper, reading as I drank:

PRESS RELEASE
The Museum of Twentieth Century Fashion presents
FLATTERY: The Muse
The Clothes, Times and Loves of Rohan Rickwood.

Stella Avery and The Museum of Twentieth Century Fashion have the honour of presenting the definitive exhibition of Rohan Rickwood's clothes and designs, taking you through a whistlestop tour of his infamous Year of Dresses, and beyond.

Rickwood – who died tragically earlier this year in a helicopter accident – spent a lifetime dedicated to enhancing and celebrating the female form. His clothes were finely tailored – no detail was too small for his attention – and were executed with wit and an obvious love of the body.

Every one of Rickwood's finished pieces featured the intricate details so beloved of this most hands-on of designers. Extra stitches on pockets or lapels or seams were added by hand in order to make a feature of the thread and the effortlessly neat Rickwoodian stitching. Colours were carefully chosen to suit each client, with only the exact one good enough for the finished article, a process which could take months to complete.

Although the designer was also known to whip up an entire outfit from scratch in just a few hours if the mood took him.

His clothes were fanciful, beautiful, exquisitely tailored, and – according to those lucky enough to own a piece – a delight to wear. But Rickwood's fashion was not just for the well dressed. Rickwood was interested in the politics of the human condition. Through his clothes he asked: What is life? What is death? What is humanity?

The clothes here are examples of his influences: Lelong, De Tommaso, De Meyer, Gernreich and Balenciaga amongst others, as well as his constant and enduring passion for Stella Avery, a woman he courted and loved despite her marriage to celebrated fashion photographer Jimmy Trowse. It is said that Rohan finally won Jimmy's blessing over an infamous poker game at his coastal home.

Not much is known about Rickwood's past. He famously said, 'My family didn't make me. I made myself in spite of them.' He refused point blank to discuss his mother and father and little is known of his ancestry – the name Rohan Rickwood was a moniker chosen by the designer himself, not his real name. In the 1970s journalist and champion of Rickwood, Christian Burne, tracked down the designer's parents, but in a shroud of secrecy would say nothing of this alleged meeting. It is known Rickwood had a sister, of whom he was fiercely protective. 'If anyone does anything to unearth, disturb or harm my sister,' he said in the summer of 1984 to a crowd of journalists at one of his favourite Soho hangouts, 'I will personally see to it that his or her life is not worth living.' His devotion to those he loved was nothing less than all-consuming, and he commanded great loyalty, evident in the fact that very little has been revealed by or about those closest to him.

But it is the clothes that stand, with or without the man.

It is the clothes that need to be seen to be believed.

Step into a world of colour, fine lines and beauty. Be awash with the bold the bright and the beautiful.

Drown in glamour and worship the sea.

Rohan Rickwood wasn't even his real name! How could that be? His name was him and he was his name. The press release didn't say whether both his names were invented or what his real name actually was – if indeed anybody knew. Would he have been the same man had he been called Rolph Rogers or Simon Simons or Peter

Pan? The reference to his parents was exhilarating. Nobody knew anything about them but they existed. I had grandparents somewhere. Grandparents who might have photos of my mother, school reports, homemade cards, finger paintings she did as a child.

And the reference to my mother, not by name, but there, mentioned, made her more real. My mother! The mermaid with the hair like mine. If he really was as protective as the flyer suggested, then it was hardly surprising her, or my, name had been left out of things all this time. Our omission was not sinister at all. He had wanted to protect us. 'If anyone does anything to unearth, disturb or harm my sister...' he had said. I felt a strong sense of pride and love that my real mother had provoked something so strong inside him. He loved her and he loved me. We were important.

'Psssst,' a voice from behind didn't whisper. It was Ronnie.

'Hey you,' I said. 'Great booze.' I held up my cocktail. I meant to be provocative but she didn't seem to notice.

'Tell me about it,' she said grinning. 'Everyone's getting sloshed – and *they're doing drugs* out back.' She came over to me and slipped her arm around my waist. I stroked the hairs on her forearm and kissed the scoop of her ear, down to the lobe. If everyone around me was going to behave like they were in *The Rake's Progress,* I didn't see why I shouldn't.

'Have you seen this?' I showed her the press release. I should have complimented her earlier. She looked good.

'Yes. I didn't know Rohan and Stella were so pretty,' said Ronnie. 'Look at these pictures.'

I had been trying not to. All around me the wire-suspended Rohans and Stellas repeated and repeated like a magnified tear-sheet of first-class Christmas stamps. I could not, had I tried, have imagined a more painful, agitating or upsetting selection of images to have thrust at me in this situation. I do not know what got to me most. Perhaps it was the black-and-white shots of them doing *The Good Life*: Rohan with the sleeves of his shirt rolled up, sun-freckled arms tight around Stella in a tank top, rolled-up jeans and flip flops.

(Diamond studs in her ears, mind you, and immaculate nails.) I remembered those shots. They'd been in a Sunday supplement I'd unknowingly leafed through in a doctor's surgery. They had been the guest stars in a feature on famous, glamorous couples who were giving up the bright lights and sway of the city for a life of cabbage patches, goats and rural-chic in the country. Fake, fake, fake, fake, fake, fake, fake…

'Dee?'

I blinked. Ronnie was pointing at another shot of the happy couple – this time in colour – which hung near the Victor Eve *Offsprung* statue. The colour of Rohan's photographed hair made me grab the hem of my cape and furiously stroke the edge of the fur. His hair took up nearly the whole top of the photo, which itself was about five foot square, and caught the light in glossy spirals, like tarnished foil. Rohan was sitting at the kitchen table – pins in his mouth, glasses at the end of his nose – his hair the colour of the thread the tricksters show the Emperor in *The Emperor's New Clothes*. He was holding onto the side-seams at the bottom of a dress – a dress made of a vivid lilac charmeuse that I remembered him buying on a rainy Wednesday from a fabric man in Soho. The dress was worn by Stella, who appeared in the photo from the bottom of her thighs to the top of her ankles. A cross section. It was a very bright picture – the colour had been enhanced with more yellow and blue and was very different in composition from the black-and-whites.

I stared at it.

The other photos had been staged for photographers. They were what Rohan and Stella deemed the world should see, but this one was different. This was taken using the timer by Rohan himself on his camera with the clunky lens. This was Rohan as I knew him, the pins bristling against his lips, the heads like silver full-stops punctuating his rare smile.

'Stella had good legs,' said Ronnie, following my eyes and draining her drink.

'She did,' I said.

But these were not Stella's legs.

These were someone else's. Much to my own disgust I would recognise Stella's legs anywhere. And these were not Stella's legs. These were the legs of somebody I did not know. Legs I was sure I had never seen before. I tried to piece together when it was taken, and thought it likely to be a late Sunday morning. There were, in the background, the remnants of pancakes with lemon and brown sugar. A Sunday treat if Stella was in the city. I used to look forward to our breakfasts, as they were not as often as I would have liked. Someone had joined him for a morning swim. Barely visible, but most definitely there, were two towels crumpled and entwined on the floor behind him, two pairs of discarded sandals upturned. I stared at the pink of the unknown woman's legs, his fingers on the dress, his thumb on her calf. I just knew it wasn't Stella. He never fitted her in the kitchen. He never fitted anyone in the kitchen.

'Fuck,' I said.

'What?' said Ronnie, turning towards a passing waiter.

I couldn't tell her. The five-foot Rohan using some other woman as a dress dummy in his kitchen was too much of a shock. It hurt because this stranger, although just a pair of legs in the photograph, was standing in the security of Rohan's domestic set-up. It was not anonymous and cold or detached as it would have been in the workroom. This woman was not a conquest to be mocked or derided. This woman was important. Important enough to go sea swimming, eat pancakes and stand barefooted on our kitchen table while Rohan dressed her. Where had Stella found it? Did she know who the woman was? And where was I at the time?

I forced myself to edge nearer and read the label. It said, 'Rohan in workshop: Stella modelling for a silk dress that is still unaccounted for'. Well that was a lie. The dress may have been unaccounted for but I knew for a fact that the woman modelling was not Stella. She would never tell *that* to the world. The humiliation would be too much for her to handle.

Ronnie came up beside me carrying two full cocktail glasses.

'I'm sorry I didn't want you to drink,' she said. 'I should have trusted you. I just worry.'

'I'm sorry I told you I hardly knew Rohan Rickwood,' I said.

'That's OK. You were in shock.' She kissed me on the back of my neck. Lovely Ronnie. There would never be surprise women barefoot on our kitchen table. Ronnie was totally trustworthy. She liked monogamy. She wanted real connection. No matter how much I tell you about her, how much I describe her reasonable reactions to every stupid thing I ever did, it would still not even vaguely portray just how ridiculously kind and empathetic and just and fair she was. This is not me, an older, wiser me, recreating her in my mind. She had her faults, but her good points outweighed them a hundred to one. I didn't deserve her. She was the nearest thing to connection I dared risk. Which meant no connection at all.

'Cheers,' we both said, smiling, drink-fuelled, with the great and not-so-good shimmering around us under sparkly lights and the flash of cameras.

'There you are!' It was Stella. She had in one hand Toby and in the other slim-trousered, navy, faille-suited Benjy Burne. He had narrow, dark-red, thick-rimmed glasses offsetting a new and messy but very particular asymmetric haircut. He carried a mini tape recorder and a battered-looking brown satchel that had probably cost him a fortune – or been sent by some fashion house looking for PR.

Stella's bit on the side.

'Darlings,' said Stella grinning. 'Isn't this great? We're opening up the main exhibit in a minute. Everyone is practically gagging to look at his stuff.'

'The man was a genius,' said Benjy, nodding.

'Do you have to talk like that?' I said to Stella, but nobody heard me. Benjy's eyes were always on the move. I thought he had the look of somebody intensely cynical about everything, but who still couldn't believe his luck at having become a part of something so dripping with glamour as both the fashion and media industries. His face said,

'Fuck you all, I know your game,' and his clothes said, 'Yes! Yes! Yes! I have arrived!'

'Benjy,' said Stella, letting go of both his and Toby's hands. 'I'd like you to look after Diana, the niece of our hero of the hour.' She pulled our hands towards each other and forced a strained hand-hold out of us both.

Benjy's eyebrows went up very high and he took my hand again, a vigorous squeeze, blinking furiously.

'I love your cape,' he said. 'Is it real fur?'

I stroked Rohan's odd gift briefly. 'I don't think so,' I said.

'Where's it from? I haven't seen anything quite like it.'

Stella's eyes widened then tightened. 'Yes…I've never seen that before…'

'I can't remember,' I said. 'Some second-hand stall on Portobello Road I think.'

'Oh, yeah, right, of course,' said Benjy, and Stella nodded in agreement. Wankers.

'Ladies and gentlemen of the press and distinguished guests,' came the confident voice of the young, freckled museum receptionist I'd made blush on my first visit. She stood on a small podium towards the back of the gallery and had a pinned-up quiff and long silver earrings which hung past her shoulderblades. I tried to catch her eye. She was exactly my type when I played at being predator. A safe bet.

'May I take this opportunity to thank you all for coming, and to say what an exciting night this is for MTCF and for lovers of fashion.'

Murmurs of agreement.

'Rohan Rickwood's clothes have been enjoying something of a renaissance for the past decade or so, a rerun of the glory of his 1970s heyday.'

Nods, ayes and strange sympathetic hums all round.

'And, of course, interest has gained fever pitch since his untimely death last month. What members of the team here have created is a tribute to his talent, his unerring dedication to fashion and well-crafted clothes, and an exposition of his two Muses: Stella Avery and the sea.'

I couldn't really believe this was happening. I clung to Ronnie to make sure she was still there, that she wasn't disintegrating and re-forming as something the opposite of what I thought she was. The room was full of bodies and nods and lights and expensive clothes and drink and electro-pop music by bands fêted by old balding men pretending to be hip. I experienced a sensation not unlike a hand on my face, covering my airways and forcing my eyes shut. What if it's me who's wrong? What if *I'm* fake? Since leaving Cowling I had not often wondered if my interpretation of events in the past, of Rohan, of Stella, of Toby, were wrong. I have always been sure that it was they who were shallow, obsessed with surface and glitter, posing as an elite and therefore becoming an elite in a world where glamour and intrigue and outrage were better than gold or money for buying a place in society. But, in a room full of hundreds of beautiful people all convinced that the display around them was the truth and the light, it was very hard not to question whether my own interpretations were exactly that – interpretations.

'So without further delay, may I introduce Rohan's wife and head of this wonderful gallery... Stella Avery...' The receptionist inflected the words in the manner of a game-show host and gesticulated self-consciously with drama-school flourish.

People clapped and whooped. Pale and perfect Stella stood up on the platform and dipped a swift bow. Quiff-girl squeezed her arm before stepping aside, while Stella smiled and held her hands up for quiet.

'Thank you Polly,' she said, and put her hands to her neck, folding the corners of the Pucci-print scarf in and out, in and out.

'I don't really want to say much,' she said quietly. 'Apart from this exhibition is something I've been working on for a long time – long before Rohan had his terrible accident.' She paused, twisting the scarf in incessant loops. 'But this isn't about gimmicks or being a *cause célèbre*.' She looked at her feet. 'It's about a man who wanted to become more than the sum of his upbringing. It's about a passion for finely made things, for colour, for texture, and most of all for the shapes and stature of women.'

There was Toby's film pitch, right there.

She had tears then. Real tears. I prised the invisible hand from my face and tried to breathe.

'I always loved Rohan Rickwood's clothes,' Stella continued. 'When I first knew him I loved to hear him talk about fabric and stitching and thread.' She smacked her lips together, and blinked among camera flashes.

'But enough of that. It is with great pleasure that I bring you our *Flattery* exhibition. Step inside for history and the sea brought to life in the lasting legacy of Rickwoodian tailoring, in flourishing swathes of satin and silk.'

With that she did what anybody but myself might have taken for a humble little nod and then moved to the side of the door, cutting a burgundy ribbon that separated the esteemed guests from the exhibition. There were actors and actresses and pop-stars and models and journalists and party-girls and party-boys high on coke and fags and champagne. They channelled in through the door, and I briefly had the pleasure of imagining the doorframe as a guillotine, chopping off the well-anointed heads of the self-congratulatory fuckwits there assembled. Ronnie would have liked it. Very eighteenth century.

Ronnie started edging towards the gallery door, riding the surge of rising heads and raised arms. She pushed through the crowd, mimicking Stella's familiar sense of urgency. I could see Benjy Burne's head dipping through the door, and I looked for Toby.

He was standing next to me.

'Hello Diana,' he said, his hands stuffed into his pockets. 'Thanks for yesterday.'

'No worries.'

'You never said which Rohan you liked best.'

'I thought it was obvious, but you obviously didn't. Neither.'

'Neither?'

'Peter Wallace is no Rohan, Toby.'

'I never said Peter Wallace was Rohan.'

'You mean…?'

'There is really only one choice. That was why I had you in there. I chose the man who reacted to you most like the way Rohan reacted to you. Treated you like he did.' I thought about Thomas Reed. He'd basically ignored me.

'No matter what you think about her, she's made this Rickwood thing a reality. She wants the truth to be known. She wants to claim something back for herself. We are all so entwined with it, it's hard to breathe. It's stifling. She doesn't want him to fade into strange coat-hanger phantoms and be forgotten. She's doing it because she cares.'

'Oh yeah, she really cares.' I rolled my eyes like a child.

'She does. You could never see that.' He shrugged. 'She wants to rediscover what was good about him, because there were plenty of good things about him. You heard her talking about it. She admires their younger selves. When they had all that potential. Before all that came later…' He paused and looked at me. So he knew I knew that she had seduced him as a boy, and he was still with her, still loved her, still slept with his arms at her waist.

'She only wishes they'd got together sooner because it would have made her more *authentic* in the eyes of the other fucking fashionistas,' I said angrily.

'You've become such a cynic. She was sold a life that was never hers. She thought she was the love of Rohan's life – she always loved him – but none of it was for her. And you never even noticed. And despite everything, despite your ice-queen demeanour, I don't believe what she says about that last day you were in Cowling. Not the bit about you.'

'What?'

'The rest of it is true. I know it is. But not the bit about you. You never shagged Sir Jimmy. If you actually talked to her you could clear the air. Find out the truth.'

'She wouldn't know the truth if it swathed her in silk,' I said. 'And I tell you one thing, I would never *shag*, as you so beautifully put it, Jimmy Trowse.'

He rolled his eyes, took my arm, and dragged me towards the exhibition. 'I know that. Speak to her. Open your eyes.'

'Oh, boo hoo,' I said. 'Poor fucking Stella. I know you love her Toby, but one day you will open your eyes and see just what a viper she really is. Wouldn't it be bloody handy if she actually *had* been sold a lie of a life? Wouldn't that make her betrayal – your betrayal – all the easier to stomach? Wouldn't it make it acceptable for her to chuck a spanner in the helicopter engine and hope for the best? *Ten-*fucking-*tare*.'

'I am going to choose to ignore that,' he said with obvious anger. 'You can't just bandy accusations like that about. If you are thinking things like *that*, well it's hard to believe you will ever see what the two of you have in common.' He started to move away.

'Oh,' I said. I wondered if he knew his beloved was being grunted all over by a *Times* style wannabe. I thought about pointing it out to him, but instead said, 'I don't think I'm going to look at the exhibition.'

'It's good,' he said. 'You should.'

'I'm not interested in Stella's Rohan,' I said. 'My Rohan is dead.'

'He's dead all right,' said Toby. He put his hand around my waist for just a second. 'He was dead a long time ago. Before you were born in fact. Now come and see these clothes,' he said. 'And the painting. We shall agree to disagree about Stella because we can. You weren't the only lonely one, you know. She was lonely. I was lonely. Being lonely makes you do things you wouldn't usually do.'

'What has any of this got to do with *you*?' Any desire or longing I'd felt died when I left Cowling. I knew that now.

'Did you never think it was odd I moved to the house next door Diana?'

'No...Well...Yes, but only because you were my only friend at school.'

'Open your eyes.' He shrugged. 'And come and see this painting.'

'The painting? What painting?' And what did he mean Rohan was dead long before I was born? What nonsense was this? Why did every single person think they knew the real Rohan? And Toby, as much as he would always stand for my childhood idea of male physical perfection, well he was less qualified to comment than most.

'Rohan's big painting of the sea. Stella's had it framed and plonked right inside the main entrance. And I'm glad you agree on the Rohan for my film. I knew you would.'

'He is the perfect choice,' I said, pretending neither of us had said the things we had. In my bag the receipt pieces etched with Richard Milk's number rustled with approval.

Rohan's big painting of the sea?

I had never seen Rohan's big painting of the sea.

At Toby's side I stepped into *Flattery* and was aware that all around me in glass display boxes were clothes made by Rohan. Not one person – other than that smug fraudster Benjy Burne – had said anything about my fur button-up cape, or guessed its origin, which kept me strong, and safe in the knowledge that *I knew Rohan better than any other damned faker in the building*. The cabinets had been set at various levels around the gallery walls, organised not into dates, but into colourways. The first corner started with black and made its way, anti-clockwise, to white on the other side. Everything in between went from navy, purple, sky blue, greens, reds, oranges, yellows, the whole rainbow. I didn't want to look at the clothes, didn't have the energy to look at the clothes, but I did at least like the fact that Stella had made a feature of just how many different coloured silks Rohan had managed to get his hands on. Colour was a big deal to Rohan – I knew colour was more important to him than clothes – and I would not have expected Stella to have noticed.

Then I saw the canvas and the whole room went still.

At first glance the entire painting was a swelling mass of ocean: thick blue-green oils recreated a sense of the sea, still and moving and full of conflicting currents. On nearer inspection the whole surface had been sectioned off into segments, as though it was a stained-glass window, broken into pieces and reassembled out of order. There was a sense of motion to it. I thought, *I'm swaying, I'm swaying*, but couldn't be sure if it was me or the effect of the blend of colours on my own orientation. In the corner, near the bottom of the painting, was a pale edge of shore. I spotted sandcastles, kites and ice cream and, I gasped, two delicate piles of clothes and shoes left neatly by the water. I scanned the sea for the figures I already knew were there. Sure enough, quite far out, beyond the rocks and away from the beach, were two people in the water, sculling to stay afloat. One had red hair fanned out like seaweed, the other was darker, on her back, her breasts facing the sun.

The label on the wall underneath the painting said it was called *Safe Sea*. There was a little annotated card next to it, in Stella's choice of font that explained,

> Before they could go public with their relationship Stella and Rohan were lovers for over ten years. They would rarely meet in London – there were friends of her husband in even the most remote corners – but would meet at his home by the sea in the village of Cowling on the south coast of England. Stella made many trips each year, and as this Rickwood painting portrays, they needed a place safe from prying, tell-tale eyes. Stella never learned to swim, and was in fact afraid of water, so the couple in the ocean are very much metaphorical. This painting was found in Rickwood's workshop after his death and has been named for this exhibition by Stella Avery.

I stared at the picture for a very long time. It was strange to see a painting by Rohan in such a public place, and I had never seen this one before. It was a snapshot of a life, a life that was secret and kept far away from the glimmer of London and the shows and the headlines. What would people think if they knew? If they really knew?

I liked the painting; the simplicity of the waves, the detail of the figures, the twinkling brilliance of the sun on the water. It was undoubtedly a beautiful painting, the sort people would put on their walls as a print – and no doubt they would do exactly that – to look at for pleasure. But it was darker than that, more unsettling, and I was shocked to see something so real amidst all the façade.

That figure in the sea with Rohan was not Stella. It was not even slightly Stella. This figure was broader, darker somehow and looked more rounded. I stared at the detail on the long hair as it spread outwards and down the woman's shoulders. I knew with a violent quake, a cricket bat to the guts, a knife through my innards, that this was the woman on the kitchen table. Rohan had been in love with someone else. Not Stella, with the pomp and the magazine photos and the glitzy dresses, but someone else. Someone nobody knew about. Somebody who ate pancakes and swam in the sea, who he kept a secret from every other person he knew. Even me.

'Toby,' I said, turning to him, my mind flicking through a hundred old memories that seemed to rearrange themselves with new meaning. A back-to-front collage that had familiar shapes, familiar sounds, familiar feelings, but were put back together the wrong way.

'Toby, that's not Stella – it's someone else.'

'Exactly,' said Toby. 'But who, huh?'

'Who?'

'Someone you would never believe. Stella thought you knew. She thought you'd worked it out…'

Stella. The shape of her body was everywhere, nipped, petite, alluring behind perspex and glass. Rohan always managed to keep my contact with Stella to a bare minimum. She was always on the outskirts of my childhood, a sketch at the corner of my life, faint lines on tracing paper. I was never allowed to get to her. The Human Broom. Yet the photo and the painting made her as much of an outsider as I was.

It must have been a joke, a strange fantasy brought on by drink or a lack of sleep. Rohan could not have been with somebody else. Somebody potentially plain and homely and normal.

'I do not believe it,' I said. 'I knew he screwed around. He always screwed around. But not another relationship. Not one I didn't know about.'

'You'd better believe it,' said Toby, but as he opened his mouth to say more I turned away. I needed to get even more drunk. I needed to get so drunk that I could not think of anything. If Rohan had been in love with someone else it changed everything. Was it someone from the village? Was it another model? Was it someone from a galaxy far far away?

I thought I might be sick, so surveyed the room for anyone I might know.

In the corner, behind a fish-tale skirt made of finest crêpe de Chine and a tray of power-sushi cut into the shape of comic-book seahorses, I saw Victor Eve nibbling the ear of his beautiful wife. At that moment I would have done anything for the sculptor to disappear into the bubble-glass gallery floor, and for the wonderful Glenys Pimm's clothes to peel away at my gaze, like foil from an expensive Easter egg. There was something about that woman, so clear and wonderful and real. I looked about for Ronnie. She was with Toby in front of a yellow gauze blouse that if you wore it your tits would definitely show through. The thought of that pushed me to go and speak to the Eves. Glenys had wonderful breasts.

Don't look at the clothes too much, that's all, I reminded myself over and over. Rohan was everywhere and nowhere. I wondered how he would feel if he were here. Everyone likes to own a dead man. Especially a famous one. But how could he have lied to me? I had been sure he had never lied to me. When did they have time to do it? How could I not have noticed. Where was *I*?

One of the good things about drink, I thought then, was that it makes you courageous, or it makes you not care about the effects of what you do. You can do anything. And if it turns out bad you can always say you were drunk. I held my glass tight in my hand like a grail.

'Dia-na!' said Victor in his Toad of Toad Hall voice. His hair was as glowing as ever, each combed channel a split in his pink scalp.

'Victor!' I said in a voice that was Stella's and was becoming mine.

'Diana,' said Glenys, not taking my offered hand. 'Good to see you again. My husband tells me he had the luck of taking you for cake at the National.'

'Yes, yes quite delightful.'

This is the way these people talk.

'Have you got any further on your quest for Diana?' Victor put his arm around his wife, who would not meet my eye, letting his fingers squeeze into her. 'Our Diana has become rather interested in the moon goddess,' he explained.

I was very busy staring at the swell of Glenys Pimm's chest in her badly cut rayon shift dress. Glenys Pimm wore cheap clothes well, and to me that is what it really means to have style. She would look good in a sack made of butcher's linen.

Suddenly Victor waved furiously at some thin, thin model and announced he was interested in her, 'purely on a professional I-want-to-sculpt-her basis.' I rolled my eyes as he strode off on his short legs, expecting Glenys Pimm to do the same, but she downed her glass of champagne and said, 'Don't get the wrong idea about Victor, Diana. I would trust him with my life.'

I felt for the wrap of cocaine in my handbag. I needed to switch off, unwind. I needed to be able to act without having to think about the effect of my actions. I took a risk and invited Glenys to the toilets to join me. She looked relieved, and we both squeezed into a cubicle, not speaking, just inhaling the powder through a shared rolled note.

'Diana, shall we go outside?' Glenys's eyes were red and watery.

'Let's.'

The air was sharp, cold, and we'd managed to get hold of two bottles of champagne. We were giggling. We walked through the flowerbeds and tried to spell out the word 'WANKY' with our high heels. We agreed this was the sum of the parts of those assembled inside the gallery's walls. The streetlights caught the fairer shades in the brown of her hair, like jewelled highlights. I am being overly romantic in my description and am trying very hard not to. I can only describe that moment, that click of time with Glenys in overblown, fantasy sentences. I cannot, even now, especially now, think sensibly about Glenys Pimm.

I leant to kiss her on the pavement behind a fake-flame torch in which she tried to light her cigarette. It was not that I wanted to have sex with her. I just wanted to be close to her. To feel her near me.

'It's fake!' I said. 'You'll get no hot sparks there.'

'Damn it, I will!' she said, giggling, breathy, and continued to suck on the unlit cigarette. She seemed young. Younger than me.

'Come here,' I said. I was obsessed with getting my head on her shoulder.

She didn't argue. She is a good thirty years older than me and yet she was nervous. When I pushed my cheek against her mouth her lipstick smeared into my skin and I thought I could feel it burn me. In a normal situation I would have restrained myself from going straight to the chest, but with her, my hands were straight into her dress under the gap in the armpits. Because it didn't fit her properly there was just enough room for me to slide a hand in far enough to grab her and to press her nipple. And then I just let her hold me. It wasn't sexual. It was something else. Something warm and – this surprised me – almost safe.

'Stop!' she said. The stars in her hair fell to the pavement and crunched under our shoes.

'Why?' I said, eager.

'There's Victor!'

I looked over my shoulder, scared, but my conquest's husband was nowhere to be seen.

'No there's not,' I said, angry, hand back at the gap under her arm.

'No, I mean, there is Victor to consider,' she said. 'And by no stretch of the imagination is this at all right. Especially not with you.' She was shaking. Her face and neck were red.

I pretended I had wanted to seduce her. The reality was more terrifying than that. I had just wanted to be held, nothing more. I didn't want anything from her. Just comfort. Just connection. 'We all take a bit of what we fancy where we dare,' I said in Stella's voice.

'*I* don't,' she said, pushing me away and wiping her mouth harshly with the back of her arm. Lipstick was everywhere, like blood and Vaseline and wine.

'You do now, Doll,' I said. I don't know what got into me.

'Look, Diana, I think you're marvellous, I really do. Just like the painting. But I'm straight as a protractor's hypotenuse. I love Victor. And you…*you are*…I'm not sure what I am doing. I used to be so…'

'*Sure* you love Victor,' I said, wiping my own mouth.

'I do.'

'OK. Whatever you say.' I paused. 'And I love Ronnie. But I don't see why we shouldn't be talking.'

'Because,' she put her hands against her face. 'You know Victor used to think that...' she stopped. She pushed her hair straight and correct. Pushed me out of the walnut strands. 'But he's not. He was wrong. He knows that now. I couldn't have...'

'Wrong about what?' I said. I thought of the sea, then.

'Look, forget it, my most wonderful girl.' She laughed and pulled out her lipstick from her mint-green handbag and started reapplying without a mirror. 'Just remember that you are worth more than this crap...And we will always have Paris.'

'We most certainly will that,' I said. I felt relieved we hadn't gone further. Maybe Glenys Pimm could become a friend. I was short on female friends. I was short on friends.

The air was clear.

Glenys put her arm around my middle and we strode, like schoolfriends in an Enid Blyton novel, to the gallery's swishing glass doors.

'At least now I know,' she whispered into my ear.

'You know what?' I said.

'That I'm definitely a man's woman.'

'That doesn't make me feel better,' I said, although for many reasons it did.

We still had the bottles of champagne, and took one each and kissed our goodbyes. She wiggled off, just like Marilyn Monroe in a terribly cut dress, with more sex appeal than any of the rest of them.

I will always remember the feel of her lipstick, yielding like waxed fruit.

'*There* you are!' It was Stella. I wondered what it would be like to be held by her, then righted myself. Drugs always do that to me, make me want things I would normally consider with disgust.

'How many wankers does it take to fill a gallery?' I said.

'You're fucked,' she said and laughed, because so was she.

'I probably have to go,' I said. 'I have no control over my actions.'

'Is that a bad thing?' she said, puffing on an unlit cigarette that she wedged gracefully into her coral cigarette holder.

'Yes it is. I like to be an armchair critic. Not a part of a bloody Bacchanal.'

'You've been hanging out with academics too much,' she said. 'You should just enjoy yourself.'

I thought of Rohan's imposing six-foot *Safe Sea* canvas.

'I know you couldn't swim,' I said. 'It would have messed up your hair-do.' I immediately put my hand over my mouth. It was unlike me to say what I actually thought to Stella's face.

'I know,' she said. 'I know a lot of things.'

'Not now,' I said, then, 'I really have to go home. We need to be out by midday tomorrow if I'm going to get to the campsite before closing time.' I decided quite suddenly that if I was going to Cowling I would not, under any circumstance, stay in the Cowling Place.

'What?' said Stella. I think, by this time, half of my champagne was gone and I was pretty incomprehensible.

'Tomorrow. Midday. Campsite.'

'Right,' she said. Benjy Burne appeared at her side, tape recorder whirring, glasses slightly askew.

'Have you seen my girlfriend?' I asked Benjy.

'Yes,' he said and winked. 'She's in there talking to two potential Rohans.'

'Dear God,' I said.

When I found her she was standing with her arms around Peter Wallace and Thomas Reed.

'Evening gentlemen.' They were both dressed in tailored suits with pale-blue shirts and narrow trousers. 'Any reason for the uniform?'

'Evening Diana,' said Peter. Thomas Reed did not acknowledge me. He looked about the room like a cat watching a fly. 'Coincidence.'

'Of course. Good evening so far?' I stared at Peter Wallace and could not believe I thought Toby would have chosen him. He was impossible. But as for Thomas. Well, he had said *in-love*, with a hyphen.

'Oh yes,' said Thomas, but not to me. 'Good for research.'

'Good for drink,' said Peter. 'I haven't drunk this much since, well, since Toby lived with me.'

I said nothing to this but took Ronnie by the arm.

'Would you mind if I borrowed this beautiful woman?' They both shook their heads. 'I hope to see you both later.' This could not have been further from the truth.

'We are going to Cowling,' I said. 'Tomorrow.'

'We are what?'

'Cowling. Tomorrow.'

'Me too?'

'Everyone is going. Stella, Toby, Benjy. Us.' I gripped her. 'But I don't want to go back there,' I said. 'I don't want to go to the house. I *vowed* I would never go back to the house.'

She had a slice of red paint on her elbow, like a wound.

'We don't have to *stay* in the house,' she said. 'We could stay in a hotel.' She blew me a little kiss and scraped some hair away from my face. 'If we sort out things in the house it can be in the day, when it's sunny.'

She stood in front of me, familiar but different. 'I'm quite drunk you know,' she said. She slurred her words and her right eye flickered.

I could see Rohan's eyes: grey, sad now, but knowing. I thought, 'What are you trying to tell me?' and felt wretched that I couldn't see him to find out, that we couldn't talk. All these extraneous people to sort through his things, when all I wanted was for it to be him and me sitting in the kitchen drinking too-strong coffee and playing a game of backgammon. Were you in love with someone else? Who was she? What was your real name?

When I first left home it took me a long time to get used to not having to think of Rohan before making decisions. It came as a shock to me that I could do whatever I pleased, that nothing I did would end with anger, tears or, worse, him ignoring me until

I worked out what it was I had done to him. Everything was in my best interest. He'd said so often enough. When I first came to London I found it hard to work out what, without Rohan to tell me, *was* in my best interest. I still found it hard. It was a long time before I even contemplated not being influenced by Drake. In fact, I do not know if I ever did.

I thought of the prospective journey to Cowling and remembered driving back with Rohan from London when he'd just done an interview for *Late Review* on BBC2. His second shot at celebrity was in full swing by this time. The seventies were having a revival and all the old icons were being dug out of their holes to provide talking heads for retrospectives. I was nineteen and only days from deciding to leave. He was excited and worried, smoking cigars all the way home. It was a normal day, normal sky, normal cars on the A3 doing normal journeys. Nothing spectacular. But the window of the passenger door had been wound down just a little way and there was this thin stream of a furious breeze coming into the car. I'd watched this clump of his dry, orange hair flapping back and forth, back and forth. It was like seeing him through a microscope. This patch of his hair, manipulated by errant breeze, had seemed like the most real thing I had ever seen. I watched it flutter and knew he would die one day. That things would change. I knew one day in the future that flick of coarse hair would lie flat against the head of a corpse: his body but not his body. I can still see it. I'd never wanted to touch something so much in my life. I wanted to suck up his hair like spaghetti and push my face into his scalp. Instead, I closed my eyes and let the bright sun flash at my closed eyelids through the passing landscape. Bursts of bright red, yellow and black performed a light show in the silence. I thought: the only truth in all the world is that things will change, and: *I do not know how to live without you.*

'We could camp?' I said.

'We *could*...' Bless Ronnie. She tried to sound enthusiastic.

'That's settled then,' I said. I could put off going to the house for a little longer. I wouldn't have to sleep in my old bed, or have Stella and Toby in Rohan's bed behind thin walls. The thought of that made me feel bereft.

'I think I am going to be sick,' said Ronnie.

'I'll come with you.'

'No. No. Some things are best done alone.' And she left.

And standing by *Safe Sea* was Richard Milk. He had slicked back his dark hair with gel and was wearing a slate-grey suit with lime split-line pinstripes. He reminded me of something from an eighties film. He had his hand in his back pocket and one leg cocked outwards. His large body looked astonishing in that suit. I rummaged in my bag for his receipt and my phone and without thinking sent him a text message.

Nice suit.

I watched him take his phone from his back pocket and read. He did not turn around. He tapped something in and continued to stare at the screen and press buttons.

Nice cape.

A few seconds later:

Nice legs.

A few seconds more:

Nice face.

Benjy Burne appeared from behind a suspended photograph and I jumped. Caught in the act.

'Toby was just looking for you. He's taking Ronnie home. She collapsed with the drink in front of a bolero jacket covered in ostrich feathers.'

Ostrich feathers? Just the thought of them appalled me.

'I have to go home,' I said. 'Was she OK?'

'Yes. Yes. She was fine.'

Richard Milk appeared brandishing two full glasses. Even in my heels he was a good five inches taller than me. I laughed at the thought of Drake. *You are too tall anyway, to ever be truly loved. Your legs are too long. Your arms are too long. You are too long.* Well, ha! Drake, look at this. Richard Milk is *taller* than me. Ha!

'I have to go home,' I repeated, disappointed.

'This is just like Cinderella,' said Richard. 'Can I take one of your shoes?' His broad shoulders shook with a laugh.

'What?' I laughed.

'You heard.'

Benjy raised an eyebrow but I said nothing. 'I shall see you tomorrow. Bright and early.'

'Me?' Richard puffed out his chest.

'No me,' said Benjy. 'We are going on a road trip.'

'Just the two of you?'

'Don't be silly,' I said. 'Now goodbye!' As I staggered off I pulled off one of my heels and put it in his hand. 'And I warn you it only fits me.' I laughed, amazed that I'd really given him my shoe.

As I turned my back on them Richard touched my arm and Benjy started to introduce himself. I staggered out towards the street, but by the door, drinking from a bottle of champagne with a long straw stood Stella's pretty receptionist. Polly, the girl I'd made blush. I turned but Richard and Benjy were far behind me. Richard Milk was swinging my heel by its strap.

'Hello there Polly,' I said, taking her hand in what I thought was a roguish manner, kissing her on the knuckles. I was instantly Drake, leaning against the Mercedes, one arm dangling, a glint in my eye.

'Hello Diana,' she said. I was pleased she knew who I was. I was about to say something charming, alluring, or a splash of flattery, when she passed me a matchbook with a telephone number on it.

'If you ever find yourself with time on your hands, call me,' she said. 'We could go out for cocktails.'

Why were people suddenly shoving their phone numbers at me here, there and everywhere? I was too far gone to be cynical. I truly believed, as I slid the matchbook into my handbag front pocket and said, 'I will. Don't you worry,' that maybe I was irresistible. As I stumbled towards the glass doors she may have said something else, but I didn't hear her because I was using every last bit of concentration to stop myself falling into a crack in the pavement.

By this time the whole gallery seemed like a Hieronymus Bosch painting – and in front of its vast glass façade I spewed pale, bubbly sick straight into the disarrayed flowerbed.

13

In the morning I made myself toast and Marmite and called Ronnie on her mobile. She hadn't come home and I hoped she had not seen me trying to stick my face against Glenys Pimm's plump lips. Not long before, I had been entirely faithful to her for five years. Not that trying to embrace Glenys Pimm was exactly cheating.

'Hell-o you,' said Ronnie. She sounded awful.

'Hey Sweets,' I said, chirpy. 'I missed you last night.'

'I'd like to say the same but I was too drunk to miss you,' she laughed.

'Drink is a tempting thing, isn't it?' I said. Vindication.

'Yes. Yes it is.'

'So where are you, dirty stop-out?'

'At Toby and Stella's,' she said. 'I conked out in the taxi on the way home and lost my keys.'

'Poor thing,' I said. 'I may as well meet you at theirs then.'

'That would help my poor head,' she said. 'Could you pack me some things?'

'Of course,' I said. 'Anything in particular?'

'Um, I can't think. My whole self feels like it's been body-slammed by a concrete walrus.'

We laughed.

'Don't worry. Camping is my speciality. I'll pack you right.'

'Oh cripes,' she said. 'We're camping.'

'Too right we are,' I said. 'Love you,' and hung up. It felt good, for once, to be the less hungover. The number of times she had told me off for my hangover; no, not told me off, just stood there with a knowing, self-satisfied look on her face; no, not that. Just the number of times she had done the right thing. I could never live up to her. It wasn't in me.

I finished a leisurely breakfast. I listened to Classic FM and danced around our kitchen to Sibelius and Rimsky-Korsakov. I read a text message from Richard Milk that said,

Last night I slept with your shoe on my pillow and I liked it.

I smiled. I opened the windows and set out my cape on the kitchen table. I looked at it carefully. It was obviously a sign, from Rohan to me. It was a sign that he loved me best.

As a child I did not have many friends. I found the whole experience of getting to know people, trusting them, extremely difficult. At least I did once I started secondary school. It was not because I did not have it in me to make friends – I was not particularly shy or cold. But because other children's lives were so very different from my own I would leave out entire chunks of my life from conversation, a pretence that my home life was similar to theirs, which I found exhausting and distressing – and occasionally boring.

I remember Louise Brooking's twelfth birthday as a turning point, a multi-coloured, slow-motion day when the pretence became unbearable and I no longer had the energy to lie to others, or myself, that I was the same as other children.

Her parents had adorned the whole house with helium balloons, bright foil hearts and candy-coloured diamonds. Girly, sparkly adornments squeezed to the brim with parental love. They had made biscuits and cakes and sandwiches and pizzas in their oven, and had filled bowls with M&Ms and Maltesers and Frazzles and Flumps. Their house had come as a shock. A semi-detached red-brick box on an estate full of other semi-detached red-brick boxes. A well-trimmed lawn. Hanging baskets. A swing and trampoline in the back garden, Swingball, bikes, two cats, guinea pigs and rabbits in straw-stacked hutches. They had a living room with a frieze running around the middle of the wall all slate grey and pink, a matching sofa and armchairs, a rug, a TV, a stereo, photographs on the walls in bright frames of Louise and her brother at many ages, in bonnets, with blankets, at the seaside, in school uniform.

In the kitchen, magnetised to the fridge were school letters, timetables, reports, pictures in crayon and a To-do list which read, I remember vividly: 'Make Louise and Josh's packed lunch. Tuesday Wind Band practise. Buy new reeds for J's clarinet. Thursday Guides. Saturday afternoon shopping in Brighton with L – new shoes for ballet.'

These words, written by Louise's mum in felt pen, were more than alien. This concept of a household centred around the children made me want to laugh and cry. I wanted to rip the pictures from the walls, draw moustaches on Louise's three-year-old self smiling sweetly in her father's arms, burst the helium balloons and – I surprised myself with my own vitriol – shit in their cartoon-character-covered beds and poison the guinea pigs.

I could not enjoy the party. There were ten girls there, as well as myself, and they talked about after-school clubs, boys they liked, where they were going on holiday with their mums and dads and brothers and sisters. I had no idea why I had been invited, some kind of oversight I thought, until Louise said, passing me three pink Party Rings on her fingers, 'So do you know if Toby Farrow has a girlfriend?'

Ah, I thought, imagining spearing the rabbit with my sausage on a stick. I have been invited because of Toby. This happened a lot at school. Girls would befriend me, if only for the afternoon, in the transparent hope of getting information about the blue-eyed, football-playing, floppy-haired beauty who was my best friend. It made no sense to anybody – including myself – that we were friends. I was strange, odd-looking and frumpy with my oft-unwashed school uniform covered in unidentifiable stains and my short hair, often cut by myself, which hung over my ears like forgotten foliage.

'I don't think so,' I said. 'At least not since he finished with Christina Lewis.'

'Oooh,' said Louise. 'Do you think you could put in a good word for me?'

'Of course,' I said, deciding quite firmly that I would do nothing of the sort and pushing all three Party Rings into my mouth in one go. Nobody ever just likes me for being me, I thought bitterly. It is always because I am Toby's friend, or Rohan's niece or because I am good at my school work and can help with homework.

What do you expect, came Drake's voice in my head. *I'm the only one who understands you.*

The whole party passed by like Chinese water torture. I felt humiliated, sorry for myself and confused with every laugh and giggle and friendly word these girls shared. But even the experience of that, of the true friends chattering and the parents loving and the pets being fluffy and adorable, was nothing compared to what happened at the end of the day. When all the other parents came to pick up their girls and I was the last one standing.

Louise's mum and dad, at first, were friendly, smiling, pouring me a glass of milk and offering extra slices of birthday cake. The time wore on.

'Does your uncle have a telephone number?' said Louise's dad eventually. He was a tall man with neatly kept hands and a tidy moustache. His clothes came, I thought, from Littlewoods and his trousers were short and showed off his towelling socks. He wore a V-neck jumper with pastel-coloured diamonds on it, of which I thought he should be ashamed.

'778220,' I said automatically.

I heard him turn the dial in the hallway and his wait as there was no reply. I knew there would be no reply. Rohan hardly ever answered the phone. That was usually me.

'He must be on his way,' said Louise's dad cheerily, but I knew, with an overwhelming sense of shame, that Rohan had somehow forgotten. Not because I was unimportant. Not because he didn't care. But because something else had come up, something that was vital and necessary or inspiring and because of that, because of whatever this situation was that had jumped into Rohan's consciousness, my need to be picked up from Louise Brooking's house at seven o'clock was forgotten. But I did not say any of this to Louise's mum and dad because I knew they would get the wrong idea and think badly of Rohan. And I hated anyone to think badly of Rohan. I often found myself lying about Rohan's actions because I knew, innately, that people would not understand his character and misinterpret his active and sporadic nature as neglect.

Sure enough, as the time passed, interspersed with lots of whispering and not-so-subtle adult sign language, Rohan still did not appear. My shame consumed me. *Please do not think that I am so unimportant that my uncle has forgotten me. Please realise he is a very particular kind of man and this says nothing about him or me or how he feels about me. Please just put me out in the garden and pretend you never met me. Please don't stand there, all of you, in your pyjamas holding cups of cocoa looking at me as though I am some abandoned child on the news or in a movie. Please Rohan, just turn up and prove them all wrong.*

In the end it was Trudy who came. Trudy in her thick cords and striped shirt. Trudy with a jumper tied round her waist and her hair pulled back into a loose bun and her red cheeks flushed with the cold, her Land Rover keys jangling in her capable hands.

'I am so so sorry,' she said quietly to Louise's parents in the hallway. 'Diana's uncle was held up in London and did not have your telephone number with him. The train broke down. He is still out there somewhere. He managed to get hold of me and here I am. Better late than never.'

Louise's dad looked relieved. 'I knew there had to be a good explanation. You're here now.' He called out to me. 'Diana! Someone is here for you.'

I came out from the kitchen with my mini carrier bag of party swag – stick-on earrings, lipstick, eye glitter that I would never dare wear – in one hand and my coat in the other.

'Hello Trudy,' I said, grateful to see her, although surprised.

'Hello Diana. Let's get you home.'

I was not surprised either to arrive at the Cowling Place and find Rohan smoking in the kitchen. He had not been in London. He had been working on a very important coat, a long, high-necked, charcoal coat for a film set, a sort of greatcoat, military style, but for a woman not a man. When I eventually saw it on screen, tight about the actress's torso, fierce at her waist, I understood how he had come to choose between the coat and me. I could see the coat was very beautiful and made with precision. I understood what was important and what was not. And even though I was never invited to any more parties, it did not matter – I would not have gone anyway.

And now I found myself on a tartan, fringe-edged blanket on the beach at Cowling with my girlfriend, my best friend from my youth, and my sort-of-stepmother, and it was nothing short of inexplicable. Maybe these things have a habit of coming to pass, although I think now that I was in shock, to be there, to know that after the lunch of baguettes, mushroom pâté and cockles bought from a man on the pier further along, I would be in the old house, sorting, rummaging, foraging for keepsakes: museum pieces. For some hint of what had happened. The salt air filled me with a sort of consternation, and a sort of glee.

It was obvious that this was a terrible idea.

What made it worse was, as Ronnie – hangover intact – put her head on my shoulder and stroked my knee, I fell instantly out of love with her. A simple, loving, normal gesture from her in front of others and I suddenly felt nothing. At least not the pretence of coupledom. I suddenly longed for her friendship. Ronnie would make an excellent friend. I kissed her cheek and ruffled her hair a bit, hoping the smell of her, the touch, would nudge me back over, but there was nothing. It was all gone.

Toby and Stella were grinning at us both. Stella said, 'You two make such a sweet couple.'

I could have hit her then.

'Practically saccharin,' I said, and helped myself to more cockles.

As if the day could get any worse, a speck on the horizon was slowly emerging as a pasty-legged, product-haired, beach-ready Benjy Burne. I could see the flash of his plastic glasses and his stupid, battered satchel slung over his shoulder.

'So Benjy's made it.' I said.

'Hooray for Benjy,' said Toby.

'My right-hand man,' said Stella. 'Although I'm sure he'll tell you I am his.'

'Did anybody bring any drink?' I said.

'I thought you'd never ask,' said Toby, producing bottles of champagne and plastic cups from the picnic basket. 'Do you remember when we nicked that champagne from Rohan's fridge and came down here?' he said to me. 'Mum made us a cake and we set up a tent on the sand.'

'That wasn't me,' I said.

'Yes it was,' he said.

'No it wasn't,' I said. 'It must have been Stella.'

The two of them looked at each other, raising eyebrows.

'Hello all,' said Benjy, hair flapping in the wind.

'Champagne?' said Stella.

'Oh yes,' he said.

I could feel that suffocating hand on my face again. This is not the way I had imagined coming home. All I needed now was a TV camera and those nubiles from last night.

'Needle Rock,' said Toby, looking over my shoulder. 'It's half the size it used to be.'

I turned my head to see what he was talking about. The grey rock that we'd had as our meeting place was still there, but looked smaller, smoother, less impressive.

'Do you remember flashing Morse code from there with that workman's torch?'

'No,' I said.

'You do!' he grabbed my foot. 'We used to be able to see your bedroom window and mine from this spot.' He turned to the others. Stella was pouring Benjy champagne. 'We snuck out at all hours. It was so safe here.'

'I don't remember,' I said. 'Sorry.'

The beach was smaller than I remembered it. More stones, less sand, and the water was more grey, less clear, although the smell was almost the same, like sediment, drizzle, cured meat and whipped-up air from far away. And the seaweed still clung to the stones when the tide was out, clasping its big fronds, reminding me of sewn-on hair on papier-mâché marionettes when slumped in storage. I fell onto my back and pulled my knees up towards my chest. The sky was nearly cloudless and the sun shone upon us like a torturer's tool.

We're like a postcard,' said Stella. 'I always wanted us to all be back here together.'

Everybody – except me – clinked plastic cups and swallowed warm champagne. I was about to say that champagne didn't belong on this beach when a pink plastic ball rolled into my head. A child, small and waddling, in a purple swimming costume came over to retrieve it. She looked so very sweet and chubby and perfect. A parent's warning, 'Olivia!' came from elsewhere. 'Say sorry!'

'Sawry,' said this Olivia, who smiled shyly and ran away.

For a moment I felt inexplicably sad.

This part of the beach had changed. It wasn't as private as it once was, and there were families and children, sandcastles and discarded lolly sticks spread all the way down.

'I can't believe you grew up here,' said Ronnie. She was wearing a thin blouse with a bikini top underneath, and a pair of calf-length denim pedal-pushers. She was getting extra freckles across her nose.

'We were lucky,' I said.

'Toby's mum, *Trudy*, sometimes did Rohan's pattern-cutting – especially in the year of fifty-two dresses,' said Stella casually.

'She did?' This was new to me.

'Yes,' said Toby. 'You knew that, didn't you? She was nifty with a needle, my mum. It was idyllic here though, wasn't it Dee?'

'I suppose so,' I said. I hadn't known Trudy did Rohan's pattern-cutting. First the painting. Now this.

'She loved it here before her lesbian flit to the city,' he said to everyone else. 'She was always out here in her bikini, splashing about in the sea.'

Ronnie gasped, '*You* wore a *bikini*?'

'Yeah, yeah,' I laughed, furious, but hiding it well. Once again I would have to listen to my body being mocked.

'A lovely bright green one if I remember rightly,' said Toby. 'With a halter-neck top and frilly little pants.'

'Oi!' I sat up.

'I used to watch her from my bedroom.'

'You did not.'

'I did.'

'You so completely did not.' I grabbed for more champagne. 'As far as I remember you were hard pressed to notice I was female at all.'

'I was not.'

'You were.'

'Wasn't.'

'Was.'

'I wasn't, well not until…' he stopped.

'Not until you met Stella,' I said.

'What?'

'Not until you met Stella,' I said.

'No, no,' said Benjy Burne, pouring himself champagne. 'That's not it at all. He knew very well you were female, you silly thing. He was more than aware until his mum told him the big secret about your Uncle Rohan. She made it very clear that he wasn't to tell you anything about it…'

'*What?*' What did they know? I thought of Rohan's painting. Evidence on canvas.

Toby punched Benjy on the knee, shook his head and put a finger to his lips.

'What secret?' I sat up.

'Nothing,' said Toby. 'We all have secrets and this one isn't ready to come out. You're supposed to find it out for yourself. At your own pace.' He looked over his shoulder. 'I think we should go to the house. There is plenty of time for revelations.'

'Yes,' said Stella. 'Let's go and see if the old crow lets you in.'

I looked at them for answers, but it was clear the conversation was over; everybody, for a while at least, pretended it never happened. The five of us began to walk. Stella went in the opposite direction.

'There's a landlord I wouldn't mind letting buy me a drink,' she said. Her eyes were suddenly red and bloated. She looked like she'd been floating in the river overnight. She smiled, a sweet smile, and pushed her hair up into a ponytail, using a leather band from around her wrist to keep it in place. She had, I felt, always tried too hard to be girl-like, infantine. She looked tired and had purplish circles under her eyes. I thought of the jar baby then, realised that it must still be in the house somewhere. Maybe on the shelf above Rohan's desk. I felt I would be unable to look.

Cowling was just as I remembered it, just as I had dreamt it during the years since leaving, but it was also unalterably changed. There was no Rohan, and Rohan had been the centre of the place. Every piece of landscape, every cleft of light from right or left, every twitch of tree or grass or sand in the breeze reminded me of his time, our time. If a place can represent a person, and a person can represent a place, which way was it with Cowling? Had the place made Rohan? Had Rohan made the place? I had spent so many years trying so completely to wash away the influence of the landscape, of the man, that being back without him was vacant, empty. I looked for him, and all I could see was stretches of washed-out sand, pebbles, ice cream and scattered tourists. If I had expected a voice on the air telling me secrets, I was a fool. There was nothing alive in Cowling for me any more. There were memories that existed in my head and nowhere else.

And as for Drake…

'This place,' said Ronnie. 'It makes me think of…' she went quiet. Perhaps for once, she had no intellectual analogy, no comparison to a work of antiquity, no frame of reference. It was just an English coastal village.

'They've knocked down the abattoir,' I said. 'There used to be an abattoir.'

'Here?'

'Yes. There used to be a man who would sweep away the blood that seeped out from under the gates.'

I had forgotten about that: the daily swish and sluice of his brush and mop and vat of soapy water. The smell in the air, burning your eyelids with its chemical haze and that other stench, that rich reek of dead flesh; of blood let out before its time, the smell of dead carcass like something human and wounded and wrong.

'Ugh.'

'It sort of added something to the place,' I said. 'Hardly any tourists used to come here at first. They'd always choose Brighton or Bognor, or Bournemouth.'

I looked out to sea and remembered the many wishes I'd sent out from that beach across the water. I wondered if they were still out there, sealed pockets of my hopes, being sent out and tugged back with the tide. My ground-down mother, tumbling through the waves.

'Stella uses people,' I said quietly. The others were several steps ahead of us.

'No she doesn't.'

'She does.'

'You should talk to her. Properly talk to her.'

'She stole everything,' I said, and then, because it is always wrong to reveal your true feelings to anyone but God, I said, 'She is just a silly posh know-it-all, that's all. A faker.'

'We'll have to agree to disagree. And your world hasn't exactly been very real these past weeks.'

'She could be a viper for all you know. *Luring* your bloody eye.'

'Diana...'

So it was Diana now, and my transformation was complete.

'Did you know,' she said, lightly. 'That the French don't really have a word for lure?' Back on familiar ground, she held my hand. 'They have the verb *attirer* – to attract... it's not quite the same, is it? Luring has particular connotations... like being led, like what Hogarth said about the serpentine line... In fact gardens in the eighteenth century all had weaving paths, to make them interesting, to *lead* you through the undergrowth.'

'Really?' Who cares?

'It's a funny word. Not just a word. An un-noun-able concept.'

'A *loirre* is something to do with falconry,' I said, pleased at remembering a useful piece of information. 'Isn't it what they use to convince the falcons to come back to the falconers?'

'Ah ha,' said Ronnie. 'A *lure*!'

'Let's walk through the pines,' I said loudly for everybody. 'The back way home.'

'This is where I split too,' said Benjy unexpectedly. 'I'm never going to be lucky enough to be invited into that house while she is running it.'

Who is this *she*? I had presumed Stella would be head of the household, preening and pruning for the world to see. I thought of the photo and the painting of the woman. Was it possible this unknown lover, this true love of Rohan's life had now taken her rightful place in the bosom of his home. Was dying the only way he could allow her to cross his threshold in the bold light of day? I would find out soon enough.

'See you at the pub,' said Toby, and Benjy was, mysteriously, gone.

Before us, towards the top left of this stretch of beach, were ten tall pine trees, reaching up so high and wide that they hid everything behind them. They had grown much in the last ten years and I was not prepared for their dark, looming girth and tips reaching up so high that just to imagine them made me dizzy. High up in the sky like prayers.

Behind the pines, when the sand turned to shingle, was the Cowling Place. It was exactly the same apart from the plants, which were thick and dark. The house was still in good repair, and the tall sandstone and white bricked walls, with motifs set in bricks around the windows were familiar and unblinking.

It was the same house. There were white, hooded windowframes, pot-plants around the door, window-boxes along the ledges. Someone had tended them. The same gravel covered the sweeping front path and driveway. The grass had not been recently cut, and was smattered with pink-tipped daisies and purple clover. I saw myself, many years ago, sitting in long grass, searching for four leaves on one stem. I looked for the fruit bushes, and saw a thicket of brambles, twisting back against the iron fence.

I wanted to run at the door, at the walls, and press myself into the brickwork. I wanted to sink into the cement and old wood. I wanted to melt, and splash down into a bucket, to coat a brush to whitewash those old walls.

Seeing it then, ten years later, brought back something I had forgotten. The loneliness of it all. Life for Diana Everett in the Cowling Place was a lonely life indeed; a scavenger on the look out for scraps of affection.

Toby knocked and we waited. Who would answer the door? I had spent my life waiting behind closed doors for the answers to secrets, but within seconds there, in the frame of the open door, ten years older, greying hair pulled up in a loose bun, the same jeans and shirt and open-toed sandals, the same loose belly, the same smell of gingerbread and wet plaster, was Trudy.

14

The day after my thirteenth-birthday encounter with Drake, the day after I killed Ruskin and buried him in the sand and swam with Rohan in the sea, I could not sleep. It was the start of the summer holidays and I locked the door to my room, sat on my bed, and listened to classical music on Radio 3. I turned the dial to find strange, seemingly ethereal programmes from across the channel; exuberance in a smattering of thick vowels and throated consonants. I stared out of the window and picked skin from the soles of my feet, or doodled my name over and over on spiral-bound foolscap. I told myself I understood German.

This continued for a week. I never left my room, not to eat, nor even to piss or shit. My entire room was covered in doodles and there was a plant pot of slop in the corner. The inside of my door was thick with biro-ed leaves, a tangle of brambles, thorns, thick lustrous foliage that had sucked up reservoirs and flourished by lamplight. I picked away at the old white paint, carefully, to fill the blue edges of the flowers with creamy white blooms; to watch a flutter of snow disintegrate on thorns, and eventually settle, in clumps, on my wooden floorboards. I brushed the peeled emulsion fragments under my purple-and-blue striped rug. They stayed there. Melting.

By the end of the first week I was hungry. Ravenous. My tongue was cracked and yellow. I scribbled a series of abstract equations on the floorboards which only made sense as I wrote them: ways to work out the best times to eat if I was to avoid Rohan, Stella, Toby, lovers, clients, angry husbands, Drake. Forming Drake's name in my mouth made me wretch. *Why did nobody stop him? Why did nobody come?*

I found new times to eat, in the early hours, and crept about the second kitchen in the basement like a cat.

I licked at scraps, warmed milk in a pan and added honey or syrup. I invented new recipes to try with whatever had been left in the fridge or the bread bin. When I was feeling brave I tiptoed upstairs to the other kitchen, the one at the front of the house, carefully and with only a torch. I imagined myself the heroine in some archaic quest; I was a servant girl, I had a master who would beat me if I was caught eating his mistress's food. Or I was an orphan breaking into a rich man's house. I gorged on sliced oranges. I cut them into quarters and alternated the pieces between slices of wholemeal bread spread thick with butter, dipped in olive oil. My lips, my fingertips, my chin, smeared with it.

Some nights Rohan left the house and I went down to eat leftovers. Bits of pork or fatty bacon, scrapings of butter fried with cooked rice and chopped-up parsley. I tore the corners from old bread, pressed them down into an oven dish, sprinkled with brown sugar, raisins and a whipped-up egg, then force-fed myself on bread-and-butter pudding, laughing, greedy, the taste of the whole world on my tongue.

I made big glass bowls of butter icing that I ate neat, licked from the back of a wooden spoon. Sometimes I added cocoa, or coffee granules, or grated lemon peel to vary the flavour. The grease and sugar sent little shivers of delight straight down to my toes, throatfuls and bellyfuls of sweetness.

Succulent.

Juicy.

Drizzled.

Plump.

Slathered.

Moist.

Dark.

Smoked.

Frothy.

Hot.

Another week passed and I took it further. I became tired of my concoctions, each more elaborate than the last, and instead I crept downstairs at three in the morning to sample condiments from their jars. I used the bone-handled teaspoon: pickle, chutney, mint sauce, mustard, ketchup, horseradish, piccalilli, relish. I took out each jar, unscrewed the lid, captured a spoonful, put back the lid and moved on to the next. I gulped back mouthfuls of vinegary thickness. Tart, sour, sweet, spice. I finished an entire jar of mint sauce in a matter of minutes, all the while looking around, fearing, hoping to be discovered.

But I was clever. I knew when Rohan was around, when he went away. I imagined him coming back to the house to the smell of frying, of herbs, but with no evidence that anything had changed. I always washed up thoroughly. I thought he was leaving me to my own devices. Maybe *he* did not want to see *me*.

I pulled off the ends of cheeses and spread them with salad cream, shoving big lumps into my mouth and chewing until the cheese and the cream trickled down my throat like sour milk.

Every morning I imagined a knock and Rohan's voice, safe behind wooden panels and screws and closed keyholes, saying, 'Would you like to go for a swim?', 'Would you like something for breakfast?', 'Would you like to come with me to the city to buy cloth?'

But he did not come. Nobody came. I did not need to say anything at all.

When the walls, my desk, the floorboards, the wooden frame of my bed, and all other reachable surfaces in my room were purple with biro, I turned on myself.

It began with biro doodles on my left ankle. It was easy to draw on my own body, the pink, blotchiness of it became smooth, white, the perfect canvas when approached by the tip of blue ink; like writing on a banana skin, on the bloated fat of a baked ham. I doodled roses, thorns and twisting vines all the way up my calf, added tendrils of honeysuckle, webbed hands of ivy, studs of old man's beard.

I drew little bursts of grape hyacinth and delicate stars of narcissus and floppy daffodils which dripped dew onto summer clematis.

I defied the seasons and planted snowdrops and polyanthus and almond blossom side by side upon my belly.

I set out the perfect herb garden on my thighs: showers of dill and chives and yarrow reaching up towards my hips. I had lavender on my arms, little buds of forget-me-not in the creases behind my elbows, behind my knees. They disappeared with sweat in my sleep, and grew back, stronger, in new ink, more intricate the next day.

In my new skin I went down to the back kitchen to make myself more elaborate scrap meals. Rohan went away for entire nights, and the house was my own. I wandered around in the dark because I could, defying demons, bogie men and burglars to jump out at me in the gloom. I was afraid of nothing.

I found shrivelled vanilla pods in an old OXO tin and scraped out the seeds with the back of a spoon. I crushed them under a rolling pin, and made vanilla custard to pour over biscuits made with nothing but flour, butter and sugar. I made pancakes and added things to the batter: raisins, slices of glacé cherry, lemon juice, maple syrup, cracked pepper. I rolled them up around soft fruit from the garden – blackberries, gooseberries, raspberries – and smothered them with cream.

One day I heard Rohan turn Toby away from the door. All that existed was the hiss of the radio. Voices from far away.

At night I got bolder.

When there was no fruit left in the fridge, in the pantry, I went outside in my new suit of clothes.

I rummaged the brambles for berries, squashed raspberries under bare feet, ate gooseberries – sharp and hairy – straight from the bush to my mouth. The moon was low in the sky, a cold comfort, slivered brightness, a mother's smile.

I boiled up empty jars and made jams. The smell of burning sugar and dead fruit swelled up through the floorboards and into Rohan's study, his fitting rooms, maybe his bedroom.

Nobody came.

Rohan left me alone to drown myself in a sea of sweetness. My hair was tangled with seeds and juice. My nails were stained with bits of plump berry, or with mint sauce, or with cheese. My body was marked with berries, splashes of red, purple, brown on my feet and up the backs of my legs. Just myself and my new skin. The girl with the swirls and the scratches like stars.

I walked around in my clothes of drawn flowers, and it was not enough. The biro was blue, the entire length of my body shiny with it, like I'd been gloss varnished, wrapped up in cellophane and left to go cold in the fridge overnight.

I went into Rohan's study when he was out for his swim.

I took a box of gouache paints and three different-sized brushes. The jar baby winked at me from under a summer bonnet of glistening formaldehyde.

Petals and leaves fell from my toes and fingers.

Locked in my room by the time he came back, I painted a multicoloured garden on my body.

I knew what I was. I was not like other women. My mother was a mermaid, my father was a phantom and I would never know what it was to be held, with love, in comfort, without having to give something in return.

The food and the painting made it better.

This continued for six weeks.

One morning in September I woke up at 6.30 to the sound of birdcall. I came out of my room and washed myself with white soap in the bathroom. I walked into the front kitchen where Rohan was making porridge and a pot of tea.

'Good morning,' I said. My voice scratched out from my throat through lack of use.

Rohan picked a cup and saucer from the dresser and set it out in front of me. 'You're going to be late for school.'

And that was all we said. Nothing more, nothing less. Neither I nor Rohan mentioned it again.

'Trudy?!' I said.

'Diana!' said Trudy as she wrapped her big arms around me and held me to her. 'You look so…grown up! I could cry!'

'What are you…?' My voice was deadened by the weave of her shirt. Being that close to her I could see her hair was still long and black, but the white at her crown crackled along its length giving the illusion of grey. How could she be standing at my old front door?

'She lives here,' said Toby. 'For various reasons which I am sure she would *love* to tell you about she has inherited the Cowling Place and everything inside it.'

'And *you* are only here because Rohan left strict instructions for his exhibition,' said Trudy.

I drew back from her, gawking with my mouth open.

'He wanted Stella to organise it,' said Trudy. As though this all made great sense. 'He specifically asked for that, didn't he Tobes? Now come in and have some coffee.'

'I am Ronnie,' said Ronnie, putting out her hand as the three of us stepped into the room in single file.

'Ah yes. Ronnie,' said Trudy, shaking hands vigorously. 'I know all about you. I *approve* of you.'

How the fuck did Trudy know about Ronnie and when did it become her place to *approve*? Mind over matter. My mind controlled itself against all familiar matter in the room: the oak table, split down the middle and made by one of Rohan's friends in Portsmouth, the Welsh dresser, hung with Spode cups and mugs and set out with jugs and plates and meat dishes, the stone floor, big grey-and-green slabs with familiar dents and long-forgotten stains – all these things I made myself not notice as we stood at the table and smiled and waited for somebody else to speak.

'Coffee,' said Trudy as we all sat at the table.

'Thank you,' I said.

'I am confused,' I said. 'I didn't even know you and Rohan were particularly friends. I remember you picking me up a few times. I remember you being here sometimes, having coffee, but…'

'I know you didn't,' said Trudy. 'I went to great pains not to let it disturb you. I never had anything against *you*.'

I was thinking how much more disturbing it was to discover it now, sitting here all these years later, with him dead. But I said, 'I didn't know you had anything against *him*.'

I supposed that if Trudy was the woman in Rohan's painting then she would have resented the ongoing presence of Stella. Stella and Trudy could not have been more different. I remembered a fleeting fantasy while eating biscuits in Trudy's kitchen, that she was my mother and the four of us – Rohan, Trudy, Toby and I – lived together in the Cowling Place. Now I hated to think of him with her as much – even more – than I hated the thought of him with Stella.

'There are not always right times for things. Rohan was very busy. He had a lot of ground to cover.'

'Ha,' said Toby. 'You may as well know, Diana, that my mother and I are what you might call estranged.'

'You are?'

Ronnie just sat there, holding on to her cup. All this must have been garbled nonsense to her, as she knew so little of my story. It made me realise just how little I had really opened up to her. To think I hadn't even told her about *Drake*.

'Yes,' said Trudy. 'We very much are. But we have this truce here, just for the moment. I thought you might need him here, and I don't want any trouble.'

'You've courted trouble your whole life Mother. Why change the habit now?'

The Toby and Trudy of my childhood were so close, warm, accepting of each other. Or so I had thought. I could not imagine what could have created this hostility. And beyond that, beyond everything I had ever experienced, how could I have missed an affair between Rohan, my uncle Rohan, the man who wept and drank too much and was brilliant, and the plain and homely woman I thought was the only female I could trust?

'I don't have to have you here Son. I could prepare the actual bits and pieces for the exhibition myself and have them sent over. I would never actually have to have any of you in this house again.' Trudy's face was set in an expression I had never seen before. Any warmth I had ever known in her was gone. This new Trudy seemed like dead skin around a steel skeleton. Lifeless. I had once thought she did not have an angry or malicious bone in her body, and now…this.

'First things first. Stella changed the press release. Legally she is not allowed to leak information, however subtle, through public means.'

Ronnie squeezed my knee under the table. None of this made sense.

'It was a simple error,' said Toby.

'I'm sure. But just remember who runs this operation.'

I laughed loudly then. There were so many questions I wanted to ask but I could not, did not know how. Trudy, in my kitchen, sounding like a Bond villain was one of the most ludicrous things I had ever seen in my life.

'What's up Diana?' she said coldly. 'Cat got your tongue? I thought you'd be all over me with questions by now.'

'Have you got any gin?' I said. 'I would really like a gin and tonic.'

Trudy rolled her eyes. 'Of course. Just like him. He always drank too much. It got him into trouble. If he hadn't been a drinker this house and all its glory would never have been mine.'

'Diana's not a drinker,' said Ronnie loudly. 'She just likes a drink.'

'That, my dear, is what they all say,' said Trudy. But she poured me a gin anyway. A huge shot of the stuff in equal measure to the tonic.

'Let me show Ronnie around,' said Trudy. 'You are obviously not ready to have any proper discussion about any of this.'

'Yes,' I said.

'That would be nice,' said Ronnie.

'Of course she'll keep her eye on you,' said Toby. 'She'll make sure you don't nick an ashtray or anything.' He laughed a strange laugh.

'I can't believe I spawned a self-righteous, pernicious, ignominious little prick like you,' said Trudy. 'Award-winning director or no.' And I wondered if I was having one of my episodes again, one where the time disappeared and stretched and tricked me. But none of this encounter was imaginary. It was all real. And it made my jealous ramblings about the funeral, about Stella, about my disappearance from Rohan's life seem more pathetic and less useful than a clenched fist shaken at the sky.

'Of course,' said Trudy. 'I am sure Rohan would have liked to have shown her around himself.'

I tried to piece everything together. The best I could do was deduce Toby's affair with Stella had pissed Trudy off. Not only because Stella was the other woman in Rohan's life, but because it divided loyalties. It could have make Rohan reconsider a life with Trudy, out of pure jealousy. Jealousy is a powerful catalyst. That was the best I could come up with, and it made some sense, at that moment at least.

Trudy was, to Ronnie and to some extent me, a genial host. In the women's workroom headless bodies stood in line as though waiting for nods of approval. I should have supposed they would still be there, but I was surprised. Rohan had not updated anything. They were the same dummies he had used since I was born. Those same twisted dials. I noticed that all of them, bar one, were now set to a size somewhat bigger than Stella. Trudy.

It almost felt like a museum. A museum to my past. I wanted to feel something, but the experience was too bizarre, too inexplicable. I wanted to cry, or howl, or get angry. Instead Toby, Ronnie and myself made our way towards several large boxes of unclaimed material, patterns and paper.

'You may as well look through those,' said Trudy. 'In fact you can sort them into outfits. You may as well be useful. There is nothing I need to hide here. And I'm sure you all know how to *behave* yourselves.'

'What a dragon,' whispered Ronnie in my ear.

'She never used to be,' I said quietly. 'She used to be my favourite grown-up.'

It seemed unassembled outfits had been stuffed unceremoniously into storage without any consideration for what might go where. Some were already cut out and pinned to colour swatches of wool or cotton. Others were neatly drawn onto thin paper, waiting to be pinned onto rolls of material, to be stitched together and made whole. Everything was tangled together with loops of pale-pink thread. There seemed to be a superfluity of purple, embroidered, Art Deco flowers stitched onto white cotton patches, but no sign of where they might go.

'I thought the exhibition should have rolling stock,' said Trudy, imposing. 'It would be nice to add details to it. Then people who've visited from the beginning will always have something new to see.'

We said nothing.

'And I thought they could put some of these unassembled patterns in a display – a sort of "Rickwood process" section. It's rare to have unassembled items in such a good state of repair.'

The rest of us nodded, trying to extricate pins from the bottoms of wooden crates without ripping any piece of pattern. I was, unsurprisingly, better at this than the others. Toby set to work quietly. I did not understand why Stella was not here arguing back. Why was she letting Toby's mum order her about? Nobody ordered Stella Avery about. She had always been the lord high executioner of her own law system. No separation of powers for Stella.

Trudy *must* have been punishing her for her affair with Toby. She was punishing them now because Rohan was dead and he had missed his chance when he was alive. I could see it might be her in the *Safe Sea* painting. In real life Trudy was bigger than that floating figure, but artistic license is possible to a painter in love. But they were not, I was sure, her legs in the kitchen photo. Neither Stella nor Trudy. How many special women were there in Rohan's life? I had known about the womanising, but *relationships* were an altogether different matter.

The box I had been allocated seemed to have many pieces of the same dress inside it. I worked on autopilot. It was like stepping into the looking glass. Trudy's presence alone made everything seem surreal. In my hands was a potential wedding dress. I looked at the mannequins. I couldn't work out what shape and style the dress was supposed to be. There was no structure to the pieces I had. They were like gauze leaves. Not very Rohan Rickwood at all.

Ronnie was leaning eagerly over a thick wedge of brightly coloured illustrations. 'Look!' she said. 'In 1993 Rohan was initially going to design his entire winter collection around the phrase "family ties"!'

'What?' I said.

'Look.' She swiftly unfolded several sketches of tall, spiky models – male and female – all with the same letterbox-red scull-cap haircut and the same scarlet painted lips. Boys and girls with their arms wrapped around each other, in matching outfits. Waistcoats, blousy panelled shirts, knee-length pinstriped shorts.

'Everyone was doing that boy/girl thing that year,' said Trudy merrily, snatching them from her. 'The whole androgyny fixation.'

I looked at the drawings: clean swipes of colour, sharp lines. A birl. A goy.

'Weird,' I said, as nonchalant as possible. Trudy and Toby looked at each other.

I did not want to see any more drawings and would have preferred a trip downstairs for more gin. I also did not want it to get dark. Ronnie and I had placed our tent right near the entrance of the campsite for easy getaways, but the dark was not welcome that night. This is another good thing about drinking. It makes not being able to sleep near impossible. Passing out is better than lying awake for hours and hours with nowhere for your thoughts to go. In fact, the nights were the hardest. If I was in bed alone I could not sleep. If I was in bed with somebody else I could not sleep. In some respects I needed a body that sweated and breathed and beat near me. In others I did not have the faculties to know what to do with that body. Awake I found it hard to last till morning. That was the dangerous time. The time that I felt I was floating, gratuitous, that nobody would notice if I floated up, away, into nothing and nowhere.

'So how are you going with putting Benjamin Burne off the scent for his book?' said Trudy, looking firmly at her son.

'He doesn't know anything you wouldn't want him to know,' said Toby.

'The things I know don't belong in a book,' she said. 'We have a legacy to keep here.'

'All the best things belong in a book,' said Ronnie.

'Benjamin's father thought so,' said Toby. 'Until his admiration for Rohan stopped him from revealing the truth.' I thought of the press release. Christian Burne, the journalist who had tracked down Rohan's parents then revealed nothing of his discoveries. Benjy's *dad*.

'You think you know the truth,' said Trudy scornfully. 'But you don't even know a pinch of it. I'm good at what I do. I would not be living here if I let any Tom, Dick or Harry know the secrets I know.'

I laughed again. I couldn't help myself. Trudy had transmogrified from Bond villain to Carry On Cockney gangster.

I thought of many things when she said that. I thought of Rohan's other women. Of the men in the downstairs workroom. Of the bitter words he'd always throw up about Stella and all the women he had here. Of Stella's dog Ruskin. Of Stella's driver Drake. Of Rohan's daily swims on the beach. Of coils of russet hair, looping around my fingers, up my arms, around my chest, up my neck and into my mouth and nose. Of biting into Ronnie in the dark.

'I...' The rooms were familiar but unanticipated. I thought of cups of tea and toast in a rack. Of swimming towels bundled up on the stone floor. Of Rohan's brushes standing in an empty vinegar jar on the windowsill. Of oil paint smudged into sideboards, walls, rugs and fingertips. I thought of Rohan's hands. Of the web of skin between his thumb and first finger, stained with orange ink, puckered up and rough, from painting, stitching, rinsing things out with white spirit. I thought of Titian's Diana, pointing her bow at poor Actaeon, watching the hounds. Of me in the woods. Of the fear that she would turn towards me with her bow.

I thought of the other figure in the painting, the one I hadn't noticed during my first visit to the gallery. Small, almost in the middle towards the top, there is a clear space among the trees. There, on a horse, is a man looking into the distance. The distance, for him, is Diana. Or Actaeon and his hounds. Or, I thought slowly, the viewer. Me. Who was watching me from a horse far off in the woods? Distanced from everything. Kept separate on the high horse.

'Diana!'

I blinked to see I was face-down in a bunch of orange cloth.

'Uh?' I said. My head was full of colour: red, pink, brown, green, orange. Titian's palette.

'You've been sitting there for fifteen minutes,' said Toby. 'We've done our lot here for today.' He turned to Trudy.

I stared at him. Toby Farrow. The black of his hair had not been reshorn since I saw him at the funeral. It grew outwards, about an inch, and made his head resemble a boom microphone. He had still trimmed his sideburns, which were neat, narrow, trapeziums cutting across his face and growing almost down to his chin. His blue eyes were hardly noticeable because his pupils were so widely dilated as almost to consume both irises with black.

When his mother turned to pick up some papers from a cabinet he whispered, 'My mother is a very intelligent woman, but she hasn't got it in for you. She has never really known what to do about you. It's one of her only weaknesses. Well, that and my dad.'

'I...' All I could think of was how I had never connected with that picture of the man with my mother by the beach. Will Everett, the Guillemot Man. Oxford Don.

Who am I?

'I need to go to the toilet,' I said, standing up.

I hadn't expected Trudy's presence like a dictator. I saw on her face that she considered following me. I went straight up the stairs, past blank walls where paintings and photographs had once been, upon wooden floors that had once been carpeted with – I realise now – dramatic red carpet. A constant VIP occasion. Other than the gaps on the walls where frames had once been, everything was how I'd remembered. The lay-out. The objects. I had thought Stella would gut the place, make it regal, but it was still Rohan's house. Stella had not even had a chance to get to it. This was Trudy's home now.

I wanted to go to his study. To take back what I knew was mine. Let them make up whatever stories they wanted. Let them create a Rohan out of scraps of silk stitched to faded brocade. None of it meant anything to me. None of it was anything to me. It was suddenly all very clear indeed. I should never have got back together with Stella or Toby or any of the past. It had gone. Rohan was dead. Nothing would ever be the same again. His real life. His real meaning. The real Rohan. It was all over, and nothing would ever bring him back. Not even Malk Blancossier's film on the silver screen. And certainly not the revelation that Trudy was the love of his life.

I thought of my cape, my wonderful, vivid blue, plush fur cape.

I knew what it was! I knew where it had come from!

Rohan knew more about me than I had ever dared imagine. That last parcel to me was a message. He knew everything, yet his feelings never changed. I forced my way along the landing. I tried not to breathe in with my nose. I didn't want to smell anything. Smell is more evocative than anything we see. Even now, whenever I pass a bottle of Vosene shampoo in a chemist, I can't help but pick it up, flip open the lid and squeeze a medicated puff of air towards my nostrils. It smells of Rohan's hair. On the few times he dressed up to go somewhere important and didn't just wash himself with soap in the bath.

The jar baby was there, on the shelf above Rohan's desk. His study had been left exactly as it had been, perhaps because there was so much evidence to plunder for the book/exhibition/film. Everyone wanted a bit of Rohan to make their own. Not me. I just wanted to remember him as he was. I wanted to keep what was mine.

Amazingly the folded-up piece of paper was still there, exactly where I'd left it ten years previously. I opened it out, speedily, knowing that if I did not do so now I might never do it. Sure enough, the piece of paper Stella had given me all those years ago had not been a figment of my imagination. It had been real.

But it was not just a piece of paper. It was those five photographs of the same thing repeated over and over. Five where there were once six. The sixth had been cut out of the top, hence the missing square. My mother, my sea mother, my mother with the long red hair, stepping across sand five times on the page. Five pairs of legs, five smiles, five dogs at her feet. The sixth version of her, my version, I still carried with me in my wallet.

'I don't understand,' I said out loud. The paper was not the usual thick photographic paper. It was thin, shiny, like the page of a cheap magazine.

When I was young there was one thing that kept me going. I always knew he loved me best. All those subtle signs he sent me over the heads of lovers. The flick of his wrist as he scissored white silk, the long squeeze of his eyelids as he tacking-stitched a hem to make the most of an absent woman's legs; always holding them shut for a fraction too long. Always saying, with that look, 'Diana, although I don't say it, although I don't show it, I love you best.'

I turned over the sheet of my parents' photographs and saw three words in a big font stamped onto the back. I had ignored them that day in the workroom when I restitched Stella's green dress. I think I had let myself believe these words were the name of the developer. But now I could see I was wrong. The three bold words were 'GILDED LILY LTD'. Underneath, in smaller font, barely legible, it read, 'Providing bespoke and pre-made frames for artists, homes and business since 1924. Couple: Jessica and Daniel, provided by Shout models, Toronto.'

I flipped over the cut-up sheet to look at my parents once again. I'd always presumed the couple were on Cowling beach – as Rohan had told me – but to look at the photograph now was to see a light on the horizon, an unfamiliar light that undoubtedly had nothing to do with the South Coast of England. It was clear. This couple were not my parents. Not just the man – who I'd never believed was my true father in any case – but the woman too. My mother with the long hair. They were an ideal couple. That perfect pair strolling through a sepia afternoon were models. A couple made to inhabit a picture frame. A couple to show you what your own snaps could look like, but who would always be having a better time than you, or those you photographed, ever could.

Will and Alice Everett came with a frame. Rohan had picked out my parents for me from a choice in the framer's window. He chose a woman with overly long hair to be his sister, my mother, because he knew what children are like, their wishful thinking: long-haired princess, like in the fairytales. Killed at sea with a fondness for sand flowers. Who would ever question that?

'These are not my parents,' I said slowly. 'These are not my parents.'

I tipped papers from a nearby leather book bag onto the floor and carefully slid the jar inside. It was warm, the jar, and I felt the baby thud around inside like pickled eggs, or something heavier; like the tinned pheasant I once picked up in Ronnie's cupboard when we first started seeing each other. I had shuddered at the thump of the bird concealed inside the can, turning the whole thing upside-down, then righting it, and turning it upside down again and again. I remember being horrified but compelled by the thud, thud, thud of something whole that had once been alive and was now dead inside a tin, waiting to be torn from its manmade womb by the serrated power of a hand-held tin-opener. Ronnie had to prise the thing from my hands, laughing at me. Put it down Dee. Put it *down*.

I slipped the page of photographs into a side pocket, made sure it was zipped safe, and ran down the stairs into the kitchen. I had the bag cradled in my arms, pulled up tight to my chest. I didn't look at Ronnie or Toby, who now sat calmly at the table. Trudy had left an ivory-handled teaspoon on the surface. Rohan's ivory-handled teaspoon. I remember using it to eat porridge when I was very small. I remember Rohan gliding it towards me – heaped with oats and syrup – making the sound of a train, or a car, or an aeroplane. No!

Where was my mother? Hair past her hips, tied up with a shoelace.

I stepped out onto the front path. The gravel was the same. I kicked it and remembered kicking it in my past. It was strange to think these small, sharp, stones were the same small, sharp, stones that had been there in my old life. Through everything. My feet. Rohan's feet. Stella's feet. Everyone's feet. Even Ruskin's.

If an arrow had come out from between the pine trees and hit me in my lungs I would not have been surprised. I would have been grateful. Voices behind me made me panic. I hid the bag with the jar baby under the leaves of a tall bush. Moses in the bullrushes. I leapt up and stood with my hands in my pockets, my heatbeat so fast it was uncountable.

Behind me the voices were louder.

'We'll prepare her tonight.' I imagined myself as a dinner for cannibals, red-faced and bubbling in a big black pot.

'Maybe it's time for that barbeque and more vino,' said Toby cheerfully. I turned and nodded.

'I'll see you tomorrow Diana,' said Trudy. 'I'll explain everything then. None of it is your fault.'

I wished people wouldn't keep telling me that. I knew one thing, as Toby and Ronnie led me away from the Cowling Place. I would not be going back inside that house. I would not be going back there ever again.

15

A wood pigeon woke me up; at least I think it was a wood pigeon. *Woo whoot woooo whoot whoot.* I've never seen a wood pigeon, or at least not consciously, but my imagination has always taken the name literally; a plump wooden bird pieced together from old-fashioned clothes pegs, a hollow carcass, with glass buttons for eyes, a little motor in the belly for the whoot.

I imagined my wood pigeon as it hailed the morning, as I breathed in last night's sweat and plastic: I worried about beetles. The little black bugs that fluttered around the air vent in the roof reminded me of the inch-long wriggling carapace I'd found in my hair as Ronnie slept, although I knew there was no room for insect fear in the great outdoors. I tried my best to remember my early-teenage fearlessness when I would camp on the beach and make fires from abandoned, broken rowing boats. I was a good camper. I was safe on the beach. I laughed at the thought of Stella shitting in the woods and sleeping on the ground with only a few millimetres of groundsheet separating her from the sodden earth.

Ronnie slept with a deep, satisfied snore and her face pressed into strands of pipe tobacco and her folded sweatshirt. We didn't bring pillows. I thought we could just fold up towels and jumpers and use them instead, like I used to as a kid. It would save on space. I was right, it did, but that hadn't stopped the crick in my neck, the throb along the length of my spine, the thick ridges of towel imprint on my cheeks. I must have looked like I'd been run over by a miniature train; lattice tracks among the freckles.

Ronnie looked well slept and I was tempted to wake her. I have never been one to lie awake for long. I think too much, my thoughts wander. Ronnie had spent what seemed like forever teaching me to train my mind; to keep it focused. If I woke her I knew she would yawn and stretch dramatically, that she'd say, 'Morning my love,' and kiss me on my nose. I would feel important as she reeled me in, cupped my tangled limbs against hers and feathered kisses on my head. 'My lovely Love.'

This is what happens when you meet your girlfriend in a homeless shelter – she felt sorry for me. She must have done. It was her job.

But I didn't wake her. It would be selfish, and I thought I might take a look around the campsite. I could hear the family in the tent next door up and making breakfast. The two kids, girl and boy, were throwing something about – a frisbee? It winded the side of our tent with an ooomph. The plastic quivered and condensation appeared in the patch where we were hit. I felt a twinge of something – the lost past, the unknowable future – at the wonderful simplicity of that family. I wondered if they'd had cornflakes for breakfast, if the kids argued about who would do the washing up. Maybe the parents were marine scientists – here at the coast to take samples of creeping willow and cord grass.

'Horatio!' said the dad.

'Jemima!' said the mum.

'Sorry!' said Horatio and Jemima.

For some reason I started to cry.

Through tears I wondered what to make for breakfast. I could have woken Ronnie with a fried-up feast: eggs, bacon, sausages, mushrooms, beans, tomatoes (fresh, sliced and fried – not that horrendous slop in a tin that glistens like scooped-out hearts. Ronnie would never have convinced me to like them, no matter how hard she tried.) I could have fried some bread and made some tea. She was surprised and right that tea tastes better in the open air. I like that there are always bits of floating grass, strands of green in the brown.

But I didn't get up. I lay still in the sticky wrapping of my own sleeping bag. It was too cold last night to zip them both together, so we tucked ourselves in, trapped our limbs in our own separate nylon parcels, made our own burial chambers upon the groundsheet. I said we looked like mummies inside our soft sarcophagi. She laughed and told me those old tombs were always made of stone, decorated with etchings and complicated stories, were never soft. I refrained from saying I'd seen *The Mummy*, that it didn't take a genius or an expensive education to know about Egypt. I'd never even used the word before, was just playing, but she gave me background information: *sark*, from the Greek for flesh, *phagos*, for eating. Flesh-eating stone? It made me shiver.

She always knew so much. I liked that about her when we met. She could fill me in on all the things I had missed out on. My knowledge was like a Pollock painting; slapped on, vivid, a feeling. On my later travels I saw one of his earlier paintings, *The Moon Woman*, in the Peggy Guggenheim Collection. It was – without doubt – my Diana, Ovid's Diana, Titian's Diana: dominating the canvas, long, definite limbs, a raised knee, sprawling colours and a line – thick, black and straight – the very core of her, from her head to the bottom of the canvas. I found this reassuring.

I learned the kings and queens for Ronnie, poetic formulae that knitted my brow and addled my tongue, Latin phrases that clung like bile at the back of my mouth. I did the best I could. I tried to make myself a rational thinker, a mind in motion. Reacting with emotion had no weight with her if it couldn't be backed up with theory. That's what comes from knowing so much. Even art and beauty, for her, were intellectual puzzles to be solved.

She was still snoring, her eyelids flickered like pencil shavings by an open window. I liked her eyelashes; they were almost white, gossamer. Her flesh was like soap, large looming. She was always proud of her broad shoulders, her Romanesque thighs. I was reminded of her when I saw Michelangelo's *Awakening Giant* in Florence. Arched back, trapped, yet proud, flesh thrusting forward from un-carved marble. Awakening.

When we first got together, Ronnie showed me The Renaissance. On our first holiday she took me to the Sistine Chapel. I knew Michelangelo preferred the chisel to the brush, I had heard that from somewhere, or perhaps I could see it in his work. It was papal power which forced that now-familiar sweeping fresco out of him, when his heart was elsewhere. I knew she didn't have much truck with hearts, she couldn't trace the line of them, make a pattern. She talked about *The Last Judgement* and I stared and nodded. I watched green moss grow through the stones, nature breathing beneath manmade splendour.

I have always had a strange fascination with plants – I always thought it was genetic because of my mother. The way they grow. They coil and lean and face the sun. 'Shine on me, fill me up, pick me!' They never neglect their needs, they won't hide, they need light and shade and wind and air. They are honest and peculiar. That's photosynthesis, she would say, and I would be grateful. I had never listened in biology. I knew nothing of O_2s and CO_2s and scientific transmogrification. I thought petals and stamens were like faces, looking at sky. (We trim them back, till it seems like we've got them under control, but have you ever looked at ivy? It creeps, creeps.)

The sun was out of its case by now, hung out in the sky and hot through our blue tent. I could hear the mum washing up and the dad banging something into the ground – Swingball? Jemima and Horatio were quiet – off to wash in the shower blocks? Wriggling their toes through unruly balls of human hair? I hate communal showers, but cannot be choosy. That's what camping is all about, getting back to a state of nature, learning to do without. (I know I know, Hobbes, Locke, Rousseau…those Granddaddies of the Enlightenment, the concept of a 'state of nature', the noble savage. You see Ronnie? I was listening.)

It struck me that I was sweating too much. I jiggled in my sleeping bag, sick of stale air and sunlight made artificial through canvas. I didn't want a fried breakfast or tea. I wanted an apple, or a glass of water. I watched Ronnie sleep, oblivious. I felt angry and did not chastise myself for the first time in, well, in as long as I'd known her.

I was claustrophobic, kicked my way out of the sleeping bag, scraped skin on cold zips. I've got to get out, I thought, even though I knew I was being silly, being hysterical, not thinking things through. I knew it wasn't Ronnie's fault. She just wanted to improve me. I could see that.

Then I was out, into my shorts and T-shirt as quick as I could. They smelt musty, of me, of yesterday. I didn't care about shoes; my sandals were still soggy from our late-night run along the sea's edge. The food in the pegged-out porch sat neat in tins and jars. I knew more about Egyptian tombs than she might have thought – the tins of sausages, beans, tomatoes and mushrooms looked like four canopic jars: the vessels for the essential organs in the afterlife, set out next to the body; one for the stomach, one for the liver, then the lungs, then the intestines. No heart. What did they do with the heart? Ronnie was wrapped snug, ready for the afterlife. Life after me.

When I was out of the tent I ran across the wet grass with bare feet. I cackled and laughed and waved my hands in the air and could hear nothing but the sound of the sea. I imagined Ronnie shouting at me to come back although I knew she was still sleeping.

'Diana!' she shouted from behind me. 'Diana! Come back!'

I ran faster and did not look over my shoulder. I wanted to shout 'No!' but I was out of breath and not thinking in words. The grass under my feet turned purple and swayed, heavy with dew. Then my attention was grabbed by a little wooden bird bobbing on the tip of the branch of a tree. I smiled and continued to run, my feet wet and cold and my heart alive. I was going to explain, put it in her words so she would understand, but no longer felt the need. I called out, for no good reason the words of the wood pigeon: 'Woo whoot woooo whoot whoot wooooooooo!'

I woke up, then, sitting cross-legged in Hat Cove – the tiny piece of sand away from the main beach that Rohan and I used to visit when I was a child. It had been a dream, then, a dream about escaping from Ronnie?

I was tired and sore. Disorientated.

My lips had dried themselves shut.

They tasted of the sea.

Then I saw something peculiar: a big pile of sand and a deep, deep hole. Somebody had dug far down into the sand, had tried to find something old and hidden beneath the beach.

Confusion.

My hands were covered in cuts and dirt, and I had in my left hand a neon-pink child's spade. The hole was about three foot deep and two feet wide. Mammoth. I could not have dug a hole that big without waking up, not with only a child's spade and my fingers as my tools.

Could I?

Why would I?

My head hurt. My eyes were tight slits.

I had another terrible hangover.

The sky was matt and shadowy with grey twists of fog edging towards smudged blue. The huge clouds were gilded yellow at their tips, and this meant it was early. Early enough to sneak back into our tent without Ronnie noticing.

Before I left, I looked into the hole. It was empty. Whatever it was I'd been looking for was long gone.

I walked the mile to the campsite trying to remember. I had no memory of leaving for the beach – other than my dream and the wood pigeon. Maybe that hadn't been a dream. But a bird made of wooden pegs? That could not have been real. My abhorrence of Ronnie. That seemed, awfully, shamefully, real.

I longed for bacon sandwiches and tea.

By the time I got to the site my feet had cleaned themselves on damp grass and I rubbed my hands under the tap by the toilet block. There were not many families camping yet – it was only early June, when every hot day is followed by uncertainty – and those that were there seemed still to be in bed. There were no signs of a Horatio or Jemima or a family with Swingball. This came as no surprise to me. Dream People. Our bundle.

I unzipped the front-door flap not very quietly at all, and crawled into the warm bell of the tent on all fours. Ronnie was still wrapped up in her sleeping bag, her arms folded across her chest, eerily corpse-like, and her eyes were wide open.

'You've been gone a long time,' she said.

'I haven't,' I said quickly. 'I just went to the toilet.'

'OK,' she said. 'If that's what you say.'

'Shall I make breakfast?' I looked at the clock we'd hung from the ridge pole. 'It's 6.30.'

'I feel odd,' said Ronnie. 'There's lots I don't know about you.'

'You know the important bits.'

'You didn't want to talk about Toby's reasons for not pursuing you…'

'I know why he didn't pursue me: because a) he fancied Stella; and b) I prefer women. It's not rocket science.'

'That's not what he said.'

'He was probably just trying to get at Stella because of her thing with *Benjy* Burne. Here look at this.' My old bitterness about Stella and her part in my unhappy childhood no longer rang true. I reached into my pocket for my wallet and brought out the original picture Rohan had given me of my parents. The happy couple striding out on Cowling beach with their dog. The lie. Funny. I'd never asked Rohan the dog's name. 'My parents.'

'Your parents?' She fondled the soft paper. 'You've never shown me this before.' She looked up at me. 'You look a bit like your mother. Wait there – Stella and Benjy? Are you kidding me? Stella isn't having an affair with *Benjy*.'

'You're probably right,' I said. It didn't sound very true. The more I thought about it the more likely it was Stella actually *had* loved Rohan and it was he who had betrayed *her*. My body ached with it.

'I bet you're thinking about how I used to wear a bikini.'

'I'm not.'

'You are,' tickling her.

'I'm not,' giggling.

'I'll wear a bikini for you on the beach if you like.'

'I'm not bothered about the bikini,' pushing her hands into my hair.

'I think you are,' kissing her belly.

'Leave it out,' stroking my neck.

'No,' kissing her thighs.

I set up the gas rings out front and Ronnie fried bacon and made tea in a billy can. We both had sand everywhere. I'd covered her in it.

'What is all this stuff with Trudy?' said Ronnie.

I thought carefully about my answer. 'You know what? You have as much idea as I do. I really didn't think Trudy was Rohan's type.'

'You don't really think Stella's having a thing with Benjy do you?'

'No. Not any more.'

'Well that's a start.' She put her hand on my shoulder. 'This isn't working any more, is it?'

I did not argue with this statement and Ronnie stirred hot liquid with a bent spoon. I did not really want to get back to how we were. Trudy in the Cowling Place made no sense. We ate bacon and drank strong tea.

'We have to go to the house soon,' I said. 'Let's leave the washing up.'

'It was good, in places,' said Ronnie. 'I think we loved each other, in some way.'

I nodded. She was right, but I could not keep any of it up any longer, and finally, neither could she.

When we got to the house Ronnie let go of my hand and smiled at me.

'I'm sorry,' I said, and I meant it.

'All I mind about is the lies,' she said. 'The rest of it is different and we can sort it in our own time. We can be friends.'

'Can we?' For a moment I allowed myself to believe it. I wanted Ronnie's friendship. I wanted to know her. I didn't want to be her girlfriend but I wanted to know her. I had chosen her as my partner to cheat Drake, but I had cheated myself. I was letting him win.

'I'll go and get us coffee,' she said, and I nodded. Ronnie and I. Safe. Happy. Enclosed. If only the words would come.

But as soon as she was gone I went to the bush where I'd hid the jar baby and pulled it to me.

'I'm sorry Ronnie,' I said.

And then I ran. I ran as fast as I could. The dull thump of the jar baby against my body as I ran told me I had to leave.

I did not look back.

Trudy. Trudy. Trudy. Her name went over in my head with the pictures from Drake's magazines. How could Trudy be the love of Rohan's life? She wasn't even beautiful, and Drake had told me how important it was to be beautiful.

Trudy. Trudy. Trudy.

Trudy. Trudy. Trudy.

Stella. Trudy. Stella. Trudy.

Drake.

As soon as I arrived at Victoria I realised I had nothing with me except the book bag, my mobile and my wallet. All my most important belongings were still in the tent alongside Ronnie's, including Rohan's cape.

People bustled around me, heaving heat and sweat and dirt along with their clothes and their bags and their newspapers. I stopped at one of the coffee stands and ordered an espresso. I drank it standing in front of the arrivals/departures board. There were trains to Dover, Brighton, Bognor Regis, Portsmouth, Bournemouth, a dot-to-dot trip along the south coast. The train to Cowling was a heavy stopper. There were thirty stations to enjoy between there and the capital.

I finished my coffee and walked into a plunge of commuters and day-trippers who strode out from the midday train from Brighton. I shouldered my way through the crowd, stepping through tuts and grimaces and barging elbows. Without thinking I swiped my way into the underground. I knew where I was going. I was going to the National Gallery.

On the tube I sort of muttered under my breath for a while to make sure the train didn't stop, or get caught in a tunnel. I thought I might not survive if the train got caught in a tunnel. I said my own name over and over. Diana. Diana. Diana.

As soon as I was at the gallery I knew I had to find out her secret. There were ghosts of her everywhere, as though every artist who'd ever put paint onto canvas knew she was more powerful than they; that to paint her was to see her and to see her was to be doomed. I don't know what got into me. I was certain I could prove that every single painting in the National Gallery had elements, remnants, of Diana. I imagined that she had control over all art. That she was *the* Muse, whether anyone liked it or not.

I walked the galleries with sweat coating my arms, legs and face. I was still wearing my sandals covered in yesterday's sand, a knee-length denim skirt and a cheap yellow vest top, grubby with beach and a stain on the hem from barbequed meat. I had one of Ronnie's striped jumpers tied around my waist.

Diana was everywhere.

I saw her in Degas's *After the Bath*. Her whole back faced outwards from the canvas. There was a curve of breast, swathes of towels. She touched her neck. It was obviously her, although maybe Degas was trying to catch her out – to portray her in a house, corporeal, surrounded by walls, to prevent her movement. Maybe he hoped she could not flee?

I saw her in Cezanne's *Bathers*. A group of naked women surround one other. They feed the central woman fruit; watch her and listen. There are no men. It would be easy to think the main woman is Diana, but there is another, one woman who has her back turned towards the main group. She is against a tree, dark eyebrows, oiled into a frown. She is more like my Diana: watchful, wary, slow to trust.

I saw her in Velazquez's *The Toilet of Venus*. Blatant, naked, with the most wonderful shoulders and hips. She shows her body and watches, from her reflection in the mirror. She is doubly powerful. Though there are no water and trees for her. She looked trapped to me. Too staged. A man's delight. I didn't like it.

I saw her in Rembrandt's *A Woman Bathing in a Stream*. It doesn't take a genius to work that one out. It's all in the title. There is something in her discarded, grand robes, contrasted with her standing there in her underwear. She lifts her petticoat and I could almost see all of her, right up to the tops of her thighs. If I were there a moment longer I would have seen all of her. It is a painting of a promise.

I saw her in Constable's *The Cenotaph to Reynolds's Memory*. It wasn't a tribute to old Sir Joshua, with his theories on what makes genius in art. It was obviously a tribute to Diana. The stag wanders, stares out. The busts of Michelangelo and Raphael sit either side of Joshua Reynolds's memorial. Chieftains of his trade. The trees are exactly the same, if you compare them, as the ones in the Titian. The stag watches Raphael, but nothing happens. Raphael is just stone now, and the stag wanders, lost. Nothing, not even those great artists, can save the stag now. *I* am Diana. No man will ever have me unless I say so.

'I could set your own hounds on you,' I said to the stag. 'One arrow and you're dead.'

I went up close to the painting. The tangle of trees and the greens, browns and greys made me want to run. I could feel the trees' roots: taut, twisted, meshed with leaves and ferns and weeds. I wanted to run. So I did.

I ran about the gallery for what seemed like hours, catching arched backs, curved mouths, long limbs on canvas. Diana. Diana. Diana. Pointing. Laughing. Scorning. There was the constant flip of my sandals on wood. I was sure I had discovered some wonderful secret, something that all the art historians had failed to discover. Diana is the Muse! I had a terrible headache. In front of my eyes were bright swirls and curling black splinters that followed me wherever I looked. I had eaten nothing, had had little sleep. I kept thinking and thinking about nothing, and everything, and that maybe I was the only one to work out what everything in the whole world was about, all Art, and all Beauty, and all longing and desire.

I could see! I could see everything!

Two hours later, I found myself back in front of the Titian, twisting the ends of my fringe back and forth between my thumb and forefinger. I cried a little, could smell salt, and brandy, and Vosene shampoo.

The book bag, with the jar baby still inside, sat in my lap. I stroked the leather. It was soft, yielding and quite old, but it made me feel uncomfortable to think of the animal it had once been stretched around; containing its innards, the heart, the liver, the gut. Everything converts into something else in the end. Energy cannot just disappear. That is a scientific truth.

A gallery attendant came up beside me and asked me if I was OK, then, tentatively, if I would consider moving along, as I was putting off other visitors.

'I am not OK,' I said. 'And no I can't go anywhere else.'

The attendant – decked out in navy everything to be invisible – wandered off to find assistance. She smiled at me apologetically, but looked a little afraid.

I started talking to Diana.

'What do you think I should do?'

'Who are my enemies?'

'Were they laughing at me?'

'What has happened to Toby and Trudy? Why is the house hers?'

'Who is the person on the horse? Be careful. I don't trust him. Observing everything from far away. Getting a warped picture. Or maybe he's my saviour…the answer to everything.'

'Whatever happened to Eddie Drake?'

Other things. Things that only she would understand.

She didn't talk back.

I knew I wasn't going mad. She stood there, destined to watch Actaeon's punishment forever. Forever victorious. I wondered if that was the point of paintings: to trap something the artist can't control, to force it to make sense; to take away its unreliability, its power.

Ronnie would say I had forgotten the influence of patrons, that Art doesn't appear in a vacuum. Especially the Art of the past when the only way to do it was to be commissioned by the church or rich families who wanted to prove their own power against Rome. Why else were there so many paintings of the Grecian myths, the Roman myths, of Christianity? Why else had there been a fashion for depicting kings alongside saints, of the Virgin or Christ or any of those other big history paintings? What we think of as Art is all related to money, Ronnie would say. What the money wanted, the artists created. Has any of that changed?

I was trying to calm myself down.

I had used Ronnie. That much had become clear. It was not on purpose, but I had run to London with the vague idea that I could fix myself, that I could make myself well by a change of scenery. I would love to be able to look at that first six months and say I had stood on my own two feet, that I had learned about my true self, that I had become whole. But it would be a lie. I had gone from bar to bar, with no money, working for pennies, for rooms, for food. I would sit in pubs, with no money, waiting for someone to buy me a drink, then another. I would reward apparent kindness with whatever I was asked for. I lived in the dark and kept myself there with drink after drink and another blackout. I only ended up in the homeless shelter because I was out of money, out of options and unclean. I had made Ronnie laugh. I cannot remember what I said, but she arrived each day like a hero in a comic book. Save me, I thought. I will give you whatever you want but just save me. Our life together was not a joining of equals. I was a mollusc or a barnacle. I clung to her for my very survival and pretended I was more capable than I really was. I wonder now if she knew it really. She tries to do her best in most things. Looking after me made her feel like she was doing something good, something human. Being looked after made me feel like I must be worthwhile after all.

Two security guards came and sat next to me on the leather bench. I was hot, had lost time. One of them, a man with short, curly dyed-yellow hair, said quietly, 'Are you here on your own?'

'No,' I said quickly. 'I am here with my dad.'

'Right…' he said. 'Is he anywhere nearby?'

'He's just popped to see the Van Eyks in the Sainsbury Wing,' I said. 'He'll be back in a moment.' I felt clear-headed. Wonderful. I stood up and turned my back on Diana.

'Do you want us to find him for you?' said the other, a woman with black hair pulled tight into a bun with strands of grey hanging around her face, and warm brown eyes.

'Oh, no thank you,' I said. 'I arranged to meet him in the café. We will have cappuccinos and cake.'

'Do you think you could move along from this section, Madam?' said the man. He was smiling at me.

'Of course,' I said. 'I am sorry to have caused you any bother.'

'No bother, Madam,' said the man. 'As long as you are OK…?'

'Oh yes,' I said. 'My dad is a painter,' I said. 'He used to make clothes, but he left them behind for a life daubed in oils. We live by the sea.'

'That sounds nice,' said the man.

'Oh yes,' I said. 'Later we are going to see a play at Drury Lane. He hasn't been well, you see. But he's better now.'

'That sounds nice,' said the woman.

'Well,' I said. 'Sorry to have kept you.' I walked away, out of the door.

In the gallery canteen, Rohan and I had coffee and cake. He was telling me about how much he hated celebrity. That he had wanted to tell me about Trudy but he didn't want to upset me. He wore a blue shirt and jeans, brown sandals and a green jumper. He smelt of salt, tobacco and Vosene shampoo.

Through the window, out in Trafalgar Square, Nelson shimmied down his column and began introducing himself to tourists. For the time being, at least, he refrained from attacking the pigeons.

I sat by the fountains and watched the lions until I felt a bit better. The time in the gallery was muddled, confused. Everyone I knew in London was in Cowling – apart from people I'd worked with, and I'd already burned my bridges with them. Everything I was I knew was dead. I had nowhere to go.

I no longer wanted to know who had killed Rohan – it was an accident. Everyone said so. But I did want to know one thing. *Who am I?* In truth, it was what I had always wanted to know.

I had discarded Stella's exhibition as over-romanticised nonsense. But now I just wanted to see the clothes. Rohan's masterpieces. And his big painting of the sea.

This time I caught the bus. I pointed out Eros in Piccadilly, Regent Street, Oxford Circus to an invisible father. It was fun. I am not saying for one moment that I actually thought Rohan was there with me. It was just more entertaining to imagine what life would be like if he was. I liked the feel of my face on his left shoulder. I liked the jokes he told about people on the street. I liked the way he finally showed me that he loved me and everything would be all right. I liked the way I could, at last, say whatever I wanted without fear of his reaction. There is no harm in imagining. I was doing no harm. I surprised myself by saying, 'You know, I think I am going to go to the police about Eddie Drake.' Saying this out loud, despite the strange look the woman in the corduroy jacket beside me gave me, made me feel ridiculously free.

The Museum of Twentieth Century Fashion glinted with glass and steel in the afternoon sun, but the flowerbed at the front was being dug over. Flora had been upturned, discarded, and a shaven-headed man in a fluorescent waistcoat was digging while another was applying compost from split plastic sacks.

I thought of mine and Glenys Pimm's midnight flit into the undergrowth. The grease of her lipstick on my cheek, her sudden change of heart. I thought about my shoe on Richard Milk's pillow and smiled.

Behind the electric doors the statue was still in place. I stood next to it, looked around to make sure nobody was looking, and put my hands onto its cold arm. So narrow was this statue that I could hold its thigh in a hole made by my curled fingers.

When I first moved to London I realised the best way to pick up women was to flatter them beyond the boundaries of decency. All women want to be compared to others and come out on top. They live in fear that some über-woman is out there, striding the corridors of life with long, elegant limbs and long glossy hair. She would make anyone laugh with her intelligence and wit. She could bake wonderful cakes. Her features would be so startling that even if she had her hair cropped short, she would look *gamine* and *sensuous* instead of butch or clumsy. She could walk into a room and steal your life, your husband, your father, your entire sense of self, with just one tilt of her face, one hand through her hair.

She doesn't exist, obviously. But most women think she does. They see her in everything, just like Diana in the National Gallery.

All women want to be the winner in the war of women against all other women. Women will have sex with ugly people, dull people, people they almost hate if that person makes them feel like they are the stuff of stars and wonder. Women don't really want to have sex with someone else, a connection. They want to have sex with someone who will confirm their own delusions of grandeur, get rid of their insecurity, their self-hate. Everyone is special, God's perfect children, but *you* darling, *you* are more special than anyone else.

This was my smug theory then. Before I really knew what it was like to connect.

The gallery, in the light of day, was clear and undebauched. There was none of the pomp and glitz from the opening night, and instead of fake flames there were just sheets of sunlight mirroring themselves in all that glass. Everywhere was very clean and very bright. There were people pointing at the photographs of Stella and Rohan. I stood in front of the one of the mystery woman in the vermilion and blue shot silk dress. Rohan's thumb on her calf burned a spot in my leg and I reached down and clung to myself. What was all this about?

I stared at the dresses. They were beautiful, well-made, sometimes elaborate, sometimes simple; always perfectly executed. I wanted to read the little cards next to them, to look at the papers and documents that had also been combined with the clothing.

It was all stuff I'd heard before.

Rohan loved Stella. Jimmy Trowse was a philanderer who feigned heartbreak. They all made up in the end. For fifteen years nobody cared about the clothes of Rohan Rickwood. Blah. Blah. Blah. Then, towards the back wall, beside a periwinkle-blue, full-skirt reinterpretation of the William Travilla dress famously blasted with drain air in *The Seven Year Itch* there was a short piece on Rohan's time at university.

> The first time Rohan Rickwood made an impression nationally was for three blue ball gowns made for the May Ball at Trinity College, Cambridge in 1974. The dresses were worn by Stella Avery, Glenys Pimm and Trudy Farrow. The foursome made quite an impact, and Rickwood was inundated with requests to make dresses for stars of stage and film almost immediately.

I reread the card several times to make sure I had understood it correctly. The fever of the National Gallery was replaced with a clear head. All at once I had access to several new pieces of information that seemed unfeasibly coincidental: a) Rohan had known Stella *before* she was with Jimmy; b) Glenys Pimm had known Rohan, Stella and Trudy; and c) Trudy had been there all along.

There is no such thing as coincidence.

The gallery was full of people now. They were pointing, pointing at dresses, and all I could see was the giant photograph of Rohan and the mystery woman in his workroom.

And there, upon canvas, was Trudy, face upwards, in the sea. Rohan and her, swimming off Hat Cove.

Trust nobody, Rohan used to say. Well Rohan was dead and I would have to trust somebody unless I wanted to spend the rest of my life staring at Diana in the National.

I held the book bag to my belly and ran from the gallery. The security machine bleeped as I went past, but I did not stop. I heard someone calling, but still did not stop. I ran out onto the street, into Stella's London of sky and plants around doorsteps and no neon. I ran to the tube stop and sat on a train, rocking gently, talking to myself over and over, until I got back to Covent Garden. I wanted to see familiar things. To remind myself that my new life was better. On strong foundations.

I stood outside the flat, and only then did I realise I had come all the way back to London without bringing my door keys. I slid onto one of the communal benches and put the book bag on the table. I could see our sash windows, our windowboxes with flowers and herbs, I could see inside on the ledge the vase of peonies I had forgotten to throw away before we'd left. I wondered if their water was yellow and smelt of piss. There was nobody to get a key from. For some reason Ronnie's mother had the other, and she was in Cornwall.

I took the jar out of the bag, carefully so as not to hear the thump against the side, and looked at it. It was just a half-formed baby in a jar. There was nothing mystical about it. It didn't watch me with its big, misshapen eye. It didn't push its fingers against the glass. It was just a pink sack of membrane with unusable organs hidden under puckered, out-of-commission skin. God, it was ugly. There was nothing. A baby in the jar. No little bundle. No birl. No goy.

I looked from the jar to our flat. I used to think I knew everything.

I thought of my mother, trapped under the belly of her boat, reaching for something; air, her husband, her child. I thought of her final moments as the boat was cut into pieces against grey rocks. But maybe even that was a lie. Maybe my mother was never out at sea.

I had always thought that, maybe, just maybe, she thought of me as her lungs burst.

I thought of this as the jar baby's lid pressed into my skin and I wept. I do not know for how long I wept.

And then a date came to the forefront of my mind. How had I missed it at the launch of Stella's exhibition? A date, clear in black and white, on the press release.

'If anyone does anything to unearth, disturb or harm my sister,' he said in the summer of 1984 to a crowd of journalists at one of his favourite Soho hangouts, 'I will personally see to it that his or her life is not worth living.

But I was born in 1983 and Rohan had told me my parents had died that same year. So why had he spoken about her as though she was still in the present a year later?

I wanted to get drunk. To forget everything. Rohan had been many things, but until the past few days I had never taken him for a liar.

I rummaged in my pocket for my mobile, ignoring the missed calls and stacked-up text messages, and made a phone call.

16

I buried Ruskin in the sand behind a rock, and I buried him deep where nobody could find him.

Rohan must have gone back to Hat Cove after I'd buried him. He saw the freshly dug sand, the small mound that signified a final resting place, and dug out the dog with his bare hands. He carried the vacant body back to the house, maybe in a sack, rolled up in a cardigan, maybe just as it was; slumped in his arms like a fur coat about to be hung upon the naked shoulders of an alluring client. That would have given him the idea. Like a coat, he would have thought.

Or...

He watched me bury him. He never went back to the house at all. After he'd called out my name and I'd kept hidden, he'd knelt behind a stone, had watched me cry into the sad sack of belly; ruffle my hands through the stiffening hair, stare at the sky hoping something miraculous would happen. He had seen me call out to the clouds to make time go backwards, to make me stay in bed that morning, when I need never have swigged on Drake's brandy.

Rohan took the dead dog back to the house and skinned it himself. I tried to remember whether he had been blistered and sore around that time. If his skin problems – that only appeared after touching fur – had been seething then. If his eyes were cracked around their rims, leaking red juice like split melons. But that was the summer I had locked myself away.

I will never know how it happened or why it happened, but I know it happened. Part of me hopes it was guilt. Guilt for not protecting me. Guilt for not caring properly for me. Guilt for lying to me and relying on me. Guilt for passing me his hatred of women. Because it struck me, as I held the jar baby and wept, that he really did hate women, for whatever reason.

I knew he hated them because he was always mocking them. Because he sneered when they tried to impress him. Because when he'd bedded them he thought nothing of them and told me so. His niece. A child! Because their secrets meant nothing to him. Because he shared them with me and made them my secrets and yet kept the most important things from me. Because he spent my entire childhood trying to make me different to them. Because he thought women didn't exist without men. Because he...

'Hell-o?' There was music in the background. Voices.

'Um. Hi. Polly. Yeah. This is Diana Rickwood...You, er, gave me your number at the, er, MTCF.'

A pause. I pressed my head against the body of the phone. A cool line of plastic on my forehead. I rolled my head from side to side and let the cold soothe me.

'Diana! Of course! Hi. Yeah. How arrrre you?'

'Fine. Fine thanks.'

'You in London? I thought you'd all gone off on a Famous Five adventure.' She giggled.

'Well, sort of. I had to pop back for something. How are you?'

'Oh, yeah. I'm fine. Good. All the better for hearing from you... Are you busy?'

'Not particularly,' I said.

'You fancy meeting for a drink?'

'That would be nice,' I said. Drink.

'The Lighthouse. In W9. You know it? We've rented it. Just say my name on the door.'

'Yes,' I lied. I could always check the A2Z.

'See you soon.'

'About forty minutes,' I said, and hung up.

The Lighthouse was the sort of theme pub whose décor didn't take itself too seriously. There was something familiar about it – like the cafés further along in Cowling, where the tourists liked to go. Polly and her well-heeled friends had rented it and turned it into a rich kids' fancy-dress party. There were blue-rimmed portholes for windows, papier-mâché seagulls on the walls and the bar had been made to look like an ice-cream van. The bottles of spirits hung upside-down with flavour labels stuck over their real identities. Strawberry for Bell's. Raspberry ripple for Gordon's. Odd. It put the wrong taste in your mouth before the alcohol got there. Offputting. Each table had a mini sandpit at its centre, with miniature beach tools for building sand sculptures. My first thought was, surprisingly, 'This can't be very hygienic.'

'Diana!' Pretty Polly stood up from a bench that was also an upturned canoe. She was wearing striped shorts and a dark pink jumper with a cotton collar. She had orange children's armbands around her upper arms and diving flippers on her feet. She was at the table with two men, who both wore knotted hankies on their heads and had their trousers rolled up around their calves. Polly grinned and skipped over sand-scattered floorboards to give me a hug.

'It is so brilliant you called!' she said. Her enthusiasm was disconcerting. 'Come and meet the others. Don't you *love* this place? We've got it for a week or so.'

I wasn't keen to meet the 'others'. Two variants of Benjy Burne sat at Polly's table, drinking cocktails from fat glasses with playing cards spread out in front of them.

'Diana, this is Claxton. Claxton Jones. He writes for the *Times*, among other things.' Of course he did.

'Hello there,' said Claxton Jones. 'Pleased to meet you.'

I was just relieved to be off the street, with a reason to drink. 'Hello Claxton.'

'And this is Mani. Mani Charles.'

'The photographer?' I said, surprised. He had taken the infamous country gentlefolk photos of Stella and Rohan.

'The very same. Pleased to meet you Diana.'

'You too.'

I sat at their table, feeling luckily suitably dressed in my denim skirt, sandals and grubby top. Beach Chic.

'I haven't been here for a while.'

'It's lovely isn't it?' said Polly. 'We come here a lot. Stella too. We've decked it out as all sorts. It was a pirate ship last summer!'

I couldn't imagine Stella getting her heels grubby with industrial sand, but didn't say so.

'Gin isn't it?' said Polly, getting up to buy drinks.

'Yes please,' I said.

'Double?'

'Yes please.'

I was left with the two men, who pushed their cards into one pile and dismissed their game. I recognised the pattern on the back immediately. 'SEW WHAT for all your tailoring needs'.

'My uncle Rohan used to have that exact same pack of cards,' I said.

'That's because they're his,' said Claxton Jones, dropping them into the palm of my hand. I must have looked startled, because he then said, 'He *gave* them to me. Don't worry. I was a good friend of your Uncle Rohan.'

'You were?' I constantly forgot that Rohan's life had continued once I left Cowling. I imagined that he had turned to stone the moment I left. That his life could not go on without me.

'Oh yes. He'd chosen me to write his official biography,' he said smiling. 'It was well underway by the time he died.'

He and Mani Charles clinked glasses.

'I am trying to finish it without him, but it's tricky. There are so many things I cannot find out. There are so many things I'm not allowed to write about.'

I thought of Trudy, the incongruous sight of Trudy in the Cowling Place and her talk of legalities.

Polly stood at the bar in her wonderful shorts. She wore a duck-egg-blue silk scarf in her hair and had frayed ribbons tied around her wrists instead of bracelets: pink, yellow, green. She had the sort of coarse, frizzy hair that is often naturally blonde, but had learned to straighten it from the root and pull it up into a high, posh-girl ponytail. She had freckles across her nose, which she obviously lightened with foundation. If you know the process, the step-by-step, you can see how a beautiful woman is made. From the outside in.

'So you know Benjy Burne?' I said, taking my gin from Polly's tray.

'Ha! Of course I do. Delusions of grandeur, our Benjamin.' He laughed. 'He thinks he's going to write a grand tome about Rohan, continuing his father's legacy. What a joke.'

'I did think him rather ambitious,' I said.

'It's Stella's fault. She encourages him.'

We drank and talked about other things. Nothing to do with Rohan. I admitted, for the first time, that I had left my job without telling anybody. This provoked general handshaking and acknowledgements of bravery. Everyone agreed they would do the same with their jobs if they could afford to.

I could not really afford to, but I didn't tell them that.

We drank more. At least I would sleep well that night.

I realised early on that Polly had a sort of celebrity crush on Rohan, or at least the idea of him and his life. She asked questions about what he liked to eat, whether he did his own ironing, whether he had a favourite colour, what sort of music he listened to.

I let her tell me about herself. Her name was Polly Rousseau Eliot. She was twenty-three. She lived north of the river in a flat owned by her father's friend Jocelyn Walters – a member of the MTCF's Buyers' Board – while her father worked in Berlin, New York and Hawaii.

'Ingratiates himself horrendously,' said Claxton, back on the subject of Benjy Burne. 'Nobody takes him seriously.'

'So you like Stella's exhibition at the MTCF?'

'Oh yes,' I said. 'I like what Stella has done with colour. Colour was very important to Rohan. He was obsessed with choosing colours to be perfect against each client's skin.'

'He took colour that seriously?'

'Oh yes. He would never, for example, make one dress for one person only to let it be worn by another. He would have to make a different dress. One perfect for the new wearer.'

'How do you think he managed to make all those dresses in the famous year?'

'Help,' I said. 'And determination. He would never be proved wrong, or unable. He would rather have died.'

'Any idea who?'

'Who what?'

'Who helped him make the fifty-two dresses?'

'Me, for one.'

'*You*?'

'Yes, *me*,' I said. 'I was his finisher.' If you say something enough times you begin to believe it to be true.

'*You*. You were?'

'Yes.'

'OK...I'm surprised he found time to make any other clothes that year.'

'He always made time.'

'Do you have any theories as to why he did any of it? Why he made so many clothes? Did he really love women that much?'

I said something surprising then.

'No,' I said. 'I think it was because he hated women.'

Claxton Jones stopped and turned to look directly at me. 'Rohan Rickwood hated women? Rohan *Rickwood*?'

I stared at him. He had sandy hair, cropped short, and wore a crumpled shirt – made that way purposely from a mixture of silk and cotton – with faded jeans. He must have been in his early forties, but looked older because of his overly fashionable look. While Benjy Burne practised the flash-geeky-boy-man look, Claxton Jones was more a follower of battered banker chic.

'Um, no,' I said. 'No,' more firmly.

'Off the record I'm interested,' he said. 'I've never heard anyone say that before. Rohan Rickwood has always been seen as the new man of the fashion world. Women's clothes the way women want to wear them. Glamour, without the pain...You know...'

'I meant yes. Yes he made women's clothes because he loved women.' That's what I meant, wasn't it?

'I'm a big fan of his work. I think there's more to him than people think there is. I think his association with Stella Avery and his winning her over a game of cards with Jimmy Trowse is,' he whispered, '*degrading* somehow. Do you know what I mean?'

'Yes. No. I don't know.' Claxton Jones seemed to be saying everything I'd ever thought, out loud.

'I think we need to give Rohan Rickwood's work a chance to speak for itself.'

'Yes,' I said.

'So you think he hated women because...'

'He didn't,' I said quickly. 'But he did think Stella had bad taste.'

'But he worshipped her...'

'So it seems.'

'Is there anything else you want to tell me? I don't have to say it comes from you. This is your chance.' Claxton Jones wasn't the first to say this to me. 'You can make your case. You've been out of the loop for long enough, haven't you? Doesn't it make your blood boil that it's Stella everyone goes to when a quote's needed on Rohan? Who is Stella to Rohan Rickwood? His bit on the side, his wife, his trophy woman? What influence did he have on her? Much. What influence did she have on him? Not a lot.'

It is very odd to hear years of your own thoughts coming at you from the voice of a stranger. They made more sense in my own head, had even been true. Coming from Claxton Jones they sounded vaguely sinister. Poisonous. If I had met him just a week beforehand, before I'd seen Trudy in the Cowling Place, how different everything might have turned out. I needed time to think.

'OK, but I'd like to talk to you more.'

'If you give me your number I'll call you some time this week.'

'OK,' he said, reaching into his side pocket to pull out an aquamarine business card with turned-down edges. 'And I think we should get a proper photo of you done. It's time to put yourself out there. Maybe

Mani here would like to come and shoot you in Cowling...on home turf, so to speak.'

'Oh...I...'

'Don't worry. You'd look marvellous. We'll get someone to do you up. We could put you in one of Rickwood's dresses...let you stand by the sea...your hair all over the place...Have you ever used Henna? The similarity is startling. We can do it tomorrow. Mani?'

'Yep,' said Mani. 'I think we have everything we need.'

Everything I'd ever wanted handed to me on a plate.

I stared at the pointed collar of Polly's jumper. She smiled a lot and winked at me. She got a narrow tube of lip-gloss out of her bag and was about to apply a coat, when I said, 'Can I put that on for you?'

She looked at me. I knew that look. 'Yes,' she said quietly. 'Go on.'

She handed me the gloss, enclosing her fingers around mine for just a moment. It was an expensive brand, with slight strands of glitter suspended through it, and a brush for application.

'Pout,' I said. 'Push your lips out.'

She did as she was told. I got a buzz from that.

I squeezed the tube and pressed it to her bottom lip applying just enough pressure to make her lip curl back on itself, the smear of gloss perfect in the low lighting.

I swept a pure shot of the stuff on her top lip, paused at her cupid's bow to enjoy the definition. She had such pretty lips. I told her so.

'Don't be silly,' she said, so quietly I could hardly hear her.

'I'm not,' I said. 'You are possibly the most beautiful girl I have ever seen.'

That really did it. She leant forward – *she* leant towards *me*, not vice versa – and I kissed her gently, at first just pushed my lips against hers. She opened her mouth, and I, slowly, carefully, licked off every last squeeze of gloss. I did it gradually, running my tongue along the inside of her mouth, catching her teeth with its tip, tasting the grease and the oil and the gin.

She sighed, an audible sigh, and pulled away, wresting a hand on my left thigh. I drank quickly, without thinking. My life was about to go along a path I had always dreamt of. Everything I had ever wanted, there, right there, in that bar.

I let myself daydream what might come next if I continued to sit in this bar and become a part of the life they seemed to be offering.

I sit, wedged, in a deckchair with my hair newly Henna-ed, twisted up and sprayed high over my shoulders.

'You are gorgeous,' says Mani Charles from behind his camera. 'Gor-gee-owss.'

I giggle and shake my head. What can I say? I know I want to hear people tell me how gorgeous I look. I would have sold myself to the devil, and more besides, to have that. Just once.

My face is thick with make-up. My body, pinned into a dress the colour of pondweed, silver scales on the hem, painted and glued to my legs by a make-up artist called, in this daydream, for some reason, Fizz McArdle.

Fizz McArdle's hands on my knees, at my ankles, make me uneasy. I feel panic. There on the sand I feel exposed. What if they are making a joke out of me? What if this is some elaborate hoax and in a minute Stella and Toby and Trudy and Benjy Burne appear holding up a mirror to show how hideous I really look. I close my eyes and try to bend in the directions Mani Charles tells me to.

Claxton Jones is on his mobile watching the shoot. The sun is low in the sky, a white fragment above my eyelids. I wonder what he is going to say. Mani throws his hands up in the air.

'The light! Ah! I need to take a break.' He strides off in the direction of the jetty, furiously smoking a cigarette. Claxton Jones begins to laugh. He comes over to where I sit. I try to look attractive.

'He is a character, isn't he?'

'Yes. Look, are you sure about this?'

'Yes! Yes! Imagine how sensational you are going to look. The Designer's Niece. That's you. Revealed in all your glory.'

'Yes!'

'Great. Well...'

Fizz McArdle kneels down in front of me with her box of cosmetics. As she rummages for the requisite eyelashes I see Mani and Polly approach Claxton and start gesticulating rather wildly in front of him. While Fizz applies glue to the tips of one fringed lash, Claxton waves his arms in the air and shouts, 'Stop!'

Polly flutters prettily at the periphery of proceedings and admires my finery with a wink. She holds up a pile of papers to Claxton and Mani. Mani is delighted, but unfortunately I cannot discover what is so pleasing about Polly's bundle as my fish scales are causing mobility trouble.

After a brief discussion with Mani, out of earshot, Fizz McArdle comes over with a sponge and bowl of water instead of eyelashes.

'We've got to scrub you clean,' she says dryly. 'We're going for another look.'

I feign disappointment but am, in fact, relieved. I can see only mockery of my rock-mermaid posturing.

Claxton comes over to my deckchair, Polly in hand.

'Diana,' he says. 'We've got a new take on your photos. I hope you don't mind. It's just Mani saw you sitting out here and thought one word. *Schiele*.'

'Gesundheit,' I say, but Claxton was not Ronnie and there was no generous laugh.

'*Egon* Schiele. The German painter. He…'

'Oh, yes. Egon *Schiele*,' I say. I know Schiele's paintings: dark, disturbing and full of sex.

'Well, Mani thinks we should recreate some of his paintings as photographs. Now he's seen you out here, in this light, he wants to do a *Seated Woman with Bent Knee*.'

'He does?' This makes sense in my daydream. I see myself becoming like the girls in his paintings. This is my future.

'Yes!' says Polly. She comes to sit on my lap, mouths a sweet kiss on my cheek, then my lips. 'It would work so much better. Really subtle. It would suit your confrontational gaze.'

'My confrontational gaze?'

'Yes.'

'Is that a good thing?'

'Oh yes.'

Polly whispers into my ear, 'Trust Mani, Diana. He knows what he's doing.'

Fish scales itch my skin and I know, for a fact, at my very core that I will never be safe with these people; that I will never be happy; that it is all wrong.

'I have to go,' I said, and stood up.

'What?' Polly's hand fell from my lap and she pouted at me. 'But we've got so much to talk about!' Quietly at my ear she whispered, 'And I wanted to take you home with me and have you scorch my Egyptian cotton sheets!'

'No thank you,' I said. 'I made a mistake.'

'Pardon?' She frowned a very pretty frown.

'I made a mistake. I shouldn't have come.'

Claxton and Mani looked up at me as I started towards the door. 'When shall we schedule this interview? The photos? It will be brilliant.'

'Never,' I said. 'I'm very sorry but it seems I've wasted your time.' And I walked away.

I felt wide awake, more awake then I ever had in my life. Rohan was no longer alive. He was gone and I knew now that he had lied to me. If I could not trust him, then who could I trust?

I pulled out my phone and called Richard Milk.

17

The film has not been totally cast, but Toby has already filmed many practice shots. A perfectionist, he will, in true Malk Blancossier style, film the entire script using a digital camera and understudies, to grasp angles, light and words before other people get to add their ideas and interpretations to his.

It all begins with a shot of Cowling beach which is not Cowling beach. The sand is too white, too clean. There is no lank seaweed, no purple fronds gripping rough stones, no empty shells, grey-yellow, broken, facing skywards like old bones.

This cinematic Cowling is broad, expansive; clear like the Mediterranean yet somehow monochrome. The camera holds its gaze upon the shoreline. No boats, no swimmers, no li-lo frivolity. Just the sea, slate grey, and one tall rock to the right of the screen in the foreground. Needle Rock. Taller. Thinner. But definitely Needle Rock.

It is sinister, this Cowling, this still, white Cowling with its vacant sand and silent water. Needle Rock stands like a hunched giant, watching, waiting for something, someone. The lack of soundtrack, the silence – no stretched-out strings or melancholic piano – is cold. All you can hear is the sound of the wind, piping like an old busker's tin-whistle, long and white – like this sand – swishing about the rock like long grass.

The screen is set still like this for what feels like minutes, a wide expanse of nothing ever after.

Then a female narrator speaks over the silence. A strange voice, slow, unapologetic, triumphant yet somehow cheerless.

'I have never gained money by honest means…I have never known the feel of a pay-packet in my fingers, a salary in the bank…I made my money here on this beach…so much money, more money than one woman could ever need…But the joy was in the making of it, gathering it like driftwood, like cuttlefish, like dry sand.

It's all about watching...watching the tides of a place until you know every last pull of it, every drop, every drip, every squall, every grain.

This is not my story – it is his...this man who hid away in this empty place...And it is hers...this woman who could never join him.

And, perhaps, it is mine. Because in part, I made it happen.'

This scene ends abruptly, the concealed woman stops speaking.

For a few seconds the screen is totally white and the sound of the wind grows louder, louder; painfully loud.

Then nothing.

The boy rides his bike for ten miles just to see her. On the way it is downhill, faster than air and light and birdcall. He flies with cloth wings, his trousers tucked into his socks. Light flashes in front of his eyes in shots of yellow, black and red. The leaves on the trees, which line the road, clap him onwards. Bravo. Go to her. Bravo.

The girl sits by the lake. She has tied her red hair up with a shoelace. She eats a piece of bread with jam, maybe made from the windfall apples by her mother. The sounds of the ducks are like scratches, like the cuts on her knees after crawling over leaves and acorns in the woods. Building a den.

When the boy arrives, he brings a burst of sunlight like pictures of the atom bomb on television; cracks of light through leaves, heavenly voices, his grey cap and his scuffed shoes. He will have to clean them when he gets home.

He leans his bicycle against a tree and sits down next to her, accepting a slice of her bread. He says a quiet thank you to God for just letting her be there. For letting him be there with her. She smells of soap and coal and the swill she feeds the pigs in the garden. He wants to breathe her in, although he cannot phrase this, does not know what this might mean. But you can see it in the way he looks at her and the way he looks at the sky. He rubs his nose and tickles his top lip with his thumbnail. Smooth. Quiet. To him the ducks are the sound of cheers, a crowd to see the cycling sweat slick his fringe and his orange hair across his brow. To applaud the grey socks rolled down over her knees.

The birds in the woods make sounds, talk to each other about – what? The boy and girl play their usual game.

'Blackbird.'

'Chaffinch.'

'Thrush.'

'Starling.'

'Lark.'

Neither of them really knows what these birds sound like, although the boy can recognise a starling or a thrush when he sees one and the girl pretends a blackbird can sing like a mezzo-soprano. *Oh for the wings, for the wings, of a do-ve.*

'Parrot.'

'Dodo.'

'Buzzard.'

'Pterodactyl.'

They laugh and squawk, fall back with open arms while leaves press veins into their skin, outstretched outlines among freckles. Peeling remnants of summer.

On their backs they kick undergrowth to land on their bare legs. Twigs and broken snail shells and pinecones and the first of the conkers.

'We never swam in the lake this summer,' she says quietly. 'We always said this was our year to swim in the lake.'

'We are not allowed,' says the boy, picking up damp bark with his fingertips, crumbling handfuls into fallen pieces. 'We will get into trouble.' He immediately seems angry with himself for saying this. The camera pans to a gap in the trees, a hint of water. The wistful look on his face says he would like to swim with the girl in the lake. He should not care about trouble. He should be a man and take her to the lake and make it safe.

'Tomorrow is my thirteenth birthday,' says the girl. She sits up and looks out at the water. The newly orange leaves from the trees falls through sky, grey-red swells on the surface. Bubbles and drops where fish raise themselves, scooping water with their mouths.

'I know,' says the boy. 'I've brought you something. I didn't want to give you this at home.'

He brings the carefully folded package out of his pocket and hands it to her. He has wrapped the bracelet in a clean handkerchief. It is delicate, made of silver wands threaded on a fine chain, with modest paste emeralds set between each link. There are two charms hanging from it. Two halves of the same heart hanging on separate clasps. They are plump, these hearts. They are beating.

The camera zooms in on them as they twinkle in her fingers.

'Oh! Oh! Thank you.' She loops the metal around her wrist, lets him fasten its ends and twist it over. Green dots of light on her skin and the reflection of the leaves on the polished surface. A smile to show her wet tongue and her lovely teeth.

He swells red. Pride. A reaction like wet paint on his neck and ears.

'Will you swim with me?' She watches him, rattles her bracelet in time with the ducks.

'I don't know...'

'Tomorrow I will be thirteen.'

'I know you will. We are truly getting old.' He kisses the fine curls of hair that grow behind her left ear. He does it softly, almost as though his lips may disappear into her flesh if he lets them linger.

'I wish it could always be like this,' she says, and he nods.

They both sigh. The reeds on the lake sway softly, reaching towards the sky like the arms of the penitent; entreating a lost God.

A white screen again. And the sound of the wind.

A row of girls sit at wooden desks in a classroom. The girl from the lake is there, hair pulled up tight in a bun. She holds her pencil in her left hand and casually pushes it in and out of her mouth. A teacher at the front, a woman in green tweed suit, recites verb structures in French.

'J'ai, tu as, il a, elle a, on a, nous avons, vous avez, ils ont, elles ont.'

Beside the girl sits another pupil writing neatly on her white piece of paper. She is darker than the girl from the lake. She is wider, less confident in her skin.

'Fat lesbian,' says a girl with yellow hair behind. 'Look at the fat lesbian. Goodie two shoes. Always gets her homework in on time.' Two girls beside her laugh.

'*Lesbian*! *Lesbian*!'

The teacher does not notice. She continues to write on the board in slanted chalk, reciting her verbs, checking the clock in anticipation of the bell.

The girl from the lake puts her pencil to a scrap piece of paper. She looks at the darker girl beside her, who winces, expecting more cruel words. She is used to this. You can see it in the way she slumps at her desk, wrapping her arms about her like bird wings, a shelter from the outside.

'FUCK OFF,' writes the girl from the lake. The words are formed with a heavy flourish, like bubbles, coloured in with her blunt pencil. She turns and holds the paper up to the girl with the yellow hair, nodding her head, triumphant. The blonde girl puts her hand over her mouth, furious.

'Madame!' says the girl from the lake. 'Excusez moi, Madame!' She raises her hand in the hair, waves it as though she were waving to a friend at the station.

'Oui Madamoiselle?'

'Je ne sais pas how I say this en Francais. Mais Lucille Parker m'a donnée un lettre offensive.'

She keeps her face completely straight. The teacher strides, sturdy in her suit, her thick tights and her polished lace-up shoes and snatches the note from her guilty fingers.

'Out!' says the teacher, resorting to English. 'You! Lucille Parker! Get out! Go to the Headmistress's office. Now!'

'But…' the yellow-haired girl's face has gone purple. 'She…'

'Don't even think of answering back. To see such language. From someone who should know better… Out!'

Lucille Parker stands up from her desk and moves straight to the door. She seems not to dare look at the girl from the lake in case she bursts with rage and betrayal and humiliation.

The teacher walks back to the front of the class as though nothing has happened. There are only a few minutes until the bell, and she just wants a cup of camomile tea and a piece of shortbread.

'Thank you,' mouths the dark-haired girl, trembling.

The girl from the lake winks, leaning towards her companion suppressing giggles with closed palms.

'My name is Alice,' she writes.

'I'm Julie,' writes the dark-haired girl nodding, her face a delighted beam. She is short on friends.

'Nous sommes amies,' writes the lake girl. 'Nous sommes amies forever.'

Another white screen. And the sound of the wind.

A dinner table set with plates and knifes and tea things. A woman in a grey skirt and pastel blue blouse is pouring tea from a pot while her husband, in a black shirt and dog collar, takes his spectacles from his face and places them on the tablecloth beside him.

Three teenagers sit in a row on one side of the table. The girl from the lake, Alice, is there. So is the boy. And the dark-haired girl from the classroom. Julie.

'It is so nice,' says the woman with a warm smile and short, curled hair set neatly about her head. 'It is so nice, to have a young *visitor.*'

The three children look at her. Julie is shy. She folds her napkin back and forth between her fingers. When she picks up her fork to eat her piece of Victoria sponge it shakes in her hands. She is terrified of making a mistake. She has never been invited to anybody's house before, at least not somebody her own age. A lot rests on this moment. The camera zooms in on her dark eyes. She is squinting with the concentration of it, a slight ridge between her eyebrows and the look of someone who might burst into tears.

'I'm always saying, aren't I, dear, it would be good for our Alice and Stephen to make other friends?'

The man in the dog collar nods. He is stirring cubes of sugar into his tea with a bone-handled teaspoon.

'Just because we live in the middle of nowhere doesn't mean we are not part of civilisation... More cake Julie?'

Julie nods. She looks like more cake might make her throw up violent jam and sponge vomit onto the chequered tablecloth.

'It didn't matter when they were younger,' says the woman. 'It was good to get this parish, to live by the sea, have our children foraging away in the sand and the woods.'

Alice and Stephen's feet touch under the table. They are smiling at each other. Secret smiles disguised as general exuberance. Their ankles link while they wipe crumbs from their lips.

'But it's time for them to grow up. They are teenagers now. It isn't right for them to be scampering around in the undergrowth, picking out flowers and weed. Especially you Alice.' She smiles and sips from her thin-rimmed cup. 'Especially you... you have to learn to be more *ladylike*.'

Stephen giggles, a wet burst from his nose and lips.

'Stephen!' says the man at the head of the table. 'Not at the dinner table.'

'Sorry,' says Stephen. 'I think it is good that Alice is not like other girls. It makes her interesting.'

'That may be,' says their mother. 'But this cannot go on forever... So as I was saying Julie, it is delightful to finally meet one of Alice's schoolfriends. A real treat. More cake?'

A white screen and the sound of the wind.

A sweep of coiled orange hair – bright whorls of it, curling and moving – in close up so you cannot see who it belongs to. A song is playing, The Band's version of 'Long Black Veil', and there is the sound of a couple having sex. As the camera pans back you can see the two figures entwined on the bed. Inexperience shows in their every movement. This is not Hollywood sex, glistening, expert, skilled. This is elbow, knee, ankle sex, knocking into each other, mouths missing their targets, body parts slipping in or out of place.

The couple on the bed are not adults. They are teenagers. The iron-framed bed they are on is decorated with paper Christmas stars, reds and greens stuck with bits of sequin and cut-up food packets. The room itself is definitely the girl's: books, dolls, teddies, pictures of ballerinas, discarded knee-high school socks, jumpers, blazers, ribbons. But there are other items on the walls, on the shelves, on the carpet: plant cuttings, stems, stamens, petals, twisted thorns and dried-out seaweed. One wall is an entire mass of natural fauna, carefully cut out, dissected, set out like a roadside hedgerow. A mannequin stands in the corner, adolescent sized, with a half-made dress pinned to its torso. The dress is purple and dark blue.

The couple tear at each other's limbs much faster than the beat of the music. The frenzy they show is equalled by the words. They mouth things to each other, sometimes silently, sometimes in whispers. *I love you I love you I love…* They smile at each other, joy-filled, delighted, elated. They may be young, but they understand what they are doing. They laugh and they squirm. They grin and they wriggle. They kiss each other with happy kisses. Their school clothes lie in piles on the bed beside them, discarded mounds of navy blue.

The camera pulls back on the couple, who are now in a new position, head to tail with each other. Somebody is at the door watching them, watching Stephen and Alice commit a joyous crime on the bed. The camera pans the room, taking in clothes, pictures, flowers, decorations. It turns away from the couple, who are laughing and gasping so furiously now, whispering 'Ssshhh! Shhhh!' but unable to keep quiet. There is a girl in the doorframe watching them. Her pale face and dark eyes are like death. Blank. Empty. She has her hand over her mouth and the familiar crease between her eyebrows. The girl is Julie.

A white screen and the sound of the wind.

Alice is hunched over the toilet. Her dark hair is pulled back from her face with an elastic band. She is sweating and wayward curls cling to the back of her neck like duck down. She is being sick into a white porcelain toilet. She is holding to the rim with tight fingers and pressing into the tiled floor with her knees.

'You'll be OK,' says Julie. She has her arms on Alice's back. She is stroking her, gently. Her face has that blank look and she shows no emotion. 'You'll be all right.'

Alice turns her head, a flash of grey eyes to the camera. She is furious. She is the hunter and the hound. Her face is red and blotched; sweat covers her face like second skin. 'How can it be all right? How will this ever be right?' She is sobbing, her face twisted and mutilated with tears, anger, sorrow.

'It just will,' says Julie. She says this simply, as though it is obvious and Alice should know this. Her tone is not unlike the teacher's in the earlier scene; as though she is waiting for the bell to ring and her cup of camomile tea. Her dark hair lies thick along her spine in a plait. She pulls it over her shoulder and strokes its ridges with one hand as she strokes Alice with the other.

There is blood on the black-and-white tiles. Thick ridges of stretched-out organic matter like unset raspberry jelly. There is an island of blood, bright red, so red that it couldn't possibly be real, on the back of her nightdress. It soaks into her, clinging to her with the cotton fabric.

'Where *is* he? Where *is* he?' Alice is crying, the fury gone. There is a conch shell on the side of the tin bath. It is white and pink, its tip points downwards, downwards to the wet blood on the floor. The camera focuses on it momentarily then back to the girls at the toilet.

'You need to be quiet,' says Julie calmly. 'You don't want your parents to hear any of this. They will be back from church soon. You must be quiet.'

'Fuck being quiet!' Alice is screaming. 'Fuck all of it! Where is the baby? Where is the baby? Where is our BABY?'

She is hysterical. She falls from the toilet and writhes in the mess on the tiling. Her body shakes, convulses, spasms in all directions.

Julie sighs and pulls her plait back over her shoulder. She reaches down, big capable arms like loaves of bread, and lifts the screeching Alice up by her shoulders.

'Stop it,' she says softly. 'Stop it now.'

Alice scrunches her eyes closed and opens them again, defiant. For a moment their eyes meet. Alice wild, passion-fuelled, flame. Julie tamed, empty, ice. Alice spits at Julie. A huge, thick gob of saliva and hate.

Julie does not flinch. She holds onto Alice by her shoulders and looks her firmly in her face.

'Stop it,' she says. 'Stop it right now.' She wipes away the spit with the back of her cardigan, dropping Alice back into the blood on the floor. Alice looks up at her, broken now, the defiance gone. She trembles, damp, afraid.

'Where is the baby?' she says quietly.

'He will be back...with it,' says Julie, and as she says it the camera pans to a boy, to Stephen, at the door, holding something in his arms, something rounded and smooth, concealed with a blanket. His red hair is slicked across his face with sweat. He has been crying.

'I can't save it,' he says sadly.

'It?' Alice's anger returns. 'It? It was a *person*!'

'I can't see,' says Stephen sadly. 'I can't see if it's a boy or a girl. It's too young. It isn't fully developed.'

Alice lets her head fall into her hands.

'I'm sorry we got you into this,' says Stephen to Julie.

'That's OK,' she says. 'It's not as though I had anything much else to do.' There is something sinister in the way she says this. Her eyes swim black and wintry.

Alice stands up and steps tentatively to Stephen, whose arms are daubed with dry blood. 'I'm sorry, my darling,' she says, strangely adult now upon her feet. 'I'm not angry with you.'

'I know,' he says. 'It's all so...'

'Unfair,' she says. 'It's not our fault.'

'No.'

'Can I see her?' She reaches towards the cloth-covered thing in his arms. He shakes his head slowly, the light from the bathroom a vicious white that makes him strain to see, and his skin seem blue.

'Please?' She is a child again, large beseeching eyes, soft mouth, downturned and thin.

'I didn't know what else to do with her,' he says, peeling back the cloth.

'Oh!'

In Stephen's arms is a deformed, stillborn baby silently sculling a thick liquid inside a glass jar.

A white screen and the sound of the wind.

'Gallow.' The man with the beard and blue tie says, making a tick next to the name in his book.

Julie stands up and pushes her metal seat back under the metal table. She walks to the front of the room, slowly, methodically. The room is full of girls in groups of two, three, four. Julie is the only one who sits alone. She hunches over herself as she walks. The way she is shot – the camerawork which pulls back to show her feet, rumpled black socks and stiff lace-up shoes – sums up this girl with one word. Resigned.

'A letter, Gallow,' says the man without looking at her. 'The first letter you've ever had.' He does not smile. He pushes the letter towards her across his desk and moves on to the next name.

'Yes Sir,' says Julie. She takes the envelope from the desk and holds it tightly.

'It won't be from your parents,' says a girl with thinly plucked eyebrows and an unkind smile. 'We all know they're banged up somewhere. Bloody perverts.'

Laughter spreads around the room. Julie's face does not flicker. She keeps the same straight, plain expression with the slight ridge between her eyebrows. She walks unhurriedly back to her chair. Girls laugh and whisper around her. She does not appear to hear them. Her eyes and mouth are serene, like the Virgin Mary in nativity scenes.

She sits down.

'Peters,' says the man. Another girl stands up. A girl with an animated face and a spring in her step. A girl who is used to getting mail.

Julie Gallow pulls her dark plait over her shoulder and strokes its pointed tip between her thumb and forefinger. She slides her finger under the brown paper flap. She does not rush. The camera zooms in on her hands, her movements so slow, so laboured that the urge is to jump into the screen and rip the letter open for her.

Julie pulls out a small piece of paper and a ten-pound note. The writing, thorned italic in brown ink, says simply,

> Thank you Julie for your help and being a loyal friend. Sorry you haven't heard from us. Alice is much better and will be back at school soon. I thought you might like to buy something nice for the dance.
> All best,
> Stephen.

Julie holds the ten-pound note in her hand like it might dissolve, like a flap of new-spun lace or a spider's web. Her expression is suddenly amused, the suggestion of a smile on her lips, in her eyes, like the secrets of the universe have been revealed to her, like she finally knows her purpose. All about her girls chatter or giggle with friends. Letters from boyfriends, siblings, occasionally parents, often grandparents; ripped open, pored over, shared. There is the sense that most of the girls in the home are parentless. Their friends in the home are their family.

Julie's dark eyes do not need friends. Julie has Stephen and Alice and their secrets.

A white screen and the sound of the wind.

A woman with dark hair tied in a loose bun sits at the wooden bar of a pub. A landlord in a grey jumper and jeans with a thick beard polishes the brass of his beer pumps. There is a coal fire lit in a grate-free fireplace. There are scattered groups of men sitting at tables drinking beer. A few play dominoes. A few play cards. One man strokes an old brown dog from its nose to its tail.

The woman sits at the bar by herself, occasionally checking her watch and looking to the old oak door. The landlord refills her glass without asking if that is what she wants, a long golden pint of soapy beer. There is a man playing a guitar by the fire. He is not very good. He plays the same three chords over and over; three sad chords that have no connection to each other; discordant, tinny and flat.

'You waiting for that Wake chap?' says the landlord kindly. He looks at the dark-haired woman over his glasses with a concerned smile.

'Pardon?' The woman nips at her beer with a tight mouth.

'Ahh, you heard me, young Julie,' says the man. 'It's not like you to go soppy over a man…but…I saw you. I saw the way you looked at him on Sunday.'

Julie – this grown up, whiter version of Julie – sighs and smiles. The child Julie never smiles. This Julie sits at the bar drinking beer, happy in her own company, brave enough to be in the company of red-nosed, sallow drinking men.

'I *am* waiting for Roddie Wake,' she says. 'Not that it's any of your business, Ron.'

The landlord, Ron, laughs with one fat shake. 'Ah ha Julie Gallow. Everything is my business in this place. Every single thing.' He nods proudly. 'And our Mr Wake is trouble.'

'He is very good looking,' says Julie and laughs.

'I thought you were better than that,' says Ron. 'I thought you were beyond silly things like that.'

'Everyone has to make a silly decision one time or another,' says Julie. 'Look where not being silly got me.'

Ron sighs and turns to a sink full of lathered-up water. He picks out some rubber and metal tubes and begins to wipe them with a faded-patterned tea towel.

'He's a blackmailer, a womaniser and a cheat…and I don't say those things lightly. He'll bring you nothing but trouble. He…' Julie smiles at him benignly. She is not listening. He shakes his head slowly and whistles. He turns his head, ever so slightly, as though he is about to say something to Julie, who is now smiling broadly and taking heavy swigs of her beer, but he thinks better of it. He continues to dry the tubes and whistles as the door opens.

'Afternoon all,' says the man. He is fairly short with dark curly hair, wearing a grey woollen jacket and polished brown shoes. Various men around the pub nod and the dog whines – a nice if not unsubtle touch, making the audience think of the supernatural. This man is very good looking. He walks about the bar as though it is his. He flips his green hat from his head with a deft tap of his thumb.

'A big glass of brandy, thank you Ronald,' he says.

'As you wish,' says Ron, who drops the tubing he has in his hands back into the foamy water and picks up a wide-rimmed brandy glass.

'In my usual glass, if you will,' says the man smiling. 'I'm a regular, Ronald. It's about time you treated me as one.'

Ron shrugs, 'I forget,' he says. 'So many people come in here.'

'Ha!' The man takes the glass and takes the lot down in one. 'Keep telling yourself that Ronald and you'll sleep better at night.'

'Another beer please Ron,' Julie says, banging her glass enthusiastically onto the counter. 'I'm celebrating.'

Ron looks at her sadly as he refills her glass. Wake looks at him with a combination of triumph and conquest.

'Yes Ron, it's true. I'm to be married! I'm to be Mrs Roddie Wake!'

A white screen and the sound of the wind.

18

The woman with the charms on her wrist. The woman in the veil. The woman Rohan told me had spilt oil on her wedding dress. I knew now, without a doubt, that woman, that woman in black, did not just come to see Rohan, she also came to see me.

She must have come a little before my thirteenth birthday. I had never associated the two events before, but now I remember. Now I recall her sitting in Rohan's workroom and Rohan, unusually for him, making me take my time with the tea things. I wasn't Secret Diana that day. He allowed me to stay, to be seen. I had thought, at the time, he was just distracted. But now I think it was on purpose. He wanted her to see me. She needed to see me.

I could not see the woman's face. The veil was thick lace and hung to her collarbones. She sat with her pale hands folded in her lap, neat nails short and unpainted. She wore a long, purple velvet skirt, frayed at the hem, and lace-up boots, pointed with wooden soles. She wore a black woollen jacket with wide lapels and big buttons. None of her clothes matched. She was not of the usual type Rohan decked out in his workroom.

'How is work?' Rohan said, seemingly distracted with a roll of cream silk ribbon, curling it around his hand, back and forth between his stained fingers.

'Going OK thank you.' The woman in the veil had a soft voice, accentless. Each word lasted longer than it should do. She sounded like somebody about to cry.

'Any new developments?'

'A few. I stare at the, um, samples for hours at a time. I even dream about them.'

'Yes. I dream about my clothes,' said Rohan. 'It's like that with what you work with. I dream about them every night.'

He did not usually speak like this to his clients. Sometimes he did not utter a word when another elongated, angular woman sat in his workroom. I often listened at the door, desperate to know what adults, in particular Rohan, talked about when there was no child in the room. His usual comments were, 'Turn', 'Put out your right hand', 'An inch longer I think.'

'Sometimes I long for sleep,' said the woman. 'I dream about all the things I know can never happen. They all feel so real. Like the life I know I could have had if the world were different. If I were different.'

She was intriguing, this woman. Her talk of feelings made no sense in the emotionless workroom. I wanted to ask her what she dreamt about – shapes, colours, people, skies – that was so real to her, more real than her actual life, that she wished she would not wake up. I understood about dreams. In my dreams I lived with my parents and had a nightlight on a pink bedside table and party dresses and a hamster in a cage and bank-holiday trips to museums or playparks and a navy Sierra which my father cleaned on a Sunday afternoon with soapy water, and a pink lunchbox with a cartoon character on the front, and sandwiches and cake wrapped up by my mother.

'Other times,' she said as I headed to the door, desperate to stay but believing I had already outstayed my welcome, 'other times I dream about the darkest things. Terrible things that should never have happened in the first place replaying again and again at night.' She laughed a strange laugh. 'I wake up with outlandish sweats, cold skin, cuts in my arms where I have ground my nails deep in fear.'

I could not believe that Rohan was letting this stranger talk like this in front of me. He was still rearranging the cream ribbon, creating ruches and frills between his fingers. Back and forth. Back and forth. Stroking the silk along his hands and fingers and occasionally bringing it up to his face to stroke it along his unshaven chin.

'Wait Diana. I need you to pick some pins out of the carpet.'

'Now?'

'Yes now.'

He did not introduce us to each other and the woman continued her reminiscences of her dreams seemingly unbothered by my presence. I glanced up at her feet from my place on the carpet. Her boots needed polishing, and I could see they were old and oft-worn. I could not imagine what kind of wedding dress a woman like this would wear. Nothing flounced, ruffled or prancing. Nothing brash, loud or brazen. Nothing made by the fabulous Rohan Rickwood. I imagined her making her own dress from a pattern given free with some woman's magazine. Cut here, stitch here, trim here, iron-on edge here. Done. What was she doing in Rohan's workroom, and why was he letting me stay?

'Yes,' said Rohan. 'Dreams are potent. Day dreams, night dreams, dreams about the future…'

'It's best not to dream about the future,' said the woman, her veil flickering slightly as she breathed. 'It's best not to dream about anything.'

'You're right, of course,' said Rohan. 'And it's best to not find your dreams too early.'

The pins were deep in the carpet; some flat, unaltered, as silver and straight as they came in the packet, others crooked and bowed bent in the weave. I filled my hands with them, methodically picking at their tiny heads with my thumbnail. They glinted in the light, so many slivers of silver, discarded, forgotten. Fallen from cuts of cloth, from paper patterns, from their place at Rohan's lips. I sat with my legs crossed and leant forward, squinting to make sure none were left behind. I prided myself on getting each segment of flooring clear of them. Unpicking the burnished latticework until each patch was bare.

'How is school Diana?' I looked up at the woman in the black veil, taken aback at her sudden decision to address invisible me.

I turned to Rohan, checking to see if it was OK for me to speak to this woman who was so different from the others. He nodded to me, a quiet gesture of his head, and he smiled. I did not often see Rohan smile. Joy was not something I associated with his life. Or mine.

'It's OK,' I said. I looked back at my pins. The palm of my hand sparkled with them; all shapes, sizes, arc, bows and bends. The pins were comforting, objects so familiar to me from the day I was born.

I wanted to push them into my skin. Feel their sharp points pierce to blood. I was disconcerted by the fact I could not see her face. I tried to picture what was under the shield of lace. Imagined rushing to her, pulling it back, ripping it from her head, leaving her bare. Was she beautiful, this woman under her veil? Did she have a hideous disfiguration? Did she always wear it? Was her face so sad, so broken, so utterly destroyed by life, by her waking and sleeping dreams that to look at her was to die, turn to stone and feel the beat of her broken heart in your veins?

'Just OK? Do you have friends? What lessons do you like?'

Her crossed legs trembled. Despite the length of her skirt, which skimmed the floor, I could see her movements in the ripple of the velvet. It shimmered as she shook.

'I don't have that many friends,' I said honestly. 'I like art and history. I like drawing things in biro, tiny pictures that have lots of detail in. I like history because I like knowing about what happened in the past. I would like to know more about the past.'

Her legs shook faster. Her hands clasped together so tight that her knuckles were white and the tips of her fingers pinched pink and purple. Rohan did something then, something I had forgotten over the years, perhaps because I did not really believe I had seen it, so out of character was it. He walked over to the woman in the veil, slowly, purposefully, and put his hand upon her shoulder. Easily, his hand, his fingers, touched her. He left them there, squeezing lightly, and stood behind her. They looked like a couple in a Victorian photograph: a man standing straight, face forward, expressionless – neither happy nor sad – sombre with his hand, almost tender; an undeniable display of ownership, on his wife's shoulder.

'Why don't you have many friends, Diana? Don't you want friends?'

I looked up from my pins, tipping a handful into the pin pot. It was not often anybody asked questions about me. I wanted to open my mouth and let a thousand words about my life fall out in no particular order. I wanted this woman to hear me.

'I find it hard to make friends,' I said. 'I don't trust many people.'

'Why not?'

'I don't know…' I thought about it. 'You can't trust people very much, can you?' I started on a new square of pins, flicking up the loose ones with quick snaps of my fingers.

'I suppose you're right,' she said sadly. 'Although people usually do when they're your age.'

I could not look at her. Drake's face had appeared in my head: large, open eyes, sweat-filmed forehead, grainy chin at my face. I had not seen him since the day I ran to the beach with Ruskin. He had not been about because Stella had not been about either. I missed him, in some peculiar, dark way. Other than this one woman, he was the only one who had ever asked about me. But I had read enough stories, met enough people at school to know that Drake's wishes were not normal.

Maybe I could tell this woman. Maybe she would scoop me up in her pale hands and carry me away under her veil. I could not tell Rohan about Drake. I could not tell Stella. But maybe I could tell the woman in the veil. Maybe her black shroud was there to absorb other people's secrets.

I continued to pick out the pins. Some felt so tight I thought I would never be able to get hold of them. I scrabbled at the heads with damp fingers, strumming their lengths like the steel strings on an acoustic guitar, scraping my skin until it was pink and raw.

'I don't mind,' I said. The needles were hot and heavy in my palm. 'I'm used to it.'

The woman in the veil shook her head. Rohan's hand stayed firmly on her shoulder. She bowed slightly, the veil tipping forward and for a moment I thought I might see her face. I longed to see her face.

'You like your own company, don't you Diana?' Rohan said brightly. 'She likes her own company,' he said quietly. He put his other hand on the woman's other shoulder. He stood behind her now, and placed his arms about her neck, and for a moment she leant back, tipped her head slightly, so her crown was resting on the space between his chest and stomach.

'Is there anything you need?' she said.

I moved to my next patch of pins. I did not look up. I presumed she was talking to Rohan and that my part in the conversation was over. I was already surprised at the amount of time I had been allowed in the workroom. This was unheard of. I was usually in the shadows, hiding behind curtains and thin walls.

'Diana?' She was addressing me.

'Yes?' I dropped the pins that were already in my hand. They scattered across the carpet like a miniature game of pick-up-sticks. Tiny flashes of silver criss-crossing in random piles, purposeful in appearance like the twigs in a new-formed bird's nest.

'Is there anything you need?'

What to say? I didn't want to get Rohan into trouble. What would people think if they knew the truth about Eddie Drake? And how would Rohan look if they knew he had let it go on under his own roof. Not that he let it happen. He just didn't see it.

I made a silent list in my head. Anything I need. Barbeques in the summer. A packed lunch every day for school. Clothes that didn't make me look like a jumble-sale reject. Somewhere safe to sleep. No Stella. No Drake. No women in the workroom fawning, laughing, desperate to be made beautiful. No abattoir with its scarlet sheets bleeding out into the road. No magazines with naked women bending and glistening and mocking me with Drake's laughter. Lists on the fridge of days I needed to be taken to ballet. Being taken to ballet. Hobbies in general. Friends. Toby Farrow. I would like to hold hands with Toby Farrow. I would like the jar baby to grow and grow and burst out of its glass shell, made flesh like a real child. I want its exaggerated veins to pale beneath well-formed skin. Peaches and cream. I want to be normal. To rewind time to the day my parents fell deep into the sea and never returned. I want to hear stories about my mother, to know how she smelt, how she talked, the sound of her breath at night. I want my mother. I want...

'Not really,' I said. 'I wouldn't mind being allowed girls' magazines.' It popped out of my mouth before I had a chance to think.

'Pardon?' Rohan let go of the veiled woman's shoulders. 'You need what?'

I had forgotten myself. What had I been thinking? He would never go for magazines. I should have said I needed nothing. I did not want him to be angry with me.

'Magazines,' I said. 'But I don't want anything really. Not even magazines.'

'Rohan will get you magazines,' she said. 'Make a list of the ones you want and he will have them delivered with his newspapers.'

Rohan stood back.

'Won't you?'

'I will,' he said. I knew he never would. He picked up the roll of cream ribbon, and once again curled it around his fingers. 'It is about time Diana went to bed,' he said.

'What about the pins?' I did not want to leave the workroom.

'You can continue with them tomorrow.' He put the ribbon back down on his desk. I looked up at the jar baby above him. It was cold in the workroom. The glass appeared to be frosted around the rim, hoary silhouettes reaching downwards in distorted shapes like undiscovered continents. The liquid inside was white-blue. Three large bubbles hung lifeless around the hairless head as though the baby was trying to breathe. Or to speak. Its one big eye seemed gargantuan in comparison to its undeveloped body. An engorged black sphere in a jar full of pallid flesh, skin and veins.

'Goodnight Diana,' said the woman in the veil. I wanted to ask her if she would show me her face. The mystery of it, that hidden visage, made me imagine her with the jar baby's head. The woman's veil was hiding an engorged eye and a sack of fleshy skin.

'Goodnight,' I said. 'It was nice to meet you.'

'It was.'

'Leave the tea things until tomorrow,' said Rohan. 'Don't worry about cleaning up tonight.'

'Goodnight Rohan,' I said. I walked to the door in confusion. Whoever this woman was she had been allowed to speak to me for more time than any other visitor to the Cowling Place.

When the door was closed I listened outside. They said things that made no sense back then. They talked like conspirators. The woman was angry.

'He cannot be allowed to come back. That's it. His time is done. I'll talk to Trudy.'

'They've got this over on us. We can't do anything.'

'You've always been so weak. He has broken the law...What has he done to her? We always knew he was scum, but this...'

'She seems okay.'

'Rohan!'

Someone crying.

'I'm sorry.'

'I'm sorry.'

'I'll speak to Trudy. She can be the one nearby if necessary.'

'I'll buy her the house on the hill.'

'There. And you can pay him off. You can't go to the police.'

'No.'

'I'm so sorry.'

'We both are.'

None of this made sense. I was yet to meet Trudy, and by that time I had forgotten, or chosen to forget, this strange encounter.

That night I dreamt of dog whelks and sea slugs and rag worm and dune beetles and parched fronds of sea-holly. I dreamt of cream, silk ribbons tied up in long red hair. Rails of clothes, many blues, buttoning and unbuttoning themselves in soft lamplight, flapping in a light breeze. I dreamt of multicoloured coastal flowers, Stork's bill, Scurvy grass and Lesser sea-spurrey. I dreamt of the woman in the black veil shaking her legs in the dark, sending shivers along the purple sheen of her velvet skirt.

'Jesus Christ,' I said.

'Jesus Christ indeed,' said Richard Milk.

I stared at the now-blank screen. The jar baby was part of me. We shared the same parents. Rohan and his sister were our parents. There it was. On the silver screen.

I started laughing. Richard looked at me with a half-smile.

'Did you ever know his real name?' said Richard.

'No,' I said. 'I only found out Rohan Rickwood wasn't his real name at the exhibition.' If Rickwood wasn't his real name, then it wasn't mine either. I really had been made up of scraps and fragments.

'Nobody knows his real name,' said Richard. 'Toby hasn't even told me.'

'It makes sense,' I said. 'It makes a lot of sense.' I looked at my feet, my hands, my elbows. All of me, every last atom, made from an illegal act; a secret, furtive union that could never reveal itself, not even to me.

'It is rather, um, fruity,' said Richard, and I looked at him. 'Sorry, it's just, well…I can't believe you never knew. They all thought you'd worked it out.'

'Not even close,' I said. 'I'm grotesque,' I said, still laughing. 'I'm Frankenstein's Monster. I'm the the Lion, the Witch and the Wardrobe. I'm a jar baby.'

'What?'

'I really am not like other women. Drake was right.'

'Of course you're not,' said Richard. 'You're better. You're unique.'

'Everyone's unique.'

'Yes. But you are you. I got so pissed off the way they all talked around you about it, even Toby, even Stella – the way they bought into keeping it secret from you. They'd have kept it secret until the film première probably. Drake and Trudy's set-up still works. People still stick to their rules.'

I wondered if they all knew about what had happened to me. They couldn't have known. They would have said something. They would have done something. Was it still the secret I've always thought it was? The thin pane of glass that separated me from the rest of the world.

'If Trudy is Julie in the film, and Wake is Eddie Drake...then Toby is...'

'Eddie Drake's son,' said Richard. 'It's a thought that disgusts him. But it drives him too. Think of his name.'

'His name? Toby Farrow...there's no link. I never guessed.' I had never even slightly guessed. The day his father's shirt had disgusted me on the beach, made me nearly retch with repulsion – even then I hadn't made the connection.

Richard's wide shoulders blocked out the lamplight. The nearness of him made me blush; hot blood at my skin's surface, and my heart beat too loud.

'Look,' he said. He turned to the computer, brought up Google and typed 'anagram generator' into the box. He typed in 'Malk Blancossier'. A long list of phrases appeared.

I began to read:

BANAL SICK MORSEL
CARAMEL SNOB SILK
NASAL BLOCK MISER
CALEB SALMON RISK
BLACKMAILER'S SON.

Blackmailer's son.

'Oh,' I said. So Toby knew what his parents were. Both of them. 'I don't think my mother is dead,'

'Of course she isn't,' said Richard.

'Do you know who she is?'

'Yes,' he said. 'I wanted to tell you straight away, but I wanted you to see all this first.'

The room was warm and calm. For once there were answers. Not the kind of answers improvised by my uncle – father! – over the oak table in the sad house at Cowling. Real answers. Ones with facts and events to back them up. They may not have been the answers I expected or hoped for, but they were answers.

'I don't know. But it's great.' Richard Milk reached out and put his hand on my leg. He stroked a circle onto my jeans. 'I feel really lucky to have met you.'

'Same here,' I said. 'And not just because you've helped me with all this.' I had been so obsessed with my own past all these years I had never really asked anyone else about their own lives. At the age of twenty-nine I didn't really know anybody.

'When I have worked all this out,' I said. 'When it makes more sense to me, I would like to hear about your childhood.'

'You wouldn't,' Richard laughed. 'Nothing happened.'

'Yes I would. I would like to hear about the whole lot. Everything you remember between birth and now.' I meant it. I wanted to know everything.

'Well there's a deal,' he said. 'When this is sorted, I will bore you with the uneventful tale of my conventional childhood.'

The tide had come in. The sea was fulfilling its promise. My mother, trapped under an overturned boat these past twenty-nine years, was about to swim free, thrashing the present with her mermaid's tail.

'Do you know why I really left Cowling?'

'Because of Stella and Toby.'

'No,' I said. 'I always thought it was that. I always told myself it was that. But it wasn't. It was something else.'

'What?

I placed the book bag with the jar baby on the table and foraged for the pictures of my Canadian model parents.

'Stella gave me this. It proved my parents weren't who Rohan said they were.'

Richard let out a low whistle.

'I'd like to introduce you to somebody.' I pulled out the jar baby, different now, its message finally delivered. 'Here is me Mark 1. Here is the first born. My brother/sister... Jemima/Horatio/other.'

'Fucking Hell!' Richard Milk looked at the jar baby with his mouth open. 'It's the baby from the film!'

'Yep. It's the jar baby.'

'He kept it!'

'Yep.'

'Fuck!'

We stared at the jar baby in its sorry sack of skin. It seemed lifeless now. Its one big eye like a polished stone pushed into bread dough. Its limbs floating – not of their own accord – in the cloudy substance Rohan must have reasearched, bought and poured into the glass jar himself.

You'd think once would have been enough. The veins, never to pump blood, stuck out, old and purple but young in the limbs of a non-life. What on earth possessed them to create me? Wasn't this poor non-sibling warning enough? They were mad, my parents. Related and mad.

'But who is she?' Who is Rohan's sister?'

'Glenys Pimm,' said Richard Milk simply. 'Your mother is Glenys Pimm.'

I have a mother! Diana Rickwood has a mother! A real-life, living, breathing, speaking, mother. And it is Glenys Pimm!

19

I arranged to meet Victor outside the National Gallery. I took the jar baby with me. It made sense. The sun was out. A clear dome of blue pressed down onto the dusty, drain-aired central London grey. The air was unbreathable. I decided it was time to move somewhere clean. Not Cowling. Not the sea. Somewhere new.

'Diana,' said Victor from the stone steps as I walked towards him. He reminded me of Pan, his small frame and pointed face, and musical voice singing my name across the pavement.

'Victor,' I said. He hadn't combed his hair, so it sat, fairly fluffy, at all angles from the top of his head. He didn't look gleaming, or otter-like, and was dressed in casual sand-coloured chinos and a pair of boating shoes. His shirt, however, was immaculately pressed and tucked perfectly into the waistband, the brass buckle on his brown belt shining bright. He was a careful man, Victor Eve. Careful and meticulous. But not quite so much today.

'I know that Glenys is my mother,' I said.

'I see,' he sat on the step, his hands on his knees.

'You know about Toby's film? He's putting everything out there. How will you both live, once everyone knows?' I had other questions to ask, others that mattered more to me, but this I wanted to know. This secret had been kept for over forty years and now the world was to know about Rohan Rickwood's secret life, and Glenys would no longer be left alone. Everybody would want to know about it.

'Well, he's assured Glenys that it's being presented as a work of fiction. Nobody will make the connection, he says.' Victor sniffed. 'He won't talk to me. He knows what I think. Too much has been lost already by doing it the way they did. To change that now. Well. It wipes out the past…'

Victor pulled out a bottle of mineral water and took a deep gulp. He shook his head, put the bottle back and then handed me a photograph of himself and Glenys Pimm on their wedding day. The two of them smiling at each other, not the camera, in black and white. Confetti fell around them, like cartoon snow. They looked happy.

'She invited him to our wedding,' he said quietly, shaking his head. 'We can move on, she said. If he sees how happy I am with you. If he sees that we are in love. We can step away from the past. We can move into the future. We can escape the sea, and the lake and the things that should never have happened. Of course I should have put all ideas of this out of her head. It was bound to fail. But…I loved her and she had told me about all of it. The years of them being together, their overbearing father, the baby as teenagers and how Rohan had saved it like a morbid souvenir.'

'He could not move on. He was infamous for his treatment of women then. Sorry, Diana, but he was what they call a proper bastard. Age, size, class, none of it mattered to him. He'd fuck them anyway. She thought, or pretended to herself that he'd be shocked out of it all if he saw us marry. It sounded good on paper. And,' he paused and reached for the photograph, which he began to roll carefully, like a cigarette paper, 'I believed her.'

I had never seen somebody look so sad, so utterly bereft. More than Rohan at the kitchen table, with endless drunken sombre platitudes. I felt angry. My mother had the chance to be happy. Victor Eve was neither attractive nor particularly witty. But he must have loved her. He knew what she'd done and he still wanted to marry her. To protect her and love her. Rohan wanted to possess her. I hated him then, thought him a petulant child who couldn't get his way.

'The wedding was beautiful. You've seen Glenys. She's like nobody else. He wanted to make her dress, of course. Went on and on about it, sending her these ridiculous letters about how he'd only started making clothes for her. That he was born to make this dress. How she owed him that, if nothing else. She wouldn't let him though. He didn't know I knew, you see. He thought I was a cuckold, with no idea about the past, that she was using me to become respectable. But it wasn't like that. She did love me. She does love me.' He held the photograph up to his eye like a miniature telescope.

'She wore a vintage, navy Hattie Carnegie frock. She found it in a charity shop. He hated it. Said she looked frumpy. Frumpy! Ha! Her hair was all rolled under and pinned up and lovely. She had her red lipstick and smelt of lemons. She was mine and I was hers and the vows were beautiful and the day was beautiful and Rohan sat there with his frown and crossing and uncrossing his long legs as he kicked at the air around him like a dying dog.'

I looked at him then, eyes wide. He knew about Ruskin? He knew, then, about Drake? But he said nothing further about dying dogs. He was inside his own monologue, years of regret and anger and secrecy falling and rolling like marbles across Trafalgar Square.

'And we had a lovely tea, more my family and friends than hers of course, but lovely nonetheless. We had cake and pots of hot drinks and wine and sandwiches and bunting. Bunting! Can you imagine it? There's something about weddings that makes everybody do things totally differently than they usually would. Bizarre. We should have just gone away. Sent some pictures home. Gone somewhere sunny and supped sweet wine.'

Victor began to cry. Not a few tears, but proper silent sobs, shoulders shaking, eyes heavenwards. People walking nearby looked at him as though he was having a fit or had been let out.

'It's OK Victor,' I said, and patted him on the arm, leaving it there.

He stopped crying. 'Look at me! Crying! When you need answers!' He put his hand over mine. 'The thing is, somehow, I don't know how he did it, somehow, he got her alone. After the ceremony. When I was carrying some cake, of all things. I was giving out cake, thick slices of cherry sponge on flowery saucers and Rohan Rickwood was seducing my wife behind the bike sheds, metaphorically speaking.' He laughed a theatrical laugh.

'He what?'

'That's when you were made, Diana. The day of our wedding. Glenys had had some wine. Red wine. It darkens things. She tries not to drink when I'm not around. It takes her on unnecessary journeys.'

'Like me,' I said. I take after my mother.

'They made you, wonderful as you are, stupid as they were. Tied with their secret and that stupid Trudy Farrow marrying that brute Drake. Blackmailing the two of them from the moment the first baby was born. Of course, he didn't love her. She told him about Dinah and Gordon and that was it. He saw cash signs.'

'Dinah and Gordon?' Dinah sounds like Diana.

'Ah, yes. Rohan Rickwood was baptised Gordon Alfred Donovan. Glenys was Dinah Olive Donovan. They didn't know they'd done anything wrong. At first. Ah, so, thirteen years after the first baby, they made a second.'

The jar baby in the bag between myself and Victor Eve was a thing in a bottle from a time when I was too young to associate myself with flesh, or even with having a flesh-and-blood mother. I don't know what will happen to it. My sister, my brother, the birl/goy. Maybe it will stay on a shelf like it has done its whole life. I do not need to know now; can see it for what it is. So much more than a dead thing caught up in a jar.

'I thought you may want this,' I said and passed the bag to him. He took it without looking inside. The weight and shape of it told him what it was. The holding of it woke him from his trance.

'Gosh, I've gone on!' he said, too jolly. 'It's a lot to take in Diana. There's more to it, of course. Glenys was hoping you'd come straight over. She's wanted to tell you for years. We wanted to bring you up as our own – it should have been simple. When you were born. But somehow Eddie Drake got wind of it, and insisted that Rohan bring you up. I...'

'Enough,' I cut him off calmly. 'That's enough for now, Victor.'

He nodded. 'Of course.' His tufts of black hair drooped mournfully along with his neat moustache.

I used to think my mother was a mermaid with a slick tail. It's strange to think she was there all along, living, breathing air and not sea water. Secrets are more dangerous than truths. Truths are tangible and you can hold them in your hands until they make sense. Secrets leave room for interpretations.

'I have absolutely no idea what to do next,' I said. 'I have a feeling I need to go to the police about Eddie Drake.'

Victor said nothing, but nodded gently.

Outside the National Gallery we watched the lions still protecting the man on the column. The fountain, too blue, tempted sun-trippers to splash each other with their trousers rolled way past their ankles. What would happen to Toby, and Stella and Ronnie and Victor and Glenys and me? Who would I be now I knew who I was? The mobile in my pocket buzzed with a new message. It was from Richard Milk.

I still have your shoe x.

I smiled.

There was too much to think about, nothing and everything made sense. The whole world called out in my head like the gulls on Cowling beach. It was too much. It was too real. But one thought, a new thought, one that felt like the truest thing I had ever thought, was clear, as clear as the familiar glass jar that held the baby with the same parents as me.

The past will not defeat me.

Acknowledgements

For the editing, the fine detail and a belief in the work, thanks to Robert Hastings and all at Dexter Haven. All your work has helped make this book, so thank you.

For reading drafts, encouragement or general cheerleading thanks to Sally Alexander, Hannah Jane Walker, Catherine Sear, Gareth Hardy, Jackie Peters, Anne Peile, Frances Fairhall, Helen Mulley, Rachel Callen, Liana Hemmet, Helen Macdougall, Em Hardy, Kerry Connelly, Mark Brown, Ben Ingber, Cassie Crane, Tony Cook and abctales.com.

Thanks to Arts Council East for the Grant for the Arts, and to Writers' Centre Norwich for the Escalator award and support.

To teachers at the University of Essex, especially Herbie Butterfield, for the poetry and reading earlier, less well-crafted work and to the late Joe Allard for the Shakespeare and Art. Thanks also to Maria Cristina Fumagalli. And to Deborah Povey for taking me on my first trip to the National Gallery. Thanks to friends, teachers and colleagues at the University of East Anglia also.

Many thanks to the many family members who have supported and encouraged me: all those Websters, Scotts, Belgroves and Biffens. Thanks especially to Jodie, Jason, Hollie, Jake, Jo, Paul, Jacob, Jackie and Mick. And to my parents, Jan and Neil, who will never get to read this book, but without whom it would never have been written. And to Kaye too.

Most importantly, thanks to Adam, for the love and laughs, Aiden, for the dancing and making me a better person, and Nell, who fills each day with proper joy and laughter.